Lillian Birnbaum

PETER HANDKE

THE FRUIT THIEF

Translated by Krishna Winston

Peter Handke was born in Griffen, Austria, in 1942. His many novels include *The Goalie's Anxiety at the Penalty Kick*, *A Sorrow Beyond Dreams*, *My Year in the No-Man's-Bay*, and *Crossing the Sierra de Gredos*, all published by FSG. Handke's dramatic works include *Kaspar* and the screenplay for Wim Wenders's *Wings of Desire*. Handke is the recipient of many major literary awards, including the Georg Büchner, Franz Kafka, and Thomas Mann Prizes and the International Ibsen Award. In 2019, he was awarded the Nobel Prize in Literature "for an influential work that with linguistic ingenuity has explored the periphery and the specificity of human experience."

Krishna Winston, now retired from teaching German literature and environmental studies at Wesleyan University, has been translating the work of Peter Handke since 1993. She has translated the work of many other authors, including Johann Wolfgang von Goethe, Günter Grass, Christoph Hein, and Werner Herzog.

ALSO BY PETER HANDKE

The Goalie's Anxiety at the Penalty Kick

Short Letter, Long Farewell

A Sorrow Beyond Dreams

The Ride Across Lake Constance and Other Plays

A Moment of True Feeling

The Left-Handed Woman

The Weight of the World

Slow Homecoming

Across

Repetition

The Afternoon of a Writer

Absence

Kaspar and Other Plays

The Jukebox and Other Essays on Storytelling

Once Again for Thucydides

My Year in the No-Man's-Bay

On a Dark Night I Left My Silent House

Crossing the Sierra de Gredos

Don Juan

The Moravian Night

Quiet Places

THE FRUIT THIEF

THE FRUIT THIEF

OR, ONE-WAY JOURNEY INTO THE INTERIOR

PETER HANDKE

Translated from the German by Krishna Winston

Picador
FARRAR, STRAUS AND GIROUX
New York

Picador
120 Broadway, New York 10271

Originally published in German in 2017 by Suhrkamp Verlag AG, Berlin, as *Die Obstdiebin oder Einfache Fahrt ins Landesinnere*
English translation published in the United States in 2022 by Farrar, Straus and Giroux
First paperback edition, 2023

The Library of Congress has cataloged the Farrar, Straus and Giroux hardcover edition as follows:
Names: Handke, Peter, author. | Winston, Krishna, translator.
Title: The fruit thief : or, One-way journey into the interior : a novel / Peter Handke ; translated from the German by Krishna Winston.
Other titles: Obstdiebin. English | One-way journey into the interior
Description: First American edition. | New York : Farrar, Straus and Giroux, 2022. | "Originally published in German in 2017 by Suhrkamp Verlag AG, Berlin, as Die Obstdiebin oder Einfache Fahrt ins Landesinnere"
Identifiers: LCCN 2021050360 | ISBN 9780374906504 (hardcover)
Subjects: LCGFT: Novels.
Classification: LCC PT2668.A5 O2713 2022 | DDC 833/.914—dc23/eng/20211015
LC record available at https://lccn.loc.gov/2021050360

Paperback ISBN: 978-1-250-86292-1

P1

The translator thanks Professor Martin Bäumel for his generous and perceptive advice on interpreting a number of passages.

Man gesach den liehten summer

in sô maniger farve nie

(*Never was bright summer*

seen in such richness of hues)

—WOLFRAM VON ESCHENBACH, *WILLEHALM*

And whosoever shall compel thee to go a mile,
go with him twain.

—MATTHEW 5:41, KING JAMES VERSION

Along the way no one offered a match,

or, at the rendezvous, light.

—FRITZ SCHWEGLER VON BREECH

THE FRUIT THIEF

THIS STORY BEGAN ON ONE OF THOSE MIDSUMMER DAYS when you take off your shoes to walk barefoot in the grass and get stung by a bee for the first time in the year. At least that has been my experience for as long as I can remember. And by now I know that these days marked by the first—and often the only—bee sting of the year usually coincide with the opening of the ground-hugging clover's white blossoms, among which the bees cavort, half hidden from view.

It was also—this, too, as usual—a sunny day at the beginning of August, still coolish, at least in late morning, with persistent bluing high and ever higher in the sky. Hardly a cloud to be seen—and if one appeared, dissolved in an instant. A gentle, bracing breeze was blowing, coming from the west, as it usually does in summertime, in my imagination whisking from the Atlantic into the no-man's-bay. No dew for it to dry. As had been the case for at least a week, not a hint of moisture on my bare soles as I strolled through the yard, let alone between my toes.

They say that because bees, unlike wasps, lose their stinger when they sting, they must die as a result. In all the years before, whenever I had been stung—almost always on my bare foot—I had not seldom witnessed this process myself, or at least caught sight of the teeny-tiny, immensely powerful three-pronged harpoon from which something flaky and viscous bulged, the insect's innards, and then, before my eyes, the creature's convulsing, trembling, shivering, wing paralysis.

But on the day when the die was cast and the fruit thief's

story began to take form, the bee that stung me on my bare foot did not die. Although it was no bigger than a pea, fuzzy and woolly, with the classic bee coloration and stripes, it did not lose any sort of stinger, and, after administering the sting, a perfect bee sting if ever there was one, at once sudden and powerful, it buzzed away as energetically as if nothing had happened, as if, in fact, its action had actually increased its strength.

Being stung was fine with me, and not merely because the bee survived. I had other reasons. First of all, they say that bees' stings, again allegedly in contrast to those of wasps or hornets, are good for your health, good against rheumatism, good for your circulation, or whatever, and a sting like this—another of my imaginings—would perk up my toes, losing circulation and sensation more and more every year, going numb; a similar fantasy or imagined benefit led me to grab bunches of nettles with my bare hands, either in my yard in the no-man's-bay or on the terraces of the property in far-off Picardy, yanking them out of the loess here, the chalky soil there.

I welcomed the bee sting for another reason, too. I took it as a sign. A good one or a bad one? Neither good nor bad or even evil—simply as a sign. The sting signaled that the time had come to set out, to hit the road. Tear yourself away from the yard and the whole area. Off with you. The hour of departure has arrived.

So did I need such a sign? On that particular day, yes, even if again only in my imagination or a summer day's dream.

In the house and yard I tidied up whatever needed tidying up, also leaving various things as they were on purpose, ironed my two or three favorite old shirts—only partially dried on the grass—packed, and pocketed the keys for the place in the country, so much heavier than the keys for my house on the outskirts. And, not for the first time when I was about to set out, a shoelace broke as I was tying my ankle boots; I could not find matching socks; I found three dozen local road maps—but not the one I was looking for, and this time both shoelaces broke, and in the quarter of an hour it took to knot them together my thumbnail cracked; and in the end I balled up the unmatched socks into pairs; and suddenly I felt fine about setting out without any map at all.

Suddenly, too, I shook off the sense of time pressure into which I had worked myself needlessly, as I always did, and not only when I was about to leave home, though it proved especially debilitating then, and downright deadly during the hour before the actual departure. Not an hour more. The book of life? A blank book. The dream at an end. Game over.

But now, unexpectedly: the time pressure gone, immaterial. Now I had all the time in the world. Old though I was: more time than ever. And the book of life: open, yet a sure thing, the pages, especially the blank ones, glowing in the wind of the world, this earth, the here and now. Yes, at last I would lay eyes on my fruit thief, not today, not tomorrow, but soon, very soon, as a person, the whole person, not just the phantom fragments my aging eyes had glimpsed in all the years before, usually in the middle of a crowd, and always at a distance, and those glimpses had never failed to get me moving again. One last time?

So have you already forgotten that it is not proper to talk about "one last time," any more than about "just one last glass of wine"? Or if you must, it should be like that child who has been allowed to have "one more turn" (on a swing or a seesaw) and then cries, "Just one more!" Cries? Whoops! —But haven't you used that phrase several times already? —Yes, but in a different country. And so what if I have?

On the summer day in question I did not pack a single book, even removing from the table the one I had been reading that morning, the medieval tale of a young woman who hacked off both hands to disfigure herself and make herself unattractive to the men pursuing her. (How could a person hack off both of her own hands? Was that kind of thing possible only in medieval stories?) I also left my notebooks and notepads at home, locked them up, as if hiding them from myself—at the risk of not finding them again—forbidding myself to make use of them, at least for the time being.

Before setting out, I sat down in the yard, with my bundle at my feet, on the only chair, actually more like a stool, at a distance from the trees, and staying away from the tables, the one under the elderberry bush, the one under the linden, the one under the apple trees, the largest, or at least most inviting one. As I sat there idle, my back straight, one leg crossed over the other, my straw hat clapped on my head, in my imagination I was embodying that gardener called Vallier (or something similar) whom Paul Cézanne often painted and drew toward the end of his life, especially in 1906, the year the painter died. In all these pictures, "The Gardener Vallier" hardly has a face, and not only because of the hat shading his brow, or a face, I imagine, without eyes, and with the nose and mouth as if brushed away. All I see in my mind's eye now is the outline of the man's face as he sits there. But what an outline. Contours that make the almost empty surface of the face they surround embody, express, project something that surpasses anything a realistic rendering of a physiognomy could ever convey—or at least that face looks different and transmits something fundamentally different—an entirely different modality. Wouldn't a possible translation of my altered form of the gardener's name from "Vallier" to "Vaillant" be not "watcher," no, "observer," "watchman," or simply "the vigilant," and that, together with the half-vanished sense organs—ears, nose, mouth, and above all eyes—as if wiped away, be appropriate for all the renderings of the gardener Vallier?

Sitting there awake, but at the same time in a kind of sleep, not the ordinary kind, I was suddenly reached by a voice, so close that it could not be closer—in my ear. It was the voice of the fruit thief, asking me something, as delicately as determinedly—impossible to be more delicate and determined. And what did she ask me? If I recall correctly (after all, our story took place long ago), nothing specific; something, for instance, like "How are you?" "When are you leaving?" (Or no, it has come back to me, the memory.) She asked, "What's wrong, sir? What worries you so? Qu'est-ce qu'il vous manque, monsieur? C'est quoi, souci?" And that would be the only time in the story that the fruit thief addressed me in person. (And what, by the way, made me imagine at first that she was using the informal mode of address this one and only time?) What made this utterance special was her voice, a voice such as you seldom hear nowadays, or perhaps never heard all that often, a voice full of empathy yet free of exaggeration, and above all a voice, the voice, of patience, patience both as a character trait and even more as a form of action, unremitting activity, in the sense of waiting and also awaiting. "I wait and I await you, him, her—I await whomever or whatever, without distinction and, yes, without cessation." Never would a voice like that take on a different modulation, let alone suddenly take on a terrifyingly different tone—as seems to be the case with most people's voices (including my own), and even more strikingly women's voices. This voice, however, was in constant danger of falling silent, perhaps once and for all—heaven forbid! Come to the aid of my fruit thief, O ye powers! With that voice still in my ear years later, I am reminded of what an actor once said, when an interviewer asked how his voice helped him act the story in a particular film: that he could sense, and not only for himself, when a scene, or the entire story, had "the right tonality," and he measured the veracity of a scene or a film not by what he saw but by what he heard. Then the actor laughed and added something that let me identify with him for a moment: "And besides, my hearing is excellent—I have that from my mother."

It was high noon, high noon as it perhaps can be only in

the first week of August. All my nearby neighbors seemed to have vanished, and not just since yesterday. It felt as though they had not merely moved to their vacation homes or chalets in the French countryside or elsewhere for the summer. I imagined they had moved away for good, farther than far, leaving France to return to their ancestral homelands—Greece, over the mountains in Portugal, the Argentine Pampas, the Japanese Pacific, Spain's Meseta, and above all the Russian steppes. All their houses and cottages in the no-man's-bay stood empty, and, unlike in previous summers, during the days and nights before my departure no alarm systems had gone off, not even in the few cars left parked on the street a good while ago, motorless.

All that morning, as on previous mornings, a silence had prevailed that with the passing hours spread beyond the borders or edges of the bay, less disturbed by the ravens' occasional cries, usually three caws, than extended even farther, if possible. But now, at midday, with everything wrapped in an inaudible windless wafting, more an intangible extra stream of air without an actual current, not visible in the summer foliage or perceptible externally on one's skin, either on one's arms or one's temples—not a single leaf, even the lightest one, that of the linden, stirred—all of a sudden the silence that had spread over the area descended onto the landscape, with a jolt as gentle as it was powerful, and, in a remarkable process, occurring for only that one moment in the entire summer: the landscape, already in the grip of silence, sank or subsided, with help from the silence descending abruptly from on high, yet remained the familiar buckled, bulging, sturdy earth's surface. That took place out of earshot, sight, and sensation. And yet it was evident.

To subside into the landscape had always been a daydream of mine. And up to now it had come to pass every time during that one and only summer moment, at least for the more than twenty-five years of my being in that one location.

On that day, too, during the hour before I set out for

the Oise *département*, the long-awaited moment of even more intense silence had descended on the general stillness. It had come as usual. And yet several things were not as usual, not at all.

As usual, when I looked up at the sky, I saw the eagle—with its wingspread curved like a sickle—circling, and forming part, as it always had before, of the living image of that one moment, silently swooping in upon its conclusion. In my imagination it was the same bird of prey year after year that had taken off from the preserve it shared with falcons, buzzards, vultures, and owls in the forest of Rambouillet to the west, and was now tracing spirals over the silent bay as it made its way east to the Paris suburbs and back. As usual I saw the bird circling over my head, in circles seemingly meant specifically for this particular area, as an eagle, although perhaps it was only—why "only"?—a buzzard or a kite. "Hello, there, eagle! Hey, you! How are things? Qu'est-ce que du deviens?"

Not usual this time was that the eagle flew so low. Never had I seen it circle so close to the treetops and roofs. In all the years before, even the swallows, so high in the blue sky, had glided several space-units below the eagle. But this time the swallows were tracing their trajectories above him, and I saw them—another unusual feature—less tracing their trajectories than whizzing back and forth, less high in the blue sky than usual, darting hither and thither just a bit above the eagle.

To be sure, the surrounding area subsided as it had always done in the many years before. But this time the ground and the underground did not remain firm and bulging. For several seconds, instead of the familiar lovely hollow or basin into which I subsided, I experienced the area as collapsing, threatening to cave in, and not only on me.

On that particular day my dreamed-of silence actually crashed over me like the shock wave of a worldwide catastrophe, if only for that one second. And for a second the reasons also became clear to me, not something imaginary but graspable, tangible, unmistakable: this subsiding of the surrounding area, this silence, instead of sparking action, was menacing and mournful, a menacing silence, and at the same time terrified and deathly: silent and paralyzed with terror.

This silence expressed what the history of the last few months and years, murderously intensified, had inflicted on human beings during this second decade of what I don't mind calling our third millennium, not in France alone, though in an acute form there, and also not audible, visible, or tangible in that one moment. Yet apparent, apparent in other ways. All the white moths crisscrossing the silent yard, each by itself, seemed to me to be crashing. And then, behind the privet hedge, in the next yard over, something suddenly cried out, striking me as a death cry.

But no: enough about death. Death has no place here. The cry came from the young woman next door, who had been sitting in a wicker chair with her embroidery, quiet as a mouse. A few weeks earlier—the privet was still in bloom, giving off that distinctive privet smell—I had glimpsed her through the foliage sitting in the same place, more a vague impression than a clear image, wearing a light-colored ankle-length dress, stretched tight over her very pregnant belly. Since then not another trace of her until that cry just now, followed by laughter, as if the young woman were laughing at her own reaction to a bit of pain.

And now the cry was followed by squalling, or rather squawking, the kind of squawking only a newborn could make, startled out of his infant sleep by his mother's cry of pain. Good news! I liked the squawking. Unfortunately it did not last long. The young mother gave the baby her breast, or something else. Silence on the other side of the hedge. I would have enjoyed listening to that crying for a long time, weak though it was, as if coming from inside a grotto. Here's to the next finger-prick, *jeune brodeuse*, at this same time tomorrow! Except that by then I would be somewhere else entirely.

Nothing was the same as usual on that summer day? Nonsense: it was the same as usual. Everything? Everything. Everything was as usual. Who said that? I did. I decreed that it be so. I settled the question. It was the same as usual. Exclamation point? Period. When I peeked through the hedge again, my gaze encountered a single eye, the infant's, which stared back at me, unblinking, and I tried to do the same.

Just as it was always a day like this on which a bee stung me for the first time, similarly, *simili modo*, there appeared as always, instead of the occasional large whitish butterfly hurtling down as if from high in the sky, the butterfly couple I called the "Balkan butterflies." I had given the two of them this name because I had been hiking through the Balkan countryside long, long ago when I first encountered the phenomenon they created as a couple. But perhaps the inconspicuousness of these little creatures when they fluttered around or just quietly rested in the scraggly grass, almost invisible there, also made this name fitting.

Yes, as usual, I saw a Balkan butterfly couple dancing around each other for the first time in the year. And as usual the dance displayed a special feature that I, at least, had never noticed in any other butterfly couple. They danced up and down and back and forth, yet spent a while each time in much the same location (before they moved their dance to another spot), until the two, constantly swirling around each other, formed a threesome. You could strain your eyes, trying to keep them apart and to see what you knew were two butterflies dancing around each other; but the image of the inseparable threesome would persist. And nothing changed when I got up from my stool, as I did now, and with the pair at eye level struggled to catch the threesome in the act. Right in front of me, hardly a handspan's distance from my eyes, the two swirled around and around each other, impossible to disentangle, as three, perhaps allowing a wave of my hand to separate them for an instant, but in the next moment twirling through the air as three again.

Yet why this desire to part them, to see them as they actually were, as two? Oh, my, time, time in abundance.

I sat down and went on watching the butterfly couple. Ah, how their transformation into three in the course of the dance sparked a glow. *Dobar dan, balkanci.* Hey there, you two. What's going to become of you? *Srećan put.* Whereupon it first dawned on me how much the little couple in its lightning-fast place-changing during the dance resembled the beloved hat game you could see being played on sidewalks all through the Balkans. Deception? Delusion? And again: so what? *Sve dobro.* All the best.

Time to go! But first the usual farewell turn about the house, about the yard, with occasional walking backward. Usual? This time nothing about my rounds was usual. Or rather: I made my way around the house as I often had before an absence I expected to last a while. Yet this time I felt different: pain, at the prospect of leaving, such as had never befallen me before, or rather quite often, but now intensified to a sense of leaving for good.

Not a tree, or at least not a fruit tree, that I had not planted with my own hands. (Rather amateurishly–in fact "bumbler" was the name I had most often applied to myself, more or less from my time immemorial, and not only with respect to my attempts at manual labor.) As usual I counted the few nuts on the crooked walnut tree, in the inextinguishable hope that the four I had spied among the leaves would have been joined by a fifth nut that had previously escaped my notice. No such luck. Even the fourth had gone into hiding. At least the little pear tree, thanks also to its scant foliage, prematurely withered, boasted its original six pears; they even seemed to have grown noticeably bigger overnight, fattening into the standard commercial pear form, while the quince, on the other hand, *le cognassier, dunja*, which the year before had won the fruit-bearing championship, this year stood there bare, its leaves rust-mottled. No booty there for the fruit thief, even though every morning after the blindingly white blossoms fell I had posted myself by the quince with something more than mere hope: determined to discover, hidden in the foliage, at least one of those yellow fruits, pear-shaped yet so very different, the smallest of *dunjas*.

On the day in question that determination—"Now I'm going to find it, that one fruit, overlooked until now, on the seemingly bare tree!"—became even more fervent. Circling the quince, one step at a time, pausing, looking up, around, down, going back and forth, and so on, my determination meanwhile swelling to a raging act of will to conjure, using nothing but my own eyes, the missing fruit into the void above me, to spy, in a gap, no matter how tiny, amid all the pointy leaves, "the one and only" emerging into the light and now, now swelling and growing round. And for a fraction of a second the magic seemed to be working: there it hung, the fruit, as heavy as it was fragrant. But then . . . Still—as I told myself—in the act of peering up and peering up again I had strengthened my neck, and that would prove useful for what was to come. And furthermore: time to stop counting. "The Counter," "The One Who Counts": one of your god's ninety-nine epithets? Strike "The Counter," indeed all of those ninety-nine names, especially "The Merciful" and the allegedly even more comprehensive "All-Merciful." Away with "The Almighty"! Or rather leave the god one epithet: "The Storyteller." And perhaps one more: "The Witness," or "The Testifier." And perhaps also that other one, number ninety-nine on your list: "The Patient One." So keep the numbers after all? No, no: one name, and another, and one more. Hadn't the apples on the trees in the yard as well as others been countless, innumerable?

As I walked toward the garden gate, I turned back to the

house and made my way down the stairs to the cellar. For a long time I stood there, looking at the sacks of potatoes, the pruning saws, shovels, rakes—remembering how the rakes made sparks fly from the pebbles—the soccer table, now wobbly, the child's bed frame without a mattress, the crate containing family papers and photos, and I could not remember why I had come down there. One thing was clear: I had meant to do, take care of, attend to, fetch something, something I needed, or that was needed in general, and urgently. Not for the first time I found myself standing and staring at something, whether in kitchens, hallways, entire houses, asking myself what in the world I was doing there. And as had happened to me time and again, I was at a complete loss, and whatever it was, the thing that needed to be done simply refused to come to mind. On the other hand: something had or ought to be done. There, in the cellar, I had to act—but do what, and how? And at the same time, as I gazed at all those objects, it came to me that this situation resembled my setting out from the outskirts of Paris for Picardy, a quintessential interior, where something special had to be done, taken care of, fetched, attended to. On the way to the garden gate I had known what it was. But at this moment it escaped me. And at the same time something depended on it—if not everything, then without a doubt various things. What had been certain just now had suddenly become uncertain—which did not make it any less urgent. It was more urgent than ever. And in particular it made me uneasy, just as standing in the cellar made me uneasy. Welcome, uncertainty? Welcome, uneasiness?

One last glance, over my shoulder, at the wide-open garden gate, the entire property, mine. Mine? Revulsion, along with weariness, overcame me in view of all those possessions. Possessions: fundamentally different from what I could call my own. Or put it this way: what I called my own had nothing to do with all the stuff—this was my thought—that belonged to me, over which I had property rights. I could not assert a right to what I called my own, nor could I count on it, rely on it. And nonetheless, in some cases, it could be obtained, though differently from possessions, and likewise sustained, maintained, retained.

Similarly I had always averted my eyes from what are commonly called "works," at least from those supposed to be "mine." Even words like *study* or *workshop* rubbed me the wrong way. Over the decades I had done my thing in every room in the house—in the kitchen, and also out in the yard. But I avoided even the most fleeting glance at anything that might confront me with evidence of my activity, let alone the actual product. It did happen, however, that I occasionally, and against my better judgment, found myself drawn to a "piece of work" and briefly(!) looked it over, weighed it in my hand, and so forth. That much I could tolerate, and it did no lasting harm; indeed, sniffing at the thing could even cheer me up, if not at the same time move me, yes, grip and strengthen me. But as soon as I immersed myself in anything I had made and literally sank into it, it lost its value, and not just for the moment, and above all its fragrance. Whatever had been accomplished went *poof!* and I found myself trailing in its dry-as-dust wake, enervated, unimaginably enfeebled. So I made a point of avoiding earlier sites of work in the house and yard—even those in the woods by the "nameless pond," in the "new clearing," along the "absence path"—or tiptoed past them as if something indecent had happened there. Only when I knew these rooms and spots to be empty, without a trace or evidence of what I had created there, could I pass them without being surreptitious. On the contrary, I could slow down to take them in. True, I would still be overcome with weakness. But that enervation was not the malign, incapacitating kind. It came over me as a sort of yearning, and of all the various and contradictory yearnings of old age, it was the last, and, I sensed, most durable yearning that remained, and it was linked, and sometimes also inextricably tied, to anxiety. Yearning and trepidation.

What a relief, instead of "work" and "property," the so-called works of nature. In the past quarter century the ground in my vicinity had been dug up, piled up, leveled, smoothed out. Only I, or so I imagined, had left the soil, the garden plot, alone, thanks to my lethargy or something else. And behold: in these few decades the ground that had been pancake-flat when I took ownership of it had been reshaped, thanks to the effects of water and weather ("thanks to" again), into an entirely different surface with harmonious contours, hummocks and hollows, miniature hills and valleys as far as the horizons (my neighbors' hedges, that is), a stimulating pattern that did the heart good, at once lying there passively and actively forming a miniature Land of a Thousand Hills. The land had developed waves, up and down, more pronounced from year to year, perceptible not just to the eye but also to the feet as one walked, strolled, wandered about, and the rhythm communicated itself not only to the soles of one's feet but also to one's knees and all the way up to one's shoulders, inscribing itself there. Yes, behold how nature, that great sculptor, had imparted fresh rhythms to the leveled ground; the land now radiated rhythms, and I pictured the fruit thief making her way over hill and dale and now pausing on one of the hilltops and shielding her eyes with her hand as she gazed over a far-flung landscape, or lying down in the grass and letting herself roll down the slope as we had done as children. Yes, this was my very own. And deep inside me an image sprang up, held still for a moment, and then was gone: a particular village on the Karst, just the outer wall of a house I had seen years ago while hiking and only now registered, which only now came to life from where it had been slumbering inside me—where? in my cells? in which ones?—ready to spring up and flash by. These images keep springing up and flashing by, even today, inexplicable, mysterious, silent pictures, always devoid of human beings, from the past, usually a very long-ago past, without any connection to what is happening at the moment, not subject to remembering or intentional re-call, fluttering and flitting, flaring up, and gone in a flash, not to be measured with any standard unit of time, absent for weeks on end, then coursing through me for a single day in swarms of shooting images, without specific meaning or with completely random meaning, yet I experience them and greet them every time—especially when they have been ab-sent for quite a while and on difficult days, and even when they do not flare but just flicker and fizzle—the thought "So all is not lost."

I fished three letters out of the mailbox by the garden gate and stuck them in my bag unopened; I would read them along the way. It was clear that they were real letters, almost the rule at the height of summer, with the addresses not stamped on but written by hand, the handwriting also not simulated by a machine. In these first two weeks of August one could finally count on being left in peace by the state bureaucracy—although even that was not a sure thing. But these were ob-viously summer letters, worthy of an epistolary novel, and if they did not belong to one yet, they could have a place here. The envelopes were not the usual kind; the paper, with an inner lining, felt different, rustled, had a distinctive smell, a weight that seemed promising. I recognized the handwriting on two of the envelopes as that of friends, and at the same time the writing looked different from what I had received in previous months—larger, with wider spacing. And also the realization: So he is still around, this friend and that. The third letter, without a return address and as the recipi-ent's address only "No-Man's-Bay," presented an unfamiliar handwriting, one that struck me as not so summery. But it also rustled intriguingly and was heavier than the other two. I would open it last. And by the bye I congratulated myself, and not for the first time, on the fact that the mail carrier, by now with quite a few white strands in her hair and soon to be a grandmother, as she pedaled her bicycle along the *départementale*, had had to turn off yet again and make her way to the gate at the end of the lane, one of the few places, I thought, on her daily route to which she still delivered actual letters, at least from time to time.

No more cars on the *départementale* (which I have referred to in other contexts as the *carretera*, *magistrale*, and *tariq hamm*), and seemingly for good. Likewise the last dog in the area had fallen silent, and not merely because of the late-afternoon heat. For more than that day, indeed for the whole month, the swallows' twittering had fallen silent, and the eagle had disappeared until the next summer—if then. And on the other hand—why "on the other hand"?—this silence was not mute. The prevailing silence, a complete absence of sound, struck me as a form of deliberate keeping still. It was not that silence of the infinite spaces that caused Blaise Pascal to shudder, but a silence that only this space, here and now, radiated, yes, a general keeping still by no means resulting from any presumption of timelessness but rather from time's holding its breath, becoming self-aware, also manifesting itself from one second to the next as something material, not a chimera but simply a different kind of real time, more tangible than usual in such moments when silence was deliberately preserved from one horizon to the other, or more comprehensively than usual, a silence that was eloquent, radiant, and made one shudder, in the sense of Goethe's dictum that shuddering "is humankind's best feature." Yes, indeed, this silence between heaven and earth was compressed, like a clenched fist, which, when it opened, revealed that the clenching had been an illusion, the moment preceding the most gentle unfolding imaginable. As I stood beside the garden gate, still open, I reflected that it would be impossible to experience this kind of silence in Picardy, that sparsely settled landscape, even for one tremulous second, and not only because during the next few weeks all the fields would be filled by day, and also by night, with the roar of harvest machines, and my gaze traveled across the yard to the enamel threshold I had had made when I moved in, with the inscription, a partial sentence from Revelation, I think, in Greek letters: *Ho hios menei en ta oikia, eis ton aiona*. The son remains in the house till the end of time. Remain? Back into the house? I stepped out the gate and closed it behind me. And then I decided to lock it, something I otherwise did not do even when leaving for a longer time, instead simply letting it swing shut by itself. But now, at the second turn, the rather rusty key snapped off, taking me back to the summer day long ago in my adolescence when I was given a key to go and fetch something from the car, but the key broke in the lock, and when I came back empty-handed, my mother said proudly to the others present, "See what strong hands my boy has!" And what went through my mind this time when the key broke? "That would not happen to the fruit thief."

Along the cypress-lined lane up to the highway. In reality it was not a highway, nor was the lane lined with cypresses. But I decided to have it so, in this story and, putting myself for now in the spirit of Wolfram von Eschenbach, beyond the confines of this story. Which was more or less "true." The lane actually did slope slightly uphill to the road. Usually when I left the house, going uphill did me good, letting me feel the ground underfoot and strengthening my knees. On the day in question, however, this benefit was absent, and it was not entirely the fault of my shoes, which, as I noticed only now, were much too light—and that was fine!—for all the walking I would be doing, probably also in rugged terrain. Turn back for my boots or the thick-soled John Lobb shoes that had proved their worth over the decade?

Turning back: out of the question, who knows why—because of the key stuck in the lock? No: I could have got in through the secret gap in the wall, known only to me. Never mind. And this time the decision was not mine but the story's.

At the end of the lane a parked car, empty. "On my lane!" All of a sudden I became the proprietor who wanted to get this auto non grata out of his neighborhood, and would have gladly smashed the windshield with a rock. But the only rocks available were pebbles, pounded into the roadbed. Goodness gracious: wasn't that a doctor's car, as indicated by the metal disk with the snake of Asclepius attached to a windshield wiper? Might the doctor's car be there for me? Had things gone this far? And involuntarily I peeked in to see whether a stretcher was installed in the vehicle's rear, with all kinds of straps to tie me down for transport.

Only then did I realize that the car belonged to the nurse or therapist who had been coming once a week for years to look after my ailing neighbor in his house on the corner of the lane and the *départementale.* As she could not park on the highway, it had been agreed that the woman would park on "my" lane. That I even found flattering. It allowed me to repay with a good deed my neighbor, who, when he was still hale and hearty, perhaps too hearty, had done me wrong—without meaning to, by the way, as is usually the case these days.

He and I had got to know each other before he fell ill. He had lost his wife, a woman who looked as though she had had wrinkles all her life, and the only member of the family—they also had children, who from a young age had nothing childlike about them—who might be seen doing anything other than leaving the house, starting the car, driving off, coming back, unlocking the front door, and closing the shutters; I sometimes saw her having a cup of coffee or a glass of wine at the bar in the railway station, walking down a side street, or alone, without her husband and children, in the bay's woods, during the summer, the same time of year as now, when the blackberries were ripe, weaving among the thorny canes with a few practiced steps and dropping berries into a metal pail that she seemed to have had concealed in her clothing, surreptitiously, as if berry-picking were somehow not proper for her, the wife of this particular man and the mother of his prematurely grown-up children, and from time to time glancing in my direction, also surreptitiously, as I glanced at her from my spot some distance away, even deeper into the berry patch, such behavior actually beneath my dignity as well as hers, and at the same time both of us with an expression in the corners of our eyes suggestive of something akin to complicity, even of a momentary stolen pleasure.

The lane ended at my property, but it continued as an alley leading to a small street that ran parallel to the highway, and my neighbor drove his car down the lane and the alley to get to the side street, where he could reach his destination faster than on the *départementale*, often choked with traffic. He had no right to do this—it was my lane! maintained by me! With my own hands I spread new gravel! raked it! mowed the banks! (my exclamation points.) He simply gave himself the right without realizing what he was doing, without meaning to. And thus, especially around the bend between the lane and the alley, when my neighbor zoomed by, braking for a moment, pebbles and gravel went flying, leaving behind potholes, more or less deep, a Land of a Thousand Hills entirely different from the work of nature inside my yard, and at the sight of the potholes I, too, became a leveler and smoother as I did my weekly raking, cursing, except that in the course of the following week the succession of gravel mounds and hollows leading to the main road in a rhythm of their own were turned by the rain into a series of glistening little gravel ponds and lakes, greeting me in their old freshness.

After his wife's death days went by with no car driving

down the lane, let alone speeding. Nothing but the distant hum of the highway, which had always appealed to me, including the occasional roar or even howl. And then one morning a crunching sound in the gravel outside my garden gate that went on and on. After a pause, and then another, it resumed, steadily, sometimes here, sometimes there in the lane. What was happening? What was going on? And suddenly, without looking, I realized what it was. I opened the gate, and outside I saw my neighbor with a rake, his efficiency far superior to mine, his arm and leg movements much more professional as he filled in the ruts and potholes along the entire lane. He was crying as he worked, silently. He looked up at me and continued crying as he raked. When I went to him and gave him a hug, he sobbed in a way I had never heard anyone sob.

For a while my neighbor refrained from driving down the lane. When he used it, he did so on foot, knocking on the gate to greet me, and I returned the greeting. Then, wonder of wonders, I even saw him on foot in the bay, whereas previously he had always taken his car to go to the supermarket, just a few buildings away, or to the small-engine and hardware store, no farther than a stone's throw, or to the real estate office, a hop, skip, and jump away, where day after day he studied the trends in prices for local building lots and houses. Even to the funeral Mass for his wife in the bay's church, no farther than an arrow could fly, he had roared down the lane with his now adult children and a couple of other people in the back, all of whom resembled him to a T.

Strange to see him on foot then, as if naked, without his protective shell, positively inept, a stranger to himself, walking along the road holding a baguette or a newly repaired shoe, or on the sidewalk, or even in the woods one time, not far from the clearing with the blackberries.

For a while after that I did hear him drive down the lane again, but slowly, as if taking one step at a time, quietly, cautiously. And a while later he whizzed by, the master of an even heavier vehicle, if possible, with an engine customized to roar into action the minute he turned the key, sending gravel and pebbles flying and hitting the trunks of the cypresses—until he fell ill, and so seriously that I, who at some moments had almost seriously wished him dead (to hell with you!), promptly felt nothing but sympathy.

From a third neighbor I heard later that the other man had complained about me: he felt harassed, if not threatened, by the stillness emanating from my house and grounds, a sort of assault by stillness, torture by stillness.

All that was long ago, the hug I gave my neighbor on the gravel raked into a wave pattern—the man with the rake a Japanese temple gardener—outside my gate. And nothing had stayed with me from that hug. What proved lasting was something else, and that has remained in effect to this day and will continue to do so—so I have decided: the sound of raking (or of a metal leaf rake), unseen, and likewise the raking that continued after the hug, once I had gone back into my yard and closed the gate behind me.

A different instance of hearing a rake or a broom scraping comes back to me now. This is probably not the first time I have told this story, but never mind. This particular sound I did not hear myself but received secondhand, passed down as a piece of family history. That history concerns an adolescent, hardly more than a child, my grandparents' youngest son. Between the wars, the boy, an excellent student, had been sent off at the beginning of the new school year to a boarding school, where he was supposed to prepare for the university, the first in his extended family. A couple of weeks later those back home in the village, his father, mother, brothers, and sisters—the latter first of all, as I imagine it—were awakened during the night, long before the first light of dawn (that was how I heard the story as a child), by the sound of a broom down in the courtyard, and it was their son and brother who, overcome by homesickness, *domotožje, mal du pays,* had run away from the boarding school, and set out on foot to cover the forty kilometers, so and so many miles, so and so many versts, back to the village on a road that had hardly any traffic at this time of night, and now, in pitch-darkness, was sweeping the courtyard, to signal that he belonged there and nowhere else—without having any more education imposed on him, and that then became his fate, along with a common soldier's grave off in the tundra.

That has to be told, repeated, and linked to the story of my neighbor, sweeping, raking, and shoveling on my property, because those raking sounds, always in my ear, made me realize just now to what extent situations like that stay with one, not simply worth passing along but practically demanding to be shared and transmitted, situations that transcend the boundaries between peoples, countries, and continents, and, usually very modest, are at once entirely different from place to place yet the same the world over.

I just realized something else: with only a few exceptions I did not experience these seemingly minor happenings with worldwide import myself, but rather had them related to me, if not while I was still a baby then very early in my life, among them the story of the brother sweeping the courtyard, as well as another that both haunted me and lit the way for things to come: the tale of the retarded milkmaid whom a farmer impregnated. After she gave birth to the child, he was raised on the farm without knowing that the idiot was his mother. And one day, after the little boy got caught in a hedge and the maid came running to free him, he asked the farmer's wife, who he thought was his mother, "Mother, why does the dummy have such gentle hands?" This story, which I again did not experience in person but knew only from hearsay, I spontaneously shared long ago, and it has been picked up beyond the borders of Europe, in the United States as a blues ballad in rural Georgia, or in Siberia beyond the Yenisei River.

Stories I witnessed myself that insisted on being passed on have remained the rare exception, and perhaps even rarer are things that happened to me in person. But what can the story experienced through the fruit thief reveal? This story demands to be told, does it not? Nothing like it has ever been told, right? And is it not a story of our times, if ever there was one? Right? Or wrong? Let us wait and see.

I had left myself plenty of time, and when I reached the end of the cypress-lined lane the nurse had already driven off. After his therapy or whatever, my ailing neighbor had summoned the strength, or the determination, to see her to the door, and now he was standing there, on the top step, clutching the railing with both hands. He had been given a glass eye, but his real eye, deep in a hollow, also looked glassy, its color faded, as if to match the artificial eye, instead of the other way around. Amazing that he could see at all, yet I could tell that his one eye was taking in the highway and at the same time saw me as I turned onto it from the lane. He called a greeting to me from the top step, yet his voice sounded sepulchral, as though it were coming from a cellar or a pit. It was his voice that conjured up that image. Before his illness he had had a voice accustomed to giving orders, even if he merely talked that way and did not actually give orders, and had probably never had occasion to, at least not in his work. It had a harsh, mechanical clang to it (clang?), lacking in modulation. But in his illness he had developed a different voice, in fact several voices, many and very varied ones, with each new stage in his illness another, if possible. And when he greeted me that day as I was setting out, it felt as though up to then I had heard a voice like that only in a dream, a particular voice that had sounded one time deep in the heart of the dreamer, promptly waking him: in the same way hearing that voice in broad daylight occasioned a kind of awakening in me that took the form of a jolt. Yes: it was a dying voice, weak, feeble, hard to conceive of one more feeble, and yet: at the same time that voice was bursting with life, and piercing, though without being painful as it had been earlier when he was well, or if it was painful, in a different way.

Our exchange did not end with the greeting, however. After I had inquired how he was feeling, my sick neighbor added, saying "we" as if his answer applied to me as well, "We have a right to live a while longer, haven't we?" and as he spoke his one good eye, opened wide, was fixed on the *départementale* in its summer stillness.

In turn I received a dual image, one that fit the situation, overlaid with one that did not fit at all, a puzzling one. The first image brought a memory of a time years earlier when we—not just my neighbor and I but most of us, if not all, who lived nearby—had packed the sidewalks for the first and up to now last time because that year the Tour de France had chosen this route for its final stage on the way to the finish line on the Champs-Elysées. And the second image, the one that inexplicably intervened? A different neighbor, back in my native village, known to all as a troublemaker and an all-around bad person, had picked up a hedgehog that had wandered onto the main road, positioning his hands on both sides of the animal's soft belly, avoiding the quills, in a gesture so caring as to contradict everything we village children associated with this despised person, this monster, and just as carefully set the hedgehog down a few steps from the road in a cow pasture.

The highway, always busy at other times of year, also led to the railway station, and it was so deserted that instead of walking on the very narrow sidewalk I strode down the middle—sallying forth. On that midsummer day the highway actually presented itself, *bel et bien*, as a country road—an aspect it otherwise assumed at most long past midnight and long before dawn, and as I rarely saw it by day. Behind me this wide road rose slightly toward seemingly endless chains of wooded hills, at their base a forester's estate from centuries past, long since abandoned and overgrown with wild vegetation, yet still state property, at least in name. Making my way along on the median strip, which extended in both directions to untold distant parts, as well as to the nearby railway station, I felt underfoot the seemingly flat asphalt, which reflected the blue sky above, as a rigid bulge, on which I balanced as on a beam, the median strip serving as my guide. At the same time I set down each foot as firmly as possible, even stamping as on an elevated trail, and made the asphalt reverberate—another thing usually possible only in the depths of the night. And verily: the deserted highway echoed from my footsteps, and from the bay's forests came, in my imagination? an echo.

"Illegal!" The term suddenly occurred to me. Even more fundamental: "An illegal!"

Seeing myself as an illegal: this was not the first time. Consciousness of my illegality had to do with my way of life, but not exclusively. Being an "illegal," an outlaw, was inseparable from who I was. Why? Never mind why. Only this: on days like the present one, shortly before an attempt to put into action an intention I had long secretly cherished—don't breathe a word!—my sense of being an illegal and doing something forbidden became even more acute. Am I exaggerating, and was this undertaking that I saw as forbidden in reality just something inappropriate, unsuitable for me as a person? Yes, that it was, certainly inappropriate and unsuitable for someone like me. But I was not exaggerating: this thing that was unbecoming of me coincided with the forbidden, and in my case was one and the same. And that was what unexpectedly struck me, now that I had finally set out, with my mind made up to pull it off—not the related concern that my undertaking would hardly be of any use, would be "for the fishes," as my brother used to say, using a village expression: well, let it be for the fishes!

My illegal venture would close me out of human society, as it always had. If in the past I had found myself, often in the middle of a venture and without knowing exactly how, readmitted to society, though one different from the old, familiar one, now I was afraid, as I made my way along the deserted suburban road toward the train that would carry me into the interior, that this time I would be closed out for good. And simultaneously this thought heightened the happy anticipation of my illegal tour. At the thought of what most law-abiding people did and were up to from early to late, from morning to night, year in, year out, with one human century racing into the next, up to the present period with its breakneck speed, what seized hold of me was not my foolish, childish, positively sinful arrogance but rather something that in a past century had been called noble-spiritedness (and might be called that again, in some future century, who knows).

This noble-spiritedness came in the form of a push. Although I was limping, and not merely because my foot was swollen from my bee sting, my walking became striding. These were epic steps. And that meant: steps that drew others in. I was not alone with the sky above. I had company. Whom? What? I simply had company. I took that liberty, had that right. And did I not see the fruit thief as someone similar?

Suddenly more and more buses came along, one after the other. I hustled back to the sidewalk and watched the convoy disappear into the distance. All of them were empty, headed for nearby Versailles, where tourists, who of late included many from China, waited on the esplanade in front of the former royal residence to be picked up. As I watched them pass—for years I had enjoyed watching anything go by—I pictured myself as not heading north to the Picardian highlands of the Vexin, at first sight so inhospitable, so devoid of historical interest, or rather of any markers whatsoever, but instead west to Versailles, two or three kilometers away, and taking a hotel room there for whatever might come, close to the Carré St. Louis and the square in front of the cathedral, with bars named Espérance and Providence. It was these names at least that drew me to the former royal seat. Often, so often, and in recent years more powerfully from one time to the next, I had noticed, as I walked in that direction, engaging in the roaming and roving so necessary to me, especially along the rigidly geometric streets, elsewhere rather annoying, all of them more or less leading to the palace (which I still have not visited), that the sensation of moving through a part of the world that had sunk out of view and been scattered in all directions, something from long ago, for the moment, and beyond it as well, rejuvenated me, lent strength to my legs, light to my eyes, and a whooshing past my temples—what more could you ask for, heart of mine? Yet I had no desire to have a king or kingdom back—at least not outwardly; the return of any kind of monarchy was simply inconceivable to me. Whenever I spied, on the gigantic esplanade in front of the actually rather delicate palace, the statue of the so-called Sun King astride his horse, with his sword and the morning-star-like spurs, which this Louis XIV (not me counting) is digging into the horse's flanks as he gallops into yet another murderous war, and then another, and so forth, heading toward the sun, my thought was: no more kings! Never to lay eyes on another king! But that aside: Ah, rejuvenation. Ah, young world.

And now enough about rejuvenation, regaining youth, acting young. The only young one was the person at the center of this story, the fruit thief, a true youngblood. And that although, and also because, she has already bled a lot for her age, and from very early on. I saw her before me as I walked along, saw her without stopping reach through a fence and snag an apple from one of the trees lining the road, an early apple, rare in France, land of the most varied types of apples, pure white inside and, as the term indicates, already ripe since July. I saw the fruit thief before me? Yes, but without a face, without any image at all, nothing but a motion: saw her flex her fingers, unlike me, before she reached through the fence. I did not see her fingers either, only their dance through the air, stretching, spreading, bending, unfolding, closing around themselves—if that was any kind of image, it was a form of typography, like musical notation. And in contrast to me, she would also not have grabbed the early apple in passing but would have stopped to take it. She would not have reached through the fence surreptitiously, like a thief—with sticky fingers. Unlike me she would not have promptly tucked the apple away. Unlike me the fruit thief would not have sped off after doing the deed. But rather? Let us wait and see. I, on the other hand, crossed to the other side of the road.

There I looked into the shops, of which there were quite a few near the station, or pretended to do so. Actually there was not much to see, either because during these first two weeks of August almost all the stores and workshops had their metal shutters lowered, or because the one shop whose display window was not shuttered had gone out of business and had no need to conceal anything from passersby. The large bare glass surfaces, splattered from top to bottom with what seemed to be windborne sand and dirt from the highway—the glass all intact, not so much as a crack—were "display windows" for me in a special sense. In the past I had developed the habit of pausing briefly to look into one of them whenever I made my way to the station for a longer absence. It belonged to the workshop of an Armenian shoemaker and locksmith who had disappeared—to where?—more than a decade ago, and the charming disorder inside included the shoe-rack carousel (or what should it be called?), the winder with replacement soles (or something like that), the metal grinding machine (?), etc., not only untouched but also ready to start up again, not so much clearly visible as glimpsed through that glass smeared with sand and dirt, but promising: on the table with the grinding machine were little piles of iron and brass particles filed off the key blanks (or whatever), a mounded landscape of tiny metal crumbs and shavings, which continued to glitter and glitter even with no sun shining into the abandoned workshop. And a few steps farther on the shutters of the corner bar had been lowered more than a year ago for the last time, the old Berber who owned the bar having returned to the Kabyle in northern Algeria, *inshallah*, but there, too, I had made a habit of pausing, why?—to pound my fist twice on the metal shutter, one short, one long, and to listen to the echo inside the empty, or perhaps not entirely empty, bar. Echo? At least I imagined one, in the form of glasses still waiting to be filled, jingling, the refrigerator clanking, with one or two half-empty bottles still inside of the wine served only in the Berber bar, an off-label wine, and, I have to admit, terrible; an echo magnified by the one cat door in the wall, likewise orphaned for over a year, and oddly installed at shoulder height, forcing the widowed owner's many cats to scramble way up high to get in.

A few steps farther on, on the threshold of the square in front of the station and drawn into the action, the no-man's-bay idiot. (There were one or two others as well, and it would not have hurt to have a few more.) I had not run into him in quite a while, and had been thinking that he, too, had disappeared, in one way or another. He zoomed around the corner as he always had, but this time he was not singing and also did not bend over to pick up the trash blown by the wind toward the station, which he considered himself responsible for removing, since no one else did. He did not recognize me, or did not want to. I watched him go. He had grown old since the last time I had seen him, when I had treated him to a cup of coffee in the Berber bar, and he had screamed—he screamed every time he opened his mouth, even when he sang—that I was always so kind (which was certainly not true). Old, but wearing a stylish windbreaker and a pair of black leather pants that looked as good as new, an outfit such as only the old Johnny Halliday could permit himself to wear, and then only when acting the rock star onstage. The aging idiot crossed the square in silence, shoveling the air with his very white palms, turned toward his back, his enormous head slumped forward, his black leather pants sagging halfway down his backside, also very white.

The threshold of the square? Such a thing actually existed, in the form of the tangle of roots spreading outward from the mighty beech at the end of the railway underpass. All around the base of the tree, sections of individual roots protruded above the surface, forming, in hollows and humps of various depths and heights, a sort of mountain range *en miniature*, the model of a mountainous landscape. Once upon a time, more than a decade and a half ago, the fruit thief's mother had set out for the Spanish Sierra de Gredos from this very threshold, flitting from root to root like a sprinter taking off from the starting line, to seek her vanished daughter, whereas now the child herself was roaming across the French high plateau north of the Oise, on the trail, or not, of her long-lost mother, although the fruit thief had various other things in mind as well. I, too, who like the rest of the pedestrians usually avoided the roots where they branched out into the asphalt, used them on that August day as a starting point, scrambling right over them, imagining myself weaving right and then left, making my way higher and higher up, from peak to peak, lifting my knees, straddling obstacles, and finally descending into the valley, where, as I crossed the square toward the station, for a few seconds I felt in the soles of my feet the rhythm that the roots had communicated to my entire body. Although any kind of wishing had long since come to seem pointless, and I had given it up altogether: I would have wished to keep that rhythm inside me.

A man and a woman passed me. The two were walking single-file, with some distance between them, but I saw them as a couple, and that they were. And it was also the case that they were not coming to meet me but were going in the opposite direction, opposite not only to mine, no, to everything taking place just then. Only moments earlier the two had been part of the crowd, of the bustle, the surroundings, the locale; had participated more or less without a care in the world in the give-and-take of conversation, supply and demand, move and countermove. And now, at one blow, all that was over. Only moments earlier they had been walking side by side, if not hand in hand, under the towering, cloudless, blue summery sky. And now they were slinking, the man a few steps behind the woman, toward the railroad underpass, their eyes terribly wide and neither of them blinking. The blue sky was mirrored equally in the two sets of eyes, and those eyes not only displayed the identical form but also the same celestial blue, except that both mirrors were blind, literally uncomprehending, from sheer misery and despair—hopeless, irrevocable. The way the woman in front and then the man behind dragged themselves along, neither one of them all that old, there would never be, for her as for him, any possibility of reaching a destination, let alone home. No refuge, no asylum would take them as a couple: prohibited—against the house or home rules and against all rules in general. To be sure, they would still lie side by side, who knows where, but never again, *plus jamais*, sleep with each other in a bed, no matter how shabby—over and done with any dream of a bed for me and him, for her and me. When had the world ever seen such a lost couple. And yet the two formed a couple, perhaps like no other, and perhaps the best imaginable, though also unlike those usually described as "beautiful," "photogenic." From the way the woman scuffed along it was clear that she was aware, without turning to look, that the man was scuffing along behind her, no possibility of a happy ending. Should I help these two? Impossible: they would not have registered any offer of help, or would have taken it for yet another threat. I did not exist for them. No one in the world existed for that accursed couple. Helpless, helpless. Did anyone like the fruit thief exist for them? Might that mute procession of misery have been distracted by the sight of her and her style? But wasn't the fruit thief usually very inconspicuous? Not likely to be noticed? But what if precisely such inconspicuousness could give the couple new eyes?

For the time being: keeping my own eyes on the ground as I walked. Water from the hoses used to clean up after the open-air market trickled over the slightly sloping square. The booths already dismantled, and water pooling in the sockets for the poles. Coolness rising into the early afternoon heat, a breeze with a hint of fishy odor. Pigeon tracks leading from the damp areas, back and forth, to the dry ones. But that day my attention was drawn more to the many iron plates in the paved surface of the market and station square. From year to year their numbers had multiplied, in the no-man's-bay as all over the world: plates for the sewer system, then plates over underground electrical cables, television cables, telephone lines, gas conduits, fiber-optic cables, also automated barriers that would shoot out of the ground in case of a terror attack, and God only knows what else. Now I noticed in particular that according to their markings—stamped, engraved, or molded into them—the majority of the steel or iron plates and grates had been manufactured in Picardy, near the area toward which I was headed. Over the decades I had encountered them in many European countries, especially in their capitals, these markings with the manufacturer's name—Norinco—what might that mean?—most often on manhole covers for drains and sewers, and in the course of time I had almost developed a craving to see this lettering, stamped or raised, at my feet in foreign cities, and whenever I saw that word it made me briefly feel at home or at least cheered me up.

The Norinco brand, in combination with the place name Méru—I occasionally felt patriotic stirrings for that region—seemed to have a monopoly on manhole covers and the like for the whole country and beyond its borders to the oversea *départements*, from the Caribbean to the Papuas in the Pacific and up into the far north, in the enclave of Saint-Pierre et Miquelon near Newfoundland. The very prospect could make one weary.

Furthermore, over the years almost all the massive, heavy covers had worked their way out of their moorings in the tar and asphalt, and now often came loose in a matter of weeks. Yes, it seemed to me that more and more they had not been seated firmly when they were installed. The result: whenever a pedestrian stepped on one, it caused a banging, crashing, booming, repeated by the next Picardian iron plate, and on all the sidewalks, streets, and squares one heard that banging, crashing, booming, seconded by other pedestrians stepping on the plates, and especially by cars and even more so by trucks, a seemingly interminable, grim, cast-iron Norincoish racket exploding underfoot.

On the day of my departure, however, the racket occurred primarily inside me. I was familiar with all the loose covers and avoided them as I crossed the bay's main square, zigzagging as if in a slalom. Besides, no one else was out and about, either on foot or in cars. At one point I heard a crash in the world outside me, a thunderclap from underground so powerful that it not only echoed across the square as it lay there in its August stillness but also into the wooded hills on the horizon, the heights above the Seine. The trio of police officers guarding the entrance to the station spun around with one accord (one of them was a woman), their submachine guns at the ready, and stared in my direction. It turned out I had caused that crash, stepping on a Norinco cover that only the day before had been firmly welded in place and seamlessly embedded in concrete.

Because of market day only a few cars were parked nearby, on the far side of the square, and they seemed to have been there a long time. These vehicles likewise had a connection to the area for which I was setting out. All of them were rental cars, small, inexpensive models without any fancy accessories, only the bare minimum. Their license plates all displayed the code for the Oise *département*, my destination. What code? Look it up on the internet. And check the following: I heard once that the majority of rental cars in France were registered in that particular *département* for the purpose of giving it some tax revenue to compensate for its small number of industrial plants and corporate headquarters. Whether that was true or not: at any rate, these cars, washed and waxed to make them look new, even if they were not, all had Oise plates and were available to rent. But what were they doing here in the no-man's-bay? How had they ended up here, forming a small squad? For whom or what were they waiting, lined up along the side of the square? They stood there, seductively empty, as if on a starting line, with the sun shining into them and quietly magnifying their interiors.

But look! Look over here! In the window of the one bakery of the three around the square that was open in August hung a poster announcing that the flour used for the bread baked there came from a mill in the town of Chars, located in the middle of the landscape that was also my destination, part of which belonged to the Île-de-France, a second part, farther to the north, to Normandy, and a third, farther to the east, to—guess what!—Picardy. In the days of the kings, the Vexin area, with vast fields of wheat and rye and hundreds of mills, had been known as the "breadbasket of Paris." Now, of all those mills, only one remained in operation, in Chars, on a river called the Viosne, but this one mill took up half the village. I promptly went in and bought a loaf of bread made from that local flour, and for my house in the country accepted a copy of the mill poster, lying there rolled up as if waiting for me.

Time to stop for a bite to eat before getting on the train. Oh, dear, had I forgotten: the Hôtel des Voyageurs, along with its bar, had closed long ago. How refreshing it had been to sit on its terrace on a summer day, in the lovely shade cast by the plane trees, watching the trains pull into and out of the charming little station, barely visible through the leaves. Now only a few homeless occupied the hotel's rooms, most of whose windows were covered with sheets of cardboard, people stranded in the no-man's-bay, all of whom, grown old and without family members—or at least none who would acknowledge them—needed care, daily, hourly, and had been warehoused by the state, left to fend for themselves in that quasi-ruin.

So today there they were, all of them, or rather four instead of last week's five (the fifth had died the previous day), huddled on the steps outside the former bar in the still lovely shade of the plane trees, and the one or two of them a bit less in need of care were sitting upright and turned their heads to look; they were pretending to be, or actually were, the caretakers of the two or three others, slumped over, their heads lolling on their chests. The one who had died and was still lying upstairs in his wretched hole, his corpse gradually being discovered by flies, would be buried at state expense, as was customary in such situations for the inhabitants of the former Hôtel des Voyageurs. Only these few remaining companions out on the steps would attend. A relative, a brother, sister, ex-wife, children—if there were any—had never turned up at the bay's one cemetery.

These asylum recipients huddled close together, most of them locals, born in the no-man's-bay and never having left, except perhaps for military service. Impossible to tell whose crutches belonged to whom. And which of them might not need crutches? Or for which would a crutch be no help? A . . . I cannot bring myself to use the new term . . . was out of the question for people like this. And they looked more than sightless; they looked eyeless. But when I said hello to them, all their faces lit up, and I noticed, not for the first time, that it was the grimmest faces, the ones belonging to people who day in, day out refused to favor not just me but anyone with a glance, that suddenly, in response to a greeting at the right moment, beamed with a friendliness that bore no resemblance to the standard greeting-card kind (though that kind might show up, too, at the right moment).

They waved me over, and I crouched down beside them, between the one whose bald head displayed a deep scar, from a blow with a machete, that ran from his brow to the back of his head, and, on the other side, once he had made room for me, the man wearing dentures he had removed that morning from the one who just died. He stressed that he had not taken them "right away, not until this morning," and he showed me how the dentures, unsecured with adhesive and never going to be secured, constantly slipped, especially when he was speaking, from side to side and from front to back, on his upper and lower gums, bare for so long now. All four derelicts were smoking and drinking, passing around one bottle, and when it made its way to me, I, too, put the bottle to my mouth and took a swig of the supermarket wine, not even the cheapest, and then another. All this happened some time ago, yet I still have the taste in my mouth, less of the wine than of the cigarette smoke, which, unintentionally blown into the bottle, had blended with the wine. —It sounds as though those two swigs weren't enough for you, and you're keen for a repeat. —Already happened.

But what haunts me in a different way is this: that from the faces of these outcasts, Jean-Jacques-Louis-*sans-pays*, now that they were so close to me, from behind their unfeigned friendliness something else emerged, something from which—thanks to films, television, photography, especially in close-ups, blown up to make enormous posters and Titian-sized paintings—any trace of reality had been forcibly removed. This "something" was called "hunger." And now, looking back, I can see that this hunger communicated itself to me from only one of the faces. But how authentic it became, despite having seemingly been illumined so often in the third to sixth world that it had become part of a nonworld. This was hunger, here and now!, not in the third world but in the first. I could no longer believe the thousands and tens of thousands of homeless huddled on the sidewalks of Paris with pieces of cardboard propped in front of them bearing the falsified or genuine handwritten assertion: "J'ai faim." But this mute hunger was real. Hunger, the condition, the suffering, the need? Yes, and furthermore all that reached out to me from the face of that one man as something that transcended the condition of mere passivity. It was a special hunger, and in it vibrated at the same time an absolute, boundless hungering. The man was hungry, ravenous, for food, and not just since that morning. And in addition he hungered. (I would not have been able to express that to him in French; his language had no such verb . . .) And for what did he hunger? Again: no "for what." He hungered, and hungered, and hungered. And could anything be done? For the moment, yes. That for the moment he be alive. He is alive.

And after that you went to the one bar on the square still open during the summer, to rinse the taste of smoke out of your mouth with a different wine? —True: I did go there. To have a glass, "Just one, really." I took a seat on the terrace, here/there called Trois Gares (after the three railway stations in the vicinity), in the shade, less inviting than under the plane trees, joining the other undeterred midsummer guests. All of them had tables to themselves. The Macedonian was describing his detour on the way home to Ohrid. The Portuguese carpenter was holding forth on his belief that after death the soul lived on somehow. The Romanian mason pooh-poohed the idea. The Polish woman was weary from working the night shift at the retirement home. The market vendor's assistant from Martinique wanted to party with the rest of us before heading back. The Scotsman was rooting against the rich Protestant fans of the Glasgow Rangers and for the poor Catholic fans of the Celtics. The young Russian woman from the university residence hall was reading Leo Schestow, in French, to learn the language. The Algerian barkeep was demonstrating how long he could stand on one foot, and he helped me with the pronunciation of the Arabic word for patience, *sabr.* The oldest among the regulars, the only Frenchman, was immersed in a pamphlet, and when I, the Austrian, asked him what it was about, he said, "It's about the Battle of the Somme, exactly a hundred years ago, with a million casualties." Before answering he had stuck his finger in the page he was reading so as not to lose his place, a passage he then handed to me, which began, in English, with "And then . . ."

None of the regulars there on the terrace of the Trois Gares seemed to take the slightest interest in me. Of course they said hello when I joined them and asked how things were going, but I did not bother to answer; no one would have listened. Even my unfamiliar duffel bag–they usually saw me with no more than a small backpack–did not arouse their curiosity. Yet it was a military duffel bag, inherited from that brother of my mother's who was buried in the tundra, the swastika replaced by a multicolored tangle of embroidery, and the moth holes darned. Before sitting down at my table I had pushed the bulging bag onto the terrace with my feet, with exaggerated slowness, as if wishing the others would ask where I was going and why I had such heavy luggage. But the folks at the other tables took as little interest in my travel plans as in my well-being. And nonetheless I knew they were with me, and likewise, at least perhaps for the rather short time we spent together, I with them. With respect to these strangers, about whom I was not all that keen either to find out where they came from and how life was treating them just then, a phrase occurred to me that at an earlier stage in my life, back in my own country, and especially during my youth there, had always struck me as rather offputting, dismissive of me, and that phrase was "people like us." In this case, however, "people like us" signified a kind of solidarity, as free as it was casual. Without expressing opinions, indeed sometimes contradicting or interrupting one another, "people like us" here were fundamentally in accord. They might not want to know anything about one another, but they were open to one another. I knew, or perhaps just imagined it again, that I could reach out to all of them, if I wanted to and the moment was right. Once reached by whatever was at stake, not for me alone but in general, they would open up, and again not just alone.

These few reachable people constituted the exception in the no-man's-bay, if not worldwide. In recent decades I had come to recognize that the overwhelming majority of two-legged creatures commonly known as "humans," whether members of the yellow, white, black, or any other race, belong to the race of unreachables. A majority, or the vast majority—impossible to define it in percentages—cannot, or perhaps never could, be reached by anyone or anything, and certainly not by me or someone like me. Nothing surprises them. Nothing makes them prick up their ears. No ray, no reflection gets through to them. These unreachables lack entirely the capacity for what was once referred to as "keeping your eyes or ears open," even when it comes to "Mother Earth," whether the natural or the human world. To express it comprehensively or "globally": the race and mass of the, of my, unreachables lacks a capacity for resonance. Nothing, not even the vanished legendary heavenly terrestrial music of the spheres, if it returned and showered its tones on them from on high and from underground, would find an echo chamber in them, not even a dull one like inside a privy.

This characteristic of unreachability among my contemporaries, or whatever they should be called, became apparent to me, among other ways, when I observed that the places where they carry out their various activities, their surroundings and environment, mean nothing to them, and this is not their fault; my people are also not to blame for their unreachability. Just look at the square in the no-man's-bay, with its railway station and the surrounding shops, banks, and offices. With the possible exception of the baker, most of those who work or have business there live somewhere other than in the no-man's-bay—somewhere else entirely. Not once have I seen these people who live elsewhere, these bank tellers, driving-school instructors, station clerks, life-and-death-insurance agents, small-animal vets, pharmacists, and public-safety officers, other than "on duty," as the phrase has it. ("He had no choice but to intervene, he was on duty.") No one who came or was sent to the bay on business or for work could ever be seen, whether during the lunch break or after work, just strolling around town, let alone looking at anything—true, there was nothing "sightworthy" there—or, and this would have been delightful, making the area unsafe. At most those very young ticket agents, boys and girls from far beyond the heights above the Seine, might step outside the station for a moment to smoke a cigarette. And if you asked the police officers, and not just those from the elite unit but also those who patrolled the square in peaceful times, where such-and-such was, they would just shrug, strangers there themselves, and without really looking at the person asking the question, but rather, in their role as unreachables, gazing past him; the Romanian mason, or was it the Portuguese carpenter, liked to joke that the police are like women—when you need them they aren't there, and when you don't need them they fall all over you.

Perhaps you have noticed that I refer to the unreachables as "mine": "my unreachables." Does this indicate that they mean something to me, that I regard them as my people, even these unreachables, they of all people? That is how it is. *Ita est.* In my eyes they all matter to me, these however many billion unreachable two-legged creatures, every single one of them, to the very ends of the earth. I know, or I think I know: no one and nothing can get through to them, nothing true, nothing beautiful, and certainly nothing once known as "godawful beautiful," not one of them. But I, I want to get through to them, have wanted to for a long time, one and all of them. Or let me put it this way: I have always wished, passionately, that I could get them to be reachable, to cock their ears, to open up, to respond (even without words), whether as two-legged creatures, one-legged creatures, amputees, or even crawling on all fours, for all I care.

At the same time I realize that this longing of mine—it is more than a mere wish—is bare nonsense without the veiled dance of sweet illusion. I have experienced this: animals, especially when they register a voice and a rhythm meant for them, usually open up and listen, which can already be a form of response. The same can never be said for you, my unreachables, you crowns of creation. Yes, I have experienced this: not just one bird or another—especially this raven and that—has pricked up its ears to listen to me, but also now and then a snake, a toad, a hornet. And perhaps the snake responded by slithering away more slowly than usual, the toad seemed to pause for a moment before hopping away, the hornets stopped zigzagging through the air in front of me and instead circled around me, showing off their special hornet yellow, their wings whirring unthreateningly, as if they were shielding me from the high-pitched whine of the stinging wasps, and thereby making it clear that hornets, in contrast to you wasps, are creatures that know how to keep their distance, and furthermore, so entirely different from you, have a sense of decorum.

A long time ago I imagined I was creating something that would get through to a person once it reached his ears, even if he were lying bound and gagged in a pitch-black closet. And now? Now I imagine that you hordes of unreachables, born unreachable to anyone and anything and from that time on placing one foot in front of the other during a long life, getting increasingly long and perhaps in the not-too-distant future immortal, would be reachable—would become my reachables—only in such a closet, without light, bound and gagged and without another soul near. Only in such a place would you actually listen, would you give an answer—if only a whimper—instead of in your overly distinct voices, like those from loudspeakers, ultrabright, inescapable, blaring. A place where you would no longer be on duty, you unreachables. —Arrogant thought! Prideful! —No, noble-spirited, again and again.

The last place before my journey began, which would take me straight across Paris to the Gare Saint-Lazare and from there onward in a northwesterly direction to Picardy, was the children's playground next to the bay's railway station, located right beside the tracks, from which it was separated by a tall fence. I had grown fond of it over the years, and not precisely because of the children. Besides, it was hardly used during the summer holidays, and at that particular hour I thought at first it was completely empty. I sat down on a shady bench by the swing and ate my purloined apple. It was juicy, tart and at the same time soft, and tasted like old times. As usual in the early afternoon, and especially during these two summer months, trains were infrequent, and the most noticeable sound was the wind in the treetops.

The two swings were rocking slightly, perhaps from the wind, perhaps from a child who had been swinging a short while ago. The swing set stood in full sun, and the shadows the swings cast on the ground seemed to move faster than the swings. Suddenly, from the sand at my feet, the eagle suddenly took off, the one that had circled over my house and grounds that morning, though now in the form of a small butterfly, with markings on its wings like those of an eagle's plumage. Only then did I notice, behind the swing set, on another bench, in deep shadow, half hidden by shrubbery, a woman, a young one. Her face looked familiar, and she smiled in my direction as if she recognized me as well. I searched my memory, and at last it came to me: the woman sitting there, not in her usual place, was the cashier from the supermarket on the lower end of the railway-station square.

She was wearing her red work-smock but had taken off her clogs or slippers, as well as the "work socks" that went with them, now draped casually over the shoes she had kicked off. The dark-skinned woman's hairdo was the same as always, yet it looked different. Everything about the cashier seemed different. It was just the end of her lunch break, yet a different person sat there, lapped by light and shadow, a person transformed, a being, reminding me of the time I had heard someone exclaim of a child, "That's no child; it's a being!" Just so the sight of the young woman filled me with amazement and caused me to experience something I had often experienced and recognized time and again but always lost sight of: the insight, yes, that transformation is always possible.

A transformation like that was the opposite of distortion; it amounted to an elevation, an opening-up, a movement from the defined to the undefinable. It could not be summoned at will, but it was also within my power. I had orders to bring this about; to transform was a commandment, one of the commandments between numbers eleven and thirteen. The commandment in question—paradoxically?—was liberating like no other. But was it not the purpose of every commandment to create freedom, in the form of a well-regulated world?

Seeing the cashier from the supermarket transformed also transformed me, *mutatis mutandis,* and memories came flocking back of not a few similar transformations, beginning with the director of the largest of the banks on the square, whom I had come upon not that long ago in the middle of the bay's woods, on the edge of a secret little clearing, almost overgrown. He, who in his director's suite was always flawlessly groomed, with his Dior or other costly perfume wafting over the threshold, his fingernails looking as though he had them manicured hourly, his hair gelled in waves, was sitting there in the tall grass, drenched in sweat, his hair disheveled, as he spooned soup out of a metal canteen, the kind with a screw-on top that keeps the contents warm all day, and in earlier times, or perhaps to this day in some countries, would be given to workers by their wives for their shift. The banker was leaning quietly against a tree trunk, and now and then brought the spoon to his lips empty, meanwhile gazing around the clearing, as if it were his secret realm, but not in an improper or forbidden sense; rather, its secret nature was what made it the best possible place in the world for him at this hour. Upon catching sight of me, he scrambled to his feet with a welcoming smile and, just as in his office, held out his hand to me from a distance, the gesture the same and yet entirely different, and said, his voice expressing unfeigned surprise, the very thing I had on the tip of my tongue: "Well, well, well; look at that! Fancy meeting you here, in the middle of the woods!"

Involuntarily I peered in the direction of the bench where the cashier was sitting to see whether she, too, had a canteen at her feet. But what gleamed from the shadows were only her naked soles up on the bench, constantly flexing, and bright against her dark legs. The young woman was neither tapping nor swiping her mobile telephone. Nor was she applying makeup, with a pocket mirror or anything else, as I often saw young women doing in the Métro, especially in early evening. She did not lean back, did not close her eyes. She displayed neither tiredness nor alertness. She did not open and close her pocketbook. She did not glance from beneath lowered lashes. She did not bat her lashes or raise her eyebrows. She did not run a finger over her lips. She did not pull her smock down over her knees or hike it up. She did not play unapproachable or receptive. She just sat there, flexing her feet, quietly occupied with herself yet not self-absorbed. And although she neither looked at me nor expressly looked away from me, it was clear we were confidants, just for now or for good, sharing a secret in the moment and for the future.

She got up from the bench and made her way back to her cash register in the supermarket. As she was leaving, she waved to me, and I waved back. As she strode off in a straight line, it was striking the way her long, slim arms swung, making it look as though she were weaving back and forth. The last glimpse I had of her revealed her tugging at the belt around her hips, again and again, up and down, back and forth, with barely perceptible movements, as if only with her fingertips. That did not create the impression that she wanted to attract attention and put on a show; on the contrary, it seemed as if she were trying to make herself invisible. I had caught the fruit thief performing similar magical gestures.

Up to now I had made a practice every time I set out of walking backward for at least a few paces, on the lane, on the highway, and especially when leaving the playground by the railroad tracks, but this time, once I reached the platform, I walked straight ahead. It was no contradiction that on the train I took across Paris to the station where I would change trains I sat with my back facing in the direction in which we were traveling. I had made this my duty for whenever I used public transportation, whether buses or trains; I was convinced that I saw more this way when I looked out the window, or saw differently. And if you ask me whether I would have preferred to have a window seat on planes where I could face backward, the answer is: yes.

As the train pulled out of the station, I noticed for the first time that the almost deserted suburban platform was blanketed in wilted leaves, blown here from who knows where. Yet the previous day I had seen the platforms and the railyard swept clean by the summer wind; a particular pleasure to walk along the tarred platform and then step onto the much longer sandy strip, having heard just moments earlier the familiar clattering, clacking, and clicking of the passengers' footwear, and now, all of a sudden a change, as the footsteps, even those of the most pointed and tough-as-nails ladies' shoes, the tongs or tangs, or whatever they were called, designed to torment one's ears, continued on their way calmly and peacefully to the farthest ends of the platforms, making a many-voiced crunching, as if we were all there not for a short ride to Paris on one track or an even shorter one to Versailles on the other, but about to take a train from a station in the desert, and from there? To who knows where.

One day later, however, during the hour of my departure for the trip into the interior, when I looked out the window as the train began to move, I imagined that from the ankle-high leaves that had covered the sand, instead of the promising crunching beneath people's soles, there would come nothing but a racket, and of the clusters of bathing hollows pecked by the railway sparrows into the sand, increasingly numerous toward the end of the platform, which only yesterday had been whirring with innumerable sparrow wings, stirring up little clouds of sand and dust all along the platform, accompanied by frenetic squawking and peeping, all that could be seen today were the pre-autumnally fallen leaves clogging the bathing hollows, the leaves motionless except when their stalks were ruffled occasionally by the wind.

Now nothing about my trip or my plans seemed obvious anymore. And that was all right! Had things ever seemed obvious to me? Never. Not even once. And wasn't it fitting that almost immediately after leaving the station the train plunged into the long tunnel, strangely long for a stretch so close to Paris?

Something else had caught my eye as the train pulled out and I looked out the window at what was behind us: something in the sky above the no-man's-bay was different, and not only since that day, and likewise something was missing, that, too, not a new phenomenon. First of all, the planes, numerous as usual, crossing the blue sky in all directions, their wing lights blinking everywhere, and leaving noticeably short contrails, as if that were a feature of summer, made an unusually peaceable impression, perhaps also because they were flying at such a high altitude that the sight of them suggested the old word *airship*. Such peaceableness, if one reminded oneself of the current state of affairs, in which one side as well as the other had declared "war," struck me as all the more astonishing, until I realized that there was nothing to be seen or heard of the large military air base that bordered this part of the outskirts, and that this had been the case for some time: no rattling and rumbling of helicopters flying low over the roofs, no sudden roar of fighter squadrons seemingly shooting forth from the treetops. The local airspace, "our airspace," I thought involuntarily, was deserted, with the exception of those passenger planes way up in the stratosphere. Where had all the military aircraft gone, the bombers, the fighter jets? Of course: they were stationed closer to Paris, deployed right on the edge of the imperiled city, ringing the metropolis, along with the combat and war machines of other military air bases, cheek by jowl. But where? Along the outer boulevards? Camouflaged under grassy banks on either side of the expressways? Ready for sudden vertical takeoffs, or whatever they were called? Whereupon I, as the train was still gliding through the tunnel toward Val Fleury, the Valley of Blooms (or something like that), had exhausted my entire strategic vocabulary or bla-bla-bla before even getting properly started.

After disembarking at the Pont de l'Alma, in the middle of Paris, I made my way across the bridge to the Alma-Marceau Métro station, from where I would continue on to the Gare Saint-Lazare. How fast the Seine flowed there, through its narrows and around the bend, as if it were backed up, a torrent like a mountain brook's, accompanied by a rushing sound, perhaps the only one in the city. This spot had always captured my attention, and did so especially on this day, more briefly than usual but all the more intensely.

In the Métro, bodies crammed in like sardines. As I had experienced before, and not all that seldom, in Paris at least, all the faces on the subway appeared beautiful, noble, from the brows to the eyes to the mouths, and even the noses, in all sorts of configurations, seemed "beautiful." Except that this time, unlike other times, I did not need to peer through my subway car, *la rame*, and into the next one: here, in close proximity, all the faces were beautiful in the Métro lighting, and I enjoyed the smell of the bodies, if they smelled at all, and however they smelled.

Outside the Gare Saint-Lazare, amid the milling crowd, the old man was sitting on his plastic stool, as usual when I took the train from there to the country; in my eyes he was something of a Lazarus, though not a saintly one. It was not just his disheveled hair, with a few remaining blond streaks; the whole person looked as if he had survived the shower of ashes, as if he were surrounded by a layer of ashes up to his bare ankles. Yet he was always smiling, at no one in particular, and also not to himself. Five years earlier, when I took my first trip to Picardy, to Vexin, he had been sitting in the middle of the sidewalk in exactly the same way, with thousands swerving to avoid him, and he had had the exact same sign around his neck, which read not "J'ai faim!"—"I'm hungry"—but "J'ai 80 ans, aidez-moi!"—"I'm 80 years old, help me!"—the difference being that now 80 had become 85, just as in previous years it had been 81, then 82, and so forth. And now, for the first time, when I had already passed him, I turned back, as I usually found myself doing with beggars, and gave him something, not necessarily as the Lazarist benefactor but rather as if I almost—no, in all seriousness—wanted to receive something in return, for instance in the form of a specific smile, a kind of traveler's blessing. The blessing did not materialize.

Inside, the station was swarming with beggars. And they were different, not quiet, mute, passive beggars but active, raucous, demanding ones. Accosted from behind at the ticket machine, in the middle of typing in my data (or whatever it should be called), I kept making mistakes, until finally I snapped at one of them, saying he should let me finish, whereupon the beggar, who had just been begging in robotic fashion, recoiled in the most visceral, human way, actually retreated a few steps, and apologized softly, whereupon I felt sorry for him and gave him something, too, despite having missed my train in the meantime. (Another would come along fairly soon.)

Should I interpret his backing away as the necessary traveler's blessing? I was still deliberating when the next beggar accosted me, and then another. I did not give them anything; after all, I had "given already," and "twice." From left and right curses rained down on me: "Shame on your mother! May your fingers get leprosy! May you be crushed between the train and the platform! Death to your children! May you sleep in quicksand! A rotten tooth as your talisman! A moldy apple for supper! Your last path paved with dog poop! Your remains dumped in the drain of a lion's cage!"

As these words echoed in my head, I wondered: Had all this been the missing traveler's blessing? Yes, I decided, and already I felt I was being propelled forward, lifted up and carried over the crowd, which was swelling in this early evening hour, and at the same time I remained steady and firm on both feet, my eyes fixed, amid the masses of passengers, on the station floor, which seemed empty despite the pushing and shoving: make way! for nothing but me and my destination.

I observed that now and then a jolt would course through all those making their way to the trains, moving quickly yet calmly as if this were their daily routine; even those who were rushing, running, kept their composure, but when the jolt occurred, a regular stampede would erupt that somewhat resembled flight, a truly panicked running-away, which, however, never lasted, and after a few steps quiet returned.

What was that about? With my eyes fixed on the empty floor amid the crush, I saw no crowds or masses. Had they never been there? And every time I looked up, that proved to be the case: at eye level I saw and heard only individuals. Or how about this: I both heard and saw each person separately. The general din had resolved itself into a single sigh, and what a sigh. In the eyes of another passenger, rushing with the throng along the long concourse, called the *salle des pas perdus*, hall of lost steps, toward his train, I could read pain, a particular and particularly powerful pain that prompted him to slow down or even come to a complete stop, which, however, was out of the question. A pain? Pain. "Pain" pain. And that would persist, and nothing would ever assuage it.

The railyards of the Gare Saint-Lazare are divided between those for local trains serving the outskirts and those for long-distance trains, the trains to Normandy, primarily to the sea, to the Atlantic at Le Havre, Deauville, Fécamp, Dieppe. Neither local nor long-distance trains went to my destination. My train took a spur that ended in the middle of the countryside, far from Paris and about equally far from the ocean. Would I have preferred to be one of those passengers heading to the trains that went to the sea? Those days were behind me. As I boarded my train, I remembered a dream I had had the night before. For this particular train, in the dream I had needed a boarding pass, as one usually does only for a plane, and I had forgotten mine, or at least did not have it on me. It was too late to get a new one; the train would be leaving any minute now, and it was the last train going in my direction, and not only for that day—the last one ever.

In fact this was the last train (of the day) to Picardy's Vexin county. Not many trains traveled the route—how many? I knew that at one time—hardly any in midsummer—how many?—hadn't you decided to swear off counting?—and this last one was leaving Paris in almost broad daylight, although it was early evening already, Daylight Saving Time, and that meant that the daylight stubbornly refused to break, as people, or rather I, needed to have happen after a certain hour. And once past the megalopolis's limits, from Argenteuil on, the train would stop at every one of the many stations—how many? no answer—most of them mere whistle-stops. By the time I reached my destination, it would not be night yet, not even dusk, but the quality of the light would be different, finally, and not solely because of the advanced hour.

The train had been packed when it left the station, after having been delayed repeatedly by passengers racing through the station, people who, after their workday or whatever in Paris or wherever, were determined to catch the train to get home, or wherever. Squeezed together, if possible even more tightly than in the Métro, we sat, or for the most part stood, everywhere in the double-decker cars, too small for the crush, and many of us, me included, huddled on the stairs, while the folding seats at the entrance and exit doors were also occupied, some of them by two passengers. Eventually, after jerking forward several times and halting, as if it could not be expected to handle so large a load of passengers, the train began to move at last, sounding a departure whistle of several minutes' duration. In the silence after the whistle stopped, when no one spoke and not even a mobile telephone rang, nothing could be heard in the cars but the polyphonic chorus of gasping and wheezing from those who had rushed to the platform and jumped on at the last minute or, incapable of jumping, had been pulled in by those of us already on board, and the gasping in unison drowned out the occasional rattling and panting, and the whistling sounds from deep inside lungs that suggested a bellows about to burst.

As usual during the summer, our train had none of the free newspapers available at other times of year in all cars. Anticipating that, at the station I had bought the *Parisien*'s local edition for the Département de l'Oise, so as to have the weather report and the regional section, and now I studied the paper as I crouched on my step, folding each page in half vertically to read it—there was not enough room to hold a paper open, even a small-format one like the *Parisien*. As usual the weather forecast bemoaned the appearance of even the tiniest cloud on the horizon, and a rainy day, summer showers, or a steady downpour was portrayed as a major threat—not to crops but to city-dwellers' vacation plans, and almost any wind, including summer breezes, was feared, viewed as an undesirable headwind. The next column over offered my horoscope: "Elements manifesting themselves at the last minute could throw a wrench in your plans." And the fruit thief's horoscope? "You have become indispensable. Beware of abusing your power." The regional section carried a report about a little girl who had been playing by the road in a village when she was abducted by a bachelor farmer. She was found unharmed on the remote farm where he lived, and in court the kidnapper testified that when he invited the girl to get into his car he was thinking, "This girl, this child, won't do anything bad to me!" (His sentence: ten years behind bars.) Another local story from the Oise featured a policeman who spent his free time tracking down pencil sharpeners from around the world; the collection in his basement now comprised tens of thousands of items; he had started collecting as a child because he was shy. Then, skipping ahead unintentionally, as I so often did, to the national and international news, I read that the man who had murdered the elderly priest in his church near Rouen (Normandy) had had "indescribably gentle eyes" after cutting the priest's throat. A death-row inmate in Texas—where else?—had been proven innocent an hour before his execution, and once more I found my throat constricted with tears. But on the same page I read about the serial killer who targeted young women, virgins exclusively, because he wanted to see the terror in their virginal eyes as he strangled them, and he himself experienced just such a long-drawn-out death, eye to eye with a female executioner and strangler, herself a virgin. And look, on the page before that: the Aral Sea, almost completely dried out, is filling with water again!

Argenteuil, Cormeilles, Herblay: more and more passengers getting off, hardly any getting on; the majority of the passengers lived in the suburbs, and for them the train functioned as a local. Then came Conflans, a town, as its name suggested, on the *con-flans*, the confluence of the Oise and the Seine: was that still a suburb? It looked like a suburb, but of what—Paris? The city's proximity hardly perceptible. And then came, farther to the north, Pontoise, the city of bridges on the Oise, the old royal seat perched atop limestone and gypsum cliffs high above the river, with the presence still palpable in the cathedral—if you wished—of Saint Louis, Louis IX, the king who wore a woolen cap instead of a crown, the most childlike of kings. Not a hint of suburban character there.

The cars had not emptied out entirely, but many seats

were available, and one could leave the stairs and have a seat to oneself, at some distance from the handful of other passengers. We sat? We read? We looked out the train's windows? We sighed? No sense of a "we" of any kind. No more "we" on this day. "No milk today, my love has gone away"? But why could I not take my eyes off the others? And certainly not off the women, especially the young ones?

It had become noticeably brighter in the cars, open to each other all the way to the first car behind the locomotive, where I sat with my back to the direction of travel, and the last one in the rear, where behind the glass door the tracks unfurled behind us; bright from the more and more sparsely settled landscape after Pontoise, and even more noticeably after Osny and Bossy d'Aillerie, with cultivated fields only now and then, like last outposts in the increasingly untended landscape—the route followed the river upstream through the valley of the Viosne; bright from the empty spaces in the train, becoming more numerous from one stop to the next and reminding me of white areas on maps—only old ones?—bright from the clothing and even brighter from the bare skin of all the young women sitting by themselves in one or two cars; it seemed as if, with the exception of the occasional older to old man, e.g., me, from the front of the train to the door in the rear these were the only passengers.

My eyes, scanning from woman to woman, straight through the short train's few cars, were searching for something. I felt pressured, compelled, to discover in these women. Discover what? Just discover. But time and again I failed, with each of the young women. There was nothing to discover, nothing at all, at least not for me. I usually found women in veils properly—or improperly—off-putting. But I also felt, I knew, that the unveiled face of a beautiful and also a less beautiful woman had the ability like nothing else on earth to uplift me and my heart. Yes, long live the heart, long live the hearts! And there was no need to bring Paradise into it, to paraphrase the saying that nothing promised Paradise as reliably as the scent of musk, the beauty of women, and the glow of eyes in prayer. Not once in my life had the unveiled face of a woman awakened anything like sexual desire in me, let alone so-called lechery. From time to time an open, tranquil face like that had awakened me, true, but that was always a sanctified time, yes, and her face awakened me to myself, yes. Away with all you veiled and disguised ones, for God's sake.

But as I looked at the young women on the train, I wanted their faces, or at least some of them, to be hidden behind veils, thick, dark ones, rendering them invisible. With veiled faces—depending on the veil—there could be something to intuit, and if you were lucky, that intuition could turn into clear perception, a different kind of clarity. These women, however, all these faces, and not only these, offering themselves openly for all to see, seemed without exception (exception, however tiny, show yourself!) masked to me, that was how obsessed I was with detecting even the smallest thing I could recognize, that would speak to me. In my youth I once saw someone in a masked procession not wearing a mask, and I thought, "Only the one without a mask is marching proudly," and then, "I want never to see masks again."

And now, wherever one looked, there was one masked face, one disguised body after another. Not an eye that lent itself to being recognized in any way. No hairline revealed itself to be alive, even when the airstream briefly ruffled a lock of hair. Not a freckle that might, upon closer inspection, turn into two. No collarbone inspired any insights. No half-bare chest, no exposed navel, no polished fingernail suggested anything, made an impression, affected one. Affected me and my person? Affected the space, intervened in the plot. Didn't it happen from time to time that especially in the presence of strangers, someone's story, no matter whether it was a man's or a woman's, in the twinkling of an eye took on form as language, as image, image as language, as a verbal image, a single word-image, which, even if it did not correspond to the facts as experienced, stood for life writ large? The women's masked faces and disguised bodies did not express anything—anything that gave rise to an image, no matter how fragmentary. They permitted no concept or imagined notion or, heaven forbid, fantasy, about any life that might be hiding behind those masks, or had been, or would be.

I felt myself flying into a kind of rage, on the verge of chastising these women because they bore no resemblance to what I thought they should be. Mute though I was, I must have developed the evil eye. For the young woman sitting closest to me abruptly turned as if she were trying to get away from me, even though two rows of seats separated us. And again I was on the verge of opening my mouth and shouting what I was thinking: "Don't imagine I want anything from you! No man, no one dreams of getting anything out of mummies like you. And supposing someone did: woe unto the poor men who land in your clutches, you false majesties. In no time flat, when you masked women go on the warpath, you'll flatten them. You're all on the wrong track—on one that leads nowhere. But at least you've noticed me."

Away from her and her fellow warriors, away from the ladies' club. The train's lower deck was empty. But a second glance—no, several glances—revealed that someone was there after all. Or was that just a heap of clothing, forgotten, left behind on purpose, cast off? Half sitting, half lying there, not on one of the regular seats but on one of the jump seats, was something alive, a living being, a person. The pile rose and fell in a regular rhythm. The person, stretched out on that very narrow fold-down seat, was sleeping the gentlest slumber imaginable. A strand of hair that had fallen across the person's eyes blew to one side with a particularly strong exhalation and revealed the sleeper's whole face.

Shock: suddenly I had the fruit thief before me. The shock had two sources: first that she was there in the flesh, my fruit thief, and also that it could not possibly be she. I knew, of course, that she was not far from here, in this very area, this very region, but it was impossible for her to be the woman sleeping there, for me to run into her at this particular moment, on the same train.

Hard to believe, but you must believe me: the shock felt sweet. When I took a few steps back at the sight of the young sleeper, I was not recoiling; it was an expression of pleasure, a pleasurable shock. And it gave me pleasure to back away and observe her and her surroundings, in expanding circles.

Descriptions of faces, of this kind or that, have always rubbed me the wrong way; they seem to be trying to impose specific impressions instead of letting the impressions form themselves. So here I will mention only that the young woman's temple displayed the same curved veins as the fruit thief's, perhaps only now, when she was fast asleep, and she seemed as "young and fresh" as the fruit thief–which would perhaps also change–what a transformation!–when she opened her eyes, without losing the appearance of youthfulness.

More remarkable, or remarkable in a different way: how the jump seat on which this young woman was sleeping, from her slumped-over head to her feet stretched far out in front of her, had been turned into her very own. It seemed as if it was not she who had molded herself to the seat but the other way around, and the entire space had become hers, with the car's floor converted, as it were, into a place where she could stash her luggage, of which there was a great deal, rough and to my eyes dark and wintry like her clothing, as if she were on her way to undertake a one-woman scaling of a snow-covered peak, and in Picardy of all places, with rolling terrain at most but not a peak in sight. And remarkable, too, that her legs, splayed as she slept, signified nothing but legs splayed as in any human creature's sleep.

My sweet shock turned to astonishment as I observed her. Only now did I realize that the young woman had chosen a place to sleep located directly under the stairs to the upper deck. Astonishment because now a specific memory came to me: the fruit thief's mother had begun her long-ago search for her missing daughter far from home, in Spain's Sierra de Gredos, to be precise, and in the end it had become clear that the child—which she still was for all intents and purposes—had been in her mother's neighborhood the whole time, even on her mother's property, disguised as a boy and living in a former gatekeeper's lodge, and at the time that had reminded me of another story, a very old one, actually more of a legend: the legend of Alexius, who returned after years in foreign parts to his parental home in the guise of a beggar, not recognized by his family, and took refuge in the enclosed space under the stairs, nameless, admitting to being the long-lost son only in the hour of his death.

Hadn't the young girl had a similar name, or been given one by her mother at the moment of the "mother-and-child reunion" that Paul Simon once evoked in a song: "Alexia!"—never mind what her real name was. "Alexia!" Ah, so many maps, with a level of detail otherwise found only on military maps, lay open all around the sleeper on the train. A daydream, mine, at the sight: "All those maps to help her search for her mother . . ." And further: "But why does she also need geological survey maps, depicting all the rock formations and strata in Picardy, layer upon layer of deposits going back ten, fifty, a hundred million years?"

The sight of the sleeper surrounded by her stuff became too much for me. I withdrew into another car, the one at the very back of the train. Out of the corner of my eye I then glimpsed the young woman getting off in Chars, the town with the mills, already in the county of the Vexin but still in the Île-de-France region, on the border with Picardy. I made a point of not following her with my eyes. I had seen enough for now.

By the exit from the station in Chars, the last stop in the Île-de-France before Picardy, the usual inspectors were waiting, as if ordered up—by whom? not by me. After Chars a new rate zone began, and tickets for the previous stretch were no longer valid. According to the warning placards, quite menacing, posted in the train, anyone who stayed on board for even a short distance with an old ticket was a "lawbreaker" and had to expect a hefty fine, if not a jail sentence.

In Chars the couple of passengers getting off, and presumably also the fruit thief's double, had already been required to show their tickets. I had averted my eyes, as if something in me rebelled at seeing a person without a ticket being humiliated by these uniformed officials; the mere spectacle of the six of them (6!) blocking the exit, after all six had donned their so-called uniform caps in unison, impelled me to look away, away, to gaze in a different direction entirely, and when I noticed one of the young women on the train or another doing the same, that created a little something we had in common. I regretted the opinion I had formed of them earlier. Sheepishly I turned back to them in my mind, all of them.

When the train left the station again, the six-person inspection squad had come on board. At first they bunched together at the entrance to the car, just letting themselves be seen. For a while they did nothing but talk loudly among themselves, more loudly than even the loudest passengers in any train in the world, and they kept laughing raucously, the women among them—equally represented—even more raucous, yet all of them sounding disingenuous, as if they were merely egging one another on with their laughter.

Then, as if on command, they fell silent and spread out through the car, but in such a way that each one was covered by a fellow inspector, male or female; you could never tell—on this particular stretch an inspector had been slapped five years earlier, and ten years earlier one had been tripped up. In contrast to the earlier loud talk and guffaws, the inspectors now modulated their voices and exhibited perfect courtesy as they asked the passengers to show their tickets and identification. And they handed the documents back with utmost graciousness, holding them with their fingertips, as if they were precious items that they had turned this way and that to ascertain their authenticity, and they thanked each of us and wished us a pleasant journey, a good evening, and a restful night, their voices (the men's) suggesting pure brotherliness, and their eyes (the women's) gazing down at us from above, but by no means condescendingly, seeking our eyes as we sat at their feet. No conductor—conductors always came through singly—would have interacted with us so correctly, and in any case by now there had been no conductors for a long time, at least not on trains like the one in which we were riding; besides, had France ever had "conductors" at all, rather than, from the beginning, consistent with French official usage, *contrôleurs*?

In the end all of us still in the car, still on the train, had valid tickets. Not one of us had been exposed as a lawbreaker. Not one of us was escorted off the train at the next station, that of Lavilletertre, the first stop in Picardy. We were free people, all equals. It would have taken little for the six inspectors, in the same manner as they wished us a good evening as they prepared to leave the train, to congratulate and compliment us.

A voice made itself heard from among our thinned ranks. It belonged to one of the young women, the one, in fact, whom I had pegged earlier as an enemy, if not my archenemy—I suddenly could not remember why—was it her short hair? her muscular neck? Maybe the unusually large nostrils that kept flaring? sinewy calves that seemed to be laughing at me? or eyes that looked past me as soon as they lit on me, while a prominent chin pointed up in the air as if to say, "So what do you want? Out of my way! Beat it!"?

It was a timid voice, or one that murmured, as if speaking

to itself. The inspectors stopped. But they did not hear her. Or rather: they did not understand her. But I understood her. The young woman at the back of the car said the following: "For months on end you were on strike yet again; you call that a 'social movement' and were nowhere to be seen. For months your *mouvement social* paralyzed the country again and made things tough for the rest of us. No sooner have you ended the strike—God knows why it started in the first place—than you're back checking my ticket, checking on us, you *contrôleurs*, and that's the one and only way you're effective. A reason for your social movements, according to you in yesterday's and tomorrow's papers: you don't want, it said, and it will continue to say, to have to get up at four in the morning anymore and be insulted by passengers. And when do we passengers have to get up? And what's at stake for us? Often everything! And for you functionaries? Nothing, nothing at all. Ah, if only we insulted you even more, and not just the few malcontents among us, but all of us—shouted you down to dwarf size, dwarfs that you are—shouted you out of our way, never to be seen again. An honest-to-goodness brutal dictatorship would be better than your saccharine, velvet-gloved version. Once upon a time regicides in the name of human rights, now you're destroying the country in the name of social movements." And then the young woman added, after the six inspectors had jumped off between stations, promptly vanishing, like ghosts, "Sonorous assholes and squawking cunts, sonorous cunts and squawking assholes (*trou-de-culs sonores et connes aigues, connes sonores et trou-de-culs aigues*). And typical: wherever and whenever these assholes and cunts jump off, there's always an official vehicle waiting to pick them up. And if I tell them I can't stand them, I'm scolded: You don't love your fellow human beings! Yet how I loved my fellow human beings as a child, and still do at some moments. But because of you and the terror you spread, your special state version, I'm rapidly losing faith in human beings, in humankind altogether. And not just to think but to shout from the rooftops: Strindberg was wrong; it's not a pity about us humans. Away with us!" But she said this last thing so loudly that the entire train heard it, even the engineer up front in the locomotive.

Why was our train not moving, free now of its occupation force? The villages of Montgeroult, where the southerner Cézanne painted his northernmost landscape, and Us, allegedly a new name given after the last world war out of gratitude for liberation by the American and British troops, but actually a thousand-year-old name, lay behind us, and there was no sign of the next station or even of a village. Another strike? Or a terror alert? Far too few passengers on the train for a juicy mass attack, ripe for the headlines, and out in the country besides, nowhere near the metropolis.

But who knows? Fear was in all our bones. And it expressed itself in a heightened sensitivity to noises, not confined to one or two of us. If nothing else, we contemporaries had something in common now. I would never have thought that the sounds associated with my so-called activities could disturb anyone. At most I had toyed with the notion from time to time that as I was sharpening my pencils, polishing my shoes, peeling apples at the open window, I would hear from behind the hedge or elsewhere a neighbor or someone shout, "Quiet!" since I already startled people when I dropped something, and in the Métro passengers ducked if someone came running as the train was pulling out and yanked open the door, or if a person merely spoke louder than usual.

That had been the reaction when the train braked, then came to a stop between stations, while at the same time we heard a crash that escalated to a rumbling: for what did we have to brace ourselves now? Yet it was only a bicycle parked in one of the connectors between cars that had fallen over. But at the moment of the crash and its reverberation, all the passengers who I had assumed cared about no one but themselves sought the eyes of those sitting opposite them, including mine, and all of us exchanged glances. That by way of an addendum to the story of the fruit thief, and probably not the last—as indeed I should add that at the time of that incident in the Métro, at least during the period of heightened fear, I had a Saracen dagger in my pocket, a very short one, to be sure, in a leather sheath, and I surreptitiously fingered it, intending to train myself in its use and be ready to strike quickly in an emergency—to which I should further add that when I attempted to draw it my fingers always got hopelessly tangled, and I would have drawn the dagger far too late, or it would have remained stuck halfway out of its sheath.

No, not a railway workers' strike, and certainly not an attack. With the inspectors nowhere to be seen, had the engineer felt like getting out and stretching his legs, or something of the sort? From the time we had crossed into Picardy, there had been no more announcements over the loudspeaker, or if there had been, garbled, impossible to understand. By now the line had only one set of tracks, but no train would be coming from the opposite direction; ours the last to use the tracks that day. This was not the first time I had experienced on this stretch, not far from the last station, that the engineer took his time, especially in the couple of weeks at the peak of summer. That was perfectly fine with me, and probably with the few remaining passengers as well. And in the meantime each of us was paying attention to the others, had shaken off the reticence of the first hour of the journey. How shy we earthworms had become! Had the human world ever seen anything like our current leeriness of other humans?

Was I mistaken in thinking that the engineer, standing in the tall grass beside the locomotive, was relieving himself? I was not mistaken. And next to him, with hardly any space between them, stood a passenger, an adolescent, not much more than a child, doing the same. So I had not been the only male passenger after all? Or had the boy been riding in the locomotive? Was he the engineer's son?

The two remained standing by the tracks, talking. The women on the train had all closed their eyes. Two who had been sitting next to each other since our departure, strangers jammed in together, had kept their seats as the train emptied out, too tired to move, or who knows why, each of them preoccupied the entire time with something else or, if not preoccupied, looking away, and these two had not only closed their eyes but actually fallen asleep, and their heads had tipped toward each other. They were sleeping head to head, the two of them, and neither of them knew anything about the other, not her name or what she did for a living, and they were also not aware that they had fallen asleep head to head and were sleeping soundly; more soundly would not have been possible. In a drawing the lines of the four closed eyelids and below them the four corners of the mouths would have been parallel, four times the same downward-sloping curves. Fruit thief, make drawings of all the sleepers you encounter on your journey!

Strange, or perhaps not: how all the women in the car woke up at the same moment and pulled out their pocket mirrors to make themselves beautiful, coloring their lips more or less red, smoothing their eyebrows. Making themselves beautiful for what? And not on an excursion to the seashore but into the innermost part of the country's interior? Making themselves beautiful precisely for that—for the interior?

I got off the train and joined the father and son in the high grass beside the tracks. It turned out that the explanation for the train's stopping between stations had nothing to do with a whim on the part of the engineer. There was a power outage, which, however (see above), was not unwelcome to him. The power would come back on shortly, he said. Whereupon the father and son continued their conversation, looking forward to having supper with their wife and mother, in Trie-Château or Chaumont, I forget which, at a restaurant, and they already knew what they would order, the son a pizza margherita, I believe, and the father? That I have forgotten also.

Where our train had stopped, we were no longer down in the valley of the Viosne. We had left behind that river's headwaters and found ourselves on the Vexin high plateau, not all that high, actually, in Vexin's Picardian part (there was also a part in Normandy and one in the Île-de-France). Here, shortly before Lavilletertre (roughly translated, "village on the hillock"), one's eye no longer rested on the buckthorn growing in the water meadows but flew in all directions to the far-off horizon. A gentle, steady wind was blowing, as if independent of the seasons, from the northwest, where, if you needed to (I felt no such need), you could imagine the ocean, a hundred kilometers away, in Dieppe, with the bay of the Somme, and so forth. The sense of expanse seemed to be enlarged further by the fields spreading in all directions on the far-flung plateau, the crops, other than the corn, already harvested, and likewise by the complete absence of villages, as well as single structures, even wooden sheds, the sole exception being the television tower, or was it a water tower? atop the hardly noticeable chain of hills in the middle distance called La Molière. Most characteristic of this time of year, the height of summer, in the hour before sunset, with the whole countryside bathed in yellowish light, were the few cloud banks high overhead, piled like dunes, and behind them the all-spanning blue of the sky, at first glance tender and familiar, but looking more and more unfamiliar as one gazed up at it, yet reminiscent of something, except that the memory remained elusive, leaving one, me, us in the lurch, as this blue sky increasingly left one in the lurch, more disquieting than any specific threat.

All the more reliable, if not more homey, perhaps even

more welcoming, the land beneath, every time one looked down, away from that sky blue. This area, at least where the train had come to a stop between stations, had no flowers in bloom, its image dominated now in August at most by the omnipresent whiteness of the morning glories, twining from the grass up into the treetops. At this time of day, however, the blossoms were closed up tight—by contrast, what a gleam from their depths in earlier hours!—tightly rolled up, "like hand-rolled cigarettes with too little tobacco inside" (as the Romanian mason would have said) or easy to confuse with the "used tampons" dangling in the bushes (the Portuguese carpenter)? Even without blooms and flowers, however: how the countryside offered bouquets to me, one, us, a very different welcome in the form of the hazel and elderberry branches' silhouettes, the ash and locust fans along the tracks, outlined in black down here, far below the sky blue, but never mind!

And where did this cordial inclusion in the countryside come from? This invitation to merge with and subside into the countryside? This special form of repatriation? Listen, all of you: in the clear light just before dusk I saw the fruit thief heading across the Vexin plateau into the distance, yet as if she were close by. It would not have been necessary, but nonetheless I looked through the binoculars I had hung around my neck before leaving home (another addendum); if anyone asks, I will name the manufacturer—but first the brand name: LEGEND.

From a distance a slight figure, recognizable even to the naked eye as a woman, unmistakable, regardless of whether all these years she had imagined herself as invisible, or at least unobtrusive. From now on, for the time being, that was no longer the case. And as I turned back to the parked train, it became clear that I was not the only one to have that impression: all the women on the train had their eyes open and were following the stranger as she made her way across the stubble fields, one with envy, another with hatred, a third, as if unmasked and stripped of mystique, now just homely.

The fruit thief, carrying an obviously heavy piece of luggage, nonetheless walked briskly, now and then scampering a bit or skipping, as if she were playing hopscotch all by herself, and not only because of the uneven ground with stubble sticking up, sometimes a hindrance, sometimes liberating, but also because she, having just come from the city and being essentially a city girl, had yet to settle on a gait suitable for the special conditions here.

So she exchanged the fields for a local road, where she strode along, matching her steps to the long serpentines typical of the network of roads in Picardy, far from the high-speed roads around the capital. Now and then she bent down to pick up an unharvested ear of wheat that had blown onto the tar and gravel; she stuck it behind her ear like a cigarette. Strange, too, that instead of going in one direction she went in a circle. On the other hand she was not circling anything, was not encircling anything, and her circles became wider and wider. And then she did circle something after all: one of the small stands of trees characteristic of the Vexin plateau, in the midst of the vast fields of grain: I thought she had disappeared behind one of them when she came around the bend, holding a pumpkin or whatever under her arm like a soccer ball. Just outside the miniature forest, a striding up and down, which became a trotting, back and forth, then a sprinting: she was searching, almost in a panic, for a way in, but I could have told her that there is no way into patches of forest like that, called *clos*, just as there is no way of getting into the dense tangled woods behind temples in Japan. Both here and there the forest patches poked into the sky, treetop next to treetop, further intensifying the impression of an inaccessible fortress, a fortified town, even.

Then the fruit thief disappearing from view. But before that happened, she unburdened herself of her traveling bag, hurling it far, far away with a strength unexpected for her slight figure. Or had she thrown it to the place intended to be hers for the day, the night? (A glance over my shoulder up to the train's windows behind me: in the face of one woman a shimmer of something that might be longing?) Lowering the binoculars, I recognized, with the same kind of shock: the woman asleep earlier on the train's jump seat had really been her, the fruit thief herself. Yes, it had happened again: when those closest to me appeared in person, I saw them as phantoms, as entirely different people, pale, alien, their particular living pallor marking them as especially different. That has happened to me with my children as well. "So who is this strikingly pale unknown child who just opened the door for me?"—and only after a leap in time: "For God's sake, it's my own son!"

A humming, droning, vibrating: fear not: the power is back. Back on board and continuing the trip, after the engineer's stubbing out his cigarette underfoot (but there, too, nothing to fear: the wheat fields would not catch fire, the wheat had been harvested—though it had been the worst harvest of the last hundred years, and not only in the former royal breadbasket).

And again in no time disembarking, at the stop in Lavilletertre, a stop unlike any other, far from any visible or audible village. Waving to the individual women on the train, especially the one with the short haircut or the one with sinewy calves. But not one of them waved back or so much as blinked; as soon as the train had started to move again and things felt normal, they had gone back to being majesties, unreachable.

As the only one to get off, I thought I was alone at the station. Some deep breaths, in and out. There it stood, the little stationhouse, closed long since and boarded up. At least it had been freshly painted, and maybe it would reopen someday, but: for whom? There was no ticket counter anymore. Perhaps there had never been one? But also no ticket machine in sight—one of the unique features of the stop at Lavilletertre. Another: the shortcut to the village led uphill through a forest with so many branching paths and no signage to indicate which to take, with the result that even a *habitué*, which I allegedly was, could get lost again and again, and I had the impression the villagers preferred to go by the main road, the long way around, if they were not picked up by someone with a car.

Further unusual features of the station could be recounted. And on that midsummer day when the fruit thief's tale became ripe for the telling, a new one had turned up. The two passenger shelters, located on either side of the tracks—which at this whistle-stop became double for a brief stretch, one set used by trains going to Paris and the other by trains heading to the station at the end of the line—were occupied not by waiting passengers, for no more trains would be passing this evening, but by a *clochard* in each. *Clochard*: didn't that word apply only to the figures and disfigured beings in large cities? But then what would you call these two, slouched across from each other on the rickety benches like a matched pair? There could not be *clochards* way out here in the country, could there, the only ones far and wide? But neither were they "tramps" or "vagabonds." That was clear from the very fact that both remained motionless, one hunched over, with his eyes, if they took in anything, fixed on his shoes, not fit for walking, and his counterpart likewise not stirring, leaning at an angle, the only imaginable further movement being that he might stretch out. "SDF," the abbreviation for *sans domicile fixe*, did not fit them either. Could not having a fixed domicile actually be something to aspire to? (For someone like me, at any rate.)

Initially I had not noticed the two of them because they had not stirred when I got off the train. No head was raised in the shelter on this side or the other side of the tracks.

(*Shelter*, for the half-shredded transparent plastic structures, their roofs long gone, was not the right word.) When I then addressed one of the men, a pair of "actually very lively eyes" looked at me from a "face with a nice natural tan," and the voice in which he answered me, promptly, "on the spot," sounded "perfectly normal"; the man spoke in "a pleasant baritone."

I had greeted him and then asked—no, not about his life or former circumstances, but whether someone had passed that way before me, a young woman, neither short nor tall, neither white nor black—a bit of each. "Yes, she was here. My first thought: she's one of us—but how in the world did she get here? One glance at her was enough, though: no. She is, and she isn't. Him over there, he scares people, because he doesn't talk, mute like a dog. With that woman, he was the one who was scared, like a dog that's been beaten. Afraid of her? Don't make me laugh." And he really did laugh, his laughter remarkably childlike. "The way she zigzagged across the tracks, back and forth, once very slowly, once with a sidestep"—he used that English word—"once running directly toward him, then toward me, but she was just looking for something. And apparently she found something, though it wasn't what she was looking for, over there in the old tool shed. What it was? I don't know. When she came out of the shed, she'd already hidden whatever it was under her coat, something rectangular. A book? It was too big for that. But if I recall rightly, books were really big at one time, weren't they? A picture? A photo? Don't ask me. Even my own questions get on my nerves. When I was young I hitchhiked across Africa one time with a snake under my shirt. Hitchhiking, that's what it's called, isn't it? That guy over there has a little ferret in his shirt pocket, a live one. Or is it a polecat? Look at it poking its head out, those piercing black eyes, those fangs. I could have used a coat like hers, with my sensitivity to cold, even in the summer. Africa! Mali. Do you know Boubacar Traoré's songs? 'Si tu savais comment je t'aime, toi aussi tu dois m'aimer.' But what she had on wasn't a proper coat, it was just a wrap. In school—a long time ago—I took German for two years, but the only word I remember is *Wetterfleck*. From my time in the Balkans I have three more words stuck in my head, supposedly German, left over from the days of the Austro-Hungarian monarchy—but I don't know what they mean: *Markalle, auspuh, schraufzier*. Goodness, how happy she was with what she'd found in the shed there. Or was she startled? Don't ask. For days I've been trying to get the door to that shed open. I've rattled and shaken it, again and again. Nothing doing. And she? One kick and the door opened? No. Not at all. She didn't kick it. She's never kicked anything or anyone. But someday she'll have no choice? And is it possible that all this time I've been tugging on the broken latch—that would be like me—and she simply pushed the door open? On the other hand, entering the shed is prohibited—didn't she read the sign—and certainly taking something met the definition of theft in my opinion, and opening the door by force would count as an aggravating factor, right? And then with the thing under her wrap she sat down close to me, showing thievish glee and also regal joy, so close that she was almost poking me, or didn't she actually poke me, *bel et bien*? Or maybe she wanted to push me away? Hog the spot for herself? No. It's been a long time since anyone sat down with me so sweetly. Sat down? Joined me! A long time? Forever, in fact. And for the first time that one over there looked in this direction. Envy. Pure, unadulterated envy. Couldn't be any purer. Till all three of us laughed, just like that, she laughing all over her face—is it still all right to say that?—and me laughing without knowing why, and him over there laughing with her and with me, as only a mute can laugh, or actually not laugh."

I made my way to the shed. The door stood wide open, and although the sun was shining in at a very low angle from the western horizon, just above the Molière, it was cold inside, almost like an icehouse. Still partly outside, I looked from the threshold over my shoulder at the "without domicile" by the tracks to Paris. He understood right away what I wanted to signal to him: the shed was out of the question as a place for him to spend the night, and in response he gave the slightest of nods, almost imperceptible. The floor of the shed was strewn with papers, with printing on them, almost exclusively numbers, and I had no need to bend down to recognize that they were bank statements or documents, recognizable by the logo on every page as belonging to a "world-famous" bank, world-famous in the sense that only hours earlier—or had it been days, if not weeks ago?—the *Parisien* had carried a feature on a "world-famous gallery-owner." Then I bent down after all and turned over a few of the papers. The back sides were blank. Or rather not: the horizontal light from the setting sun also illuminated something printed, or rather imprinted, in handwriting, invisible, as if the page had been placed underneath another as cushioning. On the floor the usual mattress, in the usual condition; less usual was the old telephone book in the farthest corner, and perhaps even more unusual the microwave oven, although the shed had no electrical socket. Or were there microwaves that operated on batteries?

Thinking that the story of the fruit thief was not a detective story or crime novel, I forbade myself to ask any more questions like that, pocketed the page with the imprint, and stepped out into the open, where I saw the station sign "Lavilletertre" gleaming in a particular blue in the last rays of the sun. The two track-side occupants had returned meanwhile to their original postures and had fallen asleep, one of them sitting, the other lying in his roofless *abri*, along with the ferret or baby polecat under his shirt, which had "Circle City, Alaska" on the chest; they were unapproachable, or no longer willing to be approached.

As I contemplated the bridge over the two sets of tracks—

with not a car or pedestrian in sight and seemingly unused from time immemorial—I, too, had nothing more to say. The sense of having nothing more to say filled me with a kind of solemnity. I felt myself becoming mute and ever more mute. So I, too, was a mute, though not like that man stretched out on his collapsed plastic bench. I stood there gazing at the land, seemingly extending to the ends of the earth, and I was completely mute, solemnly mute. I imagined the fruit thief standing beyond the bridge embankment and practicing throwing, without actually throwing anything.

The sun went down. A first breath of coolness swept over Picardy and the Vexin plateau after the summery warm day. The harvested fields, now darkening, unexpectedly appeared coated in white, from sea gulls, previously out of sight. High in the zenith, likewise white, ribbons of clouds, like foam left behind on the sand by retreating waves. Two little clouds, separated by a short distance, were struck by a ray of the sun, otherwise out of sight everywhere else, and now drifted gently toward each other and lit up at the moment when they converged. I do not know why, but that reminded me of a novel I had read when I was very young that ends with the hero seeing the clouds above his head as a dungeon from which he must free himself, as something even more intimidating than a dungeon: a citadel.

One step, and another step, uneven because of the bee sting, thanks to it; *grace à la piqûre*.

At the time in which this story takes place, the fruit thief had just returned from a journey of several months. She had spent hardly more than one day and one night in the section of Paris where she lived, near the Porte d'Orléans, and already she was on the road again, driven out of the house not only by the need to continue the search for her mother, who had disappeared shortly before the fruit thief returned from the far north of Russia, but also by anxiety for herself, very distinct in a dream, more or less fuzzy after she awoke, yet then even more compelling, if possible. But *anxiety*, or *angoisse*, was a word she never used in reference to herself. She avoided saying, "I feel anxious" or "Je suis angoissée," out of superstition—her own term, for she often said that she was "superstitious to the core"—that the moment she spoke that word the anxiety, instead of evaporating or at least letting up, would swell to become insuperable; there was no antidote to anxiety, but her superstition told her that if it went unmentioned, there might be some remedy or other.

Before her return from the taiga and tundra, stories had preceded her, or rather fragments of stories, also in the form of drawings sent to family members, though not so much to her mother, who had lost all interest in such things, and not only such things, but rather to her brother, and especially to her father. The word was that she sat for entire days, and also nights—since at this time of year the sun went down on the right? or on the left? only to come up again—along the Yenisei, Ob, or Amur rivers, or whatever the rivers in the north of Russia were called, and sketched and colored—with pencils but also with whatever she could lay her hands on, regardless of whether the colors matched those in the world in front of her—the goings-on on the rivers and, with infinitely greater dedication, as was her way, the goings-on along the banks, along the edges and in the corners of the drawings, and most lovingly of all, or at least most thoroughly, the goings-on at her feet. Meanwhile she learned Russian, the language—or so she imagined—of one line of her ancestors, one of many, and on envelopes she wrote her name in Cyrillic: АЛЕКСИЯ. In between she worked, as a waitress (in the course of which, clumsy as she could be at times, she more than once spilled soup and drinks); as a chambermaid; also at the fish markets by the riverbanks (at one of which she attracted attention and was laughed at in amazement because she was the only person far and wide without "slant eyes"); also as a tea brewer and coffee roaster (in both of which jobs she proved most successful because of her *timing*, for which the Russians used that very word, pronounced as in English); and for one long day as a mushroom hunter, having more success than all the others in the woods with her (if such an activity can be considered "work"). She reminded one man of his late wife, and another, who had initially addressed her as "my child," compared her an hour later with Sharon Stone. Another wanted to play football with her. Another rechristened her YASNAYA POLYANA. And yet another . . .

On the day after her return she heard all the voices on the streets of Paris, from Alésia to Denfert-Rochereau to Montparnasse, as those of Russians, and she repeatedly responded in Russian to a greeting or a question. Even the voices of birds in the city she heard as Slavic sounds. The coffee machines spat out Slavic consonants: *č* and *š* and the like, and this very morning it had been her own steam iron.

Alexia, or Aleksiya, actually had a different name. But that was what she was generally called, starting with the time in her youth when she had disappeared and then lived for a year on her mother's property, unrecognized (her father absent and her brother not yet born), after the saint with a similar story, St. Alexius.

Even as an adolescent, even before her year "under the stairs," the fruit thief had been a person—what to call it?—"of uncertain residential status"? "prone to wanderlust"? She vanished at least every couple of months, for days at a time, and was then picked up somewhere between the city and the country, and the authorities could never determine how she had ended up on, or even under, the loading dock of a railway freight station, in an allotment garden, in a rusted-out bus, and also often in another country, beyond the Alps, Pyrenees, Ardennes. She was considered mentally ill, and her illness had a name.

After returning, unrecognized, and then being reunited

with her mother, and with her father as well, in a different way, Alexia was healed of her wanderlust, and once and for all. That did not mean that she became a stick-in-the-mud. These days she did live most of the time in her roomy apartment, which also served as her study or work space. But she regularly took off on trips to distant parts, more or less planned in advance. She knew where she was going, and especially where she would end up, and how!: no one had a keener sense of place, a sense for the spirit of a place. On the other hand, something had remained with her from all those years of roaming around, lost and confused, but instead of burdening her it seemed now to inspire her and sometimes lent her a glow, a kind of quiet buoyancy.

The trip to Picardy, to the Vexin, was not one of her major journeys. On the map or elsewhere it did not even merit being called a journey, at most an excursion, easy to accomplish in a day, leaving Paris by car or train; many residents of Picardy covered the same stretch for work, though in the opposite direction, heading to the capital in the morning and back in the evening. For them, however, it was also not child's play.

"Also"? Did that imply that for her, the fruit thief, this trip was not child's play? Yes, that was the implication. In her eyes, what the trip promised was no game. She knew, before setting out, that this was the first real trip that would reveal her "unique style"—she had read somewhere that a journey could do that, and it was something she wanted. And in contrast to her mother, who, when she set out to look for her daughter, had wanted it to be her last journey, the fruit thief now wished it would not be her last. Yes, this trip promised something. Something good? Something bad? It just promised.

The young woman had never been to Picardy. Alternatively: perhaps in her period of wandering around, lost and confused, she had roamed and roved there, too, but her memory had retained none of the experience. The region's name, for whatever reason, had a positive resonance for her, or resonance altogether different, for example, from those of Normandy, Côte d'Azur, Alsace, Bretagne: Picardy. Without her having specific associations with knights and castles, the name, especially when she said it aloud to herself, had something knightly about it, something—what was the term?—*chivalrous*.

There was no question but that her mother, after abruptly walking out of her office at the bank she headed, would turn up in Picardy, and "precisely" in the Picardian section of the Vexin plateau. (*Precisely* and *exactly*, once her most frequently used words, had meanwhile vanished completely from her vocabulary.) No question because the Vexin had become the only place that still mattered to the lady banker, and furthermore because one of the fruit thief's superstitions had whispered the idea to her. Had she perhaps tossed a match onto the map? Lit a small paper fire and let the charred flakes blow where they wished? Have it your way. As you like it.

Before setting out on her one-woman expedition, the fruit thief had met up with her father at the Mollard, a restaurant by the Gare Saint-Lazare. After her months on the rivers of Siberia she noticed how much he had aged—and realized that he had probably been looking like that long before her trip but that she had only now become aware of it. The realization did not startle her, however. In fact, she liked what she saw. As she had always liked everything about her father, and also everything about her mother, and perhaps even more everything about her brother, her junior by a decade.

Before her father, dressed as always in a Dior suit, snagged in a few places, as if by briars, with a pocket square and English footgear, freshly polished but scuffed and with worn-down heels, got around to saying, "Russia! Tell me everything!" he described almost agitatedly, his cheeks flushing, his walk down from the Montmartre Cemetery, near which he had lived alone for a long time now, the route taking him downhill by way of the rue de Budapest, where prostitutes had smiled at him from one doorway after another, mute, ancient whores, almost grandmotherly, also heavily made-up but without any effort to look young, and their smiles, visible in their black-rimmed eyes, expressed without words that they expected or wanted nothing from him, and perhaps not from anyone anymore.

When she began to tell him about Russia, he plainly hung on her every word, almost reading the words from her lips as he leaned toward her, and repeating the ends of entire sentences like an echo. The man had behaved the same way when she was a child, also accompanying and mimicking her movements and gestures. It was clear to see, when this behavior did not degenerate into a grotesque pantomime, that if something happened to his child, if she had a bad experience, he suffered as well, endured pain, perhaps necessary pain. If the child was so tired that her head slumped over, the same thing happened to her father, without any conscious effort on his part. If the child grabbed a stinging nettle by mistake and screamed, the father let out a shriek of pain at almost the same moment, so not really as an echo. And when she received an injection in her finger, her father jumped ten to twelve times more violently than his tiny little daughter.

Strange, or perhaps not, that of all people this man had come to represent such an authority for her. Did that have to do with her feeling for family, as deeply and widely rooted as her sense of place, even extending, in the form of veneration (not a cult), to ancestors she knew only from stories or bits and pieces of stories? But why should her father be the only one of her clan whom she respected as an authority, the only one altogether, the only one in the whole world? No reply. That was how it was. It was as it was.

This fatherly authority, the only one that mattered to

her, was also always part of a game, as now, when she asked him what she should order at the Mollard. But from time to time it turned serious, and she needed his authority; felt the need of it, as if not her entire life but at least the current day and the following one, yes, whatever would follow, depended on it. And that was the case on this day. Something was at stake. What would follow was at stake.

Just as her father hung on her lips while she described her Russian adventures, afterward she hung on his when the reason for their meeting became the topic. She did not interrupt him even once with a question, keeping her wide, credulous eyes fixed on his face when he faltered and, as so often happened, did not know what to say next, when he suddenly began to babble, as he had always had a tendency to do, or said things that were just plain wrong, as she recognized immediately, without, however, correcting him: even in the nonsense he spouted from time to time, in the factual and logical mistakes he made not infrequently, the fruit thief believed there was something she needed to act on, without reservations, word for word. And the distractions, or rather the way her father repeatedly became distracted, let himself be distracted while talking, one of his specialties: this she accepted unquestioningly—see, in addition to her wide eyes, her flared nostrils—accepted them as part of the lesson being imparted to her for that day, and for life. Whenever her father's gaze wandered to the Art Nouveau mosaics on the wall and ceiling, to the flowers or peacocks or whatever they portrayed, she followed his gaze obediently, expecting a paternal pointer to emerge from among the shimmering colors, which included gold and silver. There was one mosaic overhead, however, that she sometimes looked up at entirely on her own: it depicted a garland with rich clusters of fruit. She did more than look; she became lost in contemplation of the gleaming apples, so lifelike, her head tilted back and to one side in a characteristic pose, toward the treetop.

Apropos of her upcoming journey into the country's interior in search of her mother, "into the ancient heart of France," as her father, who liked to play the geographer and historian, called it, he repeatedly offered observations, between the appetizer and the main course, between the main course and coffee, which his daughter construed as indispensable advice on her route and direction, although he did not intend them as such. (While eating or drinking the old man said not a word; for as long as she had known him, he had never done more than one thing at a time.)

"Your Isaac Babel was also in the Vexin, I believe, almost a hundred years ago, and in one of his books—if only I could remember which one—he talked about the villages there, where all you could apparently see of the peasant houses along the streets was a continuous, high, windowless wall, villages like fortresses from the time of the Hundred Years' War . . . The cheese they make in Picardy can feel like a brick in your stomach, but a few scrapings of it in a cake can give it a truly remarkable taste . . . When you're around men, put on a pair of glasses with window-glass lenses, like women in Hollywood films . . . otherwise your eyes, as was prophesied right after you were born by someone—I no longer recall whom—will 'drive them crazy' . . . If you want to find feathers from birds of prey again: buzzard feathers usually turn up on the edge of the forests there, especially where they're brushy, because when the buzzards whiz in or out, whether after their prey or not, they often lose a wing feather there, accidentally knock one off, never more than one, but the most splendid one among all their plumage; if you're lucky, an eagle's feather, a really long one, could be lying out in a field, actually far from any woods, and it, too, all by itself; on the other hand, you can often find both wings of a falcon, most likely in a small forest where the trees are planted that much closer together, and where falcons, whether out hunting or in the throes of infatuation, zoom along, close to the ground and in a straight horizontal line, and often, maybe because they're too young, or too old? crash into a tree as if blind; and when you're looking for feathers out there in Picardy you'll also come across whole corpses of hawks, together with dead pheasants, the hawks dead like the pheasants they pounced on along the cart tracks across the fields; and even entire wings of jays will fall into your lap, so to speak, and what a blue on the delicate little feathers at the base of their wings! Prized, unfortunately, for accessorizing hats in the Alpine regions; all you have to do—you'll need a sharp jackknife for your hike, by the way—is cut the wing off the jay's body (she refrained from pointing out to her father that the jay was not a bird of prey) . . . don't mention to anyone you're looking . . . was it a character in Isaac Babel of whom it was written, 'She wasn't brave, but always stronger than her fear'? I don't know, but that sentence was written by a Slav, that much I'm sure of . . . ah, the way tango partners suddenly, so suddenly, avert their eyes from each other as they dance: to avert one's eyes like that from—yes, from what? . . . your mother's alive, that I know, and she wants to be looked for, and only by you, that I know, too, and she'll respond only to your call, your voice, that I'm sure of, too, as much as one can be sure of anything . . . pay attention to items of clothing left behind on coat hooks in bars and inns: it's one of her specialties to leave things behind, shawls, hats, scarves . . . She won't perish, even if she's tempted, tempted to go to hell, to let herself go, at least for a while, as she always has been, that I'm sure of . . . and no one's going to murder her, though she's been tempted to let that happen the whole time I've known her: to meet someone she could push to the point of killing her . . . lady of terrible temptations . . . that would make a good song title and refrain in English . . . three-syllable words are more resonant and singable than two-syllable ones . . . Lord have mercy, how I've come to dislike crime novels, and how I despise their authors! Listen to this: my idea for an entirely different kind of crime novel: at the world congress of crime-novel authors a bomb blows them all up, without exception, during the plenary session—and guess who the perpetrator is? . . . it's the time of the new moon right now, you'll have bright starry nights in the countryside, and I don't want you to miss the shooting stars, not a single one, August is the month for shooting stars . . . swimming in the brooks and small rivers, Viosne, Troësne, upriver, downriver, but watch out, there are places where you can sink into the mud, what looks like a firm bottom under the clear water; watch your footing; one time I took a single step into the Troësne—or was it the Epte?—and sank in over my ribs . . . the films shown in village ballrooms, maybe outdoors now in summertime? . . . A hotel room with breakfast in Lavilletertre, Monneville, and Chaumont, not really that rustic . . . When you're walking along, don't step out of the way for anyone, not even a hand's breadth . . . no one will touch you if you don't want it, let alone lay a hand on you . . . no one wishes you ill . . . just look at them with those eyes of yours, and every one of them, even the one drunk out of his mind, as well as the weirdo famous even outside the region, and the village idiot, too—him especially—will want to be nice to you, as nice as they are, yes! will want to do something nice for you, as they've always wanted to do for someone, yes. The drunkard will bow low and let you pass, even if he topples headfirst into the thistles by the roadside. The weirdo's tongue, only a moment before lolling sevenfold out of seven mouths, will become transformed into a single angelic tongue, appearing Pentacostally as a tongue of fire above the heads of the disciples. The village idiot will hand you the malted milk ball he's been carrying around deep in his pocket for decades, waiting for just such an occasion. Nothing, nothing at all can happen to you, dear fruit thief, at least nothing coming from the outside . . . from the inside, on the other hand . . . ah, your heart: it's made to break over nothing at all, to break and ache, and likewise made to bathe you in cold sweat, in terror, from which you'll nevermore awake . . . and at the same time: no one more joyful, more filled with joy, more talented for joy, than you, fruit thief!"

Several sighs from the old man. But only the first sigh was serious; the following ones, as was usually the case when he repeated something, were just for show. Nonetheless his daughter took them seriously. She took all his utterances seriously, and more than seriously.

And this is how the father concluded the admonitions with which he sent her on her way: "Avoid facing into the light. That means: walk with the sun in your face only at high noon, when the sun is at its zenith; otherwise, in the morning and toward evening, when the sun is low, walk with it at your back. Backlighting is deceptive: it enlarges or shrinks things. A cat becomes a fox, a wolfhound shrinks to resemble a poodle; a child becomes a monster; a monster a small child. And one more thing: give yourself breathers, as many as possible. How often I've taken a deep breath and breathed more quietly whenever a dramatic story's been interrupted with 'meanwhile.' You have control over the meanwhiles. Don't let them be taken from you! It's in the meanwhiles, the in-between stretches, that things happen, take shape, develop, come into being. Searching, pausing, calling out, running, rummaging through forests, especially the smallest ones, taking a good look at the main streets, towns, villages, ponds, those especially, yes. But in the meantime it can't hurt to go around the back, behind the houses and their grounds. In the meantime, and why not for hours on end, tie and untie your shoelaces, set one foot in front of the other, keep your eyes fixed on the toes of your shoes, let your feet lead the way. And one more thing: one hot meal a day. Don't trust the bus schedules. Fold your maps properly. Put on two pairs of socks . . ."

Her father would probably have gone on in this vein for quite a while longer. But now he was interrupted because the Mollard's head waiter had shown a trio or quartet of politicians, trailed by a double quartet of journalists—if that's what they were—to one of the nearby tables. Before they had properly taken their seats, the old man said, quite loudly, addressing neither his daughter nor the new arrivals, but speaking instead into the air, "From morning to night they're served up to you on television. No getting away from them. Hour after hour the same pretentious faces, the same smug smiles, the same knowing exchanges of glances. And now they're elbowing their way into the real world, casting a shadow over the day with their dark funeral directors' and famous soccer coaches' suits and ties, continuing to simulate here in the real world, like secret society members and conspirators, an elite no one needs and a power that ceased to exist a long time ago. The only power they still have is to pursue wars with external enemies while trying to rub each other out. Beat it! Spare us, at least here in the real world. Get out of the bit of here-and-now we have left. Get out of my day. Why in God's name didn't the head waiter bring King Louis the saint and his dear, kind friend and biographer, the gentleman from Joinville on the Marne, to the next table? Having Louis and Joinville here in flesh and blood: now, that would be something else entirely, cause for celebration. But having these people here in the flesh: that's different."

His tirade went unheard. That was what the story called for. The fruit thief provided a distraction, just by being there. In addition she intentionally distracted her father—almost whispering, and thereby getting him to lower his voice, by suggestion, as it were—commenting that the coffee they had been served, Blue Mountain from Jamaica, had been roasted too dark, which explained why it tasted so bitter and ordinary, instead of having the quality unique to Blue Mountain coffee when it was roasted properly. Or she plucked at the old man's sleeve and nodded in the direction of the young waitress, making her way through the rows of tables with a tray full of drinks without spilling a drop or letting a single glass bump against another one, pointing out the difference between that waitress and herself when she worked as a server by the rivers of the taiga.

After that she was almost in a hurry to get away from her father. Once upon a time, when she still expressed an opinion on something for a change, it had been her opinion, for a change, that her mother had been right to leave her father. This opinion she no longer held, or any opinion, for that matter. Who had left whom? She did not know and also did not want to know. If asked her opinion, at most she would have exclaimed, like Jane Eyre, or was it Jane Austen? "My opinion?!" though not in consternation like the character in a nineteenth-century English novel, but casually, without much ado. After an hour with her father she had always been in a hurry to get away from him. Leave him to his amateur-historian-and-geographer mania, to his Homeric springs, or whatever. Not that his absence made her fonder of him. But with the passing years she increasingly saw him, as the end of their time together approached, as someone who in old movies, at least French ones, would have been called *le gorille*, the gorilla, in the sense of "bodyguard." But one time, when she had described his hands as a gorilla's, and he had asked her what she meant, she had meant/seen that literally: his hands as those of a human ape, and without being asked, she had added, "beautiful."

No sooner was he out of sight than he was out of her mind, and so it was this time, too, in front of the Gare Saint-Lazare. She had practically sent him packing. Heaven forbid he should see her to her train and play the bodyguard! As for watching him disappear into the crowd or turning for a last look: no. Even as a child she had never watched her father leave. He, on the other hand, when she was the one leaving: she felt his eyes on her back every time, sometimes uncomfortably so. Poor fool, watching her go. Or was this watching one of his Homeric springs?

But now she was the one trying, for the first time, to catch another glimpse of her father. "You're constantly planning, coming up with projects, projecting, giving advice. Yet you're completely at a loss yourself. True enough: if a stranger asks for directions, you have no problem giving them. But when you're the one setting out, at the first turn, you're confused: Where am I?" And as she gazed after him, her father looked like an inmate who had grown old in prison and had just been released on parole. And it came back to her that as a child she had begged him to let her open letters for him and unfold, and especially fold, maps—something her father hardly ever did successfully.

Alone at last. Those very words came to mind as she crossed the "hall of lost steps" to the train: "Alone at last!" Hall of lost steps? Of found steps! And then she wondered why she felt so relieved to be alone again after not even two hours with another human being, in fact one of very few who meant something to her; to be alone again to go on her way, free as a bird, when during all those months in Russia she had hardly ever, or never, really been in the company of others.

And then, streaming along with the crowd, free as a bird, she stopped wondering about anything. Not just her father was no longer on her mind but anything from earlier and likewise anything that lay ahead. Neither a whence nor a whither, neither clock time nor real time, and not even the present time, summer. An all-encompassing obliviousness came over her, leaving her sleepwalking in broad daylight, which, however, was also entirely different from the aimless roaming of her youth on the edge of the suburbs. She knew not only who she was but also where. Furthermore she had eyes and ears—for everything and everyone? Not that, but eyes and ears for various things that were revealed during that particular hour to no one else in the crowd. To no one else? Revealed? Where did such certainty come from? Such knowledge? —The story tells us. That's how the story goes.

She saw someone crying, and clearly and obviously for the first time in a long while, if not the very first time. A man or a woman? Not important, and besides, she paid no attention. She saw someone hiding behind a column. Hiding from the police? Hiding to surprise someone arriving on a train just then pulling into the station? Neither nor: he was hiding behind the column because that was his spot, and not just at the moment but also yesterday, all day, from the time the station opened in the morning until it closed after midnight; he had already been standing behind his column at Easter, also the previous Christmas, during Advent. She saw the old man over there on crutches, dwarflike, a hunchback, hobbling step by step through all the rushing and running, taking a brief break after every step, and now, with his crutches splayed in front of him, clutching a railing or a barrier, incapable of taking another step, his hump sticking up way above his head. And the "skeleton" about to collapse there amid all the pushing and shoving was not even that old, and ten or twenty years earlier had played soccer, professionally, in the second division, and, at the beginning of his career, the top division. He had not been rich, but from time to time had had money to spare, which a friend and advisor had cheated him out of. Just this morning he had felt hopeful for a few moments, remembering, as he stepped onto the street, a game in which, after shooting from the halfway line, he had scored his first goal, in his memory the ball flying high through the air in slow motion as the net billowed and all his teammates turned to him in disbelief, while he himself was even more in disbelief. But now . . .

Already on the platform, she had turned around and in

one of the innumerable shops located on the station's upper and lower levels she had bought a fabric bag with pockets on the front, sides, and back, which she promptly dubbed her "thief bag." Returning to the platform, she walked to its very end, out beyond the roofed area of the Gare Saint-Lazare, and, although the train was already waiting, stood there, under the open sky, which was filled with the screeching of gulls, amplified by the railroad cut and the tall buildings on both sides. White moths, fluttering into view from the darkness of the cut and zigzagging above it in the sunlight, could be mistaken at first for gulls. Transilien was the name for all trains leaving Paris for the Île-de-France region, and she, freshly back from the distant east, read the name as *Transsibirién*.

After that the fruit thief kept her eyes mostly on the tracks at her feet. At one time, not only at night but also in broad daylight like this, one could count on seeing rats scurrying between the ties. Today, as had long been the case, not a single one. She almost missed the rats down there. Such cleanliness was deadly. She "almost" missed the scurrying? Not just almost. Instead, tendrils of something green and red rose out of the crushed rock that formed the railroad bed, winding its way up the rough concrete of the bumpers and almost reaching her feet on the platform: a green plant that reminded her of a tomato vine, and then in fact was one: when she leaned over, small clusters of perfectly round ripe tomatoes literally fell into her hand, finding their way between her fingers, which she did not have to close to pluck the fruit and stash it away. Time and again in her life she had seen fruit, and splendid specimens, too, growing in the strangest places. But these tomatoes here by the tracks in this great metropolis's station . . .

Having boarded the train she promptly fell asleep. She slept soundly, without dreams, as was her way. When she woke up, the train was stopping at a station elevated above the surrounding countryside, with a view of a wide river, which she recognized only after she disembarked as the Seine. And next she saw another river, hardly a third, or even a quarter, as wide. Or was it a canal? No, it was a second river, the Oise, and the fruit thief realized that she was at the confluence of the two rivers, the spot where the Oise flowed into the Seine, and accordingly the station was called Conflans-Fin d'Oise, confluence and end of the Oise.

She had not intended to go to the confluence. While she was asleep, she had missed getting off at the previous station, Sainte-Honorine, where she was meant to change trains. But now she was perfectly happy to sit down for a while by the junction of the two rivers.

All the rivers on earth with which she was acquainted, especially the larger ones, resembled one another when they flowed through a thinly settled area, or so it seemed to her. Such places gave her a sense, more than any others, of a single planet that united all the various regions. No brook in the world had ever conveyed such an image to her, no glacial streams, lava flows, and certainly not the shores of the great oceans, whether on the eastern or western seas of Japan, the Atlantic in Brazil, or, just a few days earlier, the shore of the Bering Sea, this time, unlike the year before, not on the Alaskan side in Nome but on the opposite banks in Russia, those of Kamchatka.

Now the sight of the Seine and the Oise also transported her to the Siberian rivers where she had spent her free hours during half the summer sitting on the grassy bank, just as she was doing here. She felt the same wind blowing across the river as across the Yenisei, Ob, and Amur. The glistening silvery threads of steppe thistledown, which floated over the water, often in pairs or tangled into small clumps, also swarmed over the steppe-like angle where the Oise and the Seine met. Shoreline swallows here just as there, perhaps differing somewhat in form and coloration but making the same riverbank swallow-whirring as everywhere on the planet. The very same empty scallop shells as in the taiga, washed up on the sandy shore—no, not exactly the same. Never mind; that was how she saw them in her dissociative state. And the—only occasional—runners and bikers here: they also ran and pedaled in Siberia? That was so. Bike paths and fitness paths, *osdorovitelnye tropy*, could be found along the Yenisei, too, and the activewear was the same in both places. In her dissociative state, thanks to it and also by virtue of it, she felt as if she were in both places, with everything around her even more intensely present. Dissociated, everything there became more intense, more distinct, and that included her, as part of everything there.

Thanks to her dissociative state, she picked up on the differences, specifically those, between the two rivers directly in front of her, beyond the difference in size. She thought she recalled hearing the expression "the smell of poverty"? At any rate, the Oise smelled of poverty, its surface streaked with every conceivable and inconceivable fluid, blindly reflecting the blue summer sky, whereas the Seine, in which the Oise came to an end, *fin de l'Oise*, smelled of wealth, another familiar expression, which is to say it had no smell, with the sky's blue in the water's expanse even bluer and more bluing than the actual blue in the spheres above. An optical illusion created by the great river's capacity to fill the horizon, meanwhile swallowing up the much smaller river in the foreground as if in passing. Illusion? But given these different smells, didn't the assertion make sense that with the passage of time the waters of the Seine had been cleaned up, at least as far as the mouth of the Oise, to the point that it was safe for bathing and swimming as hardly ever before in its history, including where it flowed through Paris, and particularly to be recommended in the loops it formed there? One way or the other: as she had done before taking leave of the—infinitely colder—Siberian rivers, the fruit thief, as the story tells us, stepped into the river here, to swim in the "end of the Oise."

The time has come to explain what this "fruit thief" business is all about; time to explain how she came to be "the fruit thief."

Allegedly her father was responsible. When she was still very small, he supposedly modeled the behavior. That is not true, however. Perhaps in his early years he, like quite a few people, toyed with the idea of scrambling over walls or other barriers to get into strangers' gardens or orchards. But he never acted on the idea. He would have been too clumsy, not sufficiently athletic. Besides: whenever a small irregularity showed up in his surroundings, he would behave as if he had done something wrong, and as a result he often came under suspicion, and always unjustly. But in his own mind he felt at fault, also, and precisely, for actual offenses committed in the area, thought he deserved to be suspected of all kinds of criminal misdeeds, including robbery, rape, manslaughter, murder, and not solely in the immediate area.

She had become a fruit thief in earliest childhood during a shortish stay in the country, her very first. "Become"? On the day she climbed onto a village boy's shoulders, jumped from the top of the wall—a rather low one—into a stranger's property, scaled the tree, and surehandedly reached for and plucked the fruit that had been "burning a hole in her eyes" since the day she arrived in the area, it was as if she had not become a fruit thief at that moment but had always been one.

She did not consider herself a thief. No one had seen her as one up to now. She was called "the fruit thief" because the nickname had stuck in her family, after her baptismal name and before the out-of-the-ordinary one, used only by her mother, Alexia. She had been dubbed "the fruit thief" on the spot by the owner of that walled orchard where she had "pilfered"?—oh, come off it!—taken, pocketed the fruit, never mind what kind. He, a childhood playmate of her mother's in the village, had been sitting in the cottage that went with the orchard (not the other way around: the orchard did not go with the house), and there had involuntarily witnessed the child from the city pocketing the fruit. First he spontaneously jumped out of his chair, but then he paused and posted himself by the window to get a better look. He liked what he saw, as he later told his childhood friend, the girl's mother. He had been sitting there brooding, but now, when the little girl took the half-hidden fruit she had picked from the crown of the tree and held it up in the light, he suddenly felt cheerful, and he heard someone laughing in the cottage's single room, and he was the person laughing.

So he had come up with the name "the fruit thief." That was what he called the child as she stood at the base of the wall with her back to him, searching in vain for a way to get out; the boy who had given her a leg up was on the other side or had long since taken to his heels. "Hey, there, fruit thief!" She had turned slowly and looked at him quietly, wide-eyed, as if he were interfering with something that was none of his business. And when he played the angry property-owner and ran toward her, she merely took the fruit, which she had been holding by its stem in her teeth so as to have both hands free for climbing over the wall, and pressed it to her with those very hands. It was her fruit, not someone else's, and certainly not a forbidden one. For the child and later for the young woman, "taking possession of something," so long as it applied only to fruit and such, had a meaning entirely different from the usual one.

Stealing, robbing, thieving, thefts appalled the fruit thief. Of all types of criminals, she found only thieves repulsive. Robbers, rapists, murderers, mass murderers were something else entirely. She felt an almost addictive attraction to acts carried out in secrecy. But in her eyes, the secrecy involved in theft, of stealing, was one of the most revolting things in the world, and that included the body language that went with it. If she saw someone shoplifting in a supermarket, no matter how hard she tried to persuade herself that the perpetrator must be acting out of desperation, or that the thing being taken was almost worthless: she despised the thief. As a frequent moviegoer, which she had been for ages, after watching Robert Bresson's film *Pickpocket*, she turned against the admirable director for a while because of the sequence in the Métro, or wherever, with the gang of pickpockets, who pass passengers' wallets to each other as they make their way through the cars in a silent ballet, as if it were the height of elegance, even beauty. And toward the end of her high school years, when the girls in her class thought it was cool to swarm through department stores like a shoplifting gang, one day she could not help slapping a classmate who had boasted in front of her about some small item she had snagged, and it was the kind of slap described in those days as making her ears ring (an expression perhaps still in use). Every misdeed hurt, caused pain, each in its own way. Yet many thefts did not deserve to be called "misdeeds." Perhaps no theft ought to be called a "misdeed," and the assertion that stealing caused pain was an exaggeration, with some exceptions. But then why did a theft, as she saw it, as she was convinced, hurt in such a unique, hideous way, violating not only the victim but also a commandment that antedated any biblical one or any other?

Her fruit-thievery, however, was entirely different. Practiced under the dome of impunity, it did her heart good. And it was appropriate. And it was nice. Quintessentially nice. True, but what she did each time was undeniably crooked. This expression, too, however, had a different meaning for her. She felt at home with everything that was crooked, even slightly, sensed in it that surreptitiousness for which she hankered, especially when it was a question of crooked objects—a bent sewing needle, a crooked pencil, a crooked nail. That nail would hold better than a straight one.

If she had had her way, only crooked things would have

been produced. So did she have something against right angles and such? Yes, but even more against anything round—balls, circles, circular designs, spirals. So did she want to call the shots? And how. Or, to be more exact, that was her wish from time to time, to paraphrase Cyndi Lauper's "Time After Time."

What discoveries a fruit thief could make! In the course of the quarter century she had lived to this point, she had moved from place to place, but in each, thanks to being a fruit thief, she had managed to feel at home for a day, or maybe two—she never felt safe anywhere for longer than that.

She evaluated each place according to the spots, nooks, and crannies where a piece of fruit grew that she could grab. It took only a day and a night for her to establish an inner cartography of the fruit parameters that determined the merit of the place as a locale. It was striking (or perhaps not really) that for the most part these "trigonometric points" were just single points. Whole orchards did not serve as place markers for her, nor did greenhouses, fields, and certainly not colonies of trees or shrubs or fruit plantations, but only individual trees, a lone bush, and certainly no stands of grapes, let alone vineyards covering entire fields or hillsides: on the contrary, an isolated arbor, almost hidden behind a fence, betraying its presence only through a couple of notched grape leaves poking between the fence pickets or mesh, would mark a location unmistakably.

This kind of place-making as a function of her fruit-thievery did not depend on her being in open space, villages, or small towns. She experienced it equally in metropolises, where it often proved even more "fruitful." Various urban quarters, whether in Paris, New York, or São Paulo, became distinct quarters for her less thanks to their landmarks and their increasingly blurred transitions to entirely different quarters than thanks to her fruit thief's forays into places where, as in the children's game, it got "warm," "hot," then "boiling hot." And as soon as she arrived in a quarter, she knew that she would certainly find what she was looking for, if not specifically where, and that included quarters seemingly devoid of fruit trees. In the quarter in Paris where she lived, near the Porte d'Orléans, she found, in one of the many redesigned squares, planted with a bevy of those ginkgo trees seemingly all the rage throughout Europe—their particular fluttering shade forming a sort of curtain—behind a tree, against the windowless wall of a building, the remains of an espaliered pear from an earlier time, and it still bore fruit, though fewer from year to year, and those way up high on the trellis. "This summer it was only one pear," the fruit thief explained, "but an exceptionally large one, way, way up on the trellis, impossible to reach even on tiptoe. And along the expressway, almost out in Montrouge—" Once she began to evoke the scenes of her crime, she could not stop.

And what about winter? How did she manage in winter, when there was no fruit to be had? —"Listen, buddy: fruit grows even in winter, and plenty of it."

"What discoveries a fruit thief can make!" —What in the world does being a fruit thief have to do with discoveries? Is a treetop a place for discovering things? —To tell the truth: the fruit thief did not make major discoveries this way. But what she saw, heard, smelled, tasted, experienced in the course of her diurnal and nocturnal undertakings, and always incidentally, she could never have experienced in any other way, in short, without her place-and-time plan as a fruit thief, and thus she did experience it as a discovery; it could not be clearer. For the most part she did not need to climb to the very top of a tree; that happened only as an exception. Her discoveries took place more in passing, and they never involved the "stolen goods" themselves, the so-called main thing, but rather some incidental factor. As she set out for the place she had in mind, the special spot, always taking one detour after another—an essential feature of her forays—and as she stretched out her hand for her fruit, yes, hers, or even both hands, and as she headed home at a leisurely pace, taking different detours this time, by chance something would meet her eyes, come to her ears, cross her path, especially late at night, which she would never encounter in this form, with this unique intensity, during any other activity, and would not encounter this way in the future either. Sniffing the stolen fruit (with the exception of grapes and nuts, never more than one) was also part of these incidental discoveries: never would fruit purchased, found, or received as a gift exude a scent like the fruit she was bringing home from her theft—such an adventurous scent, a secretive scent. And the taste? The fruit thief hardly mentioned it. Apparently she left not a few of the fruits untouched, to wither or spoil.

Fruit thief, fruit thief: no help for it. And also clear: that did not mean that taking fruit that did not belong to her constituted a compulsion, an illness, or that the person engaging in this behavior was a kleptomaniac. In her case there was simply no help for it, and indeed it was just natural, right, good and beautiful, necessary and stimulating, and not merely with respect to her.

Again, what in the world: So did the fruit thief see herself as having some kind of mission? Did she wish, or even want, to see fruit thievery introduced as an Olympic sport? Not entirely nonsensical, considering all the newly adopted Olympic sports.

Once she had crossed the threshold between childhood and adulthood, she had believed for a while in something like a mission, a mission all her own, though not in the role of fruit thief or, as people used to say, "in a figurative sense." Having a mission resulted on the one hand from the fact that from one day to the next she went from being in the circle of her age mates, if also never at its center, to being on the outs, who knows why, and she did not want to know either. She did not even rate a greeting from the others, in whose group she had been included unquestioningly up to now. That she did not want to know why was of a piece with her not wanting to be a marginalized figure. "I'm not an outsider!" Now she saw herself at the center. "I'll show you all yet!"

On the other hand, she was talked into having this mission. Those who indicated to her that she had a special task to fulfill, and as time passed there were more and more of them, were always much, much older than she. These older and old folks, including those who glimpsed her only for a moment, on the street, in passing, never tired of telling her that she was "very special"—"a rarity"—"at last a young woman who's not like the others, the ones who sashay by, lacking only a price tag"—"a beauty of a different kind!"—"someone with a calling!"

During the first years of her adulthood, the person who never wearied of harping on her calling was her own father. "You have a calling, sweetheart. You have to claim your special place in the world, in the face of all others, and furthermore you have a duty. You have the duty to be powerful. You have an obligation to express the secret power within you and put it to use. You're going to let those who need it see your light, and they exist, not in the way you imagine, and with your light you'll burn off their fake eyelashes, you'll swirl it around their ears till their earrings tinkle, you'll hammer it through their nose rings. You'll embody power, a very different kind. You'll . . . you'll . . . you'll . . ."

Eventually it was precisely these litanies and prophecies of her father's that squelched the fruit thief's feeling, not long after her twentieth birthday, that she had a kind of mission. Initially she felt relieved. Yet later the sense of "I have a calling" would be replaced by something that, on the rare occasions when it popped up, upset and spurred her on even more, something that, in contrast to the "mission," pertained to her alone: a challenge, a summons, to overcome and prove, to overcome what? Herself. Challenge? Summons? Who challenged her? Who summoned her? Yes, both came entirely from inside her. But at the same time it was more than her inner voice, far more. "It's too seldom that I feel upset. Too seldom that this turmoil spurs me to action."

At the moment, however, it felt right that, after swimming in the "end of the Oise," she lay down in the grass along the bank, with her feet up to the ankles in the water. A lovely law of nature: the two big toes curling upward so noticeably in contrast to the other toes. Did everyone's toes do that? And what about apes' toes? She curled them even more on purpose. As she did so, something brushed by them, and when she sat up, she saw a mug drift by, very slowly, silvery, made of tin or aluminum. She fished it out of the water. It had a handle and reminded her of the coffee mugs in a Western she had seen once. This one had been bobbing in the water along the bank for years, for several decades. As she twisted and turned it—how light it was!—she realized it was a relic from the last great war, from the battle in that area, in August, an August like the present one, in the year nineteen forty-four, with grueling combat, advances and retreats fought one meter at a time between the forces of the Thousand-Year Reich and those from overseas. The mug had no official markings on it, and the fruit thief, tucking it into her bag, decided it had been German—German? To make up for pocketing the mug, she pulled out of the side pouch on her "combat rucksack" (the term came to her involuntarily) the pamphlet on that very battle that her father, the amateur historian, had given her for the trip: the title was "The Battle of Vexin," and the cover had a photo of a shot-up German tank; she hurled it far out into the "end of the Oise," to float down the Seine? To sink to the bottom? To sink to the bottom.

She got up to leave. Before she did so, she skipped pebbles and shells over the water, tossing them with her left hand as if for practice. Pebble-skipping on flowing water: was that possible? Yes. In response a huge fish leaped out of the "end of the Oise," a pike? a trout? a pike trout? a trout pike? Was that possible? It was. That was what the story called for. According to that, the Oise was not such a poor river after all.

At almost the same moment an excursion boat glided by, silently, as if without an engine, coming from the Oise into its confluence with the Seine, the spitting image of what she had seen in her mind's eye seconds earlier. And she promptly waved to the passengers, all of them Chinese. Or the Chinese had waved to her first, in unison, and now she waved back. How gratifying greetings exchanged by complete strangers could be. What strength and power, of a different kind, flowed from those greetings.

As she went on her way, she decided that this day would be the end of the fruit thievery. Or that she would engage in it only for memory's sake, and to get it out of her system.

In bidding farewell to the river's mouth, she had walked backward for a few paces. That accorded with her superstitious temperament. For one thing, acting on her superstition helped to kill time, or rather indulged her daily enjoyment of play (she had no need to kill time). Yet she also took it seriously. She imagined in all seriousness that actions such as walking backward, as she was doing now, ceremoniously counting the steps till she reached an uneven number, eleven, thirteen, seventeen, would come to the aid of someone far away for whom she cared. That effect could also be achieved if she tied a pair of shoes with identical bows, if she sliced bread without pausing between slices, if she walked straight through a puddle on purpose.

As she now counted her backward steps, she thought she was having a beneficial effect on her missing mother. Toward the end of this superstitious ritual it was also required that she close her eyes, which she now did. As far back as she could remember, she had experienced afterimages of all sorts of objects that lingered for an unusually long time, and very distinct ones. It even happened that the afterimage revealed something she had not perceived with her eyes open; for that her eyes had to be lightly closed, not squeezed shut. Eyes closed! And now she saw a negative of the Chinese passengers on the riverboat, their faces black, their black bangs white—so did all the Chinese have black hair?—their arms black (white shirts), raised in a wave all over the deck, and among them, also waving, she saw, or thought she saw, her mother—"unmistakable; that's her." Not missing at all! Her mother "taking an excursion, for a rest. She needs to rest. Rest from what? From the present, in particular her own." But: just as no opinions were allowed, likewise no explanations. She felt at home in the unexplained. And now she also saw the run in her mother's stocking. How could she see that? She saw it. But did stockings still get runs? Yes, they did.

The afterimage flickered and disappeared, and with it her conviction faded that in any case "All was well." But strange: at that very moment the fruit thief felt a shock go through her whole body, all the way up to her scalp and down to her up-curling big toes. Until now, until here at the spot where the Oise flowed into the Seine, she had been dawdling. And rightly so: if circumstances allowed, she would continue to dawdle. But for now: enough dawdling! The area, the region to which she was supposed to go, was waiting for her. She was needed there, and it was urgent. Having fallen asleep on the train, she had traveled west, toward the ocean. But to reach the interior she had to go north, due north. It was high time she got serious about her expedition. An adventure story? Who knows. At least that was the feeling that came over her.

And what now? Did she not hear, without a church tower in sight, something like a bell clanging, like the pealing of bells at a great distance, from just under the horizon, on certain summer evenings? Only now did she notice that she had been fervently waiting for just such a clanging during her hour on the riverbank, pining for it. So did she only imagine she heard it?

The clanging of the bell was no illusion. Except that as she listened she realized that it came less from beyond the horizons than from the foreground, getting louder and louder, from below, from the confluence of the two rivers. And as she continued to listen and the sound worked its way deeper into her inner ear, the clanging of the bell changed, all the more audible now, into thunder, though soft and very far off. This summer she had not experienced a thunderstorm yet. She had heard one described by a person who had been in the Alps and had heard the thunder coming closer and closer, the crackling turning into crashing, on all sides, behind him, in front of him, on the left, on the right, and finally booming almost simultaneously with the lightning flashes, and he had run for cover, zigzagging between the lightning bolts, "fearing for his life" . . . And as he recounted the experience, she had envied him.

On the evening of that same day she reached the Vexin. True, her stopping place was not yet in the Picardian part of the Vexin plateau but southwest of there, still in the Île-de-France, which surrounded Paris in a great arc. She not only still had far to go to reach the open, thinly settled highland, and with it Picardy, at least on foot, which, according to the fruit thief, was how most of her foray had to be undertaken; her place for the night was a proper city, a good-sized one. And it was not an old city, one that had grown handsomely or chaotically, and certainly not a former royal seat like nearby Pontoise, "Oisebridge," where the sainted King Louis had spent a few days, or a bit longer, before setting out, sick with anxiety, on the crusade in which he did not fully believe. Her place for the night was much larger than Pontoise in surface and population, one of the *villes nouvelles* in the vicinity of Paris, the capital, that two or three decades earlier had been laid out around a couple of old farmsteads or around nothing at all, then built pretty much according to plan, street by street, square by square, and this new town bore a hyphenated name, Cergy-Pontoise, as if the large new town were a mere satellite of Pontoise, the organically developed city upriver.

To her, the place was merely Cergy, not the place known technically as an agglomeration under the name of Cergy-Pontoise, which had swallowed up a few smaller, more or less old cities and former villages: Saint-Ouen-l'Aumône, where the movie house, a one-story but sprawling building with eight (or even ten?) theaters, took up almost the entire main and market square, barred to cars, and lent the square the appearance of a kraal; Osny (pronounced "Oni"), with the massive regional prison on the edge of a grim wooded gorge, where a hiker on the way from the Vexin highlands down to the Oise encountered an almost complete absence of sound and a muteness, or mutedness, coming from inside the prison walls, an airlessness, a suffocating, suffocated sensation, especially at dusk. The next town over in the Oise Valley, Auvers-sur-Oise, with the grave of Vincent van Gogh and next to it his brother Theo's, had not been incorporated into the agglomeration at the time of this story.

Cergy, disproportionately large by comparison with the other entities in the agglomeration and uncharacteristically made up entirely of new buildings, lay and lies downstream, sprawling upward from the last, and perhaps only, meander of the Oise along its high, often steep, banks, and spreading far and wide into the hills, separated from Osny, Saint-Ouen, and especially Pontoise by seemingly inaccessible strips of no-man's-land.

At any rate Cergy was not accessible to someone traveling on foot. The fruit thief knew the *ville nouvelle* of Cergy from earlier. Upon returning from her own period of disappearance, she had been persuaded by her mother the banker to study economics at the university there, which, like the entire town, was new, but she had lasted for only one semester (not even that). She knew the town less than the landscape, no, less the landscape than what had been reconfigured in the process of constructing the city, and hardly from her own observations but rather from a film by Eric Rohmer, set on the meander of the Oise, which had become an area for leisure activities and strolling, with lakes, fountains, boats, and God knows what else. She remembered the film as summery, a feeling often conveyed by Rohmer's works, with a lot of blue sky and water of the same hue, and long, animated dialogues between very young people, also a Rohmer trademark, the talk seemingly borne on the summer breeze, with the rushing of the man-made cascades providing an undertone. She had forgotten the film's plot, as indeed she was forgetful in general, perhaps a delayed effect of her "adolescent" memoryless roaming around? A tendency troubling to those who spent any amount of time with her, forgetful in an uncanny, positively worrisome way, as if she had swallowed everything they had seen together, discussed, even wondered at, admired, loved: it was all gone, irretrievably. Thus she had also forgotten, swallowed root and branch, who had sat next to her in the lecture hall, forgotten the lecture hall, the campus, and the *ville nouvelle*, and beyond the city limits her mute exclamation at the grave of the two brothers in Auvers, forgotten also the grave mounds overgrown with ivy; forgotten, back in Cergy, her childlike joy (yes) at what she had heard one spring evening on one of the new boulevards, when one of the few old men to be found in the *ville nouvelle* had exclaimed as he came toward her, "How beautiful you are, madame! ("madame," not "mademoiselle"), forgotten not just the old man but also the Boulevard des Acacias, or was it the Avenue des Mimosas?, and Cergy itself.

Reminded of her forgetfulnesses, she felt guilty about them; she was responsible for them; and if she was reminded, in the case of Cergy, for example, that there were reasons for her having forgotten her time there entirely, among them that she had not lived in the new city but had commuted daily on the local train from her mother's apartment in Paris to the campus, and in fact in all those months had not spent a single night in Cergy, she would reject that excuse, as though people were trying to talk her out of her all-encompassing forgetfulness. She was guilty. No excuses!

On the other hand, she would reply, "Yes, the way I keep forgetting and forgetting is worrisome, and must be alarming to you. But I assure you: each and every time there was one particular thing I remembered!"—"What, for example?" When asked, she usually could not say. Or it was clear from her expression either that the thing she remembered would do more than alarm, shock, or embarrass the person who had asked, serving as a reminder of that person's own guilt, or that it was nobody's business but hers.

When it came to the forgotten Cergy, she could actually say what she did recall of the *ville nouvelle*, and that was the belt of no-man's-land—impossible to cross and seemingly created by the planners to sow confusion—that surrounded the population settled in the sprawling area.

This time she had given herself permission to arrive in Cergy by bus rather than on foot. Just a summer handful of passengers from the beginning of the trip. Hardly anyone getting on or off along the whole route. The few passengers sitting by themselves, silent. The light inside the bus yellow and yellower; it would never have been that yellow in a railway car. Pre-dusk. Evening coming on. At the last station in Cergy-la-Haut saying good-bye to the driver—a woman. Each of the few passengers said good-bye and thanked her. She returned the good-byes.

What next? A question she posed once a day to no one

in particular and also not to herself: at least once a day the question had to be asked, sooner or later, as a way of taking a breath. And no sooner had the the fruit thief left the bus than she headed off, making a beeline, moving not fast, but also not slowly, like someone who knows where she is going and knows that the destination deserves that name, and also that she is expected there. Wasn't that behavior characteristic of many young women these days? No. Her demeanor was different.

Suddenly she stopped in her tracks. This was one of the many centers to be found in the new city of Cergy, a center marked by the terminal serving several bus lines and especially the local railway to and from Paris. More a station than a square—as was true of pretty much all the centers—it occupied one of the highest points in the city, which explained its name, Cergy-le-Haut. To get to the local train one had to descend several flights of stairs, going down as deep as to the Métro in Paris, and there, too, only in stations built into hillsides like Montmartre or the Buttes Chaumont.

She had stopped unexpectedly while passing, seemingly in a buoyant mood (all that was missing was skipping), this entrance to the underground. A shiver ran through her. One sob escaped her. She pressed her fist to her mouth and screamed. A cluster of people, from the stairs below or from the elevator, returning from the metropolis and elsewhere at the end of the workday, was just scattering across the square, all of them with heads bent or eyes half-closed, on the last couple of stretches on the train having traveled underground straight across the *ville nouvelle*. No one looked up, no one had heard her. Besides, she had immediately stepped to one side and pulled herself together. It was as if she had torn herself loose a moment ago, with her last shreds of strength, from something or someone invisible.

As she went on her way, briskly as before, she popped her straw hat on her head, although the sun had long since stopped blazing down, and tied the straps under her chin, with good reason: the evening wind was strong on the heights of Cergy-le-Haut, coming from the Vexin plateau. The straw hat was perhaps intended (or perhaps not) to hide the smile mixed with tears with which the fruit thief wanted to apologize to someone or something invisible for what had just happened, but it actually had the opposite effect, shedding additional light on the "Forgive me!" her moist eyes expressed.

Subsequent misunderstandings, a whole succession of them, resulting from this smiling, and continuing into the evening, when she had long since stopped smiling and just walked straight ahead, and then sat by herself. It was men—not exclusively but primarily—who thought she had smiled at them first when they saw her in the good-sized after-work crowd crisscrossing and going back and forth through the new city, at least during the early evening hours, and then thought the expression in her eyes had something to do with them.

It was as if these men, and with them those outside the city limits, had not experienced in a long, long time, if ever, that on the street an unknown woman had fixed her eye on them, him, me!—perceived me, registered me, in short, meant me. At most, gazes like that turned up on television, and there, too, extra-sharp and in close-up, primarily in commercials. But no: between the commercial gaze and the living one that fell on me: what a difference! A difference, too, between that gaze and the way women in old-time films would lower their lids or sweep a man with a sidewise glance, or go so far as to wink at him, even if the woman in question was Marilyn Monroe. Or was there a similarity after all?: the eyes of the strange woman in the flickering light of the Caesar Discotheque? Or was it the Pasha Club? No, no—no similarity! A prostitute, perhaps, dolled up like the purest of the pure, as I had experienced back in the day with the Ukrainian woman, or was she a Russian, in any case also an angelic blonde, as this strange woman fortunately was not . . .

As a result of such misunderstandings, the fruit thief was addressed several times by men. But almost all the men spoke politely, or, and this included the older ones, showed boyish excitement, and what they all had in common was reticence. In the case of the only one who actually accosted her and afterward pursued her, she, like an obedient daughter, followed her father's advice, which she would not have needed, and without moving an inch out of his way but also not putting on the recommended glasses "made of window glass," she just stared, "with eyes," her own, at the man, who happened to be falling-down drunk, and the prediction proved accurate: no one wanted to do her any harm, nothing could happen to her, at least not now.

Misunderstandings? No. Or if misunderstandings did arise, of this sort: at certain moments there was something bride-like about the fruit thief. And she radiated this quality, and how. Young girls, still almost children, could radiate something, especially when several of them sat together, quietly expectant, without actually expecting anyone specific. She, however, was no longer a young girl. In a couple of years, as she said of herself, she would resemble the "eternal bride." And she had always seemed bride-like when she was by herself, but even more so in the company of other young women. At such times she came across as a self-assured bride. How could that be: no bridegroom in sight, yet such confidence? That was how it was. That was how it must have been. That is what the story calls for. Quiet confidence, and at the same time, as she sat there by herself, among strangers, or marched along, also glided light-footedly through the crowd, she suddenly started, quivered, stammered incomprehensible words (incomprehensible to herself as well), literally lost her face, making one face after another, each more childish (not childlike) than the one before, like a classic simpleton—lacking only snot dripping from her nose and spit gathering in the corners of her mouth? —At some moments even that was not missing. —But all that was not meant to be observed, was it? —No, it was. And it was lovely to observe. This bride was lovely, so lovely. —So lovely as to make one kneel in reverence? —Yes, dear contemporary. Yes, brother of mine.

Strange side effects, or not so strange after all, or side effects particular to this hour of her bride-likeness: having just arrived in Cergy and remembering almost nothing from her earlier time there, from one street and passageway to the next she was taken for someone familiar with the city and repeatedly asked for directions. It was drivers of automobiles above all who, even with a map and even, time and again, with navigation systems, had got lost in the new city's traffic patterns. When they leaned out of their cars and practically begged the fruit thief to give them directions, it was as if they had already tried several times in vain to reach such and such a square, such and such a road leading out of Cergy and to the expressways, their facial expressions suggesting that they might drive amok any minute now or give up altogether, once and for all, on trying to reach their destinations, a circumstance in which anyone other than the object of their begging might have in fact been tempted to respond, "It's hopeless." The last person to pull up next to her and ask for help was a taxi driver, not from elsewhere but from the immediate area, from the agglomeration of Cergy-Pontoise, where he had grown up, and who gave her to understand that he was not the only taxi driver in town to lose his bearings, not the only one, in his French phrase, to lose "the north." And not one of those asking for directions wanted to believe that she, too, even she, despite the way she comported herself, could not help. But the manner in which she conveyed that information, the look in her eyes and her tone of voice, at least managed to bring to his senses this person or that on the verge of going stark, raving mad.

With the approach of nightfall, the stream of cars let up; no more drivers asking for directions. Instead the number of pedestrians swelled, and those standing around or sitting all through the new city almost in masses seemed to have been there earlier but only now began to be visible, audible, taking on filled-in colorful outlines; no one had seen them arrive; at any rate, in the fruit thief's eyes that was what had happened.

In particular the zones around the stations of the regional railway now transformed themselves into the squares that had been conceived as part of the original planning and also designated as such on the city map but until now had remained unrecognizable even to the liveliest imagination. From one station to the next these squares filled—no, didn't you see?—were full of people. The streets, too, ambitiously dubbed *boulevard* and *avenue*, suddenly became extended squares. One corso led to the next, until one could imagine the entire city as one uninterrupted corso. Before nightfall and also for a long time after that, Cergy, recently founded and down to its most remote corners and outermost districts and rotundas meticulously laid out in lines and circles that covered the landscape, took on the aspect of a southern city, and one such as appeared nowhere else and certainly not in any real southern setting. Yet it was hardly surprising that this atmosphere was intensified by the northerly, already "Picardian" sky, with its long-lingering midsummer dusk. Because it was vacation time, no students around, and also no army of high-ranking or less high-ranking white-collar workers, who would have attenuated the impression or illusion of a corso, still dressed as they would have been at this time of day in suits with slim trousers and cropped jackets that left their posteriors uncovered, their skinny leather briefcases, seemingly empty, dangling from their hands; the corso impression, on the contrary, was heightened by the outfits of almost all those sitting, standing, strolling hand in hand, shuffling everywhere in the *ville nouvelle*, in saris or sarongs (or whatever the word was), in caftans (or the like), under veils of every sort.

Previously she had noticed here and there a sign on a façade that declared the place a "café." But none of these had tempted the fruit thief to enter. Now that changed, and in front of the cafés there even appeared terraces that had not been there before, "terraces" in the truest sense of the word.

On one such terrace in Cergy she sat down at a table among the other guests. Whereas previously she had attracted so much attention, involuntarily, now the fruit thief became entirely unobtrusive. It was not simply that no one noticed her anymore; she became invisible. She was used to that, and for the most part found it more than just all right—having others not see her, disappearing yet being present, being in the presence of the others! But sometimes she became invisible in a way that she did not really want. In a store, a government office, a restaurant where she needed something, urgently (or sometimes less urgently), had to get something done, where she had come in feeling hungry and thirsty—and how hungry and thirsty she could be!—she would be overlooked, repeatedly, was as if not there, and not even ignored on purpose or out of ill will by those in charge; in their eyes she, unlike all the others there who needed something, might as well be made of air. Air? If only she had at least been air to them, but no, she was nothing, did not exist, even when she simply stood or sat there, reasonably erect, in the middle of the shop, office, eatery that was otherwise empty, with no people, visitors, or guests. Not until she turned to leave, having accomplished nothing, did it sometimes happen that they noticed her at last. Then they would pounce on her from all sides, eager to be of service. And she let herself be mollified, in her usual way, as if sad and a bit ashamed, not of herself but of the others.

That was how it was on the terrace. And at long last, with a glass of wine or whatever in front of her, she changed from being invisible, overlooked, and not present to a condition that she welcomed from time to time: seeing without being seen; perceiving things differently precisely because one had become imperceptible, not seen from the outside as a scout, a spy, or, heaven forbid, a detective, not being registered by anyone, yet in the midst of others, just part of the general population.

She saw that a woman, no longer all that young, in an advanced stage of pregnancy, was expecting her first child. A veiled woman with even her eyes covered gazed intently at someone. A woman beat her dog, the replacement for her previous dog, which had recently been put to sleep because of cancer or old age. The young man who had paused in the middle of the corso and was combing his hair, first rapidly, then more and more slowly, had suddenly realized that he had just wronged someone, yes, that he had done nothing but wrong, had been wrong from the beginning, while someone coming toward him was smoothing the fringes on the sleeve of his leisure outfit with his fingers, carefully, one fringe after the other, in the belief, or superstition—"let him be, I'm like him"—that this action was providing safe conduct for his sister as she traveled through the African war zone, from Burkina Faso all the way across Mali. In a moment tears would well up in the eyes of the man over there with the menacing expression—hand over the money—(and that proved to be the case, almost, for it took longer than a moment to happen). The woman there, baring all her teeth to her unfaithful lover in a huge smile that spread over her entire face, would spit at him any minute now, and that did happen, though without spit. And one of those sitting on the terrace tossed something, without getting up, to a person sitting several tables away, and it was certain that the other person would catch it, also remaining seated, and this is what happened. And for the old man there in the evening crowd this was the last time he would go out, and the same for the ancient cat, which could hardly set one paw in front of the other, which could be discerned from the flood of speech above her, her claws scraping the asphalt as she was dragged along on a string. *Corso ultimo.* The fruit thief recognized all that without pity, also without a trace of compassion. Invisible as she was, she participated.

In the meantime she kept busy on the café's terrace, like the others—in the intervals during which they were not conversing; she tried to read (at which she did not succeed that evening in Cergy), and above all fooled around with her mobile telephone; she had her Siberian one with her, if merely as a souvenir.

She had fished it out of her fruit-thief bag in response to a signal from the depths of the bag that sounded to her like a cry for help. No sooner was it in her hand than it rang for an incoming call, or vibrated, or something. She saw her father's number light up and decided not to answer. But since she had the device in her hand, she typed, as deftly as all the young folk around her, a "text message" or "email" or . . . to her brother, who, not yet fifteen, had left his Paris *lycée*, located where else but in an arrondissement on the Left Bank, in the middle of the school year, to take up an apprenticeship as a craftsman in the countryside, in Picardy, familiar to him from childhood. He was living there in an apprentices' lodge near Chaumont-en-Vexin, where he also had classes, as in a boarding school, but was staying there through the summer as well. His sister wrote that she wanted to visit him. It would be her first visit to her little brother. The siblings had not seen each other in a year, what with the sister traveling most of the time. Her brother, Wolfram—an unusual name for a French child—responded immediately: "Come!"

After that the fruit thief felt like having another glass and especially something to eat—giving herself permission to have a proper evening meal. She could support herself on her various jobs, not only the ones she had just had along the taiga rivers, and she used her tips for a luxury now and then, also the money her father insisted that she take from time to time, which she accepted more out of childlike obedience; see her "sense of family." Besides, the café-restaurant in Cergy was not expensive; the fruit thief could be frugal without being stingy; her mother the banker praised that as thrift.

This was by the regional rail station Saint-Christophe, probably thought of as the center of all the centers in the new city, the name taken from the church that had stood there long ago, dedicated to the former local patron saint, Christopher, the ferryman who had once carried the child Jesus, growing heavier and heavier, on his back across a river by night, across all rivers, and thus here, too, across the Oise. In place of the church of Saint-Christophe there now stood something supposed to be the landmark of the new city, a steel structure in the form of an arcade at least as tall as a church tower, with a monumental round steel clock mounted on its front (twelve meters? sixteen meters? in diameter—you can check on the internet!), between whose spokes one can look up into the sky, with Roman numerals, from I to XII.

The Saint-Christophe clock had stopped that evening, however, or perhaps it had stopped some time ago. Behind the spokes of this clock, which resembled a Ferris wheel, the spokes now joined by the motionless hands, the sky, though remaining light, became an evening sky. Distant swallows swooped down against it, providing an intuition of the countryside beyond the new city. Having disappeared for a while, not merely for that one day, they now reappeared.

The next time the fruit thief looked up, deep dusk had descended, the sun long since set, and behind and in front of the transparent clock wheel, close enough to touch, whirred something that she recognized as bats from their shadows on the square below as they swooped back and forth in the streetlights. So the *ville nouvelle* had bats—some people claimed that these creatures felt at home only in old buildings, in crumbling attics, in dirt cellars. Did the city still have buildings from earlier times, from previous centuries? Nowhere had she seen, while traversing the city, any new building that had collapsed and become a ruin. That was not allowed. The city was far too proud of being a new city, and especially of presenting itself as such. Bats! Now flying for the evening out of some secret cave? Out of a mausoleum in an old cemetery, long since dilapidated but not to be touched, at least as a piece of real estate?

Her sense of place awakened, in the form of enjoyment of the place, pleasure at being in that particular spot. But that was not her first experience of pleasure here. Earlier in the day this pleasure had come over her when, despite her resolve, she had succumbed to her "fruit thievery" impulse and here and there popped something into her thief bag, unsystematically, when the occasion presented itself, with her left hand, while doing something entirely different at the same time. And furthermore, not once did this action fit the legal definition of theft. Nonetheless, in committing it, she was "the fruit thief through and through."

The fruit she appropriated this way she did not steal, for it grew wild here and there all through the new city, belonged to no one, was neither private nor public property, unless the city also laid claim to everything that grew wild in its jurisdiction, including those plants called weeds. What the fruit thief tucked into her bag, plucked, broke off, pulled up, was sold in the markets as "chives," "cress," "asparagus," "melon," "sorrel," "squash," and it had been raised for eating. All these edibles she had gathered, in modest quantities, on the way from the edge of the new city to this central square: chives by the entrance to an office building, sorrel on the perimeter of a newly built nursery school, cress along one of the few creeks flowing into the Oise that had not been covered over, more a trickle than a brook. But had the melon also been growing wild? Yes, hidden in the grass on an embankment. And definitely the asparagus: it, too, wild, like a skinny stalk of grain—growing in the middle of a city, one without meadows? There is nothing uncanny about all this? Certainly not.

And the most luxuriant wild growth in the new city, also the most delightful to the palate, had been a plant also available in its cultivated form in specialty markets—at least in Europe—"only those should be allowed to call themselves 'markets'!"—offered as a fairly costly vegetable: so-called purslane, or *pourpier*, or . . . It spread like wildfire the length and breadth of the new city, its succulent heart-shaped greenish leaves snaking through the drainage ditches along the avenues and boulevards, clambering over the foundations of government and corporate office buildings—even if modern buildings lack this feature—almost like shrubbery, cleared away annually as a weed but sprouting anew in the same places every summer, impossible to eradicate, unbelievably delicious eaten raw as a salad, "excellent with warm potatoes, olive oil, and a dash of coarse sea salt."

The fruit thief followed this advice, adding the succulent purslane leaves, the stalks of wild asparagus, and a tiny wild squash, etc., to her regular evening meal. The tomatoes from the railyard of the Gare Saint-Lazare were included. With her jackknife she cut, peeled, and chopped the ingredients over her plate, and no one paid any attention to her; although she performed these operations openly, in a deliberately ceremonial manner, her gestures seemingly meant for someone's benefit and with the terrace's lighting shining on her, she went unnoticed; it was as if she were still invisible, not overlooked but not present, as she liked it.

The next time she looked up at the giant clock, its hands were moving again. But no: she had been mistaken. The sky behind the clock had turned into a night sky, black, with no stars visible against the floodlights illuminating the square around Saint-Christophe, coming primarily from above, high above. The street, now appearing to the imagination as a diagonal cutting clear across the entire city, remained thronged as before, except that the sounds and noises made by the people walking and standing there became audible separately, at once more abrupt and more distinct. The policemen, a small army patrolling in front of the station with submachine guns, both protecting and surveilling, also more distinct.

A gentle night breeze swept down over the square and the terrace, as if through the spokes of the great clock, inaudible, unlike the voices below, and yet it was as if she heard the breeze drowning out the voices, insistently. And after this brief gust, in the next second, also seen through the spokes of the clock, suddenly shooting out from behind the clock face, the moon, almost full, appeared, surrounded by a bevy of small clouds that it lit up, its escort. So nothing would come of the nocturnal thunderstorm for which she had been hoping so fervently since her arrival in Cergy.

How conspicuous this moon was, along with the clouds wreathed around it. How it imposed its presence. And how overly distinct the sounds on the "diagonal" beneath the moon—which seemed to become fuller each time she looked up at it. Above all, the music from the cars, intentionally driving no faster than a walk, blared from their windows or the open convertible tops into her ears and pounded her head. At one time the fruit thief had been crazy about music, and in some cases she still was. The music that had made the deepest impression on her was rap. Ah, Eminem, whose real name was Marshall . . . It was only a few years ago that she had sought out one of the impoverished sections of Detroit, 8-Mile = eight miles from the center, where the rapper had spent what was described as his wretched childhood; she was hoping to catch sight of the grown-up rapper, star or not, for a moment, and all the better if at a distance.

But this night was not the time for music of any kind, whether Monteverdi, Gregorian chant, or Johnny Cash. As she sat there beneath the moon, lowering over the new city in the giant wheel of the stopped clock that marked the center of town, the pounding, hammering, and rapping (as if one were constantly being shouted at) became an additional burden on the fruit thief. She did not hear it. Otherwise she might have enjoyed it. But on this night, when it was so obtrusive, it remained as if inaudible to her.

Instead she heard something entirely different, more and more insistent as time passed, yet never in the foreground. And these were the sounds—hard to believe, or perhaps not so hard—yet altogether unclear where they came from, whether from the grassy circles around the newly planted city saplings, or from up above in their leaves? of a nocturnal chirping of crickets—*chirping* seemingly an inadequate term—and then, far, far away, owls hooting, which could be mistaken at first for cats' long-drawn-out meowing. Oh, these secret sounds amid the new city's din and roar. Soon she did not have to strain to hear them. She had them in her ear; she heard them, unlike the general racket, instead of the prevailing sounds, as the preeminent sounds. And now the preeminent sounds gave way, mysteriously and even more mysteriously, to sounds of home. The noises or calls of one midsummer cricket (wasn't that insect associated from time immemorial with hearth and home?) received a reply from somewhere else, and from somewhere else again, here, there, in the city's backgrounds, and the owls' hoots were answered not with a meowing but with a piping, which was also a gurgling, as if underwater, or that of a hookah. And when the fruit thief looked up at the clock again, the previous illusion repeated itself: the hands were working again, but this time for good; the illusion persisted, could not be wiped from her eyes. The hands were "working"? They would work anew, any minute now. At any rate they looked ready to start; the clock had been wound, in tune with the crickets' chirping, producing an unmistakable, monotonous sound that filled her ear with a mighty clock-winding, filling the length and breadth of the night.

"Ah, if only the hidden truth would prevail. If only it could become all-powerful. Seize power on earth. Without needing to be made a law, whether gentle or harsh. The hidden home truth as the prevailing force, without being written into law. But as the prevailing force would it not lose the element of secretiveness on which its strength depends? On the one hand: wasn't hidden truth already in force, long before this hour, indeed from the dawn of time? On the other hand: why, for God's sake, must I wrestle alone with these questions, and not just since this night, and not merely with these questions, but from the beginning? Will I remain alone to the end of my life, rock, rap, and the hidden truth be damned? Instead of living life to the fullest, peacefully, in harmony, thanks to the hidden truth, as yesterday and today and so forth, why do I merely survive, from one day to the next, as in wartime? But don't they say, on the other hand, that we've been at war with each other for a long time already? Yes, since my roaming around I've been nothing but a survivor. Nothing? But doesn't the fact of my survival fill me at the end of every day—and that's why I always try to stay awake until past midnight—with a kind of pride, and a strength different from when I was crisscrossing one landscape or another, which was nothing but a silent howl at being at a complete loss. Good, rich surviving, and, instead of the landscapes, battlefields: that's all right. And then again not good and definitely not at all right. Ah, that fear again. Flee!"

"Are you asleep? The question came from a friendly voice at one of the nearby tables. She looked up at the man, his face half in shadow. Was he the one? No, he was not. But at least she had not been overlooked entirely; one person had noticed her. She laughed with relief, and he laughed with her. So friendly.

She got up and left, nodding good-bye. He would not follow her; that was understood. No one would follow her. Yet she was still thinking of fleeing. And then: "No fleeing. Never again. And for the time being, keep it simple, onward. Follow Father's advice and put one foot in front of the other. Let the feet lead the way. Head toward the owls' hoots, uphill, to the place for the night." Whereupon it occurred to her, for the first time, that she did not have a place yet; up to then it had not crossed her mind.

The owls' hooting led her steadily uphill. There had to be a forest where they were calling to one another. A forest in the middle of the new city? That would be nice. That would have been nice, as in olden but enduring times, as in the old, everlasting stories. But no forest appeared in the alternation between street lighting and full-moon shadow, from time to time like twins, moon shadow as a sibling to streetlight shadow, twofold shadow "in twofold glow," as one of the old tales had it. The built-up avenues and boulevards extended as if to infinity, except that they more and more evolved into serpentines the higher they went.

When she finally reached the top, she found herself in the middle of another square, this one completely ringed by buildings in the style typical of the new city, though here a few stories higher; at second glance she recognized the center of Cergy-le-Haut, with its entry to the stairs down to the terminal of the regional rail line, where she had been earlier when she arrived toward evening on the bus. An impulse from her younger years came over her to pop into the multiplex cinema on the square and take in one of the six to sixteen films playing there in the hours before midnight, never mind which: it could be *Mission Impossible 4* or *Die Hard 12* or an animated film (since childhood she had not seen any, with the exception of one or two Japanese ones—and how comforting it was, by the bye, in the hour before midnight, "to think in numerical terms, if need be . . .").

But on this night, disappearing into a movie theater was out of the question. It would be cowardly, the fruit thief thought, the flight she had just forbidden herself to engage in. Keep following the call of the owls. Like the others, this elevated square was planted at intervals with trees—maples, planes, lindens, or the like, all of them good-sized, with straight trunks, which enhanced the impression of being not on a real, three-dimensional square but in front of a giant, horizon-filling billboard. But the owls were squawking—now and then they also cackled and babbled—somewhere else entirely, not that far off, also less from above than at almost the same altitude. In one of the trees on the square sparrows were sleeping, or also not sleeping, their presence indicated by the thousands of droppings on the pavement below and also on a car that seemed to have been forgotten there long ago, or, as she said to herself, abandoned in a tearing hurry: "The flight was continued on foot."

Why not follow the crickets instead of the owls? The problem was that now the crickets were chirping and piping everywhere in the warm night, windless even up here. No matter where she turned her head: the chirping resounded from all sides, not secretly or secretively as in the previous hour but out in the open, presenting itself without the earlier reticence, at some moments even metallically shrill, a wing-scraping like that of cicadas, seemingly coming from the forks of trees, and cicadalike scraping also from one cricket—if indeed it was one—at her feet, from a crack in the pavement.

No, the sound came from so many directions that it was impossible to pinpoint. Sticking to the owls set her course. The outlet of the square—one of few, if not the only one—at first turned out to be a detour, once she had finally found it. But then she was able to get back on course to the serpentines, where, with the owl calls, now a fluting sound, firmly in her ear, she felt at home, going in the "right direction," toward an undetermined goal. Then the serpentines unexpectedly took her, after dense complexes of new buildings, row upon row, uphill through open land, which she would have taken for the great no-man's-land around the *ville nouvelle*, the only thing she remembered from her one semester there, had it not been for the lighting, which shone down from up high onto the serpentines and the steppe brush on either side, revealing that as she followed serpentine after serpentine she remained within the city limits, under the city's aegis, for surveillance as well as protection.

The fact that the fruit thief, alone on the serpentines, which also, at least now toward midnight, had no more traffic, stopped and looked behind her on every curve, did not result from fear of being pursued. So why did she do it? She could not explain it herself. And suddenly it became clear to her after all: she actually wished that someone would follow her. Or this: she would have been "glad of it."

Then, before the last of the serpentines, a signpost bearing the name of a town, "Courdimanche" in large letters, and under it in smaller letters, "Commune de la Ville Nouvelle Cergy-Pontoise." Courdimanche, what a lovely name—Sunday Court, Court of Sunday, Sundayish Court. (If, however, her father, with his knowledge of places and words, had been there, he would have tried to explain to her that the village's name was the kind of corruption common in that region, in this case of an old Latin term referring to the *curia*, the seat, not of Sunday, *dimanche*, but of the *dominus*, the lord, the local ruler; and "Courdimanche" accordingly meant "Lord's Seat"—though for her it would have remained the Sunday Court.)

At the sight of the signpost it occurred to her that if it was not Sunday it certainly was the weekend. And now aromas wafted toward her that suggested something exotic, at least for the catchment area of the new city. "Barbecue?" No, it was not a charcoal fire, it was wood. And the wood fires were not burning in parks, also not in front yards, and also not, with all due respect to her father's advice on the route she should take, "in backyards," but inside the houses, which were village houses, the genuine article. Did such things still exist? Perhaps here and there in the countryside. But here—see the lighting and the signpost—clearly in the orbit of the new city? Let's wait and see. Why didn't anyone in Cergy mention Courdimanche to me earlier, this village way high up and at the same time in the middle? Or did I forget that, too?

The first thing she saw of Courdimanche was the church tower, sticking up above the roofs, not because it was so much taller but because it stood on the highest point in the village. The closer she came, after a steep climb past the houses that lined a narrow alley, without twists and turns, the smaller the tower became, small like the church itself, not lit up, at least on this night—although, as the oldest structure far and wide, it would have deserved to be lit up as another landmark—yet with the full moon shining on it. And then, from amid the cubes in the village at its feet, was that the voice of a muezzin? The call to prayer, the last one on Friday? Yes, it was Friday, before midnight. And then the moon, veiled for a moment by a scrap of cloud, like tulle, and shimmering like the bronze disk of a temple gong, due to boom out any minute now.

Instead owl calls again, coming from just one owl, as if from up above, behind the Courdimanche church tower. The fruit thief's pack had grown heavy as the day progressed, and now she let it slide into her hand and carried it that way to the square in front of the church: she had reached her destination for the day; she would go nowhere else this night.

The lighting in the village was perhaps just as bright as for the entire *ville nouvelle*, into which the former village of

Courdimanche had been incorporated, located on this peak, the "summit," as her father, the amateur geologist, would have called it. But among the houses and also above them a seemingly natural darkness prevailed, whereas in the other districts of the great agglomeration the artificial light had become a kind of second nature. In spite of the full moon, could that be a star behind one of what appeared to her as the traditional chimneys, complete with smoke? No, a night-flying plane. And from beneath a bush, glowing in what remained of village darkness, were those the eyes of a fox, or even a lynx? No, but at least those of a cat.

The one bar in Courdimanche was already closed, the iron shutters lowered. Or was it closed for good? Seventeen steps farther on she saw the bakery, which would open the next morning, when? "at five thirty." Another twenty-three steps farther on, at the bend in the square, the village tavern, still lit up, the dining room bathed in very white light, but already empty, or empty all evening long? A North African restaurant, the two specialties, "couscous" and "tagines," the same price, "13 Euros," as painted on the front window, all uneven numbers, "a good sign."

Farther on around the square, where the street sloped downward slightly, with a view of the river valley below, the lights of the new city stretching to the horizon, as if far below Courdimanche—"Courdimanche, Courdimanche . . . ," the fruit thief repeated to herself, almost dragging her pack on the ground—and in among the single-family houses one stood apart, and it was the only one with lights still burning, and in all the windows of the four floors (the fourth seemed to have been added on recently).

The front door was open, "wide open." The vestibule lit, if with only one bulb. She went inside. In spite of the stillness enveloping the house, she felt the presence of other people, many of them. And that was how it was. In room after room silent figures, dressed informally, almost all of them seated, on chairs and even more on benches, along the walls. The center of each room was empty, except for the last one, where a catafalque stood, and on it an open coffin. She came closer and saw the body inside, the face almost the only thing visible amid all the flowers and who knows what else that had been placed in the coffin. A strong fragrance that might have been lavender, but an even stronger smell of candle wax.

In room after room one person or another among those sitting there in complete silence had nodded to her, as if recognizing her. She was one of the mourners, taking part in the wake. An old woman came up to her, took the fruit thief's hand, and held it for a long time; tears welled up in the old lady's eyes as she gazed at the young woman standing at some distance from the coffin. The eyes of the fruit thief, the stranger to the village, had likewise moistened, as the story tells us.

She sprinkled the dead man with holy water from a jam jar holding a bunch of boxwood branches, adding to the droplets already on the ageless face of the corpse. She had flicked so much water toward him that one of the candles by the head of the coffin sputtered, almost going out, and then flared even higher. Not until she raised her arm to sprinkle the water did she notice that the entire time she had been holding in that same hand a stalk with an umbel of little dried flaxseed pods, picked up somewhere on the edge of a harvested field before her bus trip to the new city. She had forgotten the stalk in her hand, as often happened to her with objects. And what made her notice it? The sound of the seed pods, between a rustling and a rattling, never heard in this particular way, so quiet and so gentle that it made her prick up her ears, and she was not alone. For as she looked around, as if to apologize for making this unsuitable noise in a house where someone had died, one or two of the mourners nodded to her as if familiar with this kind of flaxseed rustling as part of an old custom.

She took a seat among the others on one of the benches by the walls. Without hesitation room had been made for the stranger. She was dressed in her usual way, of course, perhaps not quite right for the solemnity prevailing in the house of the deceased. But then the rest of the company was not wearing mourning clothes, either, not even the members of the immediate family; each person was wearing what he or she had had on during the day, at work or wherever. Two children brought in a tray with refreshments, finger foods and beverages in small glasses, and the stranger allowed herself to be served along with the local folk. After this, it seemed, the silence could be broken: here and there people talked, even laughed a little. But no one asked her any questions. Or perhaps in what was said questions were implied, meant for her. Yet no one addressed her directly. Besides, for a while a language was spoken in that house of the dead that she had never heard in her travels around the world, and if questions were included, without the corresponding intonation. (Her father had told her that languages exist whose speakers do not use sound markers—but she had forgotten, yet again, what people and what language he had mentioned.) Whatever the case, she understood not a word. At the same time she was certain: if she opened her own mouth and spoke, in the official national language, the others would understand her and answer as a matter of course, though possibly with an accent; after all, Courdimanche was in the heart of France, where all of them had been citizens for decades—and then there was the fact that no place-name in all of France sounded more French than this Courdimanche, right? and at the same time it was a sound like something out of a fairy tale, right? But first this unfamiliar language, strange to the ear like no other, with not a single word whose meaning she could guess, also the result of the unidentifiable sound. It did have a sound, yes. But what did it signify? Questions? No: she, too, did not ask; kept silent. For the rest of the night she would not open her mouth. No one in all of Courdimanche expected that of her, let alone demanded it. Listen, yes. But remain wordless. And Alexia felt strength flowing into her, and a sensation of peace spread through her that was not hers alone. "Ah, incomprehensible language, how beautiful it is. Don't stop speaking it, not soon, anyway, not tonight, please!" Even when someone cleared his throat in this house of mourning, it involved sounds she had never heard before. Or was it not throat-clearing at all but an entire articulated sentence? But the sneezing now and then—the night air wafted in more and more from the windows open all through the house—that was just sneezing, wasn't it, and called nothing other than "sneezing"? True: except that in the unknown language it sounded entirely different from sneezing anywhere else on earth. And true as well: in every one of the known world languages sneezing had its own sound, with different vowels and consonants, but common to all sneezes the two-syllable pattern. In this sneezing, however: a kind of three-syllable pattern, sometimes four . . . perhaps she was hearing the original sound doubled, as one sometimes sees double when one is tired, as she was, now that it was past midnight? The sound and its echo?

She laughed briefly, the laugh she had had as a child. As if at a signal the mourners switched from the unknown language into that of the country, and the dead man's wife—if that was who she was; for heaven's sake, don't ask!—invited the fruit thief to spend the night in the house, in one of the bedrooms on the top floor. And at once she was tugged by the sleeve and followed her. Only now did she notice, as she turned on the threshold to look at the catafalque once more, the framed photograph on the otherwise blank wall behind it; as so often, she noticed something only at last glance (or not at all) that others saw at first glance, and the woman of the house said—more to herself and precisely thereby getting others to listen—"Yes, when his daughter was a child, she was God to him. As long as she was a child. Not that he worshipped her. He didn't worship anything. Prayed, yes, but worshipped, no. Except that he couldn't pray, even at the very end, though he wanted to, from the bottom of his soul . . . Yes, his daughter: he'd have sacrificed everything for her, his dreams for the future—and what dreams he still had at the time! what grand ones! and carried his 'dream of greatness' around with him, day and night—his whole 'great life,' which he talked about all the time—he was positively obsessed with the idea of sacrifice, or was it a compulsion? to sacrifice himself, above and beyond his child, for something undefined, but to him worth the sacrifice, yet first of all and certainly for the child. Not just that he'd have died for his little daughter. For her sake he'd have made enemies of the whole world, would've started a war—what he called 'my kind of world war'—would've lied a blue streak, though he called himself 'too dumb to lie,' would've robbed and murdered till hell froze over, would've broken all ten, or twelve, Commandments. His willingness to sacrifice himself could seem quite harmless—but that was only how it seemed: if the child was sick, even if she just had the sniffles, he promptly saw her on her deathbed, and he felt he had to die himself—a violent death, by his own hand, because he was convinced that was the only way he could cure and save his loved one, through his own death, his own wound. He saw saving others as his calling, though not necessarily connected with sacrificing himself, and he was forever saving the child when there was nothing to save her from. But the one time she really might have needed to be saved by him, her father wasn't her father anymore. And it was long after she'd ceased to be a child, was neither her father's nor her mother's child, was no one's child. Without expressly breaking with her, he'd turned away from her. Without raising a hand to her, he pushed her away. From one day to the next he didn't want to lay eyes on her as a grown woman, or hear from her. That doesn't mean that the father and daughter never met. They continued to meet, though less often—they were living in different countries by then—still called each other 'Father' and 'Child'—he'd put special emphasis on the word and repeat it—still sat across from each other, on a train, in a restaurant, went hiking together, in the countryside and into the mountains—her countryside and its mountains—but he didn't see or hear the adult person before him or next to him; couldn't look at her anymore, not at her face and certainly not in the eyes, couldn't stand the woman's voice and tone of voice, and eventually didn't want any contact with her. 'I just don't want to hear and see her now, don't ask me why; I ask myself that every day, from early to late—why?—but no answer. The fact that nothing about her is childlike now can't be the whole reason, can't be sufficient? Or maybe it can? Goodness me! I don't know!' The person who was closest to him"—the woman of the house jerked her head in the direction of the man in the coffin—"became physically repulsive to him. A run in her stocking, an overly long nail on her right index finger, polished in a glaring color—or was it the left?—the sight of her split ends in the summer sun—made him avert his eyes. Not to mention her tattoos, one of them tiny, and visible only when she put her hair up, a ladybug or whatever on her neck: 'Now I'm supposed to be the father of someone with tattoos!' And then the expressions she used: 'winter garden,' 'exactly!' 'Sarajevo,' 'sausage,' 'toilet tissue,' 'meeting,' 'friends,' 'condo association meeting,' 'runoff election,' 'an absolute dream,' 'quality of life,' 'jew's harp,' 'pampa,' 'Evergreen: quiet! Beat it! Have a good trip!' Everything about his grown-up daughter rubbed him the wrong way; it was like the prophet Jonah and the city of Nineveh. If she wore shoes with heels, they were too high, and in flats he thought her legs looked stumpy. If she wore cornflower-blue eye shadow and put mascara on her lashes, he got bent out of shape by her 'mask,' but if she didn't wear makeup, he got even more upset that he couldn't find any trace of the face she'd had as a child; to him, her face was monstrously enlarged and disturbingly naked. Her nostrils were too big, her teeth too small, or vice versa. Sometimes her forehead was too low, sometimes too high. Her lips, which he'd just described as too full, were too thin a moment later. First her head was too long and narrow, then too round. In front of and next to the person, the 'mortal being,' as he called her, to whom all his love had once come, flowed, been directed, and thanks to whom he'd experienced and first realized what love was and how it felt—'Love exists, I know because I've experienced it,' as he said—in the presence of this person, that one lying over there felt nothing but lovelessness. Is lovelessness an emotion? Yes, but unique in the ugly and empty way it imposes itself, unlike any other emotion, no matter how awful. He hated himself for this lovelessness, became as repulsive to himself in its grip as the daughter he rejected, repulsive in a different way, had 'had it' with himself (his expression), loveless as he was, a loveless person in the way he saw the world, over it, so over it, 'ready to smash my head against the wall out of sheer lovelessness, out of lack of love.' So in the end he was the one who could have used a savior. And how he longed to be saved, how he pleaded for a lifeboat, a 'hovercraft'—as he called it, to carry him away from the ocean of lovelessness. Not a prayer. And also the return, one way or the other, of the prodigal daughter: not a prayer. A long, long time ago someone said to him, 'The child is your life's work.' And now? Neither a child nor a life's work—certainly not that. His calling recalled. Everything silent, gone with the wind. Snakes on the prowl rummage through the silence. Such lovelessness—lovelessness to the nth degree."

The woman of the house, or whatever she was, had meanwhile led the stranger up to a room in the attic and made up her bed for the night there. And at this moment, in response to her final sentence, or in general, the fruit thief opened her mouth for the first time since her arrival in Courdimanche and in the house of the deceased, and said, "Who knows?" whereupon the woman, with whom she was just then spreading the sheet, looked up, gave a long, hearty laugh, which noticeably rejuvenated her face, and replied, "Yes, you never know. And his name actually was Jonah. The Jonah of Courdimanche. But God knows, no prophet."

Suddenly the mourner had turned away and dashed out of the room, back down to the floor with the coffin; had abandoned the fruit thief without saying good night.

She sat for a while by the open window with its view of the nearby hillcrest with the church tower. Inside her the town's name echoed quietly. Courdimanche, Courdimanche . . . On the little stand next to the easy chair a basket of apples and pears, clearly grown somewhere else and purchased; she would not touch this fruit, let alone eat it. She switched off the bedside lamp. In the meantime the moon had set. Now real stars could be seen twinkling, not night planes; she could have identified most of the northerly constellations visible from the window without her father's help and interference, not only the Great Bear and Cassiopeia. But at this late hour she did not feel in the mood to visually pull the stars together into the conventional images, at the same time separating them from the stars that did not fit those images; she wanted to let the whole starry sky impress itself on her, or at least the part she could see from her window. And thus she experienced something that up to this point in her life had been and remained only an expression, read or picked up here and there: the stars gazed down on her, for the duration of a moment. And how kindly they had looked down on her, all of them together!

She closed her eyes. She expected no afterimage, and not merely because it was the middle of the night. Nor did she wish for one. That one exchange of looks, the reciprocation of her gaze by the whole starry sky, had been sufficient, and after the long and also repeatedly troubling day tranquility had—yes, stolen into her heart. Right: she had set out in search of her mother, and would resume the search the next morning. And the thought that earlier on had less troubled her than, from time to time, disturbed her a bit—or perhaps not just a bit?—and, briefly, also angered her: the thought that no one was out searching for her, for her personally: that thought no longer troubled her in the slightest.

But then an afterimage came after all, flickering and flaring behind her gently closed eyelids. Not the starry sky of the previous moment but also not the afterimage of something her eyes had registered in the course of the day. Or was it, as so often with her, something she had overlooked, something perceived only in the afterimage—see "the silhouette of her mother" on the excursion boat at the "end of the Oise"? No. What appeared now was nothing she had overlooked. It was something she would never, ever, have overlooked under any circumstances: something in writing. Had it been a carbon copy, possibly. Something in block letters: her overlooking that was harder to imagine, yet not completely unthinkable. But what now flickered and guttered on the screen behind her lids was in cursive, with all the letters seamlessly connected and intertwined, and thus the possibility that these might have gone unnoticed by her, "by me here": out of the question, yesterday as on all the days before.

Then she realized: the handwriting moving along, flaring up here and there, was not an afterimage. For these lines of writing no original image had existed in the daily and external world. These letters had not returned to bring to mind something she had missed in the day- and summer light. In particular, an element essential to an afterimage was absent—the reversals: that which had been bright in the original image would appear in the afterimage as dark, and what had been dark would glow brightly. This writing was not imprinted onto carbon paper, in no way resembled a negative; the letters snaked along, dark on dark, against a bright background. And besides, and above all: they were not already written, but instead were writing themselves only now, in the present, and uninterruptedly, in one fell swoop, line after line, before, no, behind her eyes.

Yet she could not decipher the words, not a single one, let alone an entire sentence. All she could read were single letters as the caravan of writing passed by—that was how she saw it—or occasionally two together. She opened her eyes, left them open for a while, then closed them again. The handwriting gone? erased? flown off? No, there it was again, shimmering, coming thick and fast, and still undecipherable except for one or two letters here and there. Which finally turned into a game: trying to see whether the writing would become clearer if she closed her eyes more firmly. It did not. Would keeping her eyes open longer enable her to outwit the writing, rendering it more legible when she suddenly closed her eyes, behind its back, so to speak? The writing did not let itself be outwitted. But it continued spooling.

In her young life she, the fruit thief, had seen many things, but something like this she was seeing in the night in Courdimanche for the first time. And was this not a sight for sore eyes! Who had ever seen the like, before her, or with her, in her day? Or was she the first and only one, and accordingly was she actually, no, literally, *bel et bien*, the "chosen one," "the chosen one among women," as her old father, who sometimes suffered from "senior moments," had tried to persuade her from time to time—with the result that she thought of herself as exactly the opposite? Whereupon she laughed that laugh of hers again.

Remarkable that she felt protected by that caravan of writing behind her eyes—an afterimage? A simultaneous transcript? anticipation of things to come? It was time to stretch out on the bed, unfamiliar, in this friendly foreign place, and have a good sleep. The window wide open, without curtains. After a while no more doors banging shut on the floors below. The mourners all departed. Stillness in the house of the dead, complete stillness. Sounds from outside infrequent and very far off, from way below, where the new city spread across the plain. And then after all, from close by, behind the church up here in Courdimanche, the brief calls of two owls, which finally, coming from the two nocturnal bird throats at once, formed a single sound, no longer a call but a blast.

That night the fruit thief dreamed the dream about a child, her own. She regularly dreamed—if there was anything regular to it—about a child, without it being clear that the child was hers. It was her most frequent dream, along with another that her father asserted was a family or tribal dream, passed down from time immemorial: like her, he also dreamed it, as his mother had dreamed it before him, and likewise in earlier times his mother's father, and so forth back through the centuries, a dream in which the dreamer, whether male or female, had murdered someone, and all night long the unexpiated murder would come closer and closer to being solved, bringing shame to the whole family—shame without possibility of atonement—and this dream, according to her father, went back to the darkest Middle Ages, when a founder of their tribe had committed regicide, in reality and in broad daylight. "If it had been tyrannicide: no need for the dream, without a doubt!" (For her father many things were "without a doubt.")

For quite a while she had not had that dream about being a murderer—since the end of her time "under the stairs" hardly ever. On the other hand, the dreams about a small child, a wee one, had become more frequent with the passing years. But without exception those dreams were nightmares. Whether her own child or not: the wee one had been entrusted to her. She was first in line, could not duck the responsibility. At the beginning of the dream the child was often of normal size, and only as the idyll turned into a catastrophe did it begin to shrink, and then shrank before her eyes to teeny-tiny proportions. After that the child either fell into water or, more often, it made its way, creeping and crawling, through an open door into the next room. But that was not the actual catastrophe. The water was shallow, hardly a thumb's length deep, posing no danger even to the teeny-tiny creature, and furthermore clear and still, with firm ground visible right below the surface. The next room was in the same house, identical to the room the child had just left, as if to go on playing next door. The catastrophe occurred when she looked down and saw that the little one entrusted to her, which she thought of as being right at her feet, splashing around or such, was simply no longer there in the still, shallow water, and nowhere to be found, despite her desperate groping in all directions, nevermore to be found; and when she saw that in the next room, over whose threshold the child, chortling with glee, had leaped or somersaulted or playfully stumbled barely a second earlier, not a trace of the child remained, even when she followed him almost immediately, not a sound, nothing but the empty room, and likewise, without any response when she called and called, in all the other rooms: the child gone forever. But what made the dreamer's horror worse than that of any other nightmares and at the same time drove the horror deeper and deeper, until it could not possibly go deeper and was about to crush her heart, was the absence of any trigger for the catastrophe, the absence of any action, any event, any happening that could account for the disappearance of the child, whether in the water or the next room, this disappearance for good, the impossibility of ever finding the child again. Other nightmares she forgot with time, usually by the next day, forgetful as she was, indeed endowed with a particular gift for forgetfulness. These, however, became and remained part of her day, of days upon days.

The dream about the child that came to her during that night in Courdimanche, with the dead stranger lying in repose on a lower floor, was no nightmare. The child she dreamed about was clearly her own, one to whom she had given birth. The birth itself was not at issue, nor did it provide an image. The same was true of the progenitor. But it was also clear he existed. The dream, and the story, had nothing to do with the father, or for that matter with her, the mother. To put it this way, perhaps: in the dream she was simply the spectator, seated down in the orchestra, or wherever—at any rate down below—as a witness for her child, up on the stage or in the choir loft or wherever, the child who was the sole subject of the dream story.

And what was that story? There was none. Nothing that had been shared with her, and through her—this pierced her to the core and stayed with her, beyond the duration of the dream—with the world. The child was simply there, nothing more. It was neither big nor small. It was neither black-haired nor blond. It neither stood nor sat. No question of its lying, either. Did it speak? Did it at least say something? Not a word. It, her child, had nothing to say. And just as there was no story, there was also nothing to say. How old was the child, approximately? She did not know, not even approximately. Was it a child at all, and if so, really hers, her only one, and slated to remain the only one. How sad, if not pathetic, for the child as well as for its mother and father: a lonesome only child, and the parents' constant worry and anxiety about their sole offspring. Even in the Middle Kingdom the one-child rule has been lifted, hasn't it? Neither sad nor pathetic, certainly not the latter, for any of the parties involved. No, it was bliss. With only the eternal dimension lacking. True: that was lacking. But the absence of the eternal from her dreamed bliss did not change anything. Or she did not even notice its absence. And vis-à-vis her child in the dream she also did not feel herself to be a "party," just as the child was not a party vis-à-vis her, and probably that was what filled her with bliss. The fruit thief experienced blissful moments not infrequently by day, if only fleetingly. But this was the first time that occurred in, with, and after a dream. —What does a dream like that have to convey to me? What does a dreamer like that want to convey to us? —A dream like that: it is meant for you. A dreamer like that: meant for all of you. —But a dream like that: hasn't it been dreamed not just once, but again and again since time immemorial, and by men as much as by women? —And what if it has? —And in the future it will be dreamed exactly the same, word for word, with the identical text, right? —And? Why shouldn't it? For the good of all of us, to paraphrase Wolfram von Eschenbach, or someone. —That kind of mother-and-child kingdom: Did it exist only in a dream then? Only in the kingdom-come of dreams?

Remarkable again, or perhaps not after all, how well she slept in the strange bed. One time, in the last hour of the Courdimanche night, she woke up, did not know where she was, and promptly fell asleep again, feeling even more at peace and refreshed than before.

During the period of her youthful roaming around the outskirts, the exact opposite had been the case. Startled during the night out of her sleep of sheer exhaustion under a warehouse's loading dock, beneath the roofed-over platform of an abandoned railroad station, in the last row of seats in a bus on the edge of an otherwise empty parking lot, where it had been left unlocked, God knows why, or was no longer in service: each time she had gone into a full-scale panic at not knowing where she was. She had jumped up, and, in the unfamiliar darkness—never pitch-black but just dim because of the proximity of the great city—dashed back and forth through the surrounding area. That she collided with the concrete loading dock, with the metal stanchions in the bus, with the cracked plastic wall of the passenger shelter, almost helped her overcome her disorientation. The crashing, banging, and rumbling, coming amid the racket, unlocatable and omnipresent, into which she had woken up, provided a momentary sense of location. If only the darkness had been proper darkness . . . But no: every time she woke up with a start from her coma-like sleep in a nowhere land, the night was dim, not enlivened and relieved anywhere by real blackness but rather, peer as she might and dash hither and thither, everywhere dim, dim, and yet again dim. And at the time that was what primarily sparked her horror at those nocturnal non-places: the unrelieved dimness, no matter where one looked, and the ceaseless roar that lacked any identifiable point of origin or horizon. Intern me in a camp, people—anything to escape from that dim nothingness. Never to have to experience that dimness again, either now or in the hour of my death!

This wish of hers, or whatever it was, had been fulfilled, at least the first part. Once her roaming around ended, at night she did wake up with a start now and then, here or there. But now she promptly got her bearings, knew where she was, whether in a bed, at home by the Porte d'Orléans or elsewhere, or out in the open, which still occurred, though in a different way. Waking up at night outdoors, she took in her surroundings even more distinctly, whether she had fixed them in her mind before going to sleep or not.

During that night in Courdimanche she did not get her bearings upon waking up before daybreak. That she did not know where she was was no relapse, however. She did not feel as though she had been abandoned in a nowhere land, as had been the case before; she felt surrounded by a place, a locale, in the true sense of the word, and how. The point now: not to know where I am and what the place is called. For a change, the assurance her father had given her before she set out held true: nothing could happen to her, at least not here. And these completely anonymous, boundaryless surroundings meant something else to her as well: they offered the possibility of discovery; a lot was going on here, and would continue to go on, riotously yet silently, anonymously riotously and anonymously silently. Everything discoverable already discovered? Nonsense: time and again discovery could happen, open-endedly. So go back to sleep for a while. Which she promptly did.

When she awoke for the second time, the sun, to judge by the rays hitting the wall of her room, was already fairly high in the sky, and at first the fruit thief thought the day was already half over. But it turned out to be still quite early; daylight saving time had misled her yet again, and besides, the sun had risen earlier in Courdimanche, located far above the river valley. So she could take her time. And nonetheless she was almost in a hurry to get away from there, on the one hand. On the other hand, it was important, was it not, after what she had experienced there during the night, to pay her respects to the place, in broad daylight. On the other hand again: hadn't she experienced enough for now?

This conflict overshadowed the first, if not also the second, hour of her morning. A harmless conflict? Seen from the outside, yes. Seen from the outside perhaps even a fruitful conflict? Yes. But not for her, who to this day was incapable of observing something only from the outside; that was not for her, who took anything that needed to be done or left undone equally seriously, for whom every such thing could turn into an inner sense of obligation and a problem, one that at times seemed almost insoluble. In such cases her mother the banker, who relished making decisions, or at least pretended to, would call her a female Hamlet, and sometimes meant that angrily, in angry impatience.

She felt compelled to get away, from the room first of all, and yet, already at the top of the stairs, she turned back, and not just once, and refolded the bedding, repositioned the chair, aired out the room, wiped nonexistent dust from the windowsill, picked up an imaginary hair from the floor, even sat down at the table, studied her marked-up map for the day that lay ahead, sketched, slowly and painstakingly, the hillcrest of Courdimanche with the church tower. Away! Out of the house, out of the village, out of the new city! Or should she linger a while after all? Isn't it possible that I've missed something here, and am continuing to miss it, something decisively important? And thus she could be observed, standing on the room's threshold, motionless except for her two hands, which she wrung and wrung, a hand-wringing of which she, and she alone, was capable, as if she wanted to choke one hand with the other, and herself as well.

Finally she can be seen after all on the lower floors, with her pack, her bundle, ready to set out. Then, again far "past the allotted time," standing in the room where the deceased lay in repose, by the coffin, closed now for being taken out of the house, she one among the crowd of mourners, who had reassembled. Despite all her inner disorientation, she felt at the same time a strength inside her as if she had been given the ability to raise the man from the dead. Then standing in the wide-open front door, with one foot already outside. And now, one last time, and "one more last time"? back to her bedroom, and standing stockstill in the middle, with some distance between herself and the bed, table, and chair. And now, finally seeming ready to get under way, in the early morning sun, on the broad curve in the road that at the same time forms the central square of Courdimanche, and then back up the stairs in the house of the dead, where the coffin is just being carried down: she adds a bouquet of flowers as a traditional morning gift, "picked myself" by the side of the road, to the garlands and wreaths following the dead man.

No one looked at her, let alone spoke to her, or so much as greeted her, not even the woman of the house. She, however, greeted others, or tried to: her greetings went unnoticed, as she herself did. It was as though going unnoticed this way had some connection with her inner conflict, her inability to make up her mind on the most minor things to do or leave undone, on what to do now, what to leave undone now, and so forth. And yet whenever something had been at stake in her life or someone else's, she had been the soul of decisiveness, needing no time to reflect, acting in a heartbeat, or, if it was a matter of leaving something undone, turning her back on it. It had been her decision as a daughter to become a stranger to her mother, to render herself unrecognizable during that period in the gatekeeper's lodge on her mother's estate. Her own decision likewise to set out now in search of her mother (although searching for her father might have fit the story better, except that in her case there was no father who needed to be searched for). Her own decision to drop out of the university. To set out for Alaska, to roam through Siberia: her own decision.

In the meantime the fruit thief can still(!) be seen in Courdimanche, the village enclave in the highest spot above the *ville nouvelle* of Cergy-Pontoise. She is sitting in the warm sun with her bag and baggage—which looks like a lot, and heavy, but in fact is neither—in front of the village's only bar (the trees that once provided shade are gone), and sipping slowly, slowly, as if to gain time, her coffee, or whatever it is; the croissant, without butter—finicky as she is, she has never liked butter—from the bakery across the street, long since eaten. She is wearing a sort of camouflage, which here in the densely built-up environs, with hardly a trace or a trail left of the rural open spaces, probably hides her even more effectively from others' notice than out in nature, among bushes and trees, and the airiness of her outfit seems to constitute one of the main features of the camouflage; yet the way the community of mourners failed to notice her during the previous hour had nothing to do with her clothing.

A gentle breeze was blowing across the heights of Courdimanche. O summer wind: she almost sang the words out loud. Glancing over her shoulder, she saw a haze over the new city below, not from the Oise but from the heat already oppressing the valley and, so she imagined, making itself felt a bit up here on the hill. She would have to pass through that heat later. Strange, that in the palpable absence of wind the breeze in Courdimanche originated not higher up on the crest with the church tower but rather below, an upwind that swept through the wide sleeves of her camouflage garment and from there brushed her face: her cheeks, her forehead, her temples, and finally the part in her hair.

Mobile telephone: on the screen, how else? her father's morning greeting. Then a message, in Cyrillic, from a woman at the Siberian fish market with whom the fruit thief had become friends while serving as a helper there. With the help of the Russian dictionary in her pack—remarkable, again, how many things she had in there—she managed to decode the few short sentences. Old though she was, the woman wrote, she had never had a woman friend. She (the addressee) was the first, and that would remain the case, even if the two of them (was there a dual in Russian?) never saw each other again. The mere thought of her, the woman said, gave her solid ground underfoot, something she had lacked all her life, whereas her Siberia's permafrost . . . The evening sun was already shining on the Yenisei, "and of course we two will see each other again soon." For the fruit thief this woman was also her first female friend. As a rule (another "rule"?), those of her own gender had always reacted to her with hostility if they came anywhere near her orbit, first little girls, then adolescents, then almost grown women, now young women, fixing her with a uniquely and inimitably evil, profoundly evil, eye, and one or two women who initially seemed to be wooing her as a friend had revealed themselves to be mortal enemies, out to destroy her. Reading the words from Siberia on the small screen several times, she wished she could fold up the message and stick it in a deep secret pocket in her "camouflage."

Reading on: in the book she had felt repelled by the previous day. Now was a good time for reading it, however. (Besides, part of her daily superstition involved reading—reading anything, but every word, immersing herself completely, and that would benefit someone about whose well-being she cared deeply, clearing the person's head, providing strength, if not "solid ground underfoot.")

The book told the story of a boy, an adolescent, the term used at the time, or perhaps still in use? (She read only books with stories in them, whereas her parents . . .) This boy, who had grown up without a mother, alone with his father, one morning spontaneously boarded a train and traveled to the neighboring country. Arriving in the capital toward evening, he wandered to the edge of town and took the last cable car up into the nearby mountains. At the top the boy got out and followed an alpine road, then a path, higher into the mountains, alone, into the darkness, and so forth. He came upon a mountain hut, locked up for the season. He broke a window and spent the night alone in the hut. The next morning he retraced his steps to the cable car, took it down to the capital, dawdled a bit on his way to the railway station, and then boarded a train for home. When he walked into his father's house that evening, his father had not noticed that his child had been missing for a day, a night, and another day.

She closed the book and held it a little while longer. "It's time," she thought, as she always did when it finally became possible to make a decision. Time to go, leaving the village of Courdimanche and the new city, heading north, across the Vexin plateau to Picardy? Time first to visit the old church on the hillcrest again and the forest, if it was one, from which all night long and penetrating her deep sleep the owls had called, as if to her personally, and where now—how could that be, in a forest?—a rooster was crowing incessantly.

She had already risen to her feet, with her light pack, and earlier, while she was reading, the funeral procession had passed through the square on its way to the cemetery, located among former grain fields, and without looking up from her book she had taken in everything involving that departure from the village—or so it seemed to her. A hand rested kindly on her shoulder: a farewell from the proprietor of Courdimanche's bar. She had not left her cup and plate for him to clear but had brought them inside herself and placed them on the counter. When he asked her name, she said, "Pas de nom, kein Name, no name, lâ ism!" and he did not press her.

The church on the crest that crowned the larger hill of Courdimanche was locked. She went down on her knees before the double doors and with one eye peered through the crack into the interior. The nave seemed empty, with the exception of some chunks of stone that might once have been the altar, a light-filled emptiness, intensified by the blindingly white limestone, already half crumbled into the gypsum that made up most of the Vexin plateau. She heard an echo of the voice of the muezzin that had reached her in her sleeping chamber during the transition from night to day, probably at five o'clock, coming from the direction opposite that of the first cock's crow behind the church. Or did she just imagine that?

A forest really did begin behind the church. That, at any rate, was the name she gave the dozen or so trees, with the usual underbrush. This latter was so thick, without a visible entrance, that she had to force her way in, half crawling, even jerking along on her back through the densest part, her pack and her bag in tow, so to speak. Then suddenly in a clearing, on soft ground, with no underbrush, as in a real forest, glimpsing through the surrounding thicket the area outside as if it were far off in the distance. Scrambling to her feet and standing up straight, she had the sensation of being in a corral, not a real one with real cattle tracks, even real cattle, but rather a corral in an old Western, a set built specially for the corral scene, where the final confrontation between the two mortal enemies would take place, had already taken place long ago. *Stagecoach*? *Winchester '73*? She did not remember.

Involuntarily she glanced at the ground to see if there were any traces of a struggle. A few steps farther along, a small but distinct hollow. Could that really be a bomb crater? It was. As she climbed in and lay down in the hollow, which was at least twice as soft as the ground up above, she regretted that the day before she had tossed into the confluence of the Oise with the Seine the pamphlet her father had insisted she take along, with its account of the last battle in that region, in the late summer of nineteen forty-four, between the Allies and the retreating, then once more advancing, soldiers of the "Third Reich." Did she regret it? Not really. Poking around, without a particular purpose, in the dead leaves that had accumulated in the crater from the previous year, the previous decade, and the previous century, her fingers encountered something metallic way down at the bottom, but the form they detected was round, thin, positively delicate, harmless, no fear (she had none, and was not easily startled, in contrast to her father). She picked up the object, which proved surprisingly light, even with the clumped leaves, corresponding to the annual rings in trees, that more stuffed it than filled it: a small aluminum bowl, free of rust, of course, and matching her find of the previous day, the aluminum mug on the riverbank, almost as in a fairy tale—except that both objects came from the last days of a great war. No matter: she cleaned out the bowl and stowed it in her pack with the mug. At the moment when she realized what it was, a sound had slipped out of her open mouth that she often made when about to speak, whether to herself or someone else, no matter what she had to say, and this sound was "Oh . . . ," also written that way, especially at the beginning of a letter.

This time she did not say anything more, leaving it at "Oh!" Had she perhaps been interrupted before she said more? At any rate she should be pictured sitting bolt upright now in the bomb crater. Might she be sniffing the air? No, no! She is not a detective. She is picking up on something. She looks, listens, smells, gropes all in one. Above all she looks and listens. For now it is still a game, albeit a dramatic one, about life and death, as it were. She is pretending it is wartime. She has two versions to perform, intently watching and listening to the enclosure formed by the thicket and underbrush behind the dozen trees. One version: sitting, cowering, or lying, half or completely unconscious, at any rate mute, capable at most of a nearly inaudible sighing or gasping, is a wounded soldier, one from the fruit thief's camp, one to whom she is furthermore close, her only friend, the only one *tout court*, in short: the one and only, and he desperately needs her help, and right away, or else it will be too late for him—only she can save him, she alone. And the second version? An enemy, male or female, is hiding in the bushes, no, enemies, the enemy army, war in person, and the minute she lets herself be seen in her hollow, especially at the wrong moment, with a wrong movement—but wait: in wartime wasn't every moment, every movement wrong?—she will be done for.

She practiced these two versions, alternating between one and the other, peeking though one gap after another, peering through the foliage, keeping her ears peeled, until finally, at first just in her imagination, things got serious. All the secret sounds—leaves crackling, rustling and brushing, two tree limbs bumping, scraping, scratching, stroking each other in the wind, sounds that had always epitomized peace on earth to her, yes, the possibility of eternal peace, now became transformed in her imagination into menace. These secretive phenomena whispered threats; secretiveness meant war in the offing, about to break out. And the silent yellow secret sun-nests in the bushes all around still appeared as nests, but their yellow was no longer that of the sun.

Then things got serious—and not just in her imagination? The cracking and crashing way back in the thicket, where it was most dense, could not possibly come only from tree limbs, could it, even massive ones, or possibly an entire tree trunk gradually being brought down by the wind? The crashing became a roar, became an uproar, though still in the same location. That was a human being, larger than life, or several like that, and any moment now war whoops would be heard, as if from one throat. Or no: a wild animal was rearing up from deep within the underbrush, a heavy animal, an enormous one.

Did she jump up? She stood up slowly, very slowly. She took one step back, and then another, working her way out of the crater. But she would not give ground. If she fled and thereby saved herself, on the contrary she would be lost, and everything along with her. She drew the switchblade, which she had with her, how else?, and snapped it open. The monster—it could be nothing else—now actually broke out of the bushes, "a classic stampede," she thought, and plunged straight through the belt of underbrush and into the open, where she was waiting for it.

What came shooting toward her was a rooster, a small one, dwarflike. He was the one who had crowed at the break of day. Except that this rooster was not peaceable like the metal cutouts of roosters to be seen on the roofs of French churches. She barely had time to take him in, his tail feathers erect in a war dance, and recognize him as one of the fighting cocks she knew from documentaries, when he had already rushed at her legs, ready to attack them with his beak. He did not manage to get at her, however; she dodged his beak, dodged again, until the action turned into a game, at least in her eyes. The cock, however, continued his attacks in earnest, and now she allowed herself to back away in the face of his onslaught, first one step, then another, in the course of which the little fighter flung himself at her anew every time she paused, until finally—she was almost out of the church copse by then—he was being followed at a distance by the softly cackling hen, who tiptoed out of the underbrush, his protégée, who in contrast to her rooster did not have her feathers puffed up but nonetheless outdid him in size.

Again the moment of "it's time"; "now it's time to . . ." It was time to say good-bye to Courdimanche, to the new city, which surrounded the rump village, to leave them behind and go forth into the countryside, into the interior.

Whether the road went to the right or the left, to the east or the west, all roads out of the village led downhill. She descended—it was an actual descent, that was how steep it was—on the road to the north. At the end of the village she said good-bye under a lone tree she had recognized as a pear from afar by its curled-up, dark, shiny leaves and its fissured bark. From a distance she had not seen any fruit, and, standing directly underneath and looking up, at first she did not see any either, and then there was one pear after all, dangling up high against the blue sky, swaying slightly in the summer wind, its form unmistakable—narrow on top and fat on the bottom—dangling and swaying as only a pear could. Longing gripped the fruit thief to scramble up, that very minute (high up, for the tree was quite tall for a pear), and take possession of the fruit hanging there in the crown, silhouetted against the blue of the spheres; yes, she gulped with longing; a greedy person would never have gulped that way, would not have got around to gulping in the first place.

She let it go, having forbidden herself to engage in fruit thievery over the coming days. Even without that prohibition she would have left it. It could be a pleasure to leave things alone, also a source of joy, strengthening her for what lay ahead.

Her innate or native high spirits took hold of her, and

she said good-bye to Courdimanche by running, if only for a short distance—she counted up to "thirteen" steps and then continued, an uneven number! to "twenty-three"—and, furthermore, backward, with her gaze fixed on the sign that marked the entrance to the village.

In the strip of wild vegetation around the *ville nouvelle* she saw sheep grazing, which then turned out to be blocks of limestone poking out of the crumbly, sandy soil. No music wafted from the few cars traveling both uphill and down, with the morning by now well advanced; only interchangeable or perhaps identical speaking voices reading the news on the radio, more or less the same voices in every car, all now solemn and sonorous, their tone changing, growing more upbeat as the less serious part of the broadcast began. She did not listen. For the time being no news, and as long as possible.

Halfway down and back in the new city—but who knows where—she was asked again, as she had been the previous evening, for directions, especially by pizza and sushi deliverers on scooters, all of them terribly young, and for the most part she could at least point them in the right direction. Then one of them pulled up beside her and stopped, after his vehicle had tooted at her like an ocean liner, and peppered her with questions, not about anything personal, but, in all seriousness, about the weather: "Will we finally get that storm tonight? Will there be thunder and lightning, not just heat lightning like last night?" And after that, still not moving, from the saddle of his moped, "There's been another bloodbath, another slaughter. Won't we ever have peace on earth again? My foster father used to tell me about the eighties, and sang me the songs of Johnny Cash, Johnny Halliday, Jean-Jacques Goldmann, Michel Berger: 'There was never a man like my Johnny . . . Guitar.' And I ask you: When will we ever have peace on earth? Tell me! When? When? What future? How can we go on?"

She did not respond, and the boy leaned in close, all eyes. She had never experienced such an urgent gaze, yet also such an open one, or perhaps one time after all, though open in a different way: in the eyes of someone who was dying. The boy's gaze was open as a wound can be open, and at the same time eye to eye with her, as if she were—don't ask me why—the person he trusted most in the world. And then, his last question: "Are you hungry?" And her answer now, which took the form of her stretching out both hands. Cut. Next scene.

It seemed like an accommodation that as the road approached the settled area's outer limits it became increasingly curvy, a sign that it would finally lead out of the *ville nouvelle*, by now sweltering, especially among the houses and high-rise apartments in the midday absence of wind. But instead of straightening out or curving gently into the open landscape, the road curved more and more, in ever tighter spirals. And the turn-offs she took in order to escape from the spirals soon became spirals themselves, and the roads that branched off them, promising at first, did the same, and so on? and finally a definitive dead-end: no way out of the last and tightest spiral, which, like all the other turn-offs from the main spiral, became a cul-de-sac that widened into a turnaround at the end, also opening up the possibility of getting out and getting on? no, the turnaround was sealed off by a semicircle of houses and served as a place to park cars and gain access to the houses, rather small and all brand-new but simulating a traditional style, though not one indigenous to the area, and out in "nature," so to speak, except that no road and certainly no footpath led out of this "nature," with the possible exception of the long route back to the main spiral; any escape was blocked by impenetrable hedges, hard and tough, so thorny and interwoven that they were impossible to cut through with a knife, and even she, the fruit thief, practiced in overcoming obstacles, could not find a spot to slip through, no matter how she tried.

She did try, making her way from spiral to spiral. It did not bother her to know she was being watched from the houses. But it did deter her from using maximum force to break through the hedges. And eventually her strength abandoned her. She sank down, no, toppled over in one of the turnarounds, in front of the houses surrounding it in an approximate half-circle, collapsed onto a patch of lawn as she imagined the façades of the houses bulging toward her like the shields of a hostile army. How abruptly her daily high spirits could switch to discouragement. Even on a day like this, after the splendid dream about the child, still with her since the middle of the night. Yet nothing had happened to her. She had only to turn back and board a bus; any line would take her out of the city. What was her problem? How had she failed? Why this sudden dread that the jig was up and all was lost? Her fall from a standing position, with both feet on the ground, had been so hard that she could have broken her neck. What saint should she call upon in such a case? Never again would she get up. She would go on lying there, facedown, with the ground flickering before her eyes like an old television set after the end of the day's programming.

Spells like this usually passed quickly. Often she had only to take a deep breath, and she would go back to being her usual happy self. Or by springing to the aid of someone else she would help herself. But this time she was incapable of drawing a deep breath, and not a soul could be seen far and wide who might have needed her help. Sometimes she found relief simply by going into a shop and buying something, no matter what; the process of making a purchase, exchanging money for goods, could save the day; her mother would not have had to teach her that. But here neither a shop nor a newsstand was in sight, *nouvelle ville* or not. And how about the superstitious practices that had proved their worth in especially tough situations, such as tossing a stone or a coin behind her, or balancing a stick on the tip of her index finger? She tried it; with no stone to toss, she tossed a clump of grass from the lawn; with no stick to balance, she tried balancing a ballpoint pen.

To no avail. She had become petrified into a block of stone, stuck as a stick. If she had laid a hand on anyone, even someone acquainted with all the terrors of the earth would have been shocked at the rigidity projected by this collapsed body, now transformed into a single rigid entity from head to foot; an evil aura, combined with such extreme compaction that the next moment would bring an explosion, the explosion of the bomb embodied by the figure cowering there on the patch of lawn.

To outward appearances, utmost compaction; inside nothing but weakness, seemingly terminal, irreparable. No Paradise to expect as a reward for this bomb, no Euphrates and no Tigris, to paraphrase Wolfram, would flow from Paradise after this explosion. But perhaps after other bombs and other explosions? She would have wished that her weakness might be imposed on all the other "human bombs"—making it clear to them once and for all: no Paradise! But this wishing no longer did any good, either for her or those others.

How consistently the fruit thief had lived in real time since her period of roaming around—until now. Time had never dragged for her. Nor had she ever had too little time, or none at all. Neither boredom nor lack of time were problems for her. On the occasions when she did hurry, she offered a perfect example of the proverbial admonition to make haste slowly. Her father, the amateur anthropologist, ascribed her complete innocence when it came to boredom, further "solidified" by her "angelic patience," which he differentiated from "sheeplike patience," to "the feminine," to her "birth as a woman": according to him, from the earliest days of humankind, among African tribes, it had been the women who . . . At any rate, she lived in time, with time, and thanks to time. Time to her was material, beneficial and welcome. And she also experienced "being in time" as a sport, perhaps the only healthful one, at least in the long run. How soothing the very word, the noun *time*, could be, and the expressions one could form with it: harvesttime, vacation time, summertime, breathing time, peacetime (though *wartime* was also possible), not to mention other formulations such as a timely book, a timely intervention, a stitch in time, a time to love and a time to die, time's up, to time out, just in time, and so forth . . .

In her normal condition she could have sung the praises of time, as in general she had an urge to sing, at least a song coming from the heart and meant only for her. But her current condition was untimely. And untimeliness meant wordlessness, meant loss of the power of speech. Not another word, not a syllable, not a sound, and certainly not her characteristic "Oh!" And without a word, a syllable, or a sound, no way to move on. Just as there was no way out of the cul-de-sac, there was no way out inside her. Suddenly she was no longer the young woman from the peaceful night before and the updraft of that morning but an old, old woman in a state of collapse, incapable of lifting a finger or moving her mouth, paralyzed, ripe for carting off, for the landfill. Only moments earlier "Further on up the road," the line from Johnny Cash, had been ringing in her head–and suddenly no further possible. All over. "All over?" Even this much she could not utter as she cowered on the patch of lawn. As if by way of confirmation, the signal from her mobile phone: *Temps écoulé.*

Instead of a word, a sensation, wordless, of guilt (if one can call such a thing a "sensation"). Just as she had always loved the word *time*, she had hated *guilt*, even the sound of the word. From her father, and before that from her father's father, and passed down to them from earlier generations, the concept of guilt had been presented to her at a young age as that which had marked her family and her tribe from time immemorial, its fundamental experience, and she had sworn, no, promised herself, never to let "guilt," the word or the experience, become part of her. "Guilt? Not for me. Enough of your guilt!"

And now, doubled up in a ball—not the doubling up with laughter that was her ideal—on the patch of lawn—if only a tree had been there, a single tree, a sapling she could have used to pull herself to her feet, a sapling herself—having stumbled into the trap of guilt, she, like her ancestors, felt guilty, for no good reason and above all for something for which she could not possibly be responsible.

Now she saw herself as guilty—without including herself—because she, like so many of her age and her generation, and not her generation alone, had not yet found a place in society (or whatever it should be called), or at least no secure place. Or to put it another way: in the spirit of that poet from the Balkans who wrote, "There is only room for the one who brings room with him," she had certainly brought her own room with her, but there was no demand for it in society as it existed at the time. She had learned various things, had various skills, not only playing the guitar, skiing, and driving a car. And what she had learned had become part of her, nothing dilettantish about it, and her capabilities projected a quiet authority.

But none of that gave her entrée to society, to the prevailing structures. Normally that did not trouble her. It was a matter of indifference to her, and, when she had flashes of gentle arrogance, even fine with her, and more than just fine. She was convinced that she had her place, if not in certain social circles then among those like her. She was not alone. There were others like her, and nowadays they formed the majority, and one day, in the not-too-distant future, soon, this majority, while they were still young, would create an entirely different society, free from the current pressures and also from all the shopworn "social contracts," i.e., ideologies. Of this she was certain. That was certain. Without the community of those like her: the end of the world. The world would be doomed.

But at the moment those like her seemed nowhere to be found. She lay there alone and was to blame—to blame if for no other reason than that she was lying there. To blame because no wind was blowing, and it was so hot. To blame for the one dirty, dusty window, spattered with flyspecks, among all the others that sparkled with cleanliness in the surrounding houses, as though she were the one who lived behind that window. To blame for the one withered, dead bush in all the bright green hedges: she was the one who had forgotten to water it. To blame for the one molehill on her patch of lawn; not only to blame for the burglary the night before in the neighborhood but also involved in all the crimes committed lately in the *ville nouvelle*; to blame for the failure of the bakery delivery van to cover its route through the semicircular subdivisions, when normally it honked from a distance shortly before noon on Saturdays to announce its arrival.

She still could not move, could not even stand up, let alone leave the spot. Verbal paralysis was muscular paralysis was paralysis of the swallowing mechanism was total paralysis. If she had been able to call for help, she would have called for her mother—odd, or perhaps not odd, for a young woman, and even more odd, or perhaps not, because it was precisely for her mother's sake, and possibly to come to her aid, that she had stumbled into such an impenetrable alien place.

So she waited to be carted away. An observer might have taken her for a hiker resting on a patch of lawn. From that perspective, it seemed as if she had all the time in the world. No hint that she was walled in, buried alive in untimeliness.

And in fact inside her her original patience was still functioning. The petrification, the constriction was beginning to relax, and her inner weakness was being supplemented by acceptance, and thus she experienced the weakness that had completely overwhelmed her as almost lovely. She was waiting to be carted away? Yes, but—what was the phrase used in obituaries?—"with heavenly patience." And at the same time, strange to say, or not strange after all, she told herself, or something inside her said, "No one, not a single person, has a lovelier life, a better life than mine. You people should envy me!"

How much was wasted every day, in the *villes nouvelles* as well as the old towns, the ones that had developed organically. Lying there, she saw things in sharper relief than usual, and noticed a poster at a distance, in the turnaround in front of the houses: it displayed a photo of a cat that had gone missing; she could make out all the details, from the cat's yellow eyes, blinded by the camera's flash, to the pair of hands holding the cat up to the camera by its stomach, a child's hands and fingers. A smaller poster farther off had a photo of a parrot that had flown away, it, too, seeming very close. And actually close to her, draped on the hedges by well-meaning neighbors, were a lost woolen cap, a lost headscarf, and a sweater. She peered into the hedge for the lost parrot, sure that if she looked intently enough she would catch a glimpse of it, and the same thing would happen with the runaway cat if she kept scanning the ground under the bushes; as if the urgency of her searching would help bring back what had been lost; that would result from her gaze.

The seagulls are back, circling and mewing over her and also over the shore of the Bering Sea in Alaska, very low, hardly an elbow's distance from her, as if about to dive-bomb her, while she wards off the birds by waving both arms . . . And back at the entrance to the Great Pyramid in the desert near Cairo, the woman dressed all in black, squatting in a niche, and she, mistaking the half-veiled woman for a nun, and the woman shaking her head at the coin the fruit thief places in her hand, extended for an entirely different reason . . . And back now, just as unexpectedly and then gone just as rapidly, the shadows of the water striders on the bottom of the *río* Tormes in the Sierra de Gredos, in a spot where the *río* is still a brook and flows slowly, very slowly through the high valley, the deep black shadows of the water striders motionless in the glittering quartz sand, rimmed by a multilayered halo in the colors of the rainbow . . .

Without understanding what was happening to her, and without wondering why, she found herself veritably swarmed by images, moments, momentary images, bringing back places she had experienced earlier in her life. The images flashed into view and were gone in no time. The places never appeared whole, only portions of them, which, however, were complete in themselves and had nothing fragmentary about them. They flash into view, various places from her past, sweeping and swarming into sight, offering a second chance at being perceived, a recapitulation, not from somewhere external but from inside her, and as they dive out of sight almost immediately and disappear like dolphins, they do not disappear to anywhere outside of her but rather into her interior; are not lost forever but remain constantly present within her, in her body, not to be summoned at will but at all times ready to surface, who knows how, these place-image dolphins, and if not as images of the Bering Sea, or Giza, or the Sierra de Gredos, then of another place, and yet another, in your, my, our life, which, thanks to that inexplicable—and may it remain so!—swarm of images has been rescued from many a dilemma—and may that also remain so—can continue to be helped; as for example at this very moment her life is being rescued from its dire distress, the distress of untimeliness—from time distress back into time. That such images are alive, even only as minuscule images, barely flitting by!

She got a grip on herself. She was gripped by these images, hardly more than phantoms, sweeping through her, meant for her alone. She had not leaped to her feet. She sees herself standing. She was standing. She lets herself be seen walking away. She walked away. Why had she collapsed onto the ground in the first place? She no longer knew. This place, too, she took leave of, this one in particular, surreptitiously, as was her style, tracing a secret contour with her hand. The last thing she did was to pick up a hazel branch from the ground—so even in the *villes nouvelles* hazel branches were cut—and holding it in her left hand hurled it into the distance, far ahead of herself and her route, discovering as she did so that her left arm had at least as much strength as her right one.

Straight ahead at last, and at least in an unmistakably northerly direction. Early afternoon, with her foreshortened summer shadow at her feet. North of Pontoise, in Osny, in the one unmistakable valley carved into the Vexin plateau by a small river called the Viosne, just before she reached the spot where the footpath through the riparian meadows branched off from the main road through the town, a dog joined her, escaped from who knows where, black, otherwise of an undefinable breed—at least for her, who does not know dogs—neither large nor small, neither one way nor another. The dog did have an owner; it belonged to a house in the middle of the part of town known as Osny, near the old rectory, near the even older church, the only one located almost directly on the river in the valley of the Viosne. The dog had dashed through the open garden gate to join her. Just as she was not really afraid of anything, so, too, she was not afraid of dogs. And yet every time an animal of whatever species approached her, she remembered her father's telling her that her mother had been attacked by a Great Dane when she was pregnant with her, "or a Doberman"—her father did not know much about dogs either; "at any rate it wasn't a Labrador"—and the shock had almost caused her mother to miscarry: now every time the fruit thief encountered a dog, she did not run away, and also did not back away but stopped in her tracks, as if against her will, and remained motionless, never holding out her hand to the dog as so many people did as a matter of course, and certainly not when the dog approached her slowly and deliberately, plodding, sidling up to her.

This time, too, she stopped, keeping her eyes fixed on the dog as it ran toward her. The fact that no one offered reassurance—"He won't hurt you"—let her continue quietly on her way. And the dog trotted along beside her as if it were perfectly natural, after sniffing at her, her kneecaps (not the hollows of her knees). He ran along, keeping her company. Not until she left the road and the railway tracks to head into the meadows would he turn back, she thought, and make his way home to his yard in Osny.

But instead of turning back before she reached the path through the meadows, the dog even ran on ahead of her, the tag he was wearing around his neck or somewhere jingling louder, probably also because among the poplars, willows, and alders in the meadows the sound environment abruptly became different from that among the houses along the main road and the railroad tracks. And after every bend in the path and later the trail, the dog waited for her. From time to time he also hung back, and when she looked around, he would be standing by path or trail, as if to say good-bye, ready at last to head for home; and then each time she would hear the dog-tag cymbals coming up behind her, and he would catch up with her again.

Not that she wished to be free of him. But for his own sake she wanted him to disappear homeward. How to communicate that? Up to now she had not spoken a single word to him. If she did speak, it would only bond the dog to her more firmly. Her voice alone—she could not disguise it, had never been able to speak with any voices but her very own, and was also incapable of shouting—might make the two of them inseparable.

For a while the dog vanished among the bushes in the water meadows or let himself drift down one of the many tributaries of the Viosne in the direction of Osny and his home. But then, unseen and not even heard, there he was again, standing, hardly a pace in front of her, as if he had been waiting for her for days, soaking wet, literally moss-covered from squeezing his way through the tangle of fallen trees lying every which way in the meadows, and from their dead roots to their dead crowns thickly shrouded in the woolly green moss that seemed to be everywhere (greenacre? moss green).

So the two of them hiked upriver hour after hour, heading north, on and on through the moss-wreathed riparian woods, so dense that one could not see anything but the trees, interrupted, though only briefly now and then, "for a couple of spear-throw lengths," by the river valley's villages: Boissy-l'Aillerie, then Montgeroult, Ableiges . . . After the village of Us, however, when the two of them had plunged back into the shade of the meadow canopy, which blocked most of the rays of the hot summer sun, the fruit thief came to a halt after the dog for the eleventh time stood waiting for her at a fork in the path, his eyes wide and a dead bird in his mouth, and now she opened her mouth for the first time in his presence, realizing that it was for the first time this day, that day—by now her story is far in the past—and spoke out loud (she did not count ordering breakfast and saying "Oh!" upon finding the single pear high in the tree in Courdimanche).

So she raised her voice and said to the dog, who promptly lifted his head and pricked up his ears—literally: "Oh, *you*:

I read once that you dogs sniff out the lonely, pick up the scent of the lost, track down the abandoned. Listen, you beast, I'm not lonely, and certainly not lost and abandoned. Even by myself I'm three wanderers, if not more, under the heavens. I don't need you. Tuck your tail. Heel. Run home to your mama, your papa. I don't need an escort, is that clear? I don't need affection, and certainly not of the canine variety! Out of my sight, and yesterday, sir! Beat it!"

Her voice had been not just loud but very loud—in anger. She had almost yelled, perhaps for the first time in her life. And the dog slunk to one side, letting her pass, his eyes even wider than before, opened his mouth, with the result that the bird fell out, landed on its feet, shook itself, and hopped: it was not dead, not in the slightest, not even hurt. Nonetheless the raven, for that was what it was, remained on the spot for the time being, as did she, as did the dog.

The first to move was the dog, initially taking a few steps in the wrong direction, upriver, then in the right one, downriver, toward home. He looked back one more time, then no more. He had a long way ahead of him. She, too, had a long way to go before evening. She did not look back, not once, either at the dog or at anyone else.

For a while the raven now accompanied her. It hopped along beside her, three hops at a time, as only ravens hop when on the ground, which reminded her of playing hopscotch as a child. She was tired now. But resting was out of the question, although the thick, and furthermore cushiony moss, which also covered the ground far and wide in the meadows, tempted her to lie down and stretch out. By adapting the raven's triple hops to her own gait, she gradually shook off her tiredness.

The raven flew off, leaving behind a dark black feather bordered in bluish purple—did such a color exist?—and now she walked on alone. The bluish shimmer of the feather before her eyes summoned an afterimage that reminded her that the dog had had blue eyes, though of a different blue. High in the crowns of the riparian trees there was a rippling, almost inaudible, not wind, nothing but a steady draft. Down below, in the mossy green realm, no breeze stirred. From the various branching arms in which the Viosne cut across the *vegas*—that was how she saw the meadows, recalling her time in Spain—came at most a gurgle here and there; individual arms in which the water remained stagnant, brackish: dead arms. Hard to determine, especially among the inland deltas (her father's term) that kept forming, cutting across the meadows' paths and trails, which of the watery arms was the main arm.

She picked one whose water appeared black from a distance, like that of the other branches, but when she had it at her feet was clear all the way down to the deep bottom. The fruit thief jumped in and swam a short distance upstream against the current, which took considerable strength, after which she let herself drift downstream to where her bundles were lying on the moss. She repeated that action over a long stretch of time, for that reason not quantifiable, a time unto itself. The water of the Viosne, fairly close to its source, was cold, but that did not make the swimmer shiver; the water plants below grew thickly, with long strands that wound themselves around her legs, but they were soft and light and glided apart easily; whenever she stood up she had solid ground under her feet, muddy, too, in places, but she never sank in deeper than her ankles.

Swimming in the river, letting herself drift, standing with water up to and over her shoulders, in addition to the time that resisted being calculated and above all did not need to be calculated, she experienced a correspondingly different horizon. She noticed, one noticed, things differently, and different features. One noticed? Yes, one. Yes, she. She noticed, in addition to the unusual glowing depth of the colors, and not only of the moss green, that the living creatures in the meadows—of which initially only a few appeared, and all of them small—unlike those outside ("in nature," she thought, "in the outside world"), where they usually appeared in pairs, in the plural, in swarms, always appeared here, with the exception of the swarms of gnats, in the singular: the butterfly here, the robin there, the dragonfly over here, the stag beetle over there. Even the water strider on the stagnant arm appeared alone, and stood rather than striding, as if waiting for something, like the other singular animals; even the one butterfly circled as if expectant.

Finally she also noticed—another living being—far off among alders a single wild apple tree, glowing green, on the far side of the river delta amid the uniform black of the alders, thanks to the "planetarium" formed by the thousand yellow fruit spheres amid the sparse leaves, and already the swimmer had the bitter taste of these apples on her palate; she would not need to actually bite into one, though wouldn't a real bite into the bitterest of bitterness be fitting for a day like this? Didn't the day positively demand it?

Later, still in the same stretch of time, she sat by one of the dead arms of the river that had widened to form a pond, not all that small, with her feet in the water and consumed the last slice of the pizza, or whatever it was, that the delivery boy in the *ville nouvelle* had handed her from his scooter. She was hungry, "finally," she thought, as if she had specifically wished for that, and nothing else. Earlier she had kept an eye out, if mostly out of a sense of filial duty, for the wild currants that her father, as an expert on the woods along the Viosne, had raved about before her departure for Picardy. True, she had noticed on the bushes, whose few remaining leaves, strangely, or perhaps not, were already wilted, small bunches of berries here and there, but they were long since dried up and crumpled, and lacked the proper "heart-refreshingly sour" taste. The omnipresent blackberries, on the other hand, were not ripe yet, and would never ripen.

From her apartment near the Porte d'Orléans she could see, across the street, an apartment with a balcony or terrace, planted so densely with shrubs and trees that a little forest stood there, hardly penetrable to even the sharpest eyes, breaking up the building's otherwise bare façade. Time and again she had thought she could make out from her window the movements of living beings in this forest, also parts of bodies, human ones—a hand, a face, though only a cheek or an ear of the latter. But never had she seen an entire figure, no matter how she peered, involuntarily, into that terrace forest. And every time, every morning she spent there, she searched anew. At one point, someday, he, she, the person she was looking for, would make an appearance. What she experienced with that little forest on the nearby balcony resembled what she had encountered with certain Arab gardens, meticulously tended, at once attracting and repulsing one's gaze: over time this visual searching, without any movement, even that of the wind, in the dense terrace forest, also without the gleam of a forehead or an elbow as a rebus, gave rise to a hallucination or near-hallucination, an unusual mirage, of a human figure present there, silently hidden, yet as alive as they come.

She found herself practicing that visual searching in the water meadows, the *vega*, the prairie, the *gaba-al-nahar* along the Viosne. And then from one moment to the next she foreswore it. Yes, it was an oath, a resolution, although—the thought that came to her next—her daily scanning of her environment had actually been "lovely and vitalizing," vitalizing and lovely in a way that differed from even a cinematic masterpiece. Except that what was at stake here in the forest by the river was not catching sight of a stranger, male or female, someone unfamiliar. So: enough for today: no more visual searching! Constant scanning, yes! But enough searching. And she went so far as to stick out her tongue at her searching.

She did not remain alone as she sat there, doing nothing but sitting, on and on, with her feet in the water of the riparian pond. At one point, when she was doing nothing but curling her toes, something rose out of the depths and came swimming toward her, unseen but roiling the pond's surface all the way to the opposite bank. It was an animal, but what kind? Still unseen and not even to be intuited from its outlines, it described an arc around her, creating even more powerful waves, if possible, and then proceeded, in serpentine movements visible on the surface of the water, to the middle of the pond, where it dove into the depths, suddenly leaving not a trace except furrows on the surface, which lingered for a long time on the otherwise almost motionless pond (the only thing in sight being one dragonfly that at intervals dipped into the water, making teeny-tiny splashes). In the imagination of the woman sitting on the bank, the animal was a whale, no, *the* whale, the one that had swallowed the prophet Jonah, who had begged and pleaded with God to put an end to the world, and then spat Jonah out on land after he had spent three days in its stomach. And she imagined further that the whale would, and in her opinion should, continue to shelter end-of-the-world prophets in its stomach forever. It then occurred to her that this Jonah figure had marked a sort of milestone since the beginning of her pilgrimage.

The next living being to cross her path in the *vegas* along the Viosne was also an animal. After all the animals she had encountered since early that morning she would have noticed this one but given it no more thought, whether a hare or a fox, a wild boar or even a deer, had it not seemed to her somehow special, something she was seeing for the first time. A pheasant flew among the riparian trees, not close yet also not far off, in what would be called in old paintings, for which perspective already and still played a role, the "middle distance." Despite her youth, she had come upon countless pheasants, had seen them run, flutter, and fly across open fields, and above all rise up suddenly from underbrush and plowed furrows, cackling furiously from deep in their throats, startled, or for whatever reason; but never had a pheasant of this sort and with this kind of flight crossed her path. In the sun, shining on an angle and at some distance into the trough of the meadows, this pheasant's feather dress glowed golden as it flew by, and without the sun it would probably have glowed even more golden. This golden pheasant had not been flushed from its hiding place, and uttered no cry or other sound during its flight, a long, long one through the alders, maples, and here, higher in the river valley, also beeches. The golden pheasant, large though it was, at least twice the size of other pheasants she had seen, flew without a sound. And it flew in a perfectly straight line, holding to a steady horizontal course, partway up the trees, closer to the ground than to the crowns, without once dodging a trunk or limbs, without swooping up or down, as if it had planned its course in advance. Its silent flight straight through the forest, which was widening into forests, becoming plural, seemed unending, the bird's body moving from light into shadow, then again into light, and so forth from one kind of gold to another. The pheasant's flight was the opposite of "straight as an arrow"; straight, yes, yet, as it literally presented itself to her eyes, slow, so slow. But didn't the tail feather have the form of an arrow, an unusually long one, far longer than the pheasant's body, a long, taut, feathered arrow? True; yet this arrow extending rigidly behind it served solely and exclusively to help the bird steer and maintain its course. So the golden pheasant flew silently and unhurriedly in its straight line, hewed to its passage, and continues to fly there between and behind the tree trunks in the riparian forests while this tale of the fruit thief is being told, a long time after what was, at the time, when viewed realistically, a relatively short flight, far too short in her estimation or whatever. Since then she has never seen a golden pheasant fly, and to this day has not returned to the spot where it traced its path through the air before her. But with the years, that spot in the mossy meadows has become/remained a possible destination for a pilgrimage, whether she will actually wend her way there or not.

Finally, after all the animals, a human being, though rushing past her, and a person with a connection to an animal to boot. She heard him before he came into sight: sounds somewhat like a cat's, but if it was supposed to be meowing, so inept that it could come only from a human giving a clumsy imitation. A man hove into view who, as it turned out, had been dispatched by his wife or his children or had set out on his own to look for the lost cat whose picture she had seen on posters in the new city and then upstream all through the valley of the Viosne, tacked to trees every few hundred meters. Whether sent out or not: the man clearly took seriously his search for the little animal, missing now for two long weeks. It was a matter of the heart; he had not left the house just to have a look; he had sallied forth to search, armed with detailed maps of the area; he was conducting a systematic search–his searching was fervent, more than ordinary searching; he was driven to find the lost animal, confused and cowering all alone somewhere, and to find it alive. The way he called in all directions, and the voice in which he urgently, almost beseechingly asked the fruit thief whether she hadn't . . . some sign, perhaps, a tuft of fur, maybe . . . (he showed her a sample, a bit of gray and black fur), made it clear that he would not give up, not today, not tomorrow, until . . . And when she could not help him, he hurried on at once, as if disappointed, if not indignant–not merely at her but at the whole human race, because no one, no one at all was keeping an eye out for the creature he and his family missed so sorely. And past the next bend in the river, his calling all the more furious, not at the cat but at himself and the world.

She sat in the meadow for a while longer, to see whether the whale would plow its furrow through the pond again, whether the golden pheasant would retrace its horizonal flight, whether from the underbrush the missing cat would stare up at her silently with round eyes, whether she might even spy in one of the mossy tree skeletons the yellow streaks of the escaped parrot also pictured on posters. She peeled her eyes; but no more to be seen, nothing. She had, she felt, a kind of power. But what she was trying to do here exceeded her power. Nothing but the chirping, in a monotone, impatient, of a single cricket, and that out here in the midst of nature, while the previous evening in the new city an entire chorus of crickets had rung out, resounded, fluted as if from the asphalt-covered underground, a subterranean chorus. To the woman sitting there, it seemed as though more than a day had passed since then.

Time to get under way. Who said that? Her story. Not real, current time, however? Actually yes, that, too. In the hour of her sitting there, the stretch of railway that bordered the meadows had been traversed, if by only one train—these were the hours after noon, and this stretch had little train service in any case, and not merely at the time of her story; in the sky the constant rumbling of planes, though rather subdued, and precisely because it was unbroken it eventually went unnoticed, whereas from time to time the traffic on the highway beyond the other boundary of the meadows became that much more noticeable. That the meadow moss, elsewhere spreading as if unstoppable, in one spot, not much larger than the keyhole in the church door of Courdimanche, offered a glimpse of the distant road: in this interval that was to her liking: lovely the way the cars' metallic flanks glinted from the distant lanes into the gloom of the meadows, incorporating the play of colors into the scene, each passing in a flash, cobalt blue, silvery gray, bull's-blood red.

She forced her damp feet into her shoes and tied the laces with triple knots. (Two were not permissible, but also not four.) And at the moment when she stood up and bent over to pick up her pack and her bundle, both changed position as if on their own, away from her and already hoisted into the air, not by a ghost but rather by two strong male hands, clearly with good circulation. This was no thief, no robber: that was immediately out of the question. It was the boy from that morning in the *ville nouvelle* of Cergy-Pontoise, the pizza-or-whatever deliverer on the scooter, except that he had come on foot, had secretly followed her, to the place where she had been stopped in her tracks and had lain half-unconscious on the patch of lawn, and then onward, always at a distance, staying out of her sight without actually hiding, to the Viosne meadows, where he had waited silently for the right time. Time for what? Time to help her carry her luggage, to be her porter; to offer her his services in general; also time to ask her whether she would deign to let him accompany her for a stretch; let him be her porter and companion, if possible till evening, as far as Chars and possibly even to the source of the Viosne in a pond below Lavilletertre, from the Île-de-France out into Picardy.

She uttered her "Oh," then nothing more and let things take their course; likewise she allowed the boy, unlike conventional porters, to walk beside her rather than behind, light-footed despite his burdens, as she had also been when she was carrying them.

His sudden appearance had not startled her, of course, not even surprised her. And at the same time she braced herself for various surprises. Braced? She expected them, even counted on them, as if only good surprises could come from the person at her side.

For a while the two of them walked along without exchanging a word, still heading upstream, keeping to trails and, to cross the inland deltas, old wooden bridges—they, too, swathed in carpets of moss—and making their way in wide serpentines through the riparian meadows. Where the path became too narrow for two, the boy silently let her go on ahead, while on the bridges, which often consisted of only a beam, without a railing, he went first to test its load-bearing capacity, extending his free hand behind him in case the woman needed to hold on.

He had changed his clothes for this undertaking, less for a hike or a country excursion than for weekend strolling through the center of town, the outfit of someone who from Monday to Friday had been at his post somewhere in the hinterland: a lightweight gray summer suit, a black vest, buttons covered in the same fabric rather than of gold-tone metal, a collarless white shirt, no hat (but also not the delivery boy's cap from that morning), instead of sneakers, leather oxfords (which, however, were knockoffs). He looked older than on the motor scooter, but also younger. He resembled someone, but no matter how she racked her brains, she could not think who it might be. Eminem? No. Montgomery Clift? Not him either. Her Siberian woman friend? She laughed, and laughed again after a few more steps, without his asking her why.

Even though it was broad daylight and would, to go by the date, the beginning of August, continue to be light for hours, the already dark woods along the river became more so the closer they came to the river's source. Was she mistaken, or had the single trill of a blackbird heard a moment earlier transformed itself into the deeper song of a nightingale, and all that was missing was the first bat (there could be no question of a swallow, let alone swallows in the plural, amid all the shreds, streamers, festoons of moss). The vegetation growing ever denser, the tangle increased by the dead trees lying every which way, so that instead of sun the riparian meadows were plunged into the gloom of a solar eclipse. One living tree, it, too, a singleton, had shot up so tall that the sun was trapped in its crown, an oak (the species very rare in this river valley). Both of them, she and he, had stopped at the same moment and looked up into the sun-filled crown of the oak, inaccessibly high in the heavens.

Getting out of such dark woods as a twosome, onto sun-drenched, almost treeless grassland, where the day greeted them, a perfect summer day, was something that caused both of them to sigh in relief, audibly, at the same moment. That occurred where the meadows suddenly turn into small gardens under the open sky, shortly before Chars, once a small town on the Viosne but now, in the widening river valley, a nondescript settlement with none of the features of a town but also none of a village, yet also with almost no new buildings, conveying a sense of relative antiquity.

Walking backward by a specific number of steps, as if by previous agreement—he nine, she thirteen, or vice versa—they both took leave of the riparian forests—for the time being: that same evening, though still in the lingering summer daylight, they would set out for the river's source, that went without saying, and would finally, according to the topographic maps, have no more trails and bridges, not to mention footpaths, to follow; the maps did not even show passages, indicated by small dots, to be attempted on one's own and at one's own risk.

But for the time being: now was now! The air out in the open, between and behind the little fenced-in gardens carved out of the savanna along the river and separated by broad stretches of grassland, gardens where primarily vegetables and root crops, artichokes and potatoes, grew. As for the latter, the thought that they represented something of an anachronism in this landscape: at the time of the scene playing out before the two of them, potatoes would not be cultivated in Europe for a long time, and the one who put that in words was the boy: "Potatoes: they don't fit the picture—back then Sir Walter Raleigh, who would bring them here from America across the ocean, was still on the star of the unborn!" Whereupon, for the story, the fruit thief's companion received a name that will remain his for the duration of the episode involving the two of them: "Walter," pronounced with a "V," as in Walter von der Vogelweide, which suited him very well. "Valter" and "Alexia."

Valter and Alexia, now always side by side, continued north toward the old town of Chars, through a valley almost devoid of trees, with room enough for far more than a solitary pair of walkers. They did not move like a couple, however, but kept an unintentional, completely natural gap between them—nothing more natural than this gap.

Had the railroad tracks not been there, gradually expanding into a railyard, the scenery before them could have represented a different era, one long gone according to the conventional calculation of time. This resulted from the fact that not only the church tower of Chars still stood as it had stood eight hundred, then seven hundred years, then half a millennium earlier beneath the blue sky (it would also stand under a gray, yellow, or red one)—and that now, as centuries earlier, the river plain was dotted with limestone and gypsum-stucco houses, along with not a few semi-ruins and ruins—as if they had been ruins even in their own day, though perhaps placed differently in the town's configuration, slightly off kilter. "Just the same centuries ago"? —"The same?" —"The same. Exactly the same."

What contributed most forcefully to the dual image of today-as-long-ago were the cliffs, almost vertical and in some places almost without vegetation, naked, especially on one side, "classic escarpments" (her father) plunging into the river valley from above on the Vexin plateau.

Houses, ruins, the church tower, and the gypsum-limestone grayish white escarpments, looming over the village's buildings, including the tower, by two or three stories; all consisted of the same material, whether built, grown, or deposited, and the chains of cliffs and crags, surrounding the town at their feet, imparted regularity to what at first appeared to be the chaotic irregularity of the jumble of houses below, and also provided rules, which could not be reckoned only in millennia, and likewise included—now, now, and now—the tracks and the railyard, rusting away except for two pairs of tracks in the middle, as well as the river, channeled into multi-armed canals. "Now is now" could also mean something entirely different, and "once upon a time" did not have to mean "past and gone." Oh, the same blackish lichens on the gypsum cliffs, on the square stones of the church tower, on the limestone walls of the houses, on the low stone walls along the roads leading into the town. Oh, the caves here and there at the foot of the cliffs, where cars and tractors parked next to ladder and solid-sided wagons, no longer in use.

Without breaking her stride, Alexia moved closer to her companion and, at the sign marking the entrance to Chars, took him by the hand for a few short steps. Now she was the one in the lead. She had pressed something into his hand, which he now without hesitation brought to his mouth. And already he had bitten into the apple, the pear, the peach, the apricot—no, it cannot have been that; those ripened long ago—with a crackling noise. A peach that crackles when bitten into? Yes, indeed. She had taken the fruit somehow from one of the small gardens, doing it again so openly that no one, and certainly not Valter, viewed it as theft. And "of course," to paraphrase Wolfram again, she had stolen not only that one fruit; the other, or others, the fruit thief had kept for herself.

They took the roundabout route to the Chars mills by following one of the swift-flowing channels of the Viosne, which here, unlike those in the inland deltas, rushed along loudly, almost roaring. From a distance the fragrance not only of freshly milled flour but also of freshly baked bread; a bakery had been built in one of the courtyards of the sprawling mill complex. Through the centuries many mills had been powered by the small river. The complex in Chars was the last, or at least the only remaining one, but its older buildings and newer additions filled half the valley.

Usually the mill bakery supplied only restaurants and specialty markets. No retail sales. But Alexia did not merely wish for and want one of its breads; she was positively obsessed, she had to have one, at least one. The bakery was open, but there was no one at the counter, and so the two of them stood there alone, with the thousands of different types of bread filling shelf after shelf, up to the high ceiling and behind the unattended counter—at least there was one. Valter, with an unfocused, silent look in his eyes, offered to jump over the barrier and take a loaf. Alexia shook her head, also without words. Fruit thief, yes! But bread thief? No way! Yet what a sight all the processions, the lines of bread, formed, meeting at a distant vanishing point, far back in the space.

Finally someone showing up from another part of the bakery, already shaking his head as he approaches. But then, at the sight of her standing there, her gaze fixed on all the breads, handing one to her and wishing both of them Godspeed: he has not seen a pair like this in a long time, or is he seeing one for the first time?

The center of town? The square in front of the church? No. In front of the town hall? Not a trace of a center, also no sign of the state, showing restraint for a change, almost shamefaced (wouldn't that be nice, a shamefaced state?). The gate-controlled rail crossing summarily designated as the center. Keen air there, as in fact all through this remote town of Chars, even keener here between the open railway gates, although there is just a slight breeze on this warm, silent summer afternoon, an air of abandonment and exclusion. The railyard may have been fenced at one time. Of that only a concrete post next to the gate remains, with a poster pasted to it, another one, fairly faded, like all those seen before, the photo showing a young man, with his date of death, including the day and the hour. Involuntarily Alexia crossed herself before the photo of the suicide—if that's what he was—and her companion promptly did the same, without knowing what had come over him.

It is obvious that Valter has never crossed himself before. Yet he makes the sign of the cross as if he has been doing it all his life. Looking back then, over one's shoulder, the railway gate cutting straight across the image: not only an anachronism but even more: a flaw in the town's image; a disruptive element; an alien object.

Then she invited the boy to join her "for a glass" in what at the time of this story was the one bar in Chars, the Café de l'Univers on the other side of the tracks. On the way there, they passed a house built entirely of undressed stone, hundreds of years old, where the external stone staircase, likewise of undressed stone, had an opening in its supporting wall to a niche under the stairs that might serve as a storage area, reminding Alexia of something. It felt good, strangely or not so strangely, after time spent out in more or less untrammeled nature, to be among old houses again—some of them built sharing one wall, without any space between them—and also among ruins.

The Café de l'Univers empty at this time of day. The only voices coming from the television set, broadcasting one horse race after another, many from racetracks whose names ended in "au"—Friedenau, Freudenau—but also Las Vegas . . . La Vega del río Tormes, and domestic tracks as well—Auteuil, Enghien, Vincennes. Time and again upset winners, favorites disqualified, and no bettor in the bar staring at his racing sheet and sometimes letting out a yell after the horses crossed the finish line. The proprietor not behind the bar but posted in front of the cigarette display, because at this hour and in general that would be the more likely place for a customer to turn up. This man, with years of experience running a bar and the grim, grumpy expression of someone stranded in Chars against his wishes and his way, now welcomes the two of them, after almost leaping from the cigarette to the drinks area (where he usually settled in only gradually), with a smile that even to him seems almost uncanny, that's how foreign it still feels to him. Even more than for the two guests, however, his smile is meant for his wife, who like him has hurried behind the counter to be of service, though from the other direction: not long ago a kitchen was added on, and the Café de l'Univers now includes a small restaurant, as its chef the woman who, also not long ago, teamed up with the proprietor. This woman, with her infectious enthusiasm for whatever she undertakes, not limited to preparing food in the tiny kitchen, where she whips up dishes in the smallest of spaces as if it actually were *l'univers*, has transformed the gloomy fellow, at least for now, in a way he finds so painful that he almost fears for himself, the woman, and their shared happiness; hence his smile. But for the present anyway, "An auspicious beginning, and not merely for the kitchen."

In spite of the café's emptiness, it took Valter and Alexia a good while to find a table. It must not be in the wrong place—it had to be in the right one, the appropriate one. And neither of them could decide on a table. Deciding for oneself: no problem. But deciding for the other person, almost a complete stranger: impossible. So they wandered from one of the tables, of which, by the way, there were no more than three or four, to the next, pulled out chairs, pushed them back. No spot felt right, and not merely because of the space-dominating horse-racing broadcasts (they would have tuned them out after a while, or would not have been annoyed by them). But to find a good place, a fitting one, for whatever purpose, was indispensable just now, at this point in time. Something was at stake. It was not so much a later hour that depended on it, and even less the following day, to say nothing of the future, but rather the current hour. They, he as much as she, had a challenge to meet. They had to prove themselves as a twosome.

Instead this back-and-forth by him here, by her there, crisscrossing the Café de l'Univers. Dramatic indecisiveness on the part of these two young people. Shouldn't she, a few years older, be the one to pick the place? Or, on the contrary, he, as "him"? But how he avoided her gaze, despite having sought it so fervently since that morning, including in her, the fruit thief's, absence! Any minute now he would dash out onto the street with an animal-like howl, and disappear, never to be seen again, throwing himself under a truck in the never-ending procession passing on the road (one of the main traffic arteries between the Île-de-France, Normandy, and Picardy). Seriously, yes, that, too, the young man, serious through and through, took seriously. And she, relapsing into the female Hamlet she thought she had shaken off, wringing her hands as in the old days and/or gnawing her fingertips, found herself, young as she was and just as serious as the boy, itching to strike him, her twin in indecisiveness, to clobber him out of the room with her fists, nevermore to be seen, to see him caught under the twin tires of the next truck and also the following one. How young the two of them looked from the outside, without being conscious of their youth; how young precisely in their shared indecisiveness, which assailed her as well as him, a terrible misfortune; enviably young? Nonsense: radiantly serious, contagiously young.

It was the couple running the Café de l'Univers who without meaning to helped the two overcome their indecisiveness. A door usually kept locked was opened, and A. and V. finally found a spot outdoors at a table on a wooden deck, reminiscent of a former dance floor, slightly raised above a yard littered with debris, more a junkyard than a garden. The outside area was new, just being established, if only because it was quiet, in contrast to the interior of the bar. This spot behind the building was meant for the regular patrons, *habitués*, who up to now had not turned up, they, too, perhaps just being established.

The proprietor wiped off the table and chairs, also rusty, and his "darling," as he called her, using the English word, his mouth twisted as if in pain, brought out glasses, adding some appetizers prepared for the evening meal, *amuses geules* in French; the loaf from the mill made a nice complement.

At the sight of the chef, Alexia and Valter, who had been almost mute since meeting again in the Viosne meadows, began to talk to each other. Valter, who surprisingly, or perhaps not, for a pizza-delivery boy, expertly arranged and equitably divided all the delicacies on the shared plate, remarked, "That's something I've never seen: a chef with such long hair hanging loose!" And Alexia responded, "And such straight blond hair, with two, oh, three darker strands!"

Then later, at the table on the deck, with the junk in the yard in the foreground as they looked south downriver into the valley through which they had come, they turned serious again. He talked and told stories, and she listened.

"It's nothing new for young people to take their own lives. Maybe there were always some of your and my age who, as my mother put it, 'went of their own accord,' and the young suicides were just as numerous for the most part, regardless of the time period, or whatever it's called. What puzzles me is that the young people who go of their own accord today want their voluntary death to express something about the times themselves, want to combat them, reject them, and curse them, ultimately to change them. And in that sense people like us are living, it seems to me, in a very special time period? In one of the European countries that once—that was long ago already—were described as 'countries behind the Iron Curtain,' don't ask me by whom, there lived a young man, not that long ago. His name was Zdeněk Adamec. Was? Was and is Zdeněk Adamec. No, not Jan Palach. Jan Palach was that other young person who, in the year nineteen sixty-eight, I think, to protest against Soviet troops marching into what was then Czechoslovakia to preserve the Iron Curtain, on Wenzel Square in Prague, or somewhere, took his life in public. I don't recall whether he poured gasoline on himself and set himself on fire or whether he threw himself in front of a tank, like the Chinese youths on the Square of Heavenly Peace or somewhere. Zdeněk Adamec comes from the same country, but he committed suicide, *il a commis suicide*, what a word, isn't it? later, decades after the disappearance, just like that, crumbling, dissolving into thin air, of that iron thing, without any sound like ripping, either a thump or a bump, in no way like Hitchcock's torn curtain, right? But Zdeněk's death was also meant as a protest. Pardon me for using only his first name, something I normally don't like to do, especially when it comes to people I don't know or didn't know. But with Zdeněk it's as if I'd known him. I know Zdeněk—through and through! To me he's Zdeněk, without a last name, the way Gaspard is just Gaspard, Blaise Pascal just Blaise, Chrêtien de Troyes just Chrêtien, Zinédine Zidane just Zinédine, Johnny Cash and Johnny Halliday just Johnny One and Johnny Two, Nicolas Poussin just Nicolas, Georges Bernanos just Georges, Emmanuel Bove just Emmanuel, Rokia Traoré just Rokia, and you—forgive me for using the informal *you*—Alexia. I'd never call Obama, Putin, Clinton, and whatever their names are, by their first names, if I had to refer to them, and I'd leave out their first names altogether; at most Donald Trump would be allowed, and should continue, to keep his. Zdeněk didn't leave the world in protest against anything current, against anything happening before his eyes, any injustice crying to the heavens that was being perpetrated by one country, one state, against another, by one political system that claims to be God's chosen one, and in the name of that belief marches in to destroy another system that makes the same claim, but which, at least to all appearances, in its gestures and language, treads softly, tiptoeing, as if to be considerate of its sick neighbor. Zdeněk catapulted himself out of the world to protest against the world. Against existence? Against the misfortune of being born? Against being thrown into existence, without being asked? Possibly even against the whole thing, against a universe that refused to provide a single answer, against the silence of the infinite spaces? Don't make me laugh. According to what little I know about Zdeněk, he clung passionately to life, as only a small child can cling to life. Existing, purely and unquestioningly existing, meant something to him all his life, meant everything to him. He wasn't expecting any answer to the so-called existential questions from the universe, a so-called entity that could be calculated but not understood, and he silently venerated the universe. He was, they said, someone who worshipped women, but to the end he was hardly ever seen alone with a woman. Yet as a young man he's supposed to have had something bridegroomly about him, quiet yet agitated, almost feverish, at any rate always expectant, ready, with or without a flower in his buttonhole. One time he threw his arms around a complete stranger. Another time he kissed the hand of the woman who showed him to his seat in the theater—he went to the theater almost every day, in Prague, Brno, Znaim, and elsewhere. Another time Zdeněk is supposed to have taken the arm of a statue of a saint when he was up on the Hradschin, attending Mass in the Cathedral of St. Vitus and returning to his pew after receiving Communion, with the host still in his mouth. And at the house in Brno where a poet died, he's supposed to have spray-painted on the memorial plaque a variation on a line from one of the man's poems, 'Thank you for the salt in the house.' His reading, like his theatergoing: mainly classics, only books, no newspapers, no television. His favorite activity was to crouch in the wind on the edge of forests, in the wind of the world, as he called it; 'the windcroucher' is what his friends called him; what would that have been in Czech? with what kinds of sounds? He's supposed to have remained uninformed to the end, innocent of world news, blind to all the accompanying images. 'Spare me your information!'—which caused friction with his friends. When all of Europe was hyping the profession of journalism on mega-billboards with the slogan 'Information is a calling,' Zdeněk picked up a spray can again, taking an approach entirely different from the one he'd taken in Brno, and when the Pope in Rome, the current one or another one, declared, *urbi et orbi*, 'God loves information,' Zdeněk wrote him the first letter in a series of missives to world leaders, all of which went unanswered, and ending with his death by fire, preceded by a final postal barrage, no longer addressed to particular individuals but to the entire world and signed 'Zdeněk Adamek, my mother's son.' Or am I just imagining all this? Dreamed it, early this morning or whenever? Dead, one way or the other, the Zdeněk who existed, who was there as only a Zdeněk had to be, naked as a newborn and defenseless to his death."

Here Valter was interrupted by clapping, which at the same time seemed to be clapping him off his soapbox, and by a voice saying, "Thank you for the lecture, young man." An old gentleman, who had gone unnoticed by the two of them, spoke, in a not unfriendly tone, from another table, one he had carried out himself from the Café de l'Univers into the junk-littered yard. It sounded as though he had been listening for a while but had now heard enough, and he continued to speak, a glass bowl in front of him that was full of hazelnuts, which he began cracking with steel pliers, punctuating his sermon: "Last year was declared the Year of Mercy, the one before that the Year of the Battered Woman, the one before that the Year of the Silver Thistle, and the one before that the Year of Broken Shoelaces. What will the coming year be? Who knows? For my part, I'm declaring the present year the Year of the Hazelnut. Last year the hazel shells were almost all empty, or wormy. But this year: the nuts are plump and undamaged, and in quantities I've not seen once in what will soon be eighty years, not even in the great hazel year of nineteen forty-four, with the first ripe nuts falling, like now, in August, shortly before the final battle of the world war here in the Vexin. I was still a child then, skinny as a rail. My pockets stuffed with *noisettes* were heavy as rocks, no, even heavier, pulling me toward the ground. It was a lovely way to be pulled down, a lovely weight. And then there was the rustling of the nuts as I walked, left, right, in my two pockets, such a friendly sound, and even more so when I ran—for once no running away, no taking to my heels. I ran that way of my own accord, for fun. That hazelnuts are meant above all for eating, and not just out of necessity in wartime, hardly counted at the time. But now, in this hazelnut year that beats all records, going back to at least eighteen forty-eight—for the centuries before that we have no hazelnut harvest data in even the most detailed church archives in the Vexin—eating them has at least as much value for me as gathering them from the ground, which by now gives me more trouble than it used to, and not only because I doubled in height after the end of the war. Better, however, for those like us, *nous autres, nosotros*—I'm repeating, with gratitude, the term you just used, young man—to roast the nuts before eating them, and besides, I like the taste better than when they're raw and almost as hard as rock. Look, you two, at what's special about the first ones of the year to ripen and fall out of the hazel bushes, the *noisettiers*, and not just this year. Look at this one nut, please, in the cracked shell, cracked with a special hazel nutcracker, *casse-noisette*, not an ordinary *casse-noix*, whose jaws are too far apart for hazelnuts, the little wild ones, the noncultivated ones from our region, of which four to seven would fit into a walnut shell: it's whole, striped, with a greenish-yellowish shimmer, an egg *en miniature*, like an ornamental egg made of freshly sanded wood, hazelwood, but look, now I'm lifting the tiny egg out of its shell—after cracking it, gently, not with force, because otherwise the fruit will break in half!—and what do you see? Damn it, don't you see? Open your eyes!—ah, at last you see it, you two: this mini-egg, one of the first ripe hazelnuts of the year, won't let itself be simply tipped out of the shell; it's attached. Oh, dear, my fingertips are too weak, have gone numb—your move, young lady! Take the nut between your thumb and index finger, and raise it bit by bit, millimeter by millimeter, out of the shell. That's the way. Don't shake it, though. Don't tug! One end of the nut's anchored, but the other nestles loose in the shell. Take the index finger of your free hand and press firmly on the loose end, but gently. More gently! Easy does it! And what do you two see now? Yes, the other end of the nut-egg, the one attached to the shell, that's leverage, is raised from its bed—but remains attached. By its skin? By its birth fluid to the borning fluid of the mother shell? Wrong. Look: the hazelnut isn't stuck to the inside of the shell, it's hanging from it! And what does it hang by? Right: a thread that emerges from inside the shell, where the shell nestles deep inside its neck-ruff of leaves, nourished, the shell as well as the thread, by those leaves, as the neck-ruff around the shell is nourished by its progenitor, the hazel bush; the thread—don't pick at it, for heavens' sake, or it'll tear!—which ultimately nourished the fruit, causing it—look!—to ripen, one of the first wild ripe hazelnuts of the year, if not the first, and in addition, rare for the first nuts, undamaged, no insect borings into the shell, no nibbling by worm embryos; though the mother shell has a borehole, it doesn't go all the way through, that's how hard the shell is, that's how this summer strengthened the entire shrub and the shell along with it, and the thousands and thousands of other bushes and shells in our region, and this summer, don't you agree, has been a hundred-year summer, though maybe only here in the Vexin, and only as far as the hazelnut harvest is concerned. And now, mademoiselle, separate the thread and the fruit from the shell, gently, gently snapping the connection with your fingernails. Make sure the thread stays attached to the nut, which it nourished to ripeness! In 'instructions for use' that would be in bold type, and with two or three exclamation points, and maybe also this: Now take the nut's umbilical cord—let's use the proper term now—by its loose end, between your thumb and fingertips, and slowly and carefully, millimeter by millimeter, if not by micromillimeter (there could be fibers still connecting the nut with the shell underneath, and a jerk would rip the seemingly tough thread from the nut)—hoist the egg, the nut, the hazel fruit by it—amazing how strong it is—out of the open shell. Yes, that's right. That's good: the nut is dangling quietly between your young fingers; it hasn't fallen off, as expected, and it won't fall off, even if it swings a bit now. Keep holding it and the thread steady. No shaking, no quaking. Just extend your arm. And look: the dangling becomes swinging, completely regular, back and forth, forth and back; you don't have to do a thing. Let it swing awhile. It's not like a clock pendulum. Damned clock time! I curse you, clocks. But this swinging, look, has no particular meaning. Ah, you swinging, lovely, good, dear swinging! Oh my, five o'clock already. *Cinq heures, heure de la mort!* as we said when we were children. Five o'clock, the hour of death."

The old man had suddenly stood up, almost springing to his feet, and without looking at them or saying good-bye was making his way, with his glass vessel full of cracked hazelnuts, back to his old-age home, which was not the only one in Chars; his, called Beausoleil, or something of the sort, had a view of the railyard, where the two pairs of tracks between the platforms had a metallic gleam, whereas the seven to thirteen others lay there in a dull rust-brown, for the most part just segments, flanked by thistles and other tall weeds; the seven to thirteen discarded cross-ties scattered over the dead railyard displaying the same rust tones, all lying at the same oblique angles in which they had been activated back in the day, the switches, one after the other, still poking up all across the yard as if waiting for the hands of one railroad worker or other to either depress them or raise them any minute now.

At night this railyard would remain dimly illuminated, the lights, however, placed closer to each other than the equally dim streetlights, located at irregular intervals and flickering, and he, sitting on his stool at the window in his Beausoleil or L'Age d'or, or, his own name for the rest home, Quai des Brumes, would gaze out—until his eyes closed for the nth time, though he would repeatedly force them open because he was afraid of falling asleep—at the railyard with the switches' silhouettes standing guard, and practice, gradually tuning out the snoring, also wailing, yelping, groaning, and wheezing, from the other rooms, as long as he possibly could, the activity for which he used a word in Arabic, *dikr*. That probably meant, among other things, "remembering," but to him it was "mindfulness," "being mindful." Wasn't *dikr*, as part of a religious ritual, limited to being "mindful of God"? But what he strove for was simple mindfulness, without reference to anyone or anything. "Being mindful" of the dead? No, simply being mindful.

He would spend the evening at the restaurant recently opened on the other side of the tracks, diagonally across from the railway station, closed for a decade already. The restaurant was called Tananarivo, and along with a few standard French dishes it offered primarily specialties from Madagascar in the Indian Ocean, which was where the owner had come from to Chars, along with his wife, mother, sisters, cousins, and children. According to the poster, also displayed in the Café de l'Univers, the rival establishment, this evening a Malagasy band would play for dinner, the female vocalist also from Madagascar, reservations required, a *diner dansant*. The old man had gone there in the morning and reserved a table, "for two," although he knew he would be alone, and he would also be the oldest guest by far, and furthermore the only one who lived in Chars; the others would come from somewhere else entirely, some of them even having traveled to the area for the occasion, and almost all of them born on or descended from the island of Madagascar, the women wearing garlands, as if they came from even farther away, from the South Seas, from Tahiti or wherever.

Most of them had settled in the new cities around Paris, and came by car, not just from nearby Cergy-Pontoise but also from Saint-Quentin-en-Yvelines or even farther away, from the south and the east of Paris, from Evry, from Bondy, and as he sat at his table he always felt as though those at the other tables, much larger ones, and sometimes several pushed together, were entire clans who had emigrated from Madagascar to the Île-de-France, at one table all the Malagasies from Cergy, at the next one all those from Evry, at the next one all those from Saint-Quentin-en-Yvelines. He saw it that way every time? Yet the restaurant had been in existence only a little while, not even two months. Nonetheless, a dinner followed by dancing took place every second Saturday, and he wished—yes, he still had wishes—that this pattern would be kept up at least into the winter, and perhaps, God willing, even until the next spring. And today was another of those Saturdays, and even in Chars things would get very lively, if nowhere else in town at least in this brightly lit, warm hall, where the garlands above the dancers' heads would sway in harmony with the garlands on the bodies below. Vis-à-vis the dancers twirling and swirling, with adults, children, perhaps even one or two oldsters joining in, wouldn't he be in the role of an audience member at a concert performed for money by an ethnic dance troupe on a world tour? No, he would not need to admire these dancers as a spectator, would not have to applaud at the end, would, instead of being a spectator stuck in a theater, simply look on, enjoy the dancing, freely, enjoy the dancers and at the same time himself, watching and participating. He would begin to play with the hazelnuts in his pants pocket, take them in his fist, a loose fist, and hold out his hand, full of nuts, to those dancing past him, offering the nuts for the taking and tasting—even if no one accepted his offer; is a food like that unknown on Madagascar, even in the capital city, Tananarivo? Are these things even edible? Tananarivo: the name alone draws the old man to the place; even in his youth he could not get enough of place-names. Maracaibo and now Tananarivo. On the table, the other one, in the Café de l'Univers, he had left the cracked shells, a pile of rubble, a "chaos" (the term used in geology for a wasteland of rocks left over from the Ice Age), not necessarily in harmony with the sonorous city names, or perhaps in harmony after all. No falling asleep! And then he would nod off nonetheless, and again, and again. And in one of his mini-dreams he would see himself, the old man, on a child's tricycle, riding in circles.

It is early yet, with nightfall still far off. Yet the fruit thief and her companion really should set out. They can still be seen in Chars, however, and in another eatery, the kebab place across from the Café de l'Univers. How come? Out of the spirit of discovery. Out of the spirit of enterprise. Undertaking and discovering in a hole-in-the-wall beside the highway?

That was not the plan. First they were supposed to explore the town, as if it were only proper to pay their respects to an unknown town, and this particularly unknown Chars in the most northerly part of the Île-de-France, before the transition to who-knows-where; to enter buildings, no matter which. They tried the church: closed, the next Mass not taking place until fall, after the beginning of the school year; above the bolted door a tower as wide as the kind of tower you could live in, like the tower of a mill, and above that ravens cawing with jackdaw throats, as in October. The bakery? Done. The florist's? Bouquets set out en masse in front as in a proper city: no need to go inside. The railway station: the windows boarded up, the doorways bricked up. The Tananarivo: the smell of Malagasy dishes, but no one being let in yet, with preparations for the evening's festivities under way. The caves in the cliffs along the riverbank: the openings closed off with chains. The pharmacy: what could inspire wonder in there? The only thing left to discover and thereby to show proper appreciation to the place was the kebab hut or shack, with decorative features, made of plastic, suggestive of an Oriental palace, imported to Chars from Kurdistan.

Besides, Alexia, the fruit thief, was hungry now, thanks to the appetizers, and her companion, when she mentioned the subject, declared himself to be hungry as well. But the main thing was to postpone, as long as possible, in this unfamiliar yet unexpectedly hospitable Chars, whatever lay ahead for this day in her story, no matter what it might be; it was the kind of avoidance that occurred time and again in the spirit of the fruit thief and her story, so that she would be able to recount the story afterward all the more sequentially and speedily? Sequentially? Speedily? Yet again: who knows.

The kebab palace/hut did not have an outdoor dining area, but the door was open wide, the bead curtain drawn to one side, and for Alexia and Valter a table was pushed out partway onto the sidewalk. The table was narrow, and they sat next to each other on plastic stools, leaving room beside the table for those entering and leaving the eatery, who, unlike them, had come for takeout, to eat at home or on a train. Behind them a television channel for Kurdish exiles, the sound turned down low when they arrived, while at the same time they were asked whether they would prefer a French channel instead of the Kurdish one; the two of them did not reply no in unison—the youth's response followed hers. In any case, the Kurdish soundtrack was hardly audible; the noise of the after-work traffic on the highway in front of the place swelled to an almost uninterrupted racket and roar, not sporadic in the least, as one might have expected at the beginning of August. Not until the railroad gate a few paces away closed could they make out syllables and also entire words in the unfamiliar language, amid the sudden stillness on the road: delicate, resonant sounds, almost a chirping, and that perhaps not merely as a result of the contrast between the voices and the rumbling and droning of moments earlier; yet the sequence of images on the screen, showing every imaginable product, was accompanied in Kurdish by recitations of almost nothing but numbers, for which, since they appeared with the images of the items being advertised, no translation was necessary. It was a home-shopping channel broadcasting from Düsseldorf, Luxembourg, or who knows where.

Could it be pleasurable, after the train had passed and the gates had opened, to sit surrounded by the evening racket again? It had been pleasurable even before the train passed; nice not to hear individual sounds anymore, either a voice or a noise: no throat-clearing, no coughing, no sneezing, no high heels tapping, no handbrakes being squeezed, not a single jackdaw's screeching from atop the church tower. Nothing but the steady droning, humming, rumbling, rattling, and, as an undertone, howling, filling the town and spreading over Chars into the valley, which soon was no longer a valley, not the valley of the Viosne or any other river, just as Chars was no longer the specific town of Chars but a gigantic, nameless, tumultuous echo chamber, seemingly unending? not meant to end.

That some of the trucks, especially those with tandem

trailers, also some enormous, overly long ones, sounded horns like the sonorous horns of ocean steamships in the midst of this mad rush, which, if one listened closely, turned out to be not so mad after all, was almost irritating against the backdrop of roaring and racket. The illusion created by that tooting, quite far from the ocean, threatened the beneficial effect of the general racket, diminished the pleasure it provided, as pure racket, here and now, free of any illusion. The devil take the racket here? The devil take illusions, or this kind at least. Yes, this was the road to Dieppe on the Atlantic, accordingly named the Route de Dieppe. But first, it was still a long way to the ocean, a good hundred kilometers to the northwest. And besides: at the moment no ocean was called for; no leaving here to go to the ocean. This is the place. The story takes place here and now, in the country's interior. True enough: the Route de Dieppe, Departmental Highway 915, after it leaves the Île-de-France, along the stretch that crosses the western tip of Picardy and then goes into Normandy, with Dieppe as its end point, has been nicknamed the Route du Blues, and this segment begins right up on the Vexin plateau, shortly past Chars, one American mile and so-and-so-many Russian versts before the village of Bouconvillers, where in front of the Cheval Blanc roadhouse, on the side of the Route du Blues, during the noon hour, approximately halfway between Paris and the ocean, one tractor-trailer after another pulls in and parks. Except that in the after-work tumult now, on the one hand deafening, on the other hand ear-clearing, there's not a trace of the blues, not so much as a peep of a little blues lament.

Nothing disrupting the harmony now between the fruit thief and her companion—not a word, not a look, including none of the sidelong variety directed at her by Valter, the kind with which Alexia had previously expressed her displeasure by shaking her head; a way of being stared at that, without her consciously registering it, jolted her out of her rhythm.

But now no more sidelong looks. Both of them gaze straight ahead from their plastic kebab table, toward the south, with their backs to their destination, whatever that will be, in the middle distance, beyond the cars, beyond the foliage, the mill towers, and above everything the blue, cloudless sky. No, now a cloud has suddenly appeared against the blue, a single, dark, large one. But no: it's not a cloud but rather the dark afterimage of a light green deciduous tree. And look: in the early evening bus that just passed in the endless truck convoy, wasn't the single passenger her mother? No, that could not be. For since when did her mother, the top officer in the bank, wear a kerchief over her head and sit there seemingly sunk into the seat, like an old crone, a peasant woman, if not a maid? On the other hand: hadn't her mother always considered herself "born to serve"? And wasn't that smile from the back of the bus her mother's inimitable smile, nothing mattering except that smile, and what a smile?

Then a woman passing on foot, on the opposite side of the highway, visible through the cars only intermittently, and then just parts of her visible, an arm swinging, an earring, a buttock—a young woman walking along both matter-of-factly and purposefully, a local woman. And she, too, reminded the fruit thief of someone she knew, a close acquaintance, though closely acquainted in a sense very different from the older woman in the bus just now. The woman across the road was indubitably familiar, except that she could not place her. Nothing but a vague sensation. But that sensation said: a bad person. A nemesis. An enemy! And at the same time she had jumped up and waved to the pedestrian, and she, after glancing briefly in the direction of the kebab shack, had suddenly stopped in her tracks, waved at the same moment, with both arms, and then made ready to cross to the opposite shore, darting among the cars and trucks as they sped by with hardly a gap between them.

One foot onto the road and promptly jumping back as

the next truck roared by—no slowing down possible in the unbroken involuntary convoy, and no question of braking. Another attempt, and another, and so forth: the same process, half a step forward, half a step back. At the moment crossing Départementale 915 was impossible, which then gave Alexia, after she had tried to go to meet the other woman, likewise in vain, time to think: Who was she? From where did they know each other?

That was it: they had attended the same school in Paris, had been in the same class, had taken their final exams together a few years back. And no: the other woman had not been one of her enemies, at least had not belonged to the circle that her worst enemy at that time had gathered around her. In school it had seemed to be the rule: every school year, class after class, a new enemy. Since the end of her school days: not a single enemy anywhere. Hostility, yes, aimed at her without her comprehending why, but no overt or active, lasting enmities of the sort that had previously crashed into her year after year, despite enmity's being utterly alien to her. No more enemy out to harm every hair on her head, literally: also completely mystifying to her. Did she miss the mortal enemies of the past? No, not that. Certainly not. Heaven forbid!

No, it was no former enemy who, continuing to gesture with both arms, smiling at her again and again, was waiting patiently on the other side of the Route du Blues, now and then skipping in place, apparently with actual pleasure. And yet it gradually came back to Alexia now that during all their time in school together this girl had radiated a seemingly angry, unedifying indifference, and not just toward Alexia, who periodically shared a double desk with her: an aggressive lack of interest in all their classmates; a sort of unceasing defensive barrage, fired off from the corners of her eyes but also from her spread elbows, her sharp knees. Even when she cried once, just one time, for some reason, or even without a reason—now the fruit thief saw those tears before her, more clearly and at closer range than back when it actually happened—those tears spurted from her unaltered, fixed, menacing eyeballs as part of her constant, silent curtain of fire, if possible intensifying it: Leave me be! Don't you dare touch me! Get away from me, all of you! Out of my sight! Beat it, you and your henchmen!

The railroad gates had to close again and stop the lines of trucks before the former schoolmates could finally join each other. In a period when day in, day out almost everyone hugged everyone else and hugs had become part of automatic greeting rituals, Alexia now found herself being hugged as she had not been hugged since "time immemorial" (her own), no, hugged as never before. At the same time, nothing could be more natural, for her, as well as for the other woman, for her even more so, if possible. They did not call each other by name, whether they remembered the names or not; for the moment they did not need names; did not need addresses, did not even want to know what had brought both of them to this town, unfamiliar to both of them, at this particular moment, to Chars of all places, which, though not far from Paris as the crow flies, still felt far, but was also in the factual world far, far from everything, so far that the likelihood of their meeting by chance was greater in the Atacama Desert in Chile, let's say, on an uninhabited Norwegian fjord (if such a thing exists), in a hut on the banks of the Mekong Delta, than here in front of the Chars kebab shack on the border (hardly recognized by anyone) between the Île-de-France and Picardy. Finding each other here like two beings fallen from the sky, as two who had certainly known each other for a long time by sight—and even more from looking the other way—without ever having spontaneously exchanged a proper word, that was special. That was an event, a happy one. Had they met by chance on Trafalgar Square in London, let's say, or in front of the Kremlin, or, preferably not, in Times Square in Manhattan, they would have passed each other in silence. But there could be no question of that here in this remote place, more remote and less inviting for even a short stay than could be imagined, a bad place: here, in this place, it was natural for these two to promptly change course and head toward each other and to enter into a conversation, for the first time in their lives, this, too, like the aforementioned hug, unlike any other from "time immemorial," whether something earthshaking came up or they did not get past the initial stammering and random meaningless utterances. That two people who had hardly known each other, and only in a negative way, should open up to each other: natural? Natural and wondrous; verging on the wondrous; and that had to be celebrated. And that was expressed by her former classmate in those very words: "This has to be celebrated!"

They sat down together in a corner of the kebab shack. The door was closed to block out the racket from outside so they could talk. Valter first took a seat at a table far from theirs, either because he did not want to disturb the two or because he was disappointed that the fruit thief had a friend, if only one—as though she, at whose service he had placed himself, were supposed to know no one on earth, were to be alone, without a soul in the world. And now, from the vantage point of his table, she revealed herself to be a young woman like all the others, in her facial expressions, her gestures, her whole bearing—a young Frenchwoman such as he came across by the thousands every day in the *ville nouvelle* as he rode around on his scooter. But she had only to beckon to him and already he was at the table with Alexia and her friend, as he saw her. Huddled that close together, what could the two be but good friends?

The Kurdish kebab cook had switched the television to a sports channel, where now, with the sound entirely off, a soccer match was being broadcast from Africa, Ivory Coast versus Mali. The stadium filling the screen seemed fairly squat, every seat occupied, some of them doubly, and the scene was enlivened by the billowing of colorful garments, caused by the Ivory Coast wind or by fans jumping up from their seats to cheer, sometimes those from the Coast, at other times those from Mali or farther inland. And above this squat African stadium the African sky, as mighty as it was tender! At first Valter had just pretended to be engrossed in the game, to make himself invisible to the two young women. But then his eyes really were glued to the game and to the azure blue of the African sky. Whether at the same time he kept his ears cocked for the conversation between the former classmates, the story of the fruit thief does not say. The other woman did all the talking, by the way, the one with the former seemingly evil eye.

She was telling Alexia about the men with whom she had been involved in the six or seven years since the *lycée*. She had not been involved with only a few or with several; she had gone out with many, or, as she phrased it in French, "Je suis sorti avec . . ." Over time she had gone out with so many men that she had stopped counting long ago—or she had left them uncounted from the beginning. She did not speak of any man individually, did not describe any one of them in particular, did not mention a single detail. Yet her voice, in contrast to earlier, when, if she spoke at all, it had an insultingly monotonous, lifeless sound, now vibrated in harmony with whatever she and a man had experienced together. It was a warmhearted voice, the rhythm conveyed self-confidence, and the accent in which she invoked the experience—not experiences but experience itself—had nothing local about it, especially not the sloppy casualness and coyness affected by many young women in the capital. It was an accent suggestive of pride. She felt no need to be ashamed of the countless men with whom she had gone out, that is to say slept, and, by the same token, the men with her. No shadow of guilt hung over her; instead she glowed with pride.

That came from the fact that she and the man—in her account, the many were one, a single one, the one—had experienced something that could be experienced now only with him, the one, and indeed before the two of them actually came together physically. Not a word about the act, or whatever it should be called. The tone in which she evoked what came before suggested that *this* was the experience, was an event, and what followed was no act, but . . . ? There was no word for it, but that did not change anything. What came before was decisive, and that, as she presented it to her friend, was mutual enthusiasm, felt in the same way, *simili modo*, by the man and by her, the woman. Enthusiasm for what? Enthusiasm for each other, his for her, hers for him? That came only later, often much later, eventually, last but not least. Before that came the shared capacity to feel enthusiastic about what the other one said, and often it was but a single word, spoken at the right moment, that constituted the glad tidings. Mutual enthusiasm then enjoyed in a brief silence, giving way to and replaced by the long silence of transformation. And after that the two of them united in enthusiasm by mere nothings, by the night around them; by the night rain striking the window, by the shadows of the raindrops streaming down the windows with the lights turned off; by the rain gurgling and knocking in a thousand and three gutters; by the phonograph record—at the time of this story, records were being played again here and there—spinning without sound; by an open matchbox with a single match lying in it, already used, its head charred and twisted into a fragile curve; by a print of a still life portraying nothing but a white plate with a slice of bread on it, and next to that a small pile of coarse salt; by the form of the moon under a fingernail; by the raised tail of a stray cat; by the intervals between all these mere nothings . . . And finally, then, the physical part, which of course went with the experience, was uniquely appropriate. Hunger and thirst, thirst like hunger, and the inevitable falling into each other's arms, with the man sometimes being the one who fell into her arms.

At this point the Kurdish proprietor came to their table, bringing the three of them a dessert they had not ordered, a dish he had just prepared from millet and honey, sat down with them, uninvited, and told them, without their asking, that he, as a Muslim from the borderland between Turkey and Syria, belonged to the religious community of the Alawites, whose mosques, whose prayer sites, were usually not built as such but instead recognized wherever they happened to be, especially out in nature, and that here in the valley of the Viosne he liked best to take his prayer rug, when he felt moved to pray, north into the almost inaccessible primeval forests around the river's source. The team from Ivory Coast had meanwhile beaten the team from Mali (3–1), beneath the African sky, which was dimming as evening came on—in European Chars the light was just beginning to fade—and Valter asked the host whether he might see the rug. The host brought it from the room behind the kitchen. Actually he brought two rugs, no larger than bedside mats, the patterns dark on dark, and not just dyed on. The bright streaks here and there from top to bottom were strands of the beard lichen found everywhere in the meadows along the Viosne.

Time to go. Time to say farewell to Chars (forever? that was not the plan), to say farewell to the former classmate (forever?). When the moment came to pay, the fruit thief initially pried a ruble note out of her fanny pack.

After the two, Valter and Alexia, set out, the other young woman remained seated in the kebab shack, alone at the table, while here and there groups had meanwhile come in for an early evening meal, families with small children who would be put to bed while the sun was still shining. She can be seen staring blindly into space. Why did it happen so seldom that one encountered—what was the expression?—all too familiar people in a place where one would never have expected it, and precisely there everything became good between them, between all of us, everything, and not merely fleetingly but lastingly? Why was no provision made in the world for such places where, if previous mortal enemies should cross each other's path, the great, lasting reconciliation would occur? Why, for the sake of heavenly peace, was no provision made on earth for chance, for chance encounters like this one at least?! (Question mark followed by an exclamation mark.)

She simply could not stop staring angrily into space, could not stop even though she wanted to, and how! She veritably pleaded to have someone divert her gaze to something positive—anything, anything at all. No luck. Her prayer went unanswered. Everything was arrayed against her, and worse still, more hellish, was that she was against everything, too. How homogeneous the people in the eatery appeared, down to the slightest detail. If only the faces and heads of the Kurdish clan, busy in the kitchen nook and in the lean-to behind the shack, had displayed some variety—different angles, different roundnesses, different ovals. But they were even more identical, if possible, than the guests, the nephew indistinguishable from the uncle, the nephew's daughter indistinguishable from the great-uncle, and so forth. And to make things worse, the expressions of the small children at the tables: the spitting images of their fathers and mothers, and in twenty or at most thirty years these offspring would be identical with their parents, with fully grown bodies and inherited or imitated body language, postures, and gestures, and their thighs would quiver the same way their father's did, they would tap on their mobile telephones just as the mother was doing now; they would take their parents' places, even if the man was not actually the father, and the woman—this was the impression she received as she sat there alone at her table—to the extent she briefly interrupted her telephone games now and then, was just playing the role of mother, as the child next to her would play at being the mother in twenty or thirty years, and eventually above and beyond all the kebab shacks in the world there would be only Sunday fathers or strangers as fathers, and fake mothers.

She felt an urge to cry. And again: no luck. Instead of tears, the fires of hell in her eyes. That was something at least. As a girl she had been called "the dragon" by the other children, and that had hurt. But at the moment she accepted being a dragon. Dragon: fine by her. Even a touch of triumph: I'm not like the rest of you. Why did the man from Kurdistan not come back and sit with her? Why was he standing, after all the tables had been served, behind the counter with his arms crossed, senselessly wearing his toque, a paper one at that, and gazing past her into the distance? And why, oh why, did the pleasure she had felt during the hour with her former classmate have no staying power? How she had opened up. Opened up to the world. And how easy it had been to talk. Not until she described it had she discovered what she had experienced, and in what way, and who she really was, and in what way. In that one hour she had become a different person. No, the person she really was. And as soon as it ended, alone again: all over. As if it had never been. Was that the new life, the "unheard-of element" in human history: countless experiences, encounters, events, day after day, if not hour after hour, second after second—and one hour later, one second later: as if it had never been? The main characteristic of the current time, the present: weak and ever weaker after-effects, and finally: none at all?

She raised her empty glass—a real glass in a kebab shack rather than a plastic cup? but usual here—and she was about to cock her arm to hurl it: at the glass case with prepared dishes ready to heat up in the microwave or elsewhere. It would not have been the first time. Back when she was in the *lycée*, during a class field trip to the seashore (not by way of the Route du Blues to Dieppe, by any chance?—how else?) in a café by the harbor she, having drunk more than the others and grown silent and ever more silent amid the general chatter and laughter of her classmates, suddenly took a rock she had picked up on the beach in Dieppe and stuck in her pocket because it had a hole in it that one could look right through, and hurled it at the café's front window, whereupon the inevitable happened, and the whole class was thrown out. In Kurdistan, now, mollified by the image that came flying to her from Dieppe, she put her glass back on the table, carefully, without making a sound, and ordered a refill. And at last the host sat down at the table with her again.

By now the fruit thief and her companion have been wending their way north again for some time. The early evening, which in August, with a blue, almost cloudless sky, seems to last as if the region were much farther north, was warm, and no wind stirred down in the Viosne valley among the last houses of Chars, some of them built wall to wall. Here Alexia took some of her luggage from her porter, the larger, heavier stuff, to which Valter, after a silent exchange of looks with her, did not object. He was unaccustomed to going on foot, especially so far, and his legs felt heavy. Time and again, even without obstacles, he stumbled. How light-footedly she, the older one, walked along beside him, seeming weightless despite the load. Without taking long strides, she strode along, whether among houses or out in the open. Unlike him, she did not break a sweat, as he saw when he glanced sideways to see whether she had stains on her shirt in the armpits, as he was accustomed to seeing on female stars in the movies, at least in more recent ones; Alexia, however: a classic film. As she strode along as if wearing seven-league boots, her face gleamed, but not from sweat; all that came to light on the young woman's skin were a few freckles on one cheek, not visible earlier, or were they tiny birthmarks, no larger than dots and close together, forming a constellation, three to five freckles or marks?—he could not keep track of the number—on the right cheek or the left? The longer he stumbled along beside her, the more he confused right with left and vice versa. Where was right and where left from his point of view? Or should he see right and left from hers?

The last house in Chars was a ruin, already far out into the riparian forest in the area of the Viosne's headwaters. The windows and doors all walled up, the ruin inaccessible. The exterior walls spray-painted, not that long ago, with images, symbols, and countersymbols found the world over, including certain variations, as perhaps everywhere, that merited closer inspection. In addition there were traces, almost painted over, from earlier decades (not centuries—for that the building was probably not old enough). When had the war in Vietnam taken place? Almost five decades ago, right? On the walls here, in nice, legible script, with only a few letters and syllables needing to be filled in, America was still dropping napalm on that distant country and being challenged to cease hostilities and leave the rest of the world in peace. The bullet holes, particularly numerous in one section of the wall, came from a different war, three decades earlier, from a battle in this area, the last up to now in this part of Europe, impossible to make out who had been shooting at whom, with neither a swastika nor any other form of cross discernable between and under the paintings, let alone remnants of "one Volk, one Reich, one Führer," of which Alexia in her travels to the east had encountered not a few, and not always hidden.

Left over from a time that could not be pinpointed, however, were scraps of posters on an addition to the house, a wooden shed, of which one board wall protruded from the tangle of weeds and brush. The posters had been stapled to the wall, and where the staples still held—it seemed as if they were all there, shining in a dense mass against the blackened wood—tiny wedges of poster paper peeped out from under them. On one part of the wall the staples and paper scraps came together in a way entirely different from the bullet holes in the nearby wall stones: among the thousands of other staples and also rusty thumbtacks all around them, they offered a suggestion of a rectangle, more tall than wide, with the paper fragments, they, too, thickly layered, marking the four corners, the interior of the rectangle completely free of staples, the only noticeably empty space on the wooden wall: "the place reserved for film posters back then!" as Valter exclaimed, but the explanation could just as well have come from Alexia. And so it was: on some of the larger overlapping scraps letters could be made out, two or three, even partial words, from which one could not piece together the titles of the films, but one could imagine and play with them: *L'e(nfance nue)*—"Naked Childhood," the story of a child abandoned by its parents. That was Valter's guess; and Alexia's? *Les v(isiteurs du soir)*—"The Night Visitors." But the years, as well as the decades, of the films could not be determined; that they had been shown "back then" had to be enough; and it was enough.

While they were still standing in front of the shed, first one of them, then the other flipping through the poster scraps, almost as thick as a book, trying to guess their significance, they suddenly heard a bang from inside the walled-up ruin. No, it could not have been a bang; the sound was too dull for that. And yet it had come from a blow, and not from a chunk of stone falling and hitting the ground—from a blow inside, striking the wall, and the blow had been carried out intentionally, and not by some large animal imprisoned inside (that was what it had sounded like in the first second), but by a human being.

Someone was living in the walled-up ruin there in the riparian meadows, never mind how he had got in, perhaps through an old sewer pipe? by way of the collapsed roof (although it looked impossible to clamber up)? Someone had struck the wall from the inside, not with mere fists but with something hard and heavy, as if to say, "You out there, get away from here!" The blow had been struck with ill will, if not murderous intent. Without the wall between them, the two of them outside would have had their heads bashed in without warning, with a sledgehammer or the lever of an old railway switch. Strange, that nothing came after that one blow against the wall, clearly aimed at them, and administered with such force. Then silence; what was the adjective once used with that term? *ominous*. First the young man positioned himself in front of the woman, then the woman placed herself in front of the man, and so on, both doing their utmost to avoid making the slightest noise. For the fruit thief this situation brought to mind a hike she had taken with her father years earlier, near the Yukon River in Alaska, where they had heard in the forest through which they were walking a terrible crashing coming toward them, as if made by a predator, a huge one, that could only be a bear, and her father had positioned himself in front of her, after which she had done the same for him, etc., until finally out of the forest gloom a skinny old Indian woman had emerged into the light, her arms full of mushrooms, rather small ones, but with the shimmer of porcini unique to those one finds beneath the great sky along the Yukon River. And who emerged now from the ruin in the meadows along the Viosne River north of Chars, almost exactly on the border between the Île-de-France and Picardy, a border not drawn as a mere line but rather designated as a special borderland, a borderland all its own, through which they were about to cross? No one emerged from the ruin. No one bashed in their heads. No one scratched their eyes out. No one gobbled them up from head to toe. Nothing happened after the blow on the inside of the wall. And then something after all: a murmuring, hardly audible, also incomprehensible, yet unmistakably coming from another human being. It meant something different from the blow. Not its opposite: the murmuring behind the wall was neither hostile nor in any way friendly. It was not aimed at anyone. It pertained to no one, either a person or someone or something else.

Before the two of them crossed the border country, without a path or trail, a detour was called for, out of the river valley and up to the plateau, where the treeless broad fields of the Vexin are crossed diagonally by the Chaussée Jules César (so named, whether long ago or recently, for hikers; no cars were allowed on it).

And indeed it turned out to be merely a detour. The chaussée led, slightly elevated, without twists and turns, past harvested wheat fields, and was not lined, at least not along this stretch, with the trees that one saw along chaussées everywhere else. To continue straight ahead on a uniform broad, sandy-graveled path did not fit the spirit of the expedition, although the horizons, thanks to the slight elevation of the Chaussée Jules César above the surrounding flat landscape, had a special quality, and walking along as if on a dam, though without a river or sea, with nothing but open stretches without water at their feet, also lent wings to the two of them for a moment, gave them a boost for what came next, whatever that would be.

From time to time people came toward them on the Chaussée Jules César. No one else was going in the northwesterly direction of the detour the two had chosen. One time a rider caught up with them, greeting them first, as if that were only proper for someone mounted high above them as he jounced across the land. Those on foot whom they encountered were usually walking in larger groups, primarily older folk, the younger ones among them tending to be single, having seemingly fallen in with them by chance, and mostly silent, in contrast to the others, who, all talking at once at the top of their voices, perhaps because of their age, could be heard from afar over the chaussée in a way normally characteristic of bands of bicyclists, carrying on shouted conversations so as to be heard by one another over the whirring of their spokes.

Then the Chaussée Jules César was crossed by another footpath at almost a right angle, flanked by a road sign pointing to the southwest, and painted on the sign was the familiar scallop shell indicating one of the countless pilgrims' trails to Santiago de Compostela, which passed through not just this particular area of France but the entire country, more or less in a southwesterly direction, from the Swiss Alps, the German Rhine, the Ardennes down to Saint-Jean-Pied-de-Port or thereabouts and up over the Pyrenees of Roncesvalles, and these paths had been registered and classified as pilgrimage routes, but certainly not in olden times.

Alexia and Valter turned off the Chaussée Jules César and headed in the opposite direction from the pilgrimage site in distant Galicia, going not in a southwesterly direction but in a northeasterly one, back to the valley of the Viosne at the uppermost spot where the river cut into the Vexin plateau. It was time to end the detour. Time to take leave of the wide open spaces beneath the midsummer sky, which, when they looked up to say good-bye—which they did more than once—became big and bigger and visibly began to arch until it arched into that "cope of Heaven" that indubitably *was* of ancient origin. Time to leave behind the pairs of kites, those regal birds, circling high overhead toward and away from each other, along with their monotonous, drawn-out piping, and likewise the whistling and warbling of the larks, uttered as they rose perpendicularly from the plowed furrows and traced invisible but resonant stairs of sound, trill after trill, rising story after story into the air, the "builders" themselves invisible for a long time—that was how small these birds were, how short their wings, and when one of them can finally be spied against the empty sky from which it trills and belts out its song, it is nothing but a blackish dot, which perhaps seems to quiver only in the eyes of someone trying to spot the lark up there!—but in the twinkling of an eye this dot will have been wiped away, and the next trill promptly sounds a few air-stories higher, literally in the heavenly heights, where the singer—can one really call this distant peeping song?—will not even offer itself to be seen black-dot-wise, or, to express it in the future perfect: will not have offered itself to be seen.

On this newly declared Way of Saint James, one of at least seventy times seventy in a network spread all across the country, once more only a few people came toward them, and the two were again the only ones heading in the opposite direction, the pilgrimage site far off and with every step farther behind them. Those they encountered along the path, which narrowed to a trail as it hugged the edge of the completely uninhabited headwaters gorge, were one and all actually on pilgrimage. At least that was indicated by the way they were outfitted, much the same in every case: a tall hiking stick, two thumbs thick, and seemingly oversized scallop shells, two or three dangling on a string from the pilgrim's rucksack or whatever, their rattling audible at a distance and then still audible when the pilgrim had long since disappeared beyond the horizons.

The pilgrims on the Way of Saint James, in distinction to the groups of hikers on the chaussée named for Caesar, tended to be alone, and silent. A twosome: the exception. (Never as many as three.) And when there were two, they also walked in silence. This silence resulted neither from any particular vow nor from fatigue. It was striking that these pilgrims all came along at a good clip, and even picked up the pace, if possible, after passing them. Although they remained silent, these pilgrims differed from those in the old text that daydreams of a *vita nuova*, in which the pilgrims move along "slowly," "pensively," and "seeming to have come from afar." These pilgrims really—in reality—did come from afar. But they showed no signs of that, speeding along, copying each other, in seven-league boots. They did respond when they let themselves be greeted, but they did that hastily as well, and it was as if they were perplexed as to how anyone could possibly be going in the opposite direction—yes, as if they saw that direction as not only wrong but impermissible. Yet the two wayfarers were not addressed by a single one of the pilgrims who crossed their path; at most they received an incredulous smile, perhaps accompanied by a slight shake of the head. Long ago, when she had been mistakenly going in the wrong direction on a one-way cross-country ski trail, she had received looks like that, though instead of smiling mouths, harsh words.

They soon turned off the pilgrimage path, which continued along the rim of the plateau up above, and took a side path down into the gorge that held the headwaters of the Viosne. The path had not been made by human beings, or by hunters. It was a wild-animal track that became impassable after a few steps, blocked by a blackberry thicket that instantly closed in on them. But so what: if animals had made their way through, so could she, so could he, and a few snags in their clothing, scratches on their arms and legs, did not count. They plunged on down through the gloomy thicket, no question of turning back—that was not permitted, was not licit, whether this word was still in use or not.

No sound of rushing water, no trickling of a spring to guide them. No bird sounds either, not even the softest peeping. Here, in the middle of the great cultivated high plateau that spread in all directions, and which, when they raised their heads, flashed down as if from distant skies to them amid the tangle of briars and vines, was an actual jungle through which they had to fight their way downhill, a jungle unlike one in Africa or along the Amazon, an inland-

European jungle, where, in addition to an absence of wind, there was an absence of air—as if the jungle vegetation sucked up all the oxygen—creating an atmosphere at once suffocatingly humid and bone-chillingly cold, and here they heard the sound of a cricket, a single, brief chirp, signaling the presence of a more expansive summery space, but in this natural cage not merely having fallen silent but simply no longer thinkable, become unimaginable.

And yet this environment that was none, the opposite of an environment, was good; the right thing for the time being. In this jungle cage, where one part of the cage gave way to another partial cage, they did not let themselves be ensnared. To take one step after another, keeping one's eyes open for every obstacle, could awaken all one's senses, at least for this time being, and that even filled one momentarily with a kind of lust for life. And simultaneously, not in conflict with that sensation, amid the silence of the jungle, precisely at such moments, they would have wished for some kind of racket nearby, a family of deer leaping out of their bed in the thicket, a wild-boar clan, from which a mother boar, heaving herself out of the mud, would break away and hurtle toward the two of them, grunting furiously.

Instead of bubbling spring water they found, at the bottom of the gorge, only swampy puddles, their surfaces oily, shimmering in the colors of a false rainbow; here nothing moved, nothing flowed; nothing but stagnation. The whining of mosquitos as a sign of life after all? not even that. The gorge where the Viosne had its source was not all that deep. But the complete absence of movement—not a breath of wind, not a dragonfly, no water striders—magnified the sense of a gorge, the Deep Gorge image.

From somewhere, the spot impossible to pinpoint, the mimicked meowing was heard again in the distance, the man's voice almost failing as he kept trying, all the way out here, to locate the cat who had run away from the *ville nouvelle*. And suddenly, at the feet of the two, a response: something with a tail and four legs came crawling out of the swamp: a cat? yes, but only at first glance; a response without sound: the animal opened its mouth to make itself heard, but in vain.

Then this opening of the mouth again and again, with no sound coming out, in response to the repeated meowing, in a breaking yet persistent voice somewhere in the distance, unclear where in this headwaters jungle, perhaps outside it already, on the edge of the jungle, as the man called the cat. At long last an answer after all—if it was one—not from the animal down there on the jungle floor, but from high in the treetops, knotted together by vines: the hooting of an owl, like an answering cry, and almost indistinguishable from a cat's yowling. An owl hooting in broad daylight? Yes.

The invisible searcher in the wooded background, or wherever he was standing, now reacted to the owl's cry even before it died away by calling a name, at the top of his lungs, impossible to make out, presumably that of the missing cat. He called it several times, and after a pause again and again, his voice becoming not hoarser from time to time but more resonant. The owl continued hooting, from a different spot each time, as if to mock the man seeking his pet, and the animal in the underbrush that he was looking for opened its mouth more piteously than ever, and still just as mutely, its mouth as large as its whole skull. Incapable of following its master's call, too weak to take a single step or even to stand on its four legs, the cat lay on its stomach in the muck. Its paws drawn together underneath, its face, especially around the eyes, dotted with ticks the size and roundness of juniper berries, except that instead of being blue they were pale and colorless, swollen to the point of bursting, and along with the cat's blood they seemed to have sucked up bits of fur: the cat looked like some unknown mutated creature, foreign to the animal world.

Nothing left of the vertical, clock-hand-like pupils of the cat's eyes: the tick bodies around them made the black pupils appear round instead. The only thing left of the cat's animal form was its teeth, especially the pointed eyeteeth and fangs in the mouth, which still opened and closed soundlessly. Not the cat's tongue, with its inimitable form and texture, unique in its look and feel? As if vanished from this mouth, no trace of it.

No longer capable of sustaining life, or not yet? this strange creature seemed neither dead nor properly alive, like the protoform of something not vegetative but also not animal-like. And yet it had survived, it had come far. Dozens of kilometers, eventually into this trackless waste—deriving its nourishment and hydration from swamp plants and water? And it had been making its way, from hearth and home and its life as a domestic animal, for weeks already, the posters with pictures all through the area long since yellowing, while the animal shown in the pictures hardly resembled a cat anymore, was more an indefinable being.

It was Alexia who took the animal in her arms. It did not struggle. The way it allowed itself to be picked up, it was neither a cat nor something unfamiliar. It had animal warmth and breathed without purring; nothing but skin and bones, and yet: how heavy. And it was Valter who at the same moment answered the man's calls. The young man was slight, emaciated. And yet: what a voice all of a sudden. The woman next to him almost started, that was how loud his voice was, booming and piercing, as if coming from the chest of a giant. —"Almost started"? —Yes, only almost. For at the same time this loud voice had nothing startling about it. It was not frightening, and besides, she was familiar with this phenomenon in slight people, and not merely men, though less in real life—familiar with it more in the form of song, and not just that of rappers like Eminem but also, and above all, of blues singers, and again not just of Janis Joplin, God rest her soul.

What did start, literally, was the creature in her arms. And rightly so. A good sign. It was alive, it was gradually turning back into a cat, and now the distant shouted questions became shouted answers. With both parties calling out, they came toward each other, cutting across the thicket. It took a long time before they, Valter and Alexia here, the animal-seeker from where? came together. How long? It took a long, long time, like this day, and like the story of this day. Time and again they got hung up in the blackberry brambles, and it seemed impossible to go forward or back without ripping their clothes; they found themselves shackled by vines, from which not even a Johnny Weissmuller as Tarzan could have swung free. At least the fruit thief, who was equipped for almost every eventuality, had something for this situation as well, a sort of small machete for hacking apart these self-activated cages. True: at the time in which this story takes place, jungles were springing up in the middle of Europe, more impenetrable than anywhere else on the planet. And all the while the peacefulness of the cat in the fruit thief's arms, a peace of the soul if ever there was one, and, including the ticks all around them, the animal's eyes so large, as large as a human's.

As she glanced at her companion, who kept sending his shouts ringing through the jungle gorge at intervals, she realized what she had overlooked the entire time. Or perhaps she had seen it right away, but it had not really entered her consciousness; she had not registered it properly. But now it suddenly seemed worth registering: the person next to her, the young fellow, had a skin color different from hers. He was not white, he was not "a white person." His face, if perhaps not "dark," was certainly darker, considerably darker than hers, deeply brown, and this brownness was not a tan. In ancient Egypt there were double statues of a man and a woman: the man always quite dark, the woman very white. And yet both belonged to the same people or tribe? However that might be: the one who was fighting his way at her side through this European jungle, stumbling and struggling to free himself, came, as was now clear to her, after hours, if not much longer, spent with him, from a different part of the world, was, as the police jargon had it, a "non-European type," *un type non-européen.* Did she realize that because he used his voice in such a different way? Or because his skin color began to glow so noticeably only in the jungle's half-light, in combination with the ups and downs, back-and-forths that made one sweat? Whatever the reason and however it had come about: she marveled at him and then at herself, without his noticing how she marveled at him, so preoccupied was he with shouting and fighting his way along. At any rate, "Valter" was no longer suitable for him. But then what name should he have? She tried out several, without speaking them aloud: none that seemed to fit the person thrashing through the briars with her. Below that dark face the light-colored summer suit with a few snags, so small they could still be mended.

The backs of the hands that her companion held to his mouth every time he called out to the cat's master shimmered in an even darker brown than his face, if possible, but they had pale, whitish spots, all much the same size, which made the backs of his hands looked dappled.

She now drew this pattern with her index finger in the air in front of her, as she had sometimes written in the air as a child when walking along by herself, single letters and whole words, and as she did this it seemed to her that she had had much more air back then, had had actual air space at her disposal, and that had to do with more than the fact that here, as she drew with her left hand, at the same time she had to part the jungle thicket with her right hand and hold it down.

And again what she was doing went unnoticed by the person at her side. And if he did notice, he forbade himself, or he was forbidden, to ask what her drawing-in-the-air meant. Or he understood the meaning and refrained from saying anything. After the surprises the boy had presented her with almost all day long, anything could be expected of him, if not everything.

Did they actually make progress as they hacked their way and zigzagged through the thicket? The other man's calls and responses, once almost close by, sounded the next time as if he were as far off as in the beginning. It was as if he were waiting for them and his animal in the very same spot, and could not possibly advance even one more step into the jungle, while they drifted farther from him as they attempted to reach him. Yes, what a weird source area: no rivulet that might have shown them the way to the spring and out into the open. If there was any water, it was stagnant, in random little pools that all looked alike, or perhaps were the same ones they had passed just recently and then, as it seemed more and more often, some time ago, a long time ago. And so dense were the vines that it was impossible to scale the walls of the gorge and get away from the hollow, even with the machete, its blade dull by now.

Not that the two of them lost heart. To turn back and give up on the undertaking: unthinkable. They had to make it across this wild, tangled source area. No question of anything else. And it was appropriate that the crossing should stretch on and on. At least so the fruit thief imagined. Not once on her solitary forays had she turned back. Or if she had done so briefly, it was only in order to forge ahead all the better from somewhere nearby. And that should, that had to be the case now that she had a companion, the first since she had gone places with her father late in her childhood. And her companion? He, so she imagined, thought, sensed, was of the same mind. A sentence she had read in a book by a mountain climber, to the effect that he had "never had any companions but bad ones," did not apply to him. Again she glanced sideways at him for a moment and thought, "You're a good companion," whereupon he looked back at her, as if he had understood.

Something now interrupted this process that was stretching on and on: a panting, coming closer and closer, that of a human being. It could not come from the cat-seeker, for he could still be heard calling, his voice persistent, now from far below, from a cave, now from sky-high, as if from a balloon. The panting was so loud that it filled the entire jungle, otherwise so still and lifeless; impossible to tell whether the panting came from ahead of them or behind.

And a moment later the body to which it belonged, in the flesh. The man ran past the two of them and in another moment had plunged into the thicket and disappeared. How could that be? Running in that impenetrable jungle and straight through the thicket? Yes, for the man who ran by and blindly found the one possible passageway was a person in flight. Only someone running for his life could find his way through this trackless waste or, to describe him less melodramatically, someone for whom everything, or less melodramatically, for whom at that moment, and even if he just imagined it, almost everything was at stake. This fugitive had shown himself for only a second—not wasting a glance on the jungle-wanderers, whom he swerved to avoid in what to an observer would be a positively elegant athletic manner. But this second, no, tenth, no, hundredth of a second had been enough: they were on his heels, and if he were caught, he would be done for, one way or the other. The redness of his face, at once bright and deep red, occasioned not solely by his superhuman, no, inhuman exertion. The panting not merely panting, but accompanied by an undertone of dull rustling, an overtone of shrill whistling, and vice versa, and vice versa again, still filling the jungle air both near and far when the person had long since dashed out of sight. A young person? To judge by his body, yes. His face, however, that of an old man. Just as in a vintage photograph, the faces of that group of young people who lost their way during a hike though the desert and before dying, probably without being aware that death was imminent, once more "snapped a picture" of themselves, the faces all look old.

His pursuers now hot on his heels? As if by prearrangement the two now move to block them, her companion standing with his legs in a straddle, a stance learned in or copied from the military. Nothing doing: the pursuers did not appear. Yet it looked as though even the deathly weak cat had prepared to defend the fugitive—at least tried to make its fur stand on end and to hiss—though again without making the slightest sound. On the one hand: disappointment; a further interruption would have been welcome. On the other hand: just as well, enough action for one day, enough events, in the sense in which the fruit thief, while playing with the keys on her mobile telephone that morning, had unexpectedly read a notification, under the heading of events, *événements*, reminding her that she had listed remarkably few, and didn't she want to add some? Enough events for today, or of this sort at least.

And after that? What had to happen happened? No, no: little in the story of the fruit thief happened as it had to. Occasionally something happened as it perhaps was supposed to. But as a rule what happened just happened.

The man fleeing in a zigzag through the jungle ravine—inviting a comparison with a rugby player forcing his way with his egg-shaped ball through the opposing ranks—had traced a path for the two of them out of the tangle of vines and brambles. They followed him by doing as he had done, only more deliberately, decidedly deliberately, such that if it had been a film their zigzagging, in contrast to his, would have taken place in slow motion. A couple of times they played the fugitive's role, breaking into a run for a few steps, first him, then her. Flight as a game—impossible other than for those few steps.

Eventful, then, finally, after the long stretch in the dimness of the underbrush, dimmer on the scale of dimness by several degrees, to have firm ground underfoot, unexpectedly, though still in the middle of the woods in the source area of the little Viosne River, and to emerge onto a path—not a fox or rabbit trail losing itself again immediately in the overgrowth, but a proper path, laid out with a proper roadbed, by the book—an event, *événement.*

Finally back in the sun beneath the big open sky, close enough to touch, both of which, the sun and the sky, had vanished as if forever during their time in the jungle, as though they had never existed. But the light that rose from the path would have been just as tangible without the rays of the sun. The path glowed as if for itself, with the sand, the gravel, the midsummer-empty puddles, radiating a brightness from below that passed directly, at first sight, into one's spirit, the outer brightness simultaneously bright inside. The brightness of a path—it could also be a dark one, even a black one, strewn with crushed lava rock—after a long period of being lost in a trackless waste: a particular light effect, from an as yet undiscovered and undiscoverable material, one of whose additional peculiarities was that this path, instead of running straight ahead like the Chaussée Jules César earlier, proceeded in slight, almost imperceptible curves, and in addition went gently uphill, with an elevated light portal at the end, out of the forest surrounding the source area. Paths that at least in earlier times led toward large estates, to castles, if not to a royal palace, were laid out in this fashion. But the paths here to a royal palace, which remained out of sight up to the last bend and only then presented itself in all its royal-palace-ness: weren't they actual roads, river-wide avenues, like those that mounted in long, looping curves to the esplanade in front of the horizon-wide palace of Versailles? But where did this little forest path lead? The fruit thief might have been able to find it on one of the highly detailed maps she had with her. But she did not want to know, and for her companion, as the story intended, there was no question of anything different. They were in silent agreement that they should let the anonymous path surprise them, yes indeed!

Yet they also felt the need, after the time in that wilderness, not merely nameless and confused and confusing but also resistant to any name and any designation, to be able to move at last through an area like those on her maps, where almost everything, every copse, even the bed of a long-since-dried-up brook, even a single hedge cutting across the fields, had a name, no matter if a hardly noticeable rise might be called Gallows Hill, a clearing Dead Man's Meadow, and a patch of swamp Nest of Vipers. They felt a need, if not a yearning, for the world, at least the geographical one, of names. Yes, although a source still did not come into view, let alone become audible: here at last they were standing, he was standing, on the grounds of the "headwaters of the Viosne." Viosne: the name of the river, long absent and missed, had returned once they emerged onto the path, this path. And how reassuring it was, that one name, Viosne. How it, together with the path, brightened one's mood or, why not, one's soul—lightened it.

Has the story in the meantime forgotten the cat owner and with him his lost-and-found house pet? No. There he stood, where the path ended at the edge of the jungle barrier (*clos*, the telling word for it, closed-off), impenetrable not only for him. And he let the fruit thief hand the cat over to him, as if that could be taken for granted, received the animal without a word, let alone an expression of gratitude, and without even a hasty glance at it, popped it into the basket he had ready—still not a peep from the cat—and was gone, disappearing around the first bend in the road.

From far off, when he was long since out of sight, a sob

could be heard, a burst of sobbing far louder and more piercing than his question-and-response calling during all the previous hours. He sobbed out his gratitude, to whomever. This sobbing was at the same time a screaming and shouting, the volume growing and swelling, if possible, as up on the plateau, where he had parked his car, he made a phone call to his loved ones—at last he could call them that, down in the *ville nouvelle* of Cergy-Pontoise, with the joyful tidings, stammering alternating with sobbing, and so forth, drowning out all other sounds, including the engine starting, the car shooting forward, accelerating—or whatever it is called—and thus, echoing and re-echoing, lingering for a while, and longer than a mere while, over the entire source area of the Viosne. All that mattered now was getting the lost-and-found creature home in one piece. Not too fast! Remember that everything lost and then found is in danger of being lost again! The ticks to be removed very carefully with tweezers, trying not to pull out any fur! To the vet's immediately! Damn! Saturday. The weekend, and the summer holidays besides—where was the nearest open animal clinic? But oh, one will be found. No, I'll find one, no problem. Finally I have a feat to accomplish for others, me, specifically for those who count the most—that's how it seems to me today—my near and dear. What did that fellow say once? "I'm world-famous—to my wife."

The fruit thief's hands strangely empty after carrying the runaway animal for so long through the jungle. Strange, also, that the two of them, in the clear at last, at last on a path, at last not thwarted at every step, however small, did not set out at once, not at all, but instead, facing the wilderness, remained fixated on it for a while. Impossible to imagine now how they had ever found their way out of that tangle, a tangle so total that the snarl of blackberry and wild rose brambles, yellow locusts and hawthorns, and vines as thick as one's arm (the only plants without thorns), all paradoxically now formed a veritably clear pattern, that of a natural fence, infinitely thicker and more shielding than any fence made by human hands. A kind of retroactive shuddering at the thought that they had been groping their way blindly in a zigzag through that mess only moments earlier, a terror coming over them, if only briefly, not to be compared to that of the rider over Lake Constance. Or perhaps comparable after all?

She plucked from this barrier a handful of ripe blackberries, and her companion followed her lead. Marveling again at confirming the observation that the larger and also riper berries—so sweet in the mouth—were usually hidden under the leaves, in the realm of shadows, and that those in full sun, by contrast, were either sour or starting to go bad. Between and underneath the blackberry hedges, dead or dying raspberry canes: probably they were being overwhelmed and wiped out, down to the last shoot, by the armies of blackberries, and that occurring all over, not just here.

Upon setting out the fruit thief took her first few steps backward, and again her companion followed her lead, this time almost simultaneously, of one mind with her: a kind of farewell salute to the inaccessible tangle in spite of everything, at the same time a mute *au revoir.*

On the bright path, curve after curve, making their way out of the forested source area, and, after the last gentle bend, slightly uphill, and at the top pausing on the threshold to the high plateau that stretched before them, initially with no trees and bushes in sight, in the pre-sunset summer light. Yes, for now there was no trace of trees, bushes, and above all hedges—thanks be to the heavens, arching mightily over the landscape.

Seen from that threshold: after the metropole, the *ville nouvelle*, the riparian meadows, the town on the edge of the Île-de-France, after the headwaters jungle as the strip along the border, now, as far as the eye could see, for the time being nothing but land—the land—of Picardy. And although at first glance the land, seeming to stretch to the most distant horizons—which in all directions also represented distance and made it felt as well—was empty, at least empty of human beings, and the path cutting across it, still with barely noticeable curves, across fields that appeared as one big field extending over the entire countryside, led to nothing in particular, neither a farmstead nor a village, and certainly not a castle, let alone a "royal palace," the air space above the plateau, the "Vexin" part of the Picardy "region," buzzed with names, names upon names. Over there, the chain of hills to the west: La Molière, with the villages at its, or her, feet, out of sight, called Sérans and Hadancourt-le-Haut-Clocher (with the tall bell tower). On the right, clockwise, the split in the main road, there since the Middle Ages, with one branch, now called the Route du Blues, leading to the sea, to Dieppe, the other into the interior, to Chaumont-en-Vexin. And continuing with the litany of place-names, clockwise to the north, east, and south, in a circle around the plateau: all the villages and ponds, also invisible, called Liancourt-Saint-Pierre, Lavilletertre, Monneville, Marquemont, and then, closing the circle, the other chain of hills to the south, the highest and longest in this region, the Buttes de Rosne, and at its, or their, feet the villages and ponds of Neuville-Bosce, Tumbrel, Chavençon, Le Heaulme (the helmet), and in the Rosne Hills the source, less jungle-like than that of the Viosne, of the other river in the Vexin area, the little stream called La Troësne (privet), and also innumerable brooks, one called Sauseron, and a second called Reveillon (which could also mean New Year's), a third called La Couleuvre, the adder. Names upon names, swarming up in front of them from the seemingly empty expanse of land, lending it, and the two of them as well, a rhythm.

Tired though they had been just a little while earlier, they now dashed from the rim to the land, as if taking off from a standstill from improvised starting blocks, and ran as fast as they could (we are not told who won or what they were competing for). The landscape into which they ran was, as it now revealed itself, not merely, after the Île-de-France, a different region in the state called "La France": it appeared, sweet illusion, illusion, but above all "sweet," as more, as larger, as an, as *the* other country, or simply something different. And part of that was—an even sweeter illusion?—that the state, the French one, otherwise omnipresent, or something like "the state" in general, appeared to be excluded from this seemingly empty stretch, which nonetheless echoed with names. A state: where you wish and as you please, but not here, not now, not today, and for God's or whoever's sake, not tomorrow either, not before tomorrow evening, not before tomorrow night, and thus not before the dreamed end and final chord of this story.

At one of the turnouts along the road in this area, still unpopulated except for the two of them, the fruit thief and her fellow runner stopped suddenly and continued on at a leisurely pace, side by side, but with some distance between them—room enough on the road for a dozen like them. It had been a gentle run, and neither of them was out of breath (the boy, unaccustomed to so much walking, perhaps a bit, without letting it show). Although evening had come, and again no plans had been made for the night, they were in no hurry.

Now they were on an in-between stretch—between one place where something had happened and the next place, where the next event awaited them. An in-between stretch, which normally meant a stretch where nothing happened except that one passed through it. And yet the way in which the two of them now moved between two eventful sites, even to an observer in no way resembled mere passing through. They looked, as they made their way across the landscape, to repeat the wording of that old tale, "pensive" and as if they had "come from afar." The young woman intentionally slowed her stride, which the young man next to her did not have to imitate—her gait communicated itself to him effortlessly. At the same time her strides were large, unusually large, and not merely for her, the woman. It was a striding along, taking the measure of the in-between stretch with the movements of geometers, combined with attentiveness to all the phenomena that might possibly present themselves along and around the route. It was not permissible to overlook any of these. Precisely on such in-between stretches they could offer indications that would help one prepare for what might be waiting at one's destination—that made one receptive for what was to come. Yes, already on this in-between stretch, if one remained alert to its features, including auditory images, it could happen, in the form of a premonition. What could happen? What could take place? It—whatever that might be. So: no rush on the in-between stretches. Woe unto those in too much of a hurry. Blessings upon those of you, on the other hand, who derive something useful and fruitful from in-between stretches, as well as in-between spaces, as well as in-between times, taking it slow and absorbing everything humanly possible along the way.

A lone tree along the road: a nut tree, the nuts barely visible amid the foliage, and yet each look discovers more, their shells not yet cracking open. A shrine by the roadside, black wrought iron set in light-colored concrete, a tin can with withered wildflowers at the feet of the gaunt figure on the cross. The road cutting through one wheat field, not yet harvested, from which a large herd of wild boars suddenly emerges, first crashing, then making a huge racket, and crosses the road from one section of the field to the other, promptly disappearing beneath the ears of grain, which continue to vibrate for some time, the animals' menacing grunting and growling, like that of an enormous dog, directed at the two of them, who have backed off a bit, the noises still audible for a while, falling silent only when the laggard pig, not the largest but also not the runt, still growing, has crossed the road in front of them in a wild-boar gallop. The turtle in the grass by the side of the road, dead? No, it's alive, tapping its way along as only a turtle can. The larks' trilling giving way to evening silence. The whistling of the kites dying away on high, but in its place the whistle of the last train back to Paris, sounding far off and way below as if from its cut, not visible from up here on the plateau. The summery daytime wind changing to the pre-evening and evening wind, the continuing warm breeze as if flanked and punctuated by advancing coolness. In the sand of the path, here and there ankle-deep, scattered hollows like pockmarks, made by raindrops, large and now evaporated, having seemingly fallen weeks ago, during the June rainy season.

Such single phenomena followed upon single phenomena, and at the same time uneventfulness. Uneventful covering ground and striding along. Walking in a vacuum. Idling. Idling as something fundamentally different from running on empty, the single phenomena circling each other and intermingling: kaleidoscopic walking. Kaleidoscope of in-between stretches and in-between times. A kaleidoscope like that also as a pastime? Yes, that, too—why not?

Somewhere along the way a police car came toward them, announced at a distance by a cloud of dust, the flashing lights on the roof, the siren. As it sped toward them, it slowed, then pulled even with them, driving no faster than a walk. They ignored the looks of the men in uniform. This was a phantom; there could be no authorities here. And already the policemen had passed them in silence, their faces those of mannequins in a display window.

Later a second encounter on the in-between stretch: an older woman, a teacher at the village school who wanted to use the current summer vacation to write a book, a murder mystery, what else? She lived alone, her mother, with whom she had lived earlier, having died several years ago. Being among people was something she managed only when surrounded by her pupils. In class, in front of, among, and above all in their midst, she felt and knew she was in her rightful place. She blossomed amid the throng of her pupils, like a fellow classmate. But the minute she stepped out into the schoolyard, she began to feel ill at ease. Whether she had recess duty or was just passing through: she was not sure what to do with herself. Just passing her own children, suddenly strangers now that they were outside the classroom, could cause her to stumble. And then having to be a passerby out on the street, among all the adults! Shyness was lovely, and above all could make a person beautiful. But her shyness out of doors—"outside the stall" was her private expression for it—manifested itself, to use her own expression again, as something "feral," or was, at least, nothing human—it was a skittishness, which, instead of making her beautiful, made her ugly. If a person came toward her, regardless of who it was, her head involuntarily swiveled to one side, away from the other person. If it was someone she knew, from parent-teacher conferences, for instance, where she looked everyone in the eye quite naturally, her skittishness manifested itself even more forcefully; as the person approached, her head literally whipped away, even if she had cordially shaken the person's hand just a little while earlier in the doorway to her home or in school.

It happened, and not all that seldom, that she had visitors at home, in the house that had been her mother's. She did not have any friends, but she greatly enjoyed having visitors. Hospitality—something not much cultivated in Picardy—was almost part of the aging teacher's religion. Guests never left her house without feeling that the time there—while they were surrounded on all sides, outside as well as in, by the hostess's attentiveness—had been exemplary, her hospitality contagious. But if their paths crossed the next day: see above. No greeting, however hearty, called out to her, who just the day before had been the friendliest of neighbors, could do anything to dispel her skittishness.

Fortunately for her, as well as for the village community, there was a third location, in addition to her house and her schoolroom, where her extreme skittishness lost its compulsiveness and literally dissolved into thin air. And this place was the church, whenever the Eucharist, or Mass, was celebrated. For the duration of the service her head pointed straight ahead, her eyes wide, taking in all the others in the nave, greeting each of them with a slight raising of her eyelids, silently merry, the greeting repeated afterward in words outside by the church door and giving way to general animated post-Mass chatting, in which she joined—she even prolonged it as long as she possibly could; impossible to imagine how during the week she had shied away on the street and in the public square, the strangest of strangers, from all those with whom she now congregated in a festive mood, men, women, couples with children and more children.

However: Sunday Mass was celebrated in the church less and less often. And now, during the summer months, none was scheduled at all—the next one not until school started in September. The school closed, the children gone. And the people she might have invited to her house: no one around, all those she might have considered were away, and for weeks.

The mystery she had in mind to write was to be set in this region, familiar to her since childhood, starting in her mother's house. In earlier times this area had been notorious throughout France for its many murders, and certain bookstores in Paris still carried an illustrated pamphlet with the title "Meurtres dans l'Oise," murders in the Oise *département*. Even today, according to the regional weekly, the *Oise-Hebdo*, the number of people who lost their lives to violence week after week had hardly declined, except that as a rule these killings, unlike murders, occurred without premeditation and plan, simply on the spur of the moment, in blind rage, taking the form of manslaughter, brawls, and, most often, car crashes resulting from excessive speed on the narrow roads. So hardly any murders nowadays in the Oise *département*. But for her purposes a murder, premeditated for years, was supposed to occur. She envisioned her novel as recounting a murder such as had never been perpetrated before, not in the world of facts and also not in any murder mystery. In what unheard-of way the murder would happen she did not know yet, only that the deed should be unheard-of, the acme of murders, the murder to end all murders, "the mother of murders" (that was supposed to be the title). Anyone who read her novel would become transformed thereby into the victim, and if the reader was not blown sky-high at the end and torn into a thousand pieces, rent limb from limb, then at least as a result of reading the book the reader would be infected with an incurable illness and wither away! The only thing, however, of which she was sure at this point: the scene of the crime is somewhere in the headwaters area of the Viosne, and the murder victim's corpse, or what is left of it, ends up in the jungle forest there. Now she will scope out the where, when, and how of the murder, setting out from home with her camera, flashlight, DNA test kit, and so forth to do—what is it called?—research. And the why? No why. That, too, would be one of the unheard-of features of her book.

When the future mystery author now came upon the two of them on the road crossing the Vexin plateau, her head swiveled automatically to one side, and even more violently out here in the open countryside than in the village, close to her house; it would not have taken much for her skull to be jerked backward, breaking her throat and neck (a special form of murder). Yet from the corner of her eye, also against her will, though in a different way from the jerking of her head, she registered a bit of the two young people as they walked, strode, swerved, rambled, strayed, and roamed during these early evening hours into the countryside, her, the old lady's, countryside. "O youth, O rejuvenated world." And passing the two of them, by whom, as usual, she had been greeted without responding to the greeting, she turned—this time not against her will, but involuntarily—to them and finally uttered a greeting, too, although only under her breath, inaudibly. Way back in her own youth she had once taken the train alone, as now during the holidays, to the south of France, a long trip, from night to day and back to night, that was how slow the trains were in those days (and now?). At some point she had fallen asleep and then, toward midnight, woke up at her destination—Bordeaux? Biarritz? Latour-de-Carol on the Spanish border?—with her head on the shoulder of the man seated next to her, a stranger, a soldier. Since that time she had never slept more soundly, had never woken up more beautifully. Write a murder mystery? Abuse the countryside's peacefulness for the sake of horror? Hem in its expanse with terror? Away with this sinister, disturbing stuff. In its place, reassuring, homey stuff. Betray and sell out the region's secret, the landscape's, and not only that of this landscape, for a mystery story? Demean and disgrace these places by creating false leads? Nonsense and more nonsense. A murderer, no matter who, a murder, no matter how: tasteless. A case of running amok, on the other hand . . . the tale of someone who runs amok . . . without rhyme or reason . . . a woman as the one who runs amok . . . the unheard-of story of a woman running amok . . . dear world, dear life!

Next we see the two making their way across the landscape on the bright sandy road that winds gently past the mostly harvested grain fields, the deep yellow northwestern sky ahead of them, shortly after sunset. From a distance it looks as though they are maintaining their deliberate, even, rhythmic pace, at most picking up the tempo somewhat. From close up, however, we can see that the young man has lost the rhythm. From one moment to the next he started to feel rushed, and now he is walking erratically. After a few long strides several shorter ones, almost trotting, then again one or two longer strides as he tries to slow down. The ears of wheat he has picked up from a field and now holds out in front of him, and which appear on the signposts, in threes, symbolizing this country, the former "kings' breadbasket," do not help him recover the rhythm.

All of a sudden fear had taken hold of the young man, out of the clear blue sky and from inside him as well, a great fear, an enormous one. He would be too late, the two of them would be too late. Too late for what? Too late. Too late where? Too late. The catastrophe could no longer be averted. What kind? Just the catastrophe. He, both of them, could have prevented it. But by now it was too late. Or perhaps there was still a chance, almost nonexistent, to be sure, to squeak by and turn the impending misfortune away, to come to the rescue at the last minute, the very last second, the absolutely last hundredth of a second. To rescue whom? Themselves? Someone else, a particular person? Just to rescue. To rescue. To rescue for heaven's sake! And precisely the thought of such a teeny-tiny possibility of perhaps being able to rescue oneself, as well as someone else or others, was what inflated the young man's fear to such enormous proportions. Fear: a giant crowding him out of himself more and more with every step; it was no young person stumbling along the road now but only this giant—fear.

Often and ever more often the young man's stumbling turned into headlong rushing; he skipped bends in the road by cutting straight across stubble fields. Wherever she could, the fruit thief, who remained lighter on her feet than he was, ran on ahead of him, trying, by leading the way, energetically and evenly, to pass the rhythm to him and fill her companion with calm: but in vain. Long mute in his fear, now he belted it out, sobbed as if inconsolable, or as if his last, small hope were draining away; howled, whimpered, whined, at the same time hobbling across lots, never stopping. Understand this if you can.

She understood him, whether recalling the period of her own, though different, cross-country wandering, or who knows how. Was this one of the surprises she had expected from the boy? No, not this. But the evening they would spend together was still in the offing, and with his wailing in her ear and his snot before her eyes, seemingly dribbling from several noses, she, Alexia-beneath-the-stairs, felt certain—time and again these strange certainties came to her—that this very day this person seemingly lost for all time would amaze her and in the end make her laugh out loud with sheer amazement. Now, however, she was tempted to slap his face to bring him back to the present moment.

What eventually took away his fear of a catastrophe was the thunderstorm that came on unexpectedly, with a bank of blackish clouds, which, have you ever seen this? from one moment to the next popped up behind the chain of hills called La Molière as if in time-lapse mode, bringing the first flashes of lightning, followed more slowly by a still weak little rumble of thunder. The storm was still far off. Early in the day she had wished for it, and now her wish had been fulfilled and made sense: thanks to the lightning and distant thunder, the panicked youth next to her promptly regained his composure. With a jolt that he had not been forced to administer to himself he shook off his fear and regained his serenity. From then on, he positively radiated it. Friendly thundering, lovable lightning flashes: were such things possible? It depended on who was listening and looking, and how, and at what moment.

But now the two of them are running as fast as their legs and lungs will carry them. The weather front, borne on the west wind, is closer "by a degree" with every glance at the sky. The thunder following the lightning at ever shorter intervals, and so forth—a familiar phenomenon—and for a while the two watch and listen as if spectators to an adventure. And nonetheless running is imperative. Away from the treeless high plateau, the only thing shaped like a tree being the jagged flashes of lightning. Still no rain, at most now and then a large drop hitting one's forehead and hands, almost a caress after all that walking at the height of summer. The rain pelting down only after the path begins to descend slightly and joins a through-road. In no time the two are soaked to the skin, as the expression goes. Almost at the same moment darkness comes on, a darkness as deep as if it were already late at night. Now and then a car passing, its headlights dim in the storm. The rain roaring, the windshield wipers swishing. One car stops, and the driver waves them in. They demur; being driven is out of the question for this day, but they thank him, poking their dripping hands through the open window to shake his—God forbid that he should be discouraged from stopping the next time to offer other hikers a lift.

Finally the two of them can be seen, half in darkness, on the front step of a large house standing by itself, with no other houses around, light showing in a single window on the upper floor, above which there may be one more floor, impossible to tell in the dark. The thunder and lightning: no longer dramatic, by now having died down and fallen silent amid the increasingly heavy rainfall. The dripping faces of the two are lit up at short intervals by the headlights of the cars passing on the nearby highway, or might there even be two highways, to judge by the noise level? The fruit thief and her companion standing at the door to the house are still completely at the mercy of the rain: the house, like all the old buildings on the Vexin plateau, has a solid slate roof, but it has no overhang, the stones ending flush with the walls, so they provide no protection from the rain to those outside, to say nothing of a "roof over their heads."

She rings the bell, one short, one long, and it can be heard echoing through the entire house, as if it might be empty and the doors to all the rooms open. At the same time the boy knocks, then pounds with his fist, on the front door. No response. The fruit thief presses the latch, at first hesitantly, then firmly. And again at the same time the latch was also pressed from the inside, and as the door flew open she barely avoided tumbling over the threshold into the house and onto the man standing there.

The man did not expressly block the doorway, wide enough for more than two. But neither did he give the two of them any indication that they should enter. He looked wordlessly from one to the other as the rain poured down on them, so hard that they both had to lick the water from their lips. It was as if he were trapped in a dream, which he, alone in the house, had been dreaming for a good while and now continued dreaming in the presence of the two strangers who had just arrived on his doorstep. The garment he was wearing, without actually being a nightshirt, resembled one at first.

He continued to make no effort to let them in. In the dim light coming from one of the upper stories—the ground floor behind him almost completely dark—he stared at them without blinking, standing there transfixed, conveying the impression that he might have been standing like that, behind the door, motionless, for a considerable time as well.

In certain parts of Europe it was said of women who had never found a husband or a special someone that they projected "a forbidding aura." Didn't the house owner project a similar aura in these moments? Not merely forbidding—even more than that, resistant?

His resistance was merely apparent. When the fruit thief now made short work of crossing his threshold, towing her companion behind her, his rigidity promptly dissolved, the rigidity of loneliness with which he had been afflicted since the afternoon hours of this wretched summer day, and with a perfectly executed bow, almost a dance step, he welcomed the two late guests. Although not a word had passed his lips yet, in his own head words were finally flowing, for the first time in days, in weeks.

"They've come, my long-awaited guests. They haven't left me in the lurch, not them! They've crossed my threshold, come to me, me in person, over the threshold, honoring the prehistoric shell fossils embedded in the doorstep. They have come for an evening meal and a bed for the night, and it's an honor for me to be at their service. The two have come from so far away that they deserve to be waited on by me, showered with hospitality! At last I can be a host again! Joy, you crystallize the limestone at my threshold!" And he darted, agile as only a lifelong host and innkeeper can be, to fetch towels so the two could dry themselves off.

His house had still been a hotel only a short while before, and in the mind of the host continued to be one. During the day a large sign on the façade, with every letter intact, read AUBERGE DE DIEPPE, and on the road below, which intersected with another road, stood two highway signs. The larger, more prepossessing one read DIEPPE, 100 KM, and the other, marking the split between the two roads, pointed toward CHAUMONT EN VEXIN. The auberge stood alone by the intersection of the two highways. In the fall the inn would be torn down, and it was not merely the traffic noise, continuing all night, that was responsible for the absence of guests. More specific and additional reasons for the inn's unprofitability to be found on the internet: Auberge-de-Dieppe.com, or something like that.

Nonetheless the inn, located in the spandrel between the two highways, remained secretly "in operation" even without advertised business hours, open for guests in the host's imagination up to the morning of the demolition. The cellar, kitchen, and rooms were ready for whoever might show up, and the front door was left unlocked day and night. The two refugees from the rain, however, were the first since . . . to come into the house, in need of his services as guests should be. Or no: someone else had been there, alone, and had stayed overnight, yesterday? the day before? a week earlier? Had the innkeeper lost his sense of time? Or was he living by now in a different time dimension?

However that might be: out of season or in another time: now the entire ground floor of the inn lit up in bright yet warm lamplight, light for a table and festive spread creating a single reception area, not too large and not too small, with appropriate dark nooks and shadowy niches. And now the fire laid a good while earlier glowed, crackled, cracked, rattled, and roared in the fireplace, again not too small, not too large, just right for this evening—a fireplace fire in summertime? So what? And the table, made not of ebony or marble but also not of plywood or plastic, was set, not with Limoges porcelain and crystal from . . . but also not . . . ; everything as only in old, very old stories. "Only"? Did that mean in distinction to life? to reality? No! Such things also happened in life, from time to time, and at just the right moment, and also in reality, and only then did life actually take place, did reality take place as reality, the real aspect of reality.

To me at least, as I try to narrate this story not ex post facto but before the fact, for those to whom it matters, events like those happening in the Auberge de Dieppe have happened or been vouchsafed to them repeatedly in their lives, not too often but also not too seldom—actually at those not so infrequent sacred times—along with an accompanying previous period of misery, consisting of more than merely extreme weather and storms, and such events, if I have read this correctly, have likewise happened to not a few prenarrators, between Wolfram von Eschenbach and my current time, from Miguel de Cervantes y Saavedra to Leo Tolstoy and, why not, Karl May, from Raymond Chandler and Georges Simenon to, why not, Isabel Allende, Zane Grey, and Jerry Cotton.

On that rainy night no one, no pedestrian, passed by that ex-inn encroached upon from all sides by major highways. But if someone on the skids or merely a night hiker had passed the sprawling house, what he would have seen through the windows, now lit up from front to back and from top to bottom, would have made him eager to enter at once.

The two guests had helped the host prepare the meal, uncork the wine, and bring everything to the table; and since the man was overcome time and again by his paralysis, often in the middle of doing something, on his way to the kitchen or back to the dining room, they took things completely in hand, urging him—not all that gently, but he was glad to obey—to join them at the table; and in the end they were the ones who served him. Besides, they were accustomed to that; both he and she knew exactly what to do, and they enjoyed being of service. Just this much about what the evening meal consisted of: it was freshened up with ingredients the fruit thief had plucked in passing from village gardens and front yards without her companion's noticing; on many fields in the Vexin the once omnipresent grain had given way to prairie-wide crops of green beans, peas, and turnips—who knows what distant authority had given the former cultivators of rye and oats these directives, or whatever they were; for many square miles nothing but light-colored onions poked up out of the former grain furrows—and their scent wafted over the highways—and some of the farms, many of them going back to the Middle Ages, each one a village unto itself, a fortified village set apart from the Picardian villages, were in the meantime surrounded by a sea of parsley—innumerable clumps of parsley, but only if one did not look carefully: actually seas of cilantro. For what market were these onions and cilantro plants intended? Look it up in the weekly farmers' circular.

The table cleared. The dishes washed, by hand. A nocturnal hiker would have paused now by one of the windows, seen the two young people in a corner of the dining room, near the bar, playing table soccer, while the host, finally roused from his paralysis, stood nearby as a spectator. Despite the roar of the traffic outside, the clicking of the little ball and the cheers after a goal would have been clearly audible, especially the cheers coming from the young woman. Besides, she had more occasions for cheering than her opponent. Not only did she play infinitely better than the boy, who could not keep up with her as he watched her play, let alone react. And she did not give him an opening, not the slightest one. Wouldn't she at least grant him a consolation goal? It did not occur to her. And in the next game, when the innkeeper came to the boy's aid and took over the defense, he suffered the same fate. One goal after the other from the fruit thief's wrist: a single, seemingly effortless little flip, and already the ball thudded deep into the opposing side's goal pocket, the thud echoing out over the highways and back and forth through the rushing of the nocturnal downpour.

Later, in another corner of the dining room, the jukebox playing, iridescing in the colors of an electric rainbow. This time no sound making its way outside; out there nothing but roaring, the vertical roar of the ceaseless cascades of water from the black sky, the horizontal roar of the cars and long-distance trucks. But inside dancers would have been seen in front of the jukebox, first two, with space between them, then three, and after the woman had pulled the older man onto the dance floor, she suddenly became a young girl, holding him by the elbows and showing him the steps.

What the two of them then dance, as the man gradually picks up the rhythm and the boy just quietly shifts from one foot to the other and looks on, cannot be a blues. From this point on, to be sure, the highway is a lengthened and widened extension of the Route du Blues, with this spot its junction, so to speak. But a blues—fervently pleading on the one hand, but hardly ostentatious and certainly not foot-stomping on the other—a blues in its monotonous lament, isn't really good for dancing, is it? not even a summertime blues? Or perhaps it is? Dancing with a heavy heart, with heavy feet? Or maybe a dance executed from a seated position, a sitting dance calibrated to the song, which sounds purest and most imploring when the singer simply sits there, maybe on a wobbly chair, perhaps even one missing a leg? A seated blues dancer to go with the seated blues singer?

When it comes to the boy, who has gone off to one side and sat down on a stool, rocking his torso slightly forward and back but otherwise motionless, the jukebox might well play a blues. The young woman, the girl, and the man, on the other hand, she with her hands on his shoulders, are dancing to a music that cannot possibly be a lament, the farthest thing from a blues. She dances ebulliently; the two of them could almost be dancing a round dance as they move back and forth across the room, and one almost sees several, many, other couples like them circling and whirling through the space. As ebullient as the round dance *à deux* looks, it also looks dramatic, and there is no singer suggesting a tonality and steps to the two of them, only instruments, or no, only a single instrument, a small one, playing fast, a fiddle?

And that is how it is: they are dancing to the fiddle because they, two members of the same large family, are in danger, and with them the entire family, the entire clan. They are dancing to the fiddle from John Ford's *The Grapes of Wrath*, the scene in which the mother and son, encircled by mortal enemies, dance this way to protect each other. And the mother here is danced by the young woman? And the son, Henry Fonda in the movie, by the old innkeeper? That is how it is. And the girl here protects him by leading him in the dance, and how! Protecting the man from whatever enemies may menace him? Both men? That is how it is. That is how it must have been.

The danger menacing them did not come from the outside. It came from the young person who had just been rocking his torso back and forth in the seated dance, to his blues. Now he gradually ceased rocking, sat up abruptly, and looked around, moving his whole head as he did so, while his eyes remained motionless like an owl's. Where could he begin? In what direction, at whom or what would he throw himself in his violent act? At what would he hurl himself in the next second, closing in for the kill?

The fruit thief knew what was taking place inside the boy. How did she know? From her dreams, and in general. For a long time he had been wanting to call it quits with the world, with this world. And now the moment had arrived for him to disappear once and for all. To do away with himself. Away with me. Off to Paradise, or at least the bright place where the Tigris and the Euphrates flow out of Paradise? No bright place, nothing but blackness before and behind my eyes—away with me from here to eternity, amen.

What she did not know at first: would he try to take anyone with him to death and destruction? In doing away with himself, would he also do her in? her partner in the round dance? All three of them at one blow? And she glanced around surreptitiously to see whether there were any weapons in the dining room: no sabers or swords or whatever mounted on the walls, at most afterimages or hallucinations of them, in flickering outlines cast by the crackling fire.

And then it became clear to her: his desire to leave this world applied only to himself. She and the host, the innkeeper, perhaps existed somehow, somewhere, but no longer for him. No other person counted now. Or thus: the boy could not count on anyone else. No one was for him or against him. For me, to stand by me, to hold out a hand to me, there is no one anymore, there has never been anyone. Where are they, my brothers? I have been shouting that silently forever. Where the hell are they, those bastards, those sons of bitches, those wusses, those filthy pigs, those jailbirds—my brothers? And I had to make it all the way to twenty-one—or am I twenty-two already? forgetting my own age . . . before I realized that my brothers don't exist, anywhere, not here either, not even here. What an idiot I was. As dumb as a post. Dumber than dumb.

What then also became clear to her: he was hesitating. He would hesitate for a few more owl moments. True, any minute now he might do violence to himself, after which he would be down for the count. But he was still undecided. In any case he did not want to carry out the act in silence, in a remote place, somewhere outside in the rain; instead he wanted it to take place in here, in the light, before an audience, with drums and trumpets. Even if he had only these two spectators: his act of terror against himself had to be displayed to the world. The dining room in the Auberge de Dieppe had a back wall of bare stone, large blocks, and he had enough room to get a running start and crack his head open. On the other hand, the fire in the fireplace had formed a glowing mound of embers, and he could pour the olive oil left standing on the table over himself . . .

And now the fruit thief had pulled the boy off his stool and drawn him into the couples' dance. He did not know at first what was happening, but when he looked into the others' eyes it came to him. He wanted to cry. At long last he felt the need for that, for nothing more. He did not cry. But it was enough that he had felt the need. He felt the urge to kiss the lady's hand, both hands. He did not kiss her hands. It was enough that he had felt the urge. They continued the round dance as a threesome, each with an arm around another's waist, and what had just taken place was forgotten, forgotten, too, that their feet were still damp in shoes soaked from the long walk in the pouring rain.

Then the host let them pick out rooms before he withdrew. First he laid a few more logs on the fire. The two guests sat by the fire for a long time after that, drying their shoes in the warmth. The boy asked the fruit thief how she had known what was going on inside him. She replied, "I just knew." He marveled, not at her answer but because he realized that despite their having been on the road together so long, this was the first time they had had something like a conversation. He felt impelled to use her name in his next sentence, the name she had given herself for the day just past, but he was so tired that he misspoke, and instead of Alexia said Alicia, to which she responded that if she happened to need a name for the next morning and day that would be an ideal name for shouting over a distance.

That he was an orphan she did not even have to guess. She knew that, had known it the first time she laid eyes on him in the *ville nouvelle* of Cergy-Pontoise when she met him on his motor scooter with the metal or aluminum crate in which he delivered the pizza or sushi or whatever strapped on behind him, immensely heavier than and looming over him. Heaven forbid that this crate should come loose from its moorings someday when he had to brake suddenly, and crash into his back, breaking his neck!

That he had known neither his mother nor his father had been the source of his sorrow until a few years ago. He encountered his parents only in dreams. Actually, even in his dreams a real meeting never took place; he waited for it in vain, all dream long, all night long. In every such dream he was standing in a clearing in the middle of a vast forest, and a message came to him—out of the air, through the air—who knows how, not through his ears and voiceless: any minute now his father and mother would come to him out of the forest, to no one but him, their child. Each time he was even told the place where the two of them would emerge from the forest and come to him in the clearing: from the dark gap between two particularly tall, particularly straight trees, reaching heavenward (in the dream they were usually firs). So he stood there, in the hip-high grass of the clearing, in his dream no longer a boy or an adolescent but someone of unspecified age, the embodiment of expectancy. He was filled with rejoicing as never before. His heart was about to burst with joy. At last they would come and be there, any minute now, any minute . . . And today, as he told her about it, he was overcome again by the memory of how every time the space between the firs had remained empty.

Eventually he stopped missing his parents so much. With the passing of time, their existence also disappeared from his dreams. He no longer felt sorrow, for them, for himself. Initially that worried him. He felt guilty about no longer searching for his father and mother, either during the day or in his dreams. But then came a period when he was downright proud of having no parents. The pride later gave way to arrogance and hubris. Having no family, the young man saw himself as special, standing out from the millions of people entangled in their clans and mangled by them. The freedom, by comparison, of those of us without fathers and mothers, the blissfully free air in our armpits, beneath our wings! Yes, solitary though he was, he thought of himself as "we"—we, those of us without parents, we'll show you, just wait. We, we are the world. We are the future kings of the world. And where today damnation holds sway, tomorrow those of us free of father and mother will bring salvation. We are the saviors. We are destined—yes, we have been designated—to save the world from the rot and ruin to which it seems doomed. You others, you who fancy yourselves the lords of the universe and in reality have long since become its slaves: make way for us, the only free human beings left on earth! Make way for the orphans.

In the meantime, however, he was filled with anticipation again, in the clearing in the midst of the dark wood, less in dreams than by day, and those he was waiting for, as fervently as when he was a child, were, if not his parents, relatives, yes, relatives, but not in the flesh. Just as his childhood dreams had run their course, so, too, his later arrogance. What had it brought him but delivering food, telephonically ordered, all over the *ville nouvelle* on the scooter, the Vespa, a Piaggio model (Ital.)—though this job did have various benefits (money? let's not mention that here), especially—strange, or not so strange—at night and in wintertime, in the classic three stages, from the loading and dispatching of the metal crate at the restaurant to the often quite long, dark, icy, and windy in-between stretches, with the special woolen cap on his head, copied from a miniature of Louis, the saintly king, to the not-seldom-adventurous address of the customer, and not just the address adventurous. What was the name of his scooter again, his delivery vehicle? *Aujourd'hui*—today.

And the next morning each of the two would set out alone. That was the plan. Were they sitting across from each other for the last time? Each of them had that thought, without needing to voice it. No, they would see each other again, someday in the not-too-distant future, perhaps even soon, and that would not be the last time. On the other hand, who knows, who knows? And so they sat for a while longer in silence at the cleared table, at opposite ends, and listened, of one accord, to the night rain falling outside, its rushing abraded for gradually lengthening intervals and at the same time magnified by the highway traffic, while indoors, in the inn, they heard the innkeeper talking up in his private quarters, very loudly, loudly the way some people do on the telephone? no, loudly in a different way, and it took a long time for the two of them downstairs to realize that the man was talking in his sleep, and thus, in his sleep, with no one but himself.

Although the voice echoed through the building, clearly and distinctly, what the sleeper was saying remained incomprehensible. And yet it sounded like a language if ever there was one, not a foreign, unfamiliar one but an old, familiar one, perhaps familiar from ancient times. Incomprehensible? Yes. Without meaning? Meaningless? No. This voice coming so distinctly from the top floor, without stress or strain, without ever being raised, projected an authority fundamentally different from that of any official announcement on a public square, or from a summoner-to-prayer. And this authority came from the impression that this language they were hearing toward midnight seemed to have been spoken before all other languages. At the same time the voice making itself heard in this language had nothing domineering about it. Neither this one voice nor the language it conveyed expressed any inclination to rule. Nothing was being ordered, commanded, proclaimed. The sense to be derived from it alternated instead between matter-of-factness and helpfulness: the facts are such and such, the situation is such and such, and accordingly, to the extent I have any say in the matter, this and this will be done, and gladly. What to make, then, of a third voice in the intervals, seemingly emanating from a different, much deeper layer of sleep, yet parallel to the other layer, this voice abruptly breaking through the voices of matter-of-factness and helpfulness: incoherent, beyond all languages, a stammering with an undertone of raucous laughter, then squalling, a small child's bawling that could not be pacified and would never again be appeased?

The two saw each other to the doors of their rooms, he going with her to hers, and then she going with him to his, and then he seeing her back to hers. The time had come for saying good-bye. Yes, although the fruit thief and the pizza-or-whatever delivery boy had joined forces only late that morning, they had the same feeling that this was goodbye. And each of them had the urge to give the other one some gift in parting. Something from me for you, and from you for me! Was that really necessary? Yes, it was necessary. And thus more time passed while they did nothing but stand in the inn's hallway and watch each other silently search for something that could serve as a gift. No matter what the boy dug out of his pockets: nothing fit the bill, not his jackknife, not the ballpoint pen with the restaurant's name printed on it, etc., until finally she took something from his hand, a piece of shoelace, a clothespin, a bottle opener, a metal capsule. And she? She had him give her his jacket, so she could mend the rip from the jungle thorns; she would hang the jacket on his room's door handle when she was done.

Having finished that chore, Alexia/Alicia lay awake for a long time in the room she had picked for the night. She had picked it for a special feature: it was located under a staircase, not one of the inside staircases but the one on the outer wall of the old structure, made not of wood but of stone. The room under the exterior stone stairs had perhaps been used at one time as a stall and later converted into a guestroom, entered from inside the inn and available as an overflow in case all the other rooms were taken. And now, with the house almost empty, she had chosen this particular space, the chamber under the stairs. She had been wishing for a good while that she could spend time in a space like this, even if only for one night. And now the opportunity had presented itself. Now or never. And what did she expect of lying in such close quarters, almost squeezed in, with a window hardly larger than an arrow slit? She just wanted to lie this way for a night, like her namesake Alexius.

But this chamber was no shed. Cramped though it was, it offered comforts, as well as a sense of security. To be able to twist and turn in this smallest imaginable space could enhance one's sense of freedom and independence, and the narrowness of the bed contributed to that sense. The little chamber exuded cleanliness, even without the shower tucked into one corner.

As she looked at herself in the mirror—just a long gaze into her eyes—she became aware that for a change she had not thought of her family even once all day, of either her mother or her father, or of the one who of them all was sometimes closest to her, her brother, the growing boy, the adolescent. Not only had she forgotten to think of them during the day—the three of them had not so much as come to mind, even in passing. It was as if she had forgotten all about her loved ones. They had not even existed. Mother, brother, father had left her consciousness.

And as she continued to gaze into her own eyes, she thought: As it should be! Her having forgotten her family had let good things happen to them, they had all gotten a breath of fresh air, her mother, father, and beloved brother; the latter, the one of the three perhaps most at risk, had been whisked by magic into a halfway-safe realm, for that day at least, for the time being. Of that she was certain. How it calmed her to have been rid of her near and dear so completely for the day, and furthermore it had a strengthening effect, including for her. To forget her family: an idea? And what did *idea* mean? Something that was meaningful and would remain so beyond this one day. "You'll see," she said under her breath to herself in the mirror. "We'll see!"

Nonetheless she could not resist looking at her mobile phone, her *portable*, to see if she had any messages. There were two, one from her brother, and one from her father. Her brother: "Come! I have something to tell you." Her father wrote that he had gone on ahead of her into Picardy and for the following evening would be expecting her, her brother, and, if the heavens or whatever proved gracious, also their mother, though he did not yet know where, because the place he had pictured did not exist anymore, or he had not been able to find it, which often happened with a favorite place, or he, the wannabe geographer, had got lost on the way there—typical of the "geographer without a sense of direction," an epithet that fit his entire life. From her mother, nothing. Also nothing from her friend on the bank of the Siberian river. Right now even just a word from her would have been welcome, but that morning's message still cheered her, and besides, off there in the distant east a new day had long since dawned.

The one clothes hook on the wall held a piece of clothing, apparently forgotten, a shawl? No, a scarf for wearing around the neck, made of silk. And she could tell that it had not been there long. How could she tell? Remembering all the garments left behind on coat trees in bars, restaurants, inns: usually they had been hanging there for a long time, very long. This scarf, however, looked fresh, forgotten only one or two days earlier. Forgotten? Left on purpose?

After she turned off the light, a familiar scent wafted through the little chamber under the stairs. A fragrance brushed her nostrils that did not come from outside, either from the rain or the rain-soaked fields, or from the highways. Her mother's perfume, just one whiff before it was gone, seeming to come from below, not from the bed but from the floor, its wide wooden boards, suitable for a spacious hall, but in the teeny-tiny room resting directly on the base of the wall. So her mother had been in that very room. She had not spent the night there; she had slept elsewhere. For a person like her mother the little chamber under the stairs was out of the question. (Or maybe not?) At any rate, the bed was too short for the lady banker, who was tall. Or who knows, maybe exactly right for one time, one night, a special one, *una notte speciale*? No. She had just taken a quick look around the room, was using the bank holiday, which she could declare at will—such was the degree of her motherpower—to set out on an inspection tour of every hotel and guest room, *chambre d'hôte*, in the entire country, listed on Google or elsewhere as located under a staircase, *sous un escalier*.

An inspection tour of all under-stairs lodgings: for what purpose, objective, goal? What would she do with this research on sheds, crash pads, broom closets, hideaways for deserters and Resistance fighters, holding pens for misbehaving children, death cells for those slated to be executed at dawn? Simply check out whatever came her way. Check out all these caves hidden under staircases, and in particular do research on herself.

That was where she had stood, her tall mother—as big as a giant at night to her daughter as a child—on the chamber's threshold, one foot outside, one inside, stooping almost double—so low was the chamber's door frame—and, as she looked into the interior, *el interior del morada* (Teresa de Avila's Spanish term was usually translated as "bower"), simultaneously scanning her own interior, taking in the smallest, darkest, most out-of-the-way and hidden bower among all the bowers, *moradas*, in the *castillo*, the castle, which taken all together formed her soul, *el alma*, and not hers alone. Her daughter wondered whether this bower, or this particular corner of her mother's soul, had presented itself to her during her inspection tour in the same gleaming lily-white garment in which she occasionally claimed to encounter the entire castle of her soul. At that thought her child, the fruit thief, could be heard laughing her child's laugh inside the pitch-black chamber.

Behind her closed eyelids writing scrolled by again, marched past, still handwriting, regular, illegible, at most with individual letters lighting up now and then. It seemed to her as if this parade of writing had also been filing past during the day, without interruption, not visible when her eyes were open, and she, the superstitious one, took that as a good sign for the following day. There it was, the writing, there it went, there it ran, there it flickered and flared, indecipherable, present, close at hand.

Already half asleep, she had the sensation that the rumbling and roaring of the traffic on the two highways was dwindling. Nonetheless it remained the overwhelming presence in the chamber, forcing its way through the stone walls, which had fissures everywhere. Except that in her half-asleep state the sound felt less intrusive, also a great deal clearer, and the hum of the engines seemed more and more to provide the undertone for other sounds, making them audible in the first place. Tone? Yes, tone.

The other sounds, the other tones: these were the secret ones, the sounds and tones of secrecy. Similar to the parade of writing behind closed lids, they made themselves heard afresh, fresher than ever amid the racket. They all seemed to originate in the immediate vicinity, in the chamber itself, by her feet, side, head as she was falling asleep. Strange, or maybe not strange after all, that it was specifically sounds usually ignored, if not abhorred, that counted now. Not a mosquito whining by her ear? No, not that. The rain drumming in the gutter? Nothing secretive about that. Sounds that came across as secretive on the other hand, reminding her of her half-sleep, were for instance the whooshing and swooshing of the thread as she had pulled it through the needle to mend the boy's jacket an hour earlier—or when had that been? And she experienced as secretive a sound, otherwise ignored, if not unheard, that a woodworm was making somewhere near her ear, in the bedstead, scraping away at even, melodic intervals. The scraping and rasping of a woodworm a melody? During that night, yes, a secretive one. Added to that the rising and falling hum of a fly, newborn or dying. Added to that the flapping of the curtain, too large for the tiny window, in the rainy night wind, and added to that the crackling, as it cooled, of the travel iron, with which half an hour before, here in Picardy? or half a month ago in

Siberia? she had "pressed," or what expression did they use earlier? her dress for the next day . . . and added to that . . . The secretivenesses expanded, amid the racket from outside, the space in the chamber, and not it alone; they played for her as she was falling asleep, lulled her to sleep. And this, too: still superstitious as she was falling asleep, she took it as a good sign for the following day that these secret sounds turned up again at the end of the day. —Let us see. —Us? Who are we? —We.

She dreamed that she had no other dream than of herself and him, all night long. Who was he? He was he. And all that night their becoming a couple was in the offing. A powerful and seemingly gentle drama was unfolding between him and her. It was the kind of drama in which nothing abrupt happened, all was calm, a steady swelling, building, taking possession of one by the other, of the other by the one. Not merely nothing abrupt, no single incident occurred, actually nothing at all, and again nothing, and yet again nothing. She did not touch him, nor did he touch her. They did not walk or run toward each other, did not post themselves in front of each other, did not fall to their knees in unison, did not lie down next to each other, let alone on top of each other. All that could be said of them: that they faced each other—not standing, not sitting, just facing. True, they were meant for each other and desired each other—in this context being meant for each other was identical with desiring each other, and vice versa, but any move, any action, any act was out of the question. Or wrong: becoming a couple was unnecessary. Or, to state it unambiguously: a conventional conjoining of the two sexes does not enter into it. Any sort of sexual conjoining, including a telepathic one, if such a thing exists, lay outside the domain of these two.

So the two had a domain of their own, of their very own? But what was special about this domain? It was a domain in which she, the woman, and he, the man, were rid of their separate bodies—relieved of their respective bodies and at the same time all body, purely incarnate and nothing but incarnate. In desiring each other, their two bodies had soared to being only one, single, pure being, and this one being oscillated all night long, without end, unwilling to end, back and forth, desiring and consummating, consummating and desiring. Their domain was beyond time and place, and also beyond man and woman, yet owed its power to the physical fact that it was a man and a woman whose bodies, unassisted, flowed together all night long, into a collateral body, a third one, which rendered the other two superfluous. How the two of them, the one being, needed that. Infinite need. Infinite sweetness. Hallelujah! Plentiful night, luxuriant night. But was that possible solely between a man and a woman? Solely between a man and a woman! And again, solely in a dream? No, that could not be.

The gentlest awakening in the morning, a feeling like Sunday. And it actually was Sunday, even in the narrow chamber under the stairs. Staying in bed and letting the effect of the dream linger. Such dreams had become far too rare in the meantime. Or was that true only of her? And already the dream was fading, losing the source of its strength, the feeling that grounded it.

Never in her life would she experience the consummation, even approximately, of what he and she, she and he, the man, her man, had just been/meant to each other in the dream, and not merely to each other, to the whole human world. For her, for a person like her, there was no right person, no right one for her on earth. Or she, the fruit thief, was not the right one for any man, for any right man. She had to make do with her dream until the hour of her death, amen.

But no, no amen, no "so be it, so be it for me!" No prayer of acquiescence to some alleged fate. Instead pounding the chamber's stone wall with her fist. And a sentence from a Sunday sermon came back to her, one she had heard from a priest high in the pulpit in a distant strange land—where such sermons from on high were still customary: "Infinite oscillation of love between the soul and God, that is heaven." So who said that he, her man, one of flesh and blood, had not long since begun to make his way to her? Who said that he, her man, did not exist and would never exist? She herself, she alone said that. And what she said to herself alone: was she obligated to believe it? No, not to a nunnery. No heavenly bridegroom. An earthly one!

Hallelujah! Morning light coming through a fissure in the stone wall before her eyes, pale gray. The rain had stopped, but the sun remained hidden behind clouds. Pulling open the ceiling-to-floor curtain from the arrow-slit-narrow window. The iron grille sparkling with raindrops. Pushing open the grille. A fleeting ray of sun striking the floor: she wanted to pick it up like dust. On the parapet outside one apple placed there for the night, its stem sticking up and the stem's hollow filled with rainwater. In the gutter overhead the scraping sounds of a blackbird searching for nest-building material. The morning glow, Sundayish, on the apple's round cheek, something not yet investigated, begging to be researched. Ah, so much to be discovered, beyond the supposedly world-changing discoveries. Ah, putting on her Sunday dress, freshly pressed the night before. Dressing up for the day with her earrings made by the Athabaskan woman of the Yukon in Alaska. How firm the floor felt underfoot in the narrow chamber, there in particular, even if one had to stoop to stand, indeed precisely in that position. Now church bells from who knows where, even if there had been no glad tidings for a long time, and perhaps never would be again. Oh, come on: those were no church bells calling the faithful to Mass. It was the clock in the bell tower. Normal time. Real time. Real? Down to street level, highway level. Do something! Do something! —Do something even though it's Sunday? —Do something! —But what? One way or the other:

the gray sky, with lowering clouds, filled her with desire to do something. Let it stay gray!

She promptly found something to do downstairs in the inn's dining room. The host, the former and, if he had it his way, future one, was seated at the table, and she, the guest, served him without asking, and without objection he let himself be served by the young stranger. She knew how to work the coffee machine, knew just what to do in the kitchen, as if she had been working there forever, did not need to ask where she would find the napkins, the egg spoons, the trivets, the olive oil, the pepper grinder, the salt cellar (filled with coarse salt straight from the saltworks). The tinkling of her earrings as she swept back and forth, without seeming to be in a hurry, between the kitchen and the dining room: that, too, a secret sound amid the roar of the Sunday morning traffic, especially on the highway leading to Dieppe on the Atlantic.

As he had the night before from his private quarters, the innkeeper seated at the long table in the dining room let his voice be heard, not so loud this time but clearly audible and, in contrast to before, understandable, word for word, sentence for sentence. Not clear to whom he was speaking—himself? the stranger? As he spoke, he looked straight ahead, his back very straight, craning his neck, as if to keep an eye on something in the distance and in the farthest corner of the kitchen, large even for a restaurant. Usually when someone in the dining room speaks to someone in the kitchen who is banging pots and pans around, the person in the kitchen has to run into the dining room and ask what was just said, but she did not need to do that. Even with the clatter of plates and skillets, not a single word of his tirade escaped her.

The innkeeper had begun by describing how buttoning his special Sunday shirt had exhausted him when he got up that morning. Just choosing one of the three buttons on the cuffs of the right and left sleeves—the closest, the middle one, or the farthest one, which had the advantage that if he chose it, the sleeve would lie the smoothest around his wrist, like a second skin, and a more good-looking and better skin, too. And then, after the decision, the problem of forcing the button he had chosen into the buttonhole. Yes, forcing it, for the button was either too big, or the hole was too small for the button—the shirt's special Sunday material having shrunk in the wash because the water was too hot. For a good eight minutes—that unlucky number eight—and several seconds he had struggled in the sweat of his brow to get the sleeve buttoned, and time and again the button had slipped, jumped, popped out of the hole just when he had almost pushed it through. This indication of time applied only to the easier part, however, buttoning the right sleeve with his left hand. The other sleeve took twice as much time, and cost twice as much sweat. Or had the opposite sleeve been the easier one, and the first-mentioned one the real torment? He could not say anymore. And then came the challenge of opening the vacuum-packed supplies from the food warehouse, the butter in restaurant portions, the ham, the cheese. All the packages were labeled *ouverture facile* (easy to open)—but then: a broken thumbnail, and what was opened? Neither butter nor ham nor cheese. He said he already felt discouraged and debilitated, and today was not the first time; as soon as he read *ouverture facile* on products of any sort, or *montage* or *installation facile* on devices that needed to be assembled or installed, he was positively traumatized, pardon this word, by all these things that were allegedly easy to open and child's play to operate.

He fell silent for a while and then began to speak again: "I'm not giving up my inn. And first of all I'll rename the Auberge de Dieppe, will rebaptize it, solemnly, at a festival to which everyone will be invited, from near and far—the host and party-giver requests your presence: come one, come all—rename it the Auberge de l'Interieur du Pays, the inn of the country's interior. True enough: the ocean represents distance. But in the country's interior: a different distance. And here, at my renovated inn in the country's interior it will begin anew, this distance, here it will start, this will be its starting point. How this place has found its way into my heart, this place where my father before me was the innkeeper, and my grandfather before him. Praise be to him, and praise be to the two highways, the one to the ocean and the one into the countryside. How I love it, the rumble of cars heading in both directions. And how I miss their turning off from one highway or the other to stop at my caravanserai. If they knew how beautiful I find them all in their vehicles on those crossing highways, the various profiles, the foreheads, the noses, the bald heads, the ones with weak chins: if word reached them of how beautiful they are, one and all, they would become good people, and furthermore they'd be so good as to turn in at my parking lot and let me host them, those so-and-sos, those no-goods, those goof-offs. But for the time being it will be enough if they just raise their arms and wave to me. Silhouettes waving greetings! Yes, here at my place it will begin anew, distance, also for you careless ones, you unfaithful ones, you bastards, you con men, you deadbeats, you lousy customers. But not another word about you—back to this place: look here, over there: see the rain puddle trembling in the Sunday wind. See the racing card for the steeplechase in Enghien blowing across the spandrel between the two highways. Over there in the drainage ditch, see the cattail's stalk, with the seeds blowing away. And over there: the old cow-breeding platform: ah, how the bull keeps mounting the cow and sliding off! A condom caught in the hedge. The tumbledown privy. The dog who's been taken out for his Sunday poop on the stubble field but is having trouble—how he strains. The poster from the spring before last advertising the Jules César Disco. The cross for the American soldier killed in 1944; it's leaning, and soon it will topple over. And now: the driver of a car lighting a cigarette. A woman letting her hair down. One driver who yells "Connard!" (asshole) at another. One honking at another to let him pass. One who forces others to brake suddenly. The child on the back seat waving—to whom?—ah, it's been so long since I've seen a child . . . Which brings me back to all of you, whom I invite: come one, come all. No, I'm not leaving this place. No, I refuse to give up this triangle. No, I will not let my inn die. I love this triangular intersection more than the world. Here, in this place, it not only originates, distance; it's here, before my eyes, an arm's length away, what am I saying, an elbow's length away. The triangle here: a place of refuge since early times. And that it shall be again, and remain."

Only now did the innkeeper, who had been staring straight ahead the entire time, turn his head to where she was standing in the doorway to the kitchen, and at last she saw his face, or he let her see it: not nearly as old as she had imagined, positively youthful, no—childlike, especially the eyes. And at the same time it was a face expressing something that can perhaps appear unexpectedly only on the face of an old person, a friendly fierceness, a fierce friendliness.

She joined him at the table in response to his silent gesture. "How sweet you are to join me!" he wanted to exclaim, in those very words, which he had once heard from a guest, long ago, when one of his, the innkeeper's, young waitresses had obliged, long, so long ago, by doing the same thing the beautiful young stranger had just done for him. He kept it to himself, however, as if it were not proper to speak it out loud. Instead, what he said next began with an exclamation. An exclamation! Exclaiming: at most in a dream, sound asleep, was he capable of this, which, he was certain, indeed certain through and through, and not only since yesterday, constituted the best of what a human being was capable of, next to reverential awe. Silent awe and loud exclamation.

And his exclamation came out—loud but lacking resonance, without sonority. That, too, perhaps not unusual: a substantial body, "the typical innkeeper," with a wide rib cage, thick neck, large, round innkeeper's head with plump cheeks, reminiscent of old painted inn signs—and the voice, by contrast, the exclaimer's voice, thin, reedy, as if it were simultaneously making fun of what it was exclaiming; did not really mean it; perhaps even meant to serve up the opposite of what it seemed to be proclaiming with such urgency.

The old innkeeper's exclamation, squeaked out in the voice of a first-grader on the first day of school, there in the triangle formed by the highways, went thus: "Yet how I miss having neighbors here. So many neighborhood celebrations, yet not a single real, solid neighbor."

As he continued speaking, without exclaiming, it became clear that it was less flesh-and-blood neighbors he had in mind than images of neighborliness, remembered from childhood, from old books or from who knows where. He was thinking first of neighboring houses, and not so much of doors and windows, not to mention human figures or at least their silhouettes, but almost exclusively of neighboring roofs, and on the roofs perhaps one glass tile that determined the pattern in the tiles, whether intended or imaginary, and then the line of tiles on the ridgepole, one tile overlapping the next, the lead tile or leader, and then all the ridge tiles in succession, as if confined by an invisible fence, forming a long cavalcade heading in an unnamed direction, independent of any weather- or windvane above them showing north-south-east-west. It was the roofs that provided the image and the sense, image as well as sense, image as sense, of a neighborhood, or had once provided it, and on the roofs, even more vividly than the rest, the chimneys, the smokestacks, *les chiminées,* or no, the smoke, and the ways in which it eddied from the chimneys.

A sense of community and at the same time an image of

community of a particular kind, acquired by standing at the window in one's own house and seeing above the roofs in the immediate vicinity—which became the vicinity only by virtue of being seen—in calm weather all the vertical columns of smoke in parallel, or in windy weather all the columns of smoke likewise parallel but on the diagonal, and in stormy weather parallel on the horizontal, in a near-hurricane the smoke breaking up and blowing away the moment it left the chimney, the *cheminée*, and, probably most evocative of a neighborhood, the sense-image in quiet, clear weather, when the smoke columns remain almost invisible, perceptible—more intuited than seen—only in the way the air curls and ruffles above the roofs, with the sense of belonging, as it pertains to smoke, whether in columns or swaths, from smaller chimneys in comparison to smoke from larger, more massive, taller ones, seeming inversely proportional to their outer volumes, the "spatial capacity" of the fireplaces: strange, or not strange after all. At times a veritable tenderness for the neighboring roof, even for the entire house, and, why not, its—unknown and continuing to be unknown—occupants, whenever their chimney was as narrow as a stovepipe and no larger than a flowerpot, not even as tall as a chef's toque. "Whenever"? Yes, often, so often.

And finally, after the innkeeper had remained silent for a while, he went back to exclaiming, again in that reedy voice, so suddenly that the stranger at his side started, as if at a voice of thunder: "But in truth how often, more often than often, above all when observing a column of smoke rising straight as a die into the sky, I've seen the invisible other person in the house below as Abel, and myself here as his evil brother, as Cain!" After shouting these words, he promptly turned his attention to a partially filled-out Sudoku, moving his pencil back and forth over it as if on a loom. It looked as though he was preparing in this fashion to write a letter! Except that he had no one to whom to write.

Before departing, the fruit thief withdrew for a little while to the chamber under the stone staircase. It was as if there, of all places, where there was hardly room to take more than three steps, hardly room to turn around, she could gather strength for what was to come. This little chamber, so out of the way, was to serve as an exercise room: that was how she saw it, that was how she defined it, that was what her story and that of the others called for. No equipment was needed, neither dumbbells nor a treadmill nor chest expanders. She could also spare herself her early-morning workout, which consisted of practicing with a rod as an imaginary javelin, but without hurling it; stretching her fingers rhythmically and curling them around an imaginary piece of fruit in an imaginary tree. If the chamber contained a piece of equipment, it was one that strengthened without specifically building strength: just a book. Strengthening, and, why not, strength-building reading. How did that work? A book as equipment? The one she was reading now, and went on reading, yes. Did the book read itself, like many? No, "it" did not read itself; she would be the one to read it. A decision had to be made, this very day. —But what has to be decided? —No answer. Smoothing out the page corner folded down as a bookmark the day before: it felt to her as if someone else had folded it.

As she lay on the cot and continued reading the story of the near-child who spent a day, a night, and another day in another country without his father's noticing, when he came home, that he had been gone, the story merged for the reader into another story, acquired, while she paused in her reading, a new variation, one that was not in the book but could not have come into being without the book. She continued her reading now in a standing position, like a runner at the starting line, with one leg out in front.

First of all the story became that of her brother, a decade younger than she, who was here in the Vexin, in Picardy, after prematurely leaving the Lycée Henri IV in Paris, despite having good grades, and since the end of winter had been learning the trade of a carpenter, *un charpentier.* In the episode that came to her, as if of its own accord, while she was reading, her brother did not remain alone in that neighboring country as he spent the night in the cable-railway station he had broken into. In the middle of the night someone joined him, supposedly a mountain hiker, who claimed he had lost his way in the high alpine region and had only now come upon the cable-railway station. Stretched out side by side on the bare floor, since the hut had no benches, let alone mattresses, the two strangers chatted for a while in the dark, as was customary in mountain huts, as if they were old friends.

Suddenly the new arrival broke off the conversation in mid-sentence, as he was talking about the weather forecast for the following day or whatever. Had he fallen asleep? No sleeper's breathing to be heard, no breathing at all. The silence in the pitch-black hut, however, was no deathly silence but rather one in which someone was merely holding his breath, preparing for some act, and not a good one. The hero of the story, the near-child, her dear, dear brother, was in danger, in mortal danger. No weapon available except the little jackknife that he tried to open in his pocket—but the blade jammed.

Close beside him in the dark a crackling now, which little by little increased and at the same time, as if from above, gradually came closer to the boy stretched out on the floor. At intervals, however, the crackling repeatedly fell silent, held back, was completely absent for a while—before it started up again, louder than before, unmistakably closer, now almost above his dear head, and inside the crackling, at its core, so it seemed, an even more localized crashing, banging, which a moment later would break forth and fall upon him—which the child in the dark mountain hut in the other country was almost wishing for: that was how ghostly every one of those in-between moments was, with the ominous silences, so chest-bursting.

How could she have drifted away from the book, putting her brother into the role of the world-forsaken child, into a ghost story, if not a horror story? So contrary to what she had imagined, the chamber where she was reading had not provided her after all with powers of protection?

Back to the book, to reading word for word. There, too, the crackling in the dark, the crashing, the great crash. But in the book what crashed down on the young person lying on the floor, what fell on him, turned out, when he switched on his flashlight, to be nothing but his backpack, which had been standing the whole time on the floor by his head, and then, who knows why, slowly, very slowly, began to tip until it tumbled over with a racket. Away with ghosts. No more horror. The boy was safe and sound and would get home just fine the next day, also safe and sound in another sense, with a secret that would go with him through life. Accordingly, the chamber had been the right place for reading after all. Book and chamber. And besides, she had read there at the right time. Of all the variations in the way her superstition manifested itself, was reading the most tangible? The one she trusted most? The one of which she could expect the most? One variation above and beyond all the established, all too established variations?

She had faith that with reading, through and in reading, by virtue of and thanks to it, she could protect someone and actually was protecting him, the one who mattered to her. That was both her faith and her certainty, "the certitude of faith," as it was once described.

In the certainty that with her reading she had provided her brother with reliable protection, she promptly gave him a call. Without wishing him a good morning or a happy Sunday etc., and, above all, without asking him how he was feeling, the sister/fruit thief babbled into his ear that she was about to set out to join him. She did not let him get a word in edgewise, since it was clear: he could not be in anything but good spirits, infinitely better than during the night, and the best was yet to come. Only after ending the call did she wonder why he had not burst out babbling in happy anticipation like her. What had his loud breathing in response to her babbling meant, a breathing almost like groaning? Had he wanted to tell her something?

Telling and groaning? A deep yellow shimmer shining through the fissures in the room's stone wall instead of the rainy gray light: the sun was back. And strange, or also not: she wanted the sun gone for the day ahead. No sun rays today. But the sun remained, and shone and shone. Too bad about the pale gray.

To say good-bye to the inn located between the highways—another good-bye—a glance into the room that her companion of the previous day had left in the gray light of dawn, heading back to the *ville nouvelle* to deliver food on his motor scooter, a fairly lucrative undertaking on a Sunday, when quite a few customers would open the door still in their pajamas or bathrobes in midafternoon. His room left tidy, with the table and chair aligned as if in geometric order, the blanket and sheets on the bed tucked in tightly: a bedmaking technique learned in the military, in boarding school, in the orphanage. In one corner of the room, on what she recognized as a freshly swept floor—she was an expert—something bounced, a small thing, the pom-pom that must have come loose from Valter's (that was his name again for a moment) woolen cap. She picked up the pom-pom carefully, pocketed it even more carefully, touched her forehead with one finger and pressed so hard and so long that in the middle she made a round dark spot that stayed there until the evening and perhaps even longer, a spot such as can sometimes be seen on the foreheads of Indian women.

As she left the Auberge de Dieppe, aka Inn of the Country's Interior, the innkeeper blocked her way on floor after floor, on landing after landing, from column to column down in the dining room. He did so unintentionally, involuntarily, out of a clumsiness that had temporarily come over him, and she, familiar with this sort of thing in herself, accepted it matter-of-factly, swerving exaggeratedly to avoid him, as if it were a game.

The old person was not playing. He simply did not realize he was blocking the young stranger's way. After the hour of fierce friendliness his face now showed nothing but earnestness, with round eyes uncannily large for someone his age. Bitter earnestness? Pleading, imploring earnestness.

Likewise, because she had waited on him like a servant or a maid, he kept giving her small new chores, which delayed her departure. The filters for the coffee machine had to be washed, down to the last speck of grounds, but also dried with a dishtowel—"Not that one, it scratches, the one over there!" On one of the burners in the kitchen she had overlooked a crumb from the white bread toasted for Sunday breakfast. In her sleeping chamber the little window was not latched, and the curtain was not drawn properly. And look: that spot of candlewax on the table in the dining room, and the jukebox not unplugged!

And when it came time for her to pay, he first disappeared for a long time to fetch pen and paper with which to make out the bill, from who knows where in the realm over which he had previously held sway. How's that? He let her pay him for the room? Yes, she herself had requested that; the chamber under the stairs had been worth more than money to her, and to the former innkeeper—once a businessman, always a businessman—her "wish" to pay seemed perfectly natural, or he was merely pretending, to gain time. And how the process of filling out the bill dragged on. He drew the numbers and letters, literally drawing them, wrote out the numbers in words, putting them in parentheses, even the numbers designating the date and the day, before which he inserted *dimanche* (Sunday), then the month and the year.

He needed so much time for this that she finally sat down beside him and watched him writing and drawing, until at last "Auberge de l'Interieur du Pays" had been inscribed. Whereupon he, after the young stranger—he did not want to know her name—had placed the banknote on the table (a small amount, but money was money), disappeared again for a long time to get change, at least three times longer than before. How he dragged his feet when he finally returned, and if it was intentional, it, too, was done in all seriousness, like each of his previous instructions and actions, certainly not in jest.

But then it was time to leave the old inn and step outside, outside into the fresh air, and suddenly it seemed to be high time. Otherwise it would be too late. What would be too late? Everything. Everything would be too late.

Just as she, after a silently drawn-out leave-taking, was just about to step over the threshold—which was high and wide, from a different era—a dark shadow fell over it. The innkeeper, the master of the house, was standing outside, as if to prevent her, the guest, from leaving his inn, just as the previous evening he had seemed at first to bar her and her companion from entering. In addition to blocking the door, all it would have taken would have been for him to spread his arms. But no, his arms dangled limply at his side as only arms can, old arms as well as young arms and children's arms (perhaps least of all the arms of small children), and after a moment he stepped aside to let her out.

He offered to relieve her of her luggage and keep it for her at least until that evening. She should cross the open countryside with both hands free. What gave one more freedom, was more beneficial to one's soul? He, at least, had aspired all his life to travel without being loaded down with baggage, at most with a toothbrush. She responded that it did her good to make her way across the countryside with a load on her shoulders. Without proper weight she felt something was missing. When she was traveling for a longer time, she said, the day usually did not begin to count, to mean something, to have value, until she shouldered a pack that was not too light; only then did the day become a real day, even if that did not happen until late midday or even sundown. Especially when crossing foreign countries, before the day became a day, she would experience, at the moment when she took her first step with such a load, a special light. Then she felt oriented in the foreign country, reliably, which did not happen in her own country. He then asked whether the high Vexin plateau, Picardy, and especially the *département* of the Oise constituted foreign territory for her, and she said yes. He said he had noticed something she and her companion, the one *à la peau matte* (to translate that as "with the dark skin" would be wrong), had in common, no, two things: first of all, the irregular part in their hair, those two highly irregular, if not wild, zigzags that resembled each other "to a hair," and then the veins in their temples, also alike to a hair, hers on the right side, the boy's on the left, or vice versa, forming wavy lines, several close together under and on top of each other, protruding from the skin of their brows in a way usually described as a physical manifestation of anger, but in their case already visible, swollen even when they were calm, perhaps resulting from the tiredness they had in common, except that the veins were prominent in her, the young woman's, forehead even now, as distinct as such veins otherwise appeared only on sculptures, and then only on the temples of male figures. She asked whether that meant anything, and without replying he gave her, as a parting gift, the striped feather of a buzzard, and also a wild boar's tooth, a fang almost as long as a finger, sharp, and hard as granite.

He accompanied her to the path that led away from the spandrel between the highways, the path only he, the native, knew. She allowed herself to be accompanied, as if that were proper for setting out on a Sunday, and even let him give her a leg up when they reached the stone wall that separated the path from the highway, "as in olden times," they said at the same moment, in one breath. Yet a leg up like that was not necessary; the wall was hardly shoulder-high, and was crumbling away. Alone on the path, she again walked backward for a while, without checking to see where she was and where the path was taking her, her eyes fixed on the site that had sheltered her for the night and up to now. Site? Place? Yes, there it was. That was where it had taken place. There it shimmered, the arrow-slit-small opening in the wall of the chamber under the outside staircase. Play on!

A sudden urge to swing onto the back of a horse and ride out onto the field, her very own field, "our" Sunday be damned; yet she had hardly ever ridden a horse. Instead she strode along for a while without looking up, her eyes fixed, not exactly on the toes of her shoes, as her father had advised, but rather intently on the ground—she had eyes for nothing but the ground at her feet. Seen from behind and from a greater and greater distance, she looked heavy, frumpy and dumpy even, almost a hunchback, with a military-style pack weighing her down as she trotted along, weaving a bit: hard to believe this was the same person who only a little while ago had danced through the rooms at the inn in the role of a maid.

Once again strength was her main concern: in keeping her eyes focused on the ground as she went along the path, she was hoping to draw strength from it, or recover her strength from underground. And she succeeded. That meant not looking up, at least for the time being, from the light sand of the path on which she was literally marching along. Keeping her eyes fixed on the ground. Avoiding raising her head and looking for anything. To be on guard above all: against looking up at the sky, also trying to glimpse the farthest horizon—her strength would abandon her at once. It helped that the path had no puddles from the previous night's rain in which any distant parts and, perish the thought, the sky, the high summer sky, could be mirrored, breaking her strength-rhythm as she strode along. The Vexin plateau here in Picardy consisted of porous limestone and water-absorbing gypsum, and the rain had filtered into its underground strata before the morning's sunrise.

This, too, helped strengthen her: moving along, her gaze consistently lowered to the ground, in whose depths innumerable veins of water crossed and converged before coming up to the surface as springs far off at one foot of the plateau or another. For several moments she thought the many thousands of underground runnels could be heard up above amid the Sunday stillness of the countryside through which she was plodding—one step after the other, with nothing but the sandy path before her eyes—as a single, uniform sound, a whooshing from the plateau's interior. Or did the whooshing and swooshing come from buried pipelines, their presence indicated by the yellow triangles posted along the path, that brought natural gas from Russia or wherever? Or was it oil making that sound in an underground pipeline (not the one that began on the edge of the Arctic Circle in Point Barrow, Alaska, ah, Russia, ah, Alaska)? Whether instead of rushing water it was gas or oil: that, too, lent her strength, perceptible in the balls of her feet, which felt bouncy. Should she call her friend in Siberia to give her Sunday greetings? That was not necessary now; it was as if she were greeting her just by making her way across the Picardian high plateau.

After a while she could risk stopping, raising her head, letting her eyes drift away from the path, which in the meantime had widened into a lane, dotted with horse manure (was the term *horse apples* still in use?). Her first impression from the landscape, devoid of forests, seemingly flat—unmistakably a plateau: she was in a part of the world where the part also stood for the whole, forming its center. Couldn't an impression like this arise anywhere, at a definite, undefinable moment, under certain or uncertain conditions? Not just anywhere, but yes, here and there, and thus also here at this moment.

The area, and with it the whole earth, extended to the horizons in the form of a disk, a not entirely flat one, but at the spot where the fruit thief was standing and marking the center, slightly bulging, and on its distant edges gently falling off, and her next impression was that she was on the back of a whale, balancing on its highest point, a specific whale, the one by which, according to legend, Jonah, the reluctant prophet of doom, who had been tossed into the sea to be eaten by the fishes, was swallowed, and then had days and nights in the whale's stomach, before being spat out onto land, to prepare his prophecies of doom, for Nineveh or one of the other ancient cities. Instead of the whooshing and swooshing from underground, now from deep inside the whale's belly came Jonah's cranky, petty grumbling and grousing, invoking the end of the world.

But let's keep any cosmic allusions out of the story of the fruit thief and her loved ones. Out of this story, you biblical images, especially you Old Testament ones that suggest parallels to various current situations (see prophet of doom, see end of the world). In general, avoid like the plague and cholera any infection with old stories said to be "still relevant today." If an old biblical image must make an appearance in the fruit-thief story, at most one that was not relevant then and is still not relevant today, for instance the image painted both intimately and monumentally by Nicolas Poussin (from the small Norman town of Les Andelys, near the Picardian Vexin) in which Ruth and Boaz meet in the wheat field during the summer harvest and later become husband and wife. This picture remains to be discussed in this story and will remain so to the end.

With the sun in her face she continued in an easterly direction, heading toward morning, soon to become midday. The wind, gentle after the rain, blew across the high plateau from the west, from the province of evening, where almost an entire midsummer day would pass before evening arrived. The path, another one, wound in long curves, this time actually toward a castle, one of many in the Vexin. Every village had its castle, often hidden among farmhouses and not easy to find. This one, however, stood all by itself, and an earlier castle in the same location was said to have been built by William the Conqueror. But here, too: let's leave history out of it. Another rule was supposed to be in effect: touch on historical aspects only at a remove. So the fruit thief passed up the Conqueror's castle and turned off to cross the stubble fields, choosing pathlessness, getting off the beaten track. Unlike her mother she took little interest in castles, unless they were hidden. For a year she had lived near the palace of Versailles without ever feeling drawn to see it from the inside. Her father, who as a young man had, as he said, read "everything," commented once that he still could not understand why the land surveyor, or whatever he was, in Kafka's book was so determined to reach the castle on the hill rather than staying down below in the village tavern. As for her: castles did not tempt the fruit thief because they usually had no orchards.

Any small history, with a lowercase h, is said to be unable to avoid History, so-called, with a capital H, in the sense that Oskar, the stout, violent butcher-shop owner in a famous play by Horváth, says to innocent young Marianne, "You won't be able to avoid my love!" Is that how it is? Is that how it was? Will it be like that forever? Or not? Or maybe after all? However that might be: the first person the fruit thief ran into that Sunday on her cross-country course was one who, no joke, was hunting for his father, who had gone missing during the last days of the Second World War, more than seven decades earlier, in the Vexin.

She was just passing one of the cornfields that were almost the only ones on the high plateau that had not been harvested yet, the cutting not scheduled to be done until fall. The wind was causing a frenetic rustling in the corn fronds, a rustling close to a roar, unlike any other sound. Amid this rustling a different sound now became audible, moving around in the field, coming closer, then going farther away, back and forth, forward and back. She halted on the bare field next to the cornfield, bracing herself for the appearance of an enormous animal, as she had that time with her father in the forest, a stag at least, like the one depicted on the warning signs posted on the edge of various landscapes, leaping. And just as that time it was a human being that emerged, fighting his way through the corn stalks, which towered over him, and into the clear, but in his arms this time, instead of fruits of the forest, he was holding some bones, one on top of the other, thigh bones, or what he believed to be thigh bones.

But it was not these bones that made the person so eye-catching. It was more the brightness radiating from him in the moment when he stepped out of the cornfield, which, despite the sun shining everywhere else, was dark and gloomy, almost as black as night. There was nothing to fear from this bright figure, which remained bright when the man, after uttering a brief greeting, immediately began, without transition, as if it were perfectly natural, to talk about his decades-long search for his missing father.

The son, born during the war, had grown old in the meantime. But his father still appeared to him in dreams. Earlier on, indeed until just recently, the son had searched for him as someone among the living. According to his dreams, his father was still alive, hale and hearty, just hidden somewhere, but somewhere in this very area, where in an August like this one more than seventy years ago he had been seen for the last time. Of late, however, when his father turned up in a dream, he was someone else as well, and this someone pointed not to this one spot but to the entire region, the Vexin, Picardy, as his grave. In the dream the son thought he heard his father, or whoever was standing before him, singing, in the deep voice of Johnny Cash: "Ain't no grave can hold my body down!"

But who knows: who could say that his father was not still alive? Weren't there more and more hundred-year-olds nowadays? And hadn't the son, now over seventy, just published, in the Vexin weekly, on the page set aside for poems by local residents, right before the pages with homicides and drivers killed in fiery car crashes, a poem containing the line, which, translated freely, read, "Unlikely, yes, but hit the road and get a move on"? ("Invraisemble, mets-toi en route et deviens mobile!")

And accordingly, after he had tossed the bones back into the cornfield, one after the other, over his right, then his left shoulder, as if performing a ritual, he pulled out a photograph of his father as a very young man, as he had been doing for decades, and held it up to her face, convinced that it would enable her, the *randonneuse*, the wanderer, to recognize the one he was seeking. She would help him find his father. It had to be. His father could not remain lost and gone to the end of time. No pain more painful, no grief more grievous than that for the disappeared. It was not his father he was mourning, however, but his father's child. And nothing cried louder to the heavens than the lamentation for a lost child.

He saw it in the eyes of this stranger: she was his ally. She had earnestly committed his father's features to memory. If tears now came to his eyes, they would come to hers as well. But he did not weep. He did snuffle loudly, but out of confidence (different from hope, which he despised as so much hot air). As he turned away to continue his search, he gave her a hug, and she tolerated it, without, as he had experienced over and over in his life, and as one could witness when hugging occurred on television, patting his shoulder to tap out some emotion, like the opening bars of a piece of music, or "channel" it.

For a while she continued on her way, no longer heading due east, but with the sun sometimes in her face, sometimes on her right, sometimes on her left, crisscrossing the landscape, with nothing specific to tell or, to use the formula in old epics, "without any occurrences worthy of telling." But at the same time it was clear that in the course of this uneventful traversing of the landscape without fixing one's eye on, let alone observing, anything in particular, images would be transmitted to one and be absorbed, images that had nothing in common with photographic or painted ones of any kind, and certainly not biblical ones. These were profane images of the places and locales one passed, of places one did not register specifically but only in passing. If afterimages refused to form when one intentionally focused on or observed a person or object, the same rule applied to images of places in the world that did not call attention to their unique characteristics, did not offer details that jumped out at one. They became images only if one had not been conscious of them when in their presence. They coalesced only after the fact, but, in contrast to the usual afterimages, long after the fact, much, much later, often years and decades later, and not in one's eyes, behind one's eyelids, but all through one's body. Some morning or evening in the future, let's say eight years from now, the young woman making her way across the countryside without focusing on anything in particular would bend her arm in a room somewhere and only then register the wrought-iron roadside crucifix that she is passing at this moment, an image of past, present, and future all in one. Yes, strange, or perhaps not, an image of the future. She would step out of her room onto the balcony by the Porte d'Orléans or in another location, and from the hollow of her knee an image would well up and fill her being: the image of the water tower in Gypseuil, which she has just left behind, her thoughts elsewhere. She will take one step to the right on her balcony, and one bright wave, with a few foamy bubbles on the surface, in the brook called Reveillon, just beyond the village of Reilly, on the threshold of the village of Delincourt, will flash through the body and soul of the woman there on the balcony, emanating from the bottom of her foot or somewhere. She will lower her head and become aware of the rabbit hutch, long since empty, in the hamlet of Tumbrel, of a donkey's foal, alone and forsaken under a tree near the town of Vallangoujard, of a swallow's nest under the eaves of the church in Montjavault. She will spread her arms and feel the presence of Sarah Bernhardt's former estate on the Buttes de Rosne, the highest elevation on the Vexin plateau, with a view from outside of a wall of bookshelves, where a volume of Antonio Machado's poems will meet her eye in hindsight, its title *Los Soledades*. She will stand on tiptoe and find herself gazing at the laundromat on the edge of Chaumont-en-Vexin, with all the machines open and empty, except for one in whose drum a wad of blue, the color of a worker's overalls, turns to the left, then to the right; turned; will have turned. And images like these, afterimages from previous years and decades, if she let herself dwell on them, unlike the hourly and daily afterimages, would mean every time: "Play on. The game isn't over yet. You're in the game, my friend, still in the game."

The fruit thief was not crisscrossing the plateau but walking in widening spirals, as a sort of mirroring, at ground level, of the kites high in the sky, circling each other while at the same time steadily moving away and onward. In one of her spirals, marked by a cart track, someone caught up with her on a yellow bicycle, which she at first took for a postal bike. Could that be, a postal bike on a Sunday? And it turned out to be one after all, and the rider was a female mail carrier in uniform, wearing a broad-brimmed mail carrier's hat.

Upon the wanderer's stepping aside and greeting the cyclist, the woman stopped and explained, in answer to an unspoken question, that her husband, the regular *facteur*, had been sick for a week—nothing serious, just a summer flu—and she was the substitute, finding time only now, on Sunday, to make the rounds. Not a single letter in the mail, however. The preprinted official forms and tax documents in the panniers on either side of the bike were so heavy that pedaling, especially on the bumpy tracks through the fields and over the long stretches between towns, became arduous—could these materials be referred to as "letters," or only as "mail"? Still, she did have postcards to deliver, a small number, not many, sent by people from the area, few of whom—summer was harvesttime—were giving themselves vacations elsewhere, the majority in places for which there were no postcards; a very few cards came from tourist destinations farther away, or simply from Paris, with motifs such as the Sacré-Coeur, Notre-Dame, and the Eiffel Tower conveying pictorial greetings. Almost all the cards came from within France, which the substitute mail carrier regretted, since she and her husband collected stamps, but only foreign ones. On the other hand, the domestic, French stamps were often not canceled, so they could be removed and reused. Only in three Vexin villages did she have cards from other countries or even continents to deliver, and all three of them had far more colorful stamps than the French cards, and were also, in particular those from countries she had never heard of, at least three times larger (she would ask the recipients, on behalf of her husband as well, to remove them, carefully, with steam if possible). One card, from the Kingdom of Lesotho, was destined for Monneville, the second, from the Republic of Kosovo, which according to the stamp—a single-colored number in scarlet, portraying the country's flag with its double eagle—was just celebrating the one-year anniversary of its founding ("since . . ."), was intended for the hamlet of Montherlant, near the castle called Marivaux, and the third, whose stamp depicted two rugby teams huddled together, came from one of the Fiji islands, recently become independent, its name in unrecognized letters (if it was indeed script), and was addressed to the habitués of the bar Chez Pepone in Lavilletertre; Pepone with one P.

Afterward it seemed as though the mail carrier was also riding from village to village in spirals, going on ahead as if to show the stranger the way. Time and again, when she stopped at a house in a village, she seemed to be waiting for the woman on foot to catch up, as if she were breaking a path along part of the route, one spiral section after the other. That impression was deceiving, however, for the *factrice* kept stopping to drop off mail, almost exclusively government forms, demands, threats, warnings—here, too, the state omnipresent, its merciful absence in the countryside only apparent—but in the process she was happy not to run into many of the occupants of the houses and farms in the flesh, and on a Sunday, to boot.

Afterward there came a time when the stranger on foot caught up with and passed the local mail carrier as she parked her bike by house after house, after which the bicyclist caught up with the pedestrian, after which . . . and so on and so forth, from one village, from one jurisdiction, as it was once called, to another. The two did not say another word to each other, finally not even exchanging glances. And yet it was clear that for the duration of their route something like a commonality existed between them, which each of them was experiencing for the first time, unique in a number of ways. This solidarity was cheering, even when the letter carrier got not a little cross at having to pedal up inclines on the high plateau, hardly noticeable to the eye, but feared by bicyclists, even those in the Tour de France, as *faux plats*, false flatland. But so what: spiral after spiral she and the young stranger formed a duo. And the substitute mail carrier remembered how long ago, when she was young, she had hitchhiked through Scotland, and one night, in a hotel by the railway station—ah, all these railway hotels, officially affiliated with the stations—in Glasgow or wherever, she had looked out the window of her room under the eaves and past the railroad yard, and spotted the post office—ah, all the railway post offices in large cities—and how she had watched, hour after hour, as, in a hall lit up as bright as day, an entire army of men, older ones—she saw their bald heads shining—in long gray jackets sorted mail, mail which, of that she was certain, was entirely different from today's. And the pedestrian, overtaking her, or being overtaken by her, was thinking for her part of a similar yellow bicycle, the mail bike, that for more than a year now had been chained day and night to the iron fence by the entrance to the Métro station at the Porte d'Orléans, and that she had seen there only three days earlier—so little time had passed since then?—after her return from Siberia, a yellow postal bike, a letter carrier's bike just like this one, except that it was missing its rear wheel, or was it the front wheel?, and there it stood, the postal-yellow one-wheeled bicycle, and stood and stood, with its rusted chain, redgreengrayblueblack, its slit-open saddle, its jammed pedals. But why did this sight make her feel stronger, more confident? Just because of the color? That indestructible yellow?

In parting—yet another parting . . . the substitute mail carrier asked the other woman whether she did not have a letter, or at least a postcard, to entrust to her; the mail would be dispatched the first thing tomorrow from Chaumont-en-Vexin. It sounded more like a plea than a question. And look at that: the hiker did have a letter on her, scribbled as she walked along, paused, resumed walking, the address in two different scripts, Latin and Cyrillic, the stamp already pasted on, along with an airmail sticker. As she looked back at the mail carrier then, who was almost old now, gray-haired, she saw her with her children, all of them small, almost infants.

Then another stretch in the fruit thief's story during which nothing, in the old formula, "worthy of telling" happened, or at least none of what happened narrated itself as it was happening. But was there ever a time when happenings narrated themselves? No. And will happenings to come narrate themselves? No, and again no. The happenings that this story is narrating become that solely thanks to the narrator. It does not happen without him. Stories that narrate themselves: I, the reader, have no use for them.

Thus, in ever-widening spirals, the fruit thief had gradually neared the northeastern edge of the plateau, with Chaumont located on its slope, and at its foot, the only city in the Picardian Vexin. Very few cars on the narrow road along its upper rim, but these moving at excessive speed, racing along as if they were pursuing someone or were themselves being pursued. They seemed to be in a greater hurry than the planes in the blue sky overhead, although these were more numerous, taking off in rapid succession from the Beauvais airport, nearby as the crow flies and specializing in vacation excursions and flights to remote countries not included in the routes served by large airports and major airlines. Along one stretch of road, between the village of Liancourt-Saint-Pierre and the hamlet of Le Vivray, looking from the rim of the plateau in a northeasterly direction, one could seemingly see far past Beauvais, with its cathedral and airport. The fruit thief had stopped by the side of the road, and imagined she was seeing beyond all of Europe's borders, and then she really could see the Urals and beyond them all of Siberia; instead of a plane taking off there she saw a Siberian eagle, a fish eagle. Those were no plane's wings that rose and leveled off over the earth's horizon but the huge bird's wings, whose span exceeded any others'. As it approached, the eagle turned back into a plane, a rather rickety one, flying low, but to make up for that the pilot in the cockpit had his eye on her, only and exclusively on her, the young woman standing below and staring up at his aircraft: he bobbed the plane's wings, the left one and then the right one, waving to her, even if she merely imagined that.

What a pronounced hump that road along the rim had down its middle, as did the other small roads in the region. Whenever a longish gap occurred in the traffic, she walked on this crest, and it felt like balancing, if not exactly on a tightrope, then on a beam. Her old father came to mind; she pictured him as not far from there at this moment, somewhat befuddled yet enjoying himself thoroughly as he made his way across the lea—almost every landscape was a lea to him—stumbling, tripping, getting bogged down (so she imagined). She had always imagined herself witnessing her near and dear this way in their absence, had been there to observe their sleeping, walking, also toothbrushing, shoelace-tying, radio-dial-turning, and the more profoundly absent her mother, father, brother were, the more impossible to reach by telephone or such, the more tangible they became as she imagined them from afar—an involuntary game, which, however, could suddenly turn into alarm and fear, felt for the others.

Now she imagined her father bumbling along a highway with a possibly even bigger hump down the middle and, suddenly overcome by dizziness, losing his balance, not that good in any case, and falling into the ditch and breaking his neck. A deadly fall on a smooth road: could that happen? In her imagination, yes, like many other things. And now another one of the people had come to mind whom she had so gloriously forgotten the previous day—her loved ones. What had someone of her own age lamented to her once: "The old father-and-mother story: why does it never end?" Was it supposed to?

A horn honking: repeated, at considerable intervals, from all different places, it took on a melodic quality. It was not meant for her, yet she felt as if it were—until she realized that she had heard something similar before, only yesterday, from the baker's van on the outskirts of the *ville nouvelle*. And already she was running toward the honking, which in the meantime sounded farther away, as if off on side roads. She had to get to the car, had to see the bread car on Sunday, had to buy a loaf of bread or whatever. And besides, she was hungry again, had forgotten to eat anything that morning, so caught up was she in her service role at the inn (another of her forgetfulnesses).

Although now on an open stretch with no houses nearby, the car kept on honking, on and on, as if the baker were looking for her, only for her. And he stopped the vehicle at once, with a child, his son, on the passenger side, and got out to show her his wares, displayed in the cargo area when he opened the hatch in the rear. At the sight of the loaves—round, oval, four- to eight-cornered, the baguettes—thick ones, thin ones, even some as thin as a rope—there was no need for him to wax lyrical about the bread's freshness, about its smell, its fragrance: the bread itself, this thing, these things here in such an unusual place, on a side road like a distant, uninhabited steppe, with the steppe's characteristic wind, sufficed: it was as if one were seeing bread and breads like this for the first time, the bread "bread": object, shape, name all in one. And those elements produced a fragrance after all, even if the bread, the individual breads, had not necessarily all been baked by a master baker, even if the person in question was not necessarily the best baguette-baker in the canton of Chaumont, the best ficelle-maker in the *département*, the best traditional baker in Picardy.

Nonetheless this baker did have his specialty. If others offered bread with raisins, figs, kiwi, also simply walnuts or hazelnuts baked in, he offered a wheat bread studded with beechnuts. "Beechnuts": what are those? As the name indicates, or perhaps does not make clear, beechnuts are the fruits of beech trees, similar to nuts but much smaller even than walnuts, also smaller than hazelnuts, and not egg-shaped like those but, as their German name, *Buchecker*, suggests, angular, three-cornered, and pointy, tiny pyramids enclosed in thin shells of the same shape, and these in turn enclosed in a husk, a very spiky one; further details and also photos available on the internet. His beechnut bread, according to the baker on the side road in the steppe, was an innovation in the world, if not yet market-tested. One problem: a single loaf called for hundreds, or at least several heaping handfuls of beechnuts. Only in that way did the bread, with the beech fruits first rinsed, then roasted, acquire its taste, unlike any other, a taste unheard of for bread, that lingered on one's palate for days, unique among fruit breads, an effect perhaps comparable only to the world's best coffee beans. Collecting the beechnuts was very tedious, however. Many of the shells turned out to be empty, and before one had gathered the hundreds needed for one loaf . . . But he felt confident. "A bread like this has to be brought to market. The market is waiting for my beechnut bread. There's never been a bread like this! Here, have a taste!" And she tasted it, not saying a word, and then again later, agreeing completely, and she wanted to tell the beechnut-bread baker, but he had long since driven on, and the baker's car's honking was far off in the distance.

Only after he was gone did she see that the steering wheel of the bread-delivery vehicle was dusted with flour. And likewise only then did she realize that when the baker shook her hand in parting (yet another farewell) he had flour on his fingers, and only now did she feel the effects on her own hands, a "granular" sensation. So apparently the baker had jumped in his car right after work, handwashing not necessary. How many features of others one noticed only in retrospect, but then all the more vividly, when they unexpectedly swept toward one in a swathe, an animating one.

But at the same time she remarked to herself, "How trusting all these strangers have been whom I've met during the three days I've been on the road! How each of them confides in me on the spot, at the same time making claims on me, as if I were entirely at their disposal, existed for no other reason. Not one of them wants to know anything else about me. Not one asks me anything, let alone asks about my well-being, how my life is going. Where I come from, why I'm roaming through this area, with this heavy load on my back: not one person seems to care. Yet more and more I feel the absence, powerful and even painful, of questions about myself, even just one, for instance about my earrings. Where I bought them. Whether someone gave them to me. And, why not, what they cost. In the past, wherever I was, someone would at least ask about my 'accent'; in every region, every country, including my own, I immediately attracted attention with my 'slight accent,' as they said, and they wondered where I came from, because that accent was never taken for the local one. Here, however, I'm not asked about my accent, as if the people in this area didn't feel entirely comfortable with their own. Have I turned into a ghost in the course of these three days, perhaps a dear one, a welcome one, because otherwise people wouldn't confide in me so unhesitatingly, but a ghost nonetheless, and a phantom to myself as well? True: as I've walked people have waved to me from trains and buses, far more often than ever before, as just happened with that pilot, waving from his cockpit, and that made me feel spoken to and also recognized as a certain, known quantity. But why hasn't anything similar happened to me face-to-face, and if at all, less and less during these three days? Am I nothing but a medium to others?"

At the foot of the Vexin plateau, on the wide prairie of Chaumont, with the Troësne flowing through it, the fruit thief stumbled on a Sunday Mass being celebrated outdoors. Her brother in his construction trailer would have to wait for her a while longer. She knew, or thought she knew, that he did not mind waiting, or at least under some circumstances, that he even enjoyed a certain kind of waiting. When his sister had picked him up from school when he was younger, she had made a point of coming late, sometimes so late that he was the only one left waiting in his classroom or in the schoolyard. But it still could happen that he would ask her, his eyes shining, why she was there "so soon," or even snap at her.

She could have avoided the outdoor Mass. But when she looked down from the edge of the plateau and saw the congregation gathered by the river around an improvised altar and the priest, and the Introit made its way to her ears, it was like the honking of the bakery car earlier: she had to be there. She had to take part in the celebration of the Eucharist. It called to her, and something inside her called back. It was a call of hunger and thirst, and a call of zest. Rushing downhill, straight down the slope, head over heels, to those clustered in a ragged semicircle around the table, determined not to miss a single phrase, a single word of the Old, the New, and the Eternal Testament. In her haste, she tripped over a root and fell, picked herself up and hurried on. She had not hurt herself, or, according to her mantra, nothing could happen to her. Or could it? For a long time now she had not been so sure. Was that no longer a mantra but a maxim?

Neither the priest nor the members of the congregation looked up as she joined them, but without a word they made room for her in the semicircle, not really necessary with so few people there. This was the one Sunday in the year when Mass was celebrated at this spot. The tradition, going back centuries, was fading. (How many Sundays after Pentecost? Remember: no counting!) People still came from all over the region, some from beyond the borders of the *département*. But one could count them on the fingers of two hands, or, she fantasized, on the rungs of a not very tall fruit-picking ladder, and besides, the majority of them were old, ancient, elderly folk who needed help every time they had to change their position, especially from standing to kneeling and back, those helping them being almost as old, but less frail. At times they all seemed to have fallen asleep on their folding chairs, clutching their crutches, but the moment it was a question of standing up or falling to their knees they were wide awake. She was by far the youngest in the circle. In a daydream, one of those particularly distinct ones, fostered and perhaps brought on by the rhythm of the Mass, the reading of Scripture, the "Lift up your hearts!" the transubstantiation of the bread and wine into the body and blood, she saw herself transformed into the weary and heavy-laden around her, frail like them, if not on the verge of collapse. Break, O heart. And in a subsequent daydream she was back in Siberia, at an Orthodox service, had tied a kerchief over her head like all the women in the windowless, cramped chapel, and at the end had the sign of the cross traced on her forehead by the priest with his thumb, dipped in anointing oil. Now it was the time for making the sign of the cross. Was it time? At her feet, the grass rippling in the wind. The fields beyond the Troësne, in the heart of the country's interior, white with gulls, tall ones with long beaks, and among them, much larger and taller, a gray-and-black cormorant. Or was that an albatross standing there? Were albatrosses black?

After the Mass she stayed in the circle for a little while. No one spoke to her. No one showed any sign of wanting to confide in her, and no one asked where she was coming from and where she was going. The others' conversations also seemed trivial, mundane: weather, where to have lunch and what to order. No need existed anymore for talking, asking questions, inquiring, recounting. After the reading of Scripture and the ritual they all seemed to be purely in the present, reveling in a lively, buoyant, shared jolliness, including those who might die tomorrow, or even today. This jolliness would remain in effect, God or whoever or whatever willing, for a while longer, until the next Mass, in case I, you, we should still be around to experience it. A hundred-year-old lady slapped a ninety-nine-year-old gentleman on the buttocks. Another couple of oldsters smooched until their lips plumped up and their withered cheeks flushed. A cripple suddenly hoisted himself out of his wheelchair; he soon sank back, but still. A mute regained the power of speech, uttering only one word, but still. The brook, a tributary of the Troësne, whooshed by for one tremulous second like the Jordan—if indeed that river had ever whooshed. Here there was no need for saying good-bye, either formally or formlessly, no need for a formula like "See you later." Without having been expressly taken into the community of these others, one belonged to it, and not just for the time being.

"Does a community like that meet my needs?" she wondered, already far away and standing on a beam that served as a footbridge, without a railing, over the prairie river, the Troësne, quite narrow but all the deeper. And the reply: "A community like that can be a pleasure, pure, unadulterated pleasure. But it doesn't meet my needs."

That marked the beginning of what much later, when words for it finally occurred to her, she dubbed "the hour of hopelessness." The Troësne flowed calmly and rapidly at her feet, a tangle of aquatic plants in its depths shimmering green and undulating evenly in the current. An otter swam upstream, its fuzzy head showing above the water only as far down as its little black eyes, while its tail, serving as a rudder, left hardly visible waves in its wake. When she took one step on the beam, the otter promptly dived out of sight, and in less than a second there was no trace of the heavy animal, as big as a beaver, that had just been plowing through the water. Before her trip her father had warned her against wading in the Troësne; once he had taken only a step and had sunk up to his ribs in its muddy bottom, and only by grabbing an overhanging tree limb had he been able, "if not at the last minute, at the next to last," to heave himself back onto land, back onto the prairie. Under other circumstances, whenever the fruit thief encountered a site of danger, she was always tempted to take the risk. If she felt any fear, it was always for others, not herself. Now, however, although she was standing on the sturdy, rather wide beam, she suddenly felt fear for herself and literally fled to the opposite bank, saving herself, as she perceived it, veritably "at the last minute."

Off to the animals of land and air, to the gulls, the cormorant (or was that a *héron*, a heron, standing there?). On the way, unexpectedly coming upon animals native to the country's interior, everywhere in the tall savanna grass, seemingly all genera and species gathered on the far side of the Troësne, not merely hares, foxes, deer, wild boars, pheasants—alas, no golden pheasant—quail, partridges, wildcats, wild dogs (in the process of reverting—with one or two more generations before that happened—to wolves), but also one (1) lynx, two (2) badgers, a couple of raccoons, as well as, here and there, correlated to the cultivated plants known as "garden refugees" that had emigrated into the wild, an escaped turkey and a parrot as "domestic refugees," see also, high in the crown of this huge willow (several such trees in the middle of the Troësne prairie), a peacock, wearing his crown and fanning his richly colored tail. And all these animal species were lying, crouching, standing, stalking along in the grassland, sometimes far apart, sometimes crowded together, the most varied kinds, and formed a community, by day at least—who knows whether at dusk the fox and the snake curled up quietly beside it might somehow or other lash out at each other. The hunters, and not merely those of autumns to come, as well as those of autumns past, also those of previous centuries and millennia, were absent, again somehow or other.

She disrupted this community, however, became the intruder, the foreigner, the enemy. Yet she was traversing the prairie with utmost care, avoiding any sudden movements and any noise, if possible, unless it were a whispered greeting, accompanied by a gentle gesture. In spite of these precautions: a general scattering when she took a single small step or encroached in some way on the community gathered here/there. Even the snake slithered away like greased lightning, making itself scarce; the badger scooted into its burrow, throwing up a cloud of dust, and all the animals darted off, with the exception of the fox, which took its time, turning its head to eye her, the wannabe pal; off darted the hares, the pheasants, with piercing cries, away swooped the scolding parrot, away galloped the wild boars, away flapped, last of all, the owl, who had become her escort on her journey into the interior and had been sleeping the day away in the steppe grass, its wingbeats ponderous and soundless as only an owl's can be, but that, too, was a scattering, scattering at the approach of someone who did not belong, was violating boundaries, an outlaw wherever she turned up. "Stay here!" she shouted. "Stay here, you sons of bitches!" she bawled, which merely accelerated the scattering, until finally all the animals had disappeared from the savanna, even the peacock from the crown of the huge willow. Or had she been mistaken? Had it been only a long, bushy branch in the shape of a peacock? And the gulls, along with the cormorant, heron, and albatross? Another of her daydreams? The only animal still in sight, the fly on the back of her hand, with its antennae, or whatever those teeny-tiny gesticulating things were, seeming to write in the air, mocking her. This fly had a golden gleam, allegedly a characteristic of carrion flies, and as she gazed and stared at it, it appeared to her in this moment as the "queen of the animals." A beautiful golden queen. She had to restrain herself to keep from killing this queen of the animals. "But I would have missed anyway."

Weren't there depictions of the death of the Buddha in which all the animals in the world wept for the Mahatma, torrents of tears from elephants, lions, tigers, eagles, down to the mouse, the rainworm, perhaps also dung beetles and May and June bugs: but how had all these animals got along with the Enlightened One during his lifetime? Depictions of that: none. Wept for, cried for, respected only in death?

Away from the animal world. Home to civilization, following the bank of the channelized river all the way to town. What was the title of that song from the previous century, sung by Petula Clark to America, and from there to the entire world? "Downtown." Did Chaumont-en-Vexin have a downtown, however? Besides, as a fruit thief she was out of place in a "downtown," had never been at home there and especially had never felt welcome. And how she needed, how desperate she was, how she longed to feel welcome somewhere. And besides, how would one say "downtown" in French? *Centre ville?* No. Downtown was untranslatable. (Another untranslatable concept.)

For a while it distracted her to carry her luggage on her head instead of on her shoulders; to hold the duffel bag first with both hands, then with one, and finally to balance it without hands as she made her way across the savanna, which converged with the town. A sympathetic observer might have seen the way she strode along, from time to time taking a step to one side, like a dance step, as beautiful, full of grace; someone less kindly disposed might have seen it as a mess, the movements of a drunkard, if not a madwoman;

a person of outright ill will might have described her movements as those of an enemy, of someone on the warpath against him, the lookout, about to engage him in a life-and-death confrontation.

And all three of them would have been right. The main incentive for her storming along, however, came from the war taking place inside her, not from a war against any particular person but rather from a rage deep inside against the world as it presented itself to her, at least in this desperate hour, a world she nevertheless viewed as her very own, and which she, as a young woman, a young person, claimed to possess, though in a sense different from that of any conventional property.

How did it happen, she asked herself as she staggered along in confusion, that access to the world was blocked for her and those like her, seemingly for good and irrevocably? Her father had once regaled her with an account of his childhood, according to which his parents, as refugees in a strange land, had been categorized for many years as "stateless," and thus he, too, had had the designation "Citizenship–Stateless" on his report cards, and had been ashamed vis-à-vis his classmates of his statelessness.

She, however, had no desire to belong to a state, wanted nothing to do with all the states in the world, expected nothing from any state, and likewise nothing, nothing at all from any country, no matter whether people currently praised it to the skies. All she longed for was to join with the others in the world. —"The world"? Please define that. —Theworld wastheworldwastheworld. Or perhaps this definition might do: the world was the triangular story of oneself, nature, and others. O, others! Divine others. And she regarded herself, the experienced fruit thief, she recognized herself, and had done so for a long time—aside from her thievery, her travels, her ability to intervene and be helpful—as a world expert, one of the experts who set the tone for the world, though of a different kind. –"Expert" at what? Just expert. She, a young person today, what could she possibly have to give, what morning, midday, or evening gifts, the richest of which were the morning gifts. Except that to this day her gifts had not been used, and certainly not loved. The world, her world, did not even know about her gifts and probably would not want to know about them, from now until hell froze over. Or would they, and she, be discovered someday after all? –Discovered? Like a star? –Discovered, simply discovered at last. How she had always secretly striven for success. –Success? Being in the limelight? In the glare of publicity? –Away from all that, no "publicity," none of its "glare." Just success. Giving what I have to give. Just think what I could have given my world. Just think what new songs I could have sung to her, what new stories I could have told, what new dishes I could have cooked and tasted, what new ideas I could have swiped and pocketed. I'm a main character, too. And now: the expedition a failure. Turn back? Impossible. So many placed their trust in me. And no one had faith in me.

Walking along the channelized Troësne became a simultaneous process of groping her way across the prairie labyrinth in the river's bottomland. Had she been afraid for herself earlier? Now she was afraid of herself. "Blood will flow." That ancestor in her family, the alleged murderer, storming along in that guise only when she was asleep, now appeared, in a waking dream, in broad daylight, and spoke those words in her own voice, that of a ventriloquist. For moments she even saw him before her in the oppressive air prevailing in the bottomland: the eyes of someone who had not killed only once: eyes of glass.

She lifted the hair off her neck several times, finally tugging at it so hard that it hurt, and instead of crying out in pain she laughed out loud. She wished she could be swept away to somewhere else, somewhere entirely different, onto a ferry crossing the Yenisei in Siberia, where she would be the captain and thus in safety for the rest of her life, or also merely south to the Oise, for instance to the L'Isle-Adam locks, beyond the country here, beyond the Vexin and Picardy: there, too, she would be saved from herself, employed in the control cabin, up in the switching room, with windows on all sides, where she would be on duty day and night—a job she had already held as a temp for an entire summer—as the lock-gate operator, granted asylum there, too, from the murderer's female descendant here.

Walking along blind to find her way out of the labyrinth. Eyes closed to see whether behind her lids that old reliable writing scrolled by. The writing did flicker into view again, but this time the lines piled up in a hopeless tangle—not one letter decipherable—in the form of a funeral pyre. Lying down in the prairie grass for a catnap, which in the past had always helped her recover the day's colors and forms. Sleep came at once, except that she plucked a blade of grass with which she could have pulled up the whole savanna; in her ears the prairie-wide sound of the crickets: a shrilling and clamor that no longer had anything homelike about it.

Again an anecdote her father had passed along to her darted through her mind like a will-o'-the-wisp: a young person had forced his way into a lion's lair, taken off all his clothes, and sprayed the lions with water until . . . No lions available, at most a couple of bulls, inaccessible behind barbed-wire fences, and besides, little more than calves, young bulls. At most a herd of cows accessible, and one of the uddered creatures came to her and licked her hand with its rough tongue; at least the cow then snatched at the kerchief that she willingly surrendered to her, and chewed it up. No lightning flashed out of the clear sky and struck her, as she devoutly wished might happen. One gigantic dark cloud in the form of a shark did appear, but a moment later it dissolved. She felt like a wild animal as she wound through the prairie labyrinth, an animal panting to be hunted, come hell or high water. At the sight of a dead hare drifting downstream in the Troësne, she thought: "That's me!" The Great Fall was imminent, or had it already taken place? and it only seemed that she was still on the face of the earth? And she, who could sing so sweetly when she had to, and held a tune like God knows who, now sang off key and even more off key, almost like several men bellowing in unison, and in between she groaned. As she stormed along, marching, she bellowed and groaned.

But wasn't it typical of this kind of inner hopelessness that larger as well as smaller external annoyances, the more annoying, the more effective, could counteract the hopelessness, and, in the best of circumstances, banish it altogether, offering a self-activating counterspell, a blessing? That may be. Yet for the fruit thief this principle did not work now; every external evil or mere irritation that befell her after this had the opposite effect, only magnifying her inner turmoil. Thus she stepped on a wasps' nest, and as she took to her heels the occupants caught up with her, stinging her with astonishing accuracy, like sharpshooters practicing by firing at a cardboard cutout. Then, on the edge of town, dogs leaped at her from behind the fences of one garden after the other, sending crushed rock and gravel flying into the air and clattering against the gates, with ceaseless clamor and yapping issuing from their maws as they panted with eagerness to rip her to shreds (see her imagined scene, interpreted by her mother as stemming from the fact that late in pregnancy she had been attacked by a huge dog). Weren't all animal noises—the clacking of storks, the cackling of hens, the quacking of geese—meant to merge into one sound, if not melody—with the exception of the panting and howling of these dogs, also in contrast to the silent wild dogs on the savanna? On the other hand, couldn't the barking of several dogs at night in the countryside, far off, one in a valley, the other halfway up somewhere, give a lost hiker a welcome signal, an indication of homeyness, by which to orient himself? True. But that hour passed without her hearing any such thing, even one, even some insignificant nothing—that might have helped her come to a halt in her frantic plunging ahead. But listen, sweetheart, from that house now, and now from somewhere else, way off in the distance, the tender music, the distant sound! She did take in the sounds, these as well as those, as well as the third ones, and all the tender tunes worked their way into her innermost ear and continued playing there, except that she was thinking, "I'll never get home again!"

The prairie labyrinth converged with the town labyrinth, different from the one in the *ville nouvelle*: if the ever-smaller spirals of Cergy's new housing developments had offered no way out, and escaping into the open, into the countryside, had not been possible, here all the streets led pretty much straight ahead. From all directions the center of the town of Chaumont could be seen; yet she felt as though she had to grope her way along, step by step, as earlier on the savanna.

No obstacles, however. No alley that ended at a wall. No one who blocked her way. It was early afternoon on Sunday, and not a single person in sight, not a cat. At least a sparrow, please. If only she could have bird droppings bestowed on her, as generous a blob as possible, and if possible on the middle of her forehead! Didn't some people regularly attract that kind of thing? Why couldn't she have that, too, at this particular hour?

No one whom she could have greeted and who would have returned the greeting. Added to the persisting desperation, the clumsiness had now manifested itself that, congenital or not, often plagued her except when she was engaging in her fruit-thievery and all that involved. She tripped over her own legs, bumped into the side mirror of a car as it was parking, slipped and fell where there was nothing to slip on, patted all her pockets for something she already had in her hand. That would have been hilarious to witness under some circumstances, but only from a distance. From close up, however: her face contorted in desperation. "No point to being clumsy if you can't show it"—a witty expression, but she had no one to show her clumsiness to, and no one would have enjoyed witnessing her humiliation.

Early on a Sunday afternoon, and in this godforsaken town of Chaumont, on some houses—all the houses, including those toward the center built in rows with no space between them, appeared isolated—the shutters were already being closed: a slamming here, a slamming there, and here as well as there a single hand visible for a churlishly brief moment as it reached out to pull the shutters to. The supermarket in the center: closed; the only light visible the "emergency lighting." The two bars: one closed because it was Sunday, and on the second one, which also sold smoking materials, the iron shutters were just clanking down, the final crash echoing through the silent town; otherwise she would have dashed in, just to get inside somewhere, and bought some cigarettes, not for herself but to give away. The one restaurant no longer in business, for a year already. The pizza joint: not opening until evening. The handsome Renaissance church on the slope leading up to the plateau: closed up tight. From the railway tracks up above, a train's whistle, just one toot, but so long-drawn-out as if this train were the last already, and not only for this particular day.

Onward! Away from downtown Chaumont-en-Vexin, never mind where to. Why not to the barracks complex where her brother was living, on the edge of town? No, she could not let him see her in this condition, hopelessly astray.

For the time being heading north, her tried-and-true direction—except that as she went she could glimpse her shadow out of the corner of her eye, foreshortened and thickened in the summer sun. To have to see her own shadow: adding insult to injury. But now: inside a fence, a tree full of cherries. And already she had turned off, or rather just turned, with the grace that was all her own, and already in and out again, traversing the ford between the fence and the tree that she alone detected, her fruit-thief's hand filled to the brim with cherries. What? Cherries in August rather than June? These were sour cherries, their red lighter and glassy. And popping one of the cherries into her mouth, and then another as she went on her way, hoping that all the sourness concentrated in this fruit would help.

Still no good: it was clear that these cherries were sour as only sour cherries can be. But in her mouth there was nothing sour about them; they had no taste at all, no matter how many she ate, and ate. It was as if she had completely lost her sense of taste in this hopeless hour, which went on and on. She tried again with the watercress that she found downstream along an arm of the Troësne that branched off in Chaumont: the same tastelessness in the curly leaves, usually so peppery, and the same thing with some juniper berries, famous for their bitterness. After that going out of her way to bite into the rotten spots on the drops under apple trees, piles of which she came across as she headed out of town, filling her mouth with the rotten flesh and chewing it, sucking it in, swallowing it: but only an all-encompassing sense of tastelessness inside and out. Not even nausea. If only all that rottenness had made her sick! But still nothing: physically the fruit thief felt fine, indestructibly healthy, cursed with a downright malignant good health.

Although the road led straight out of town, she felt as though she was walking off kilter, more and more so, twisting and contorting herself until she was seriously off-balance. But no, she would not fall, not this time, not today. In the middle of a green that formed a bay on the edge of town, she came to a halt and righted herself, along with her load. Never in her life had she stood up so straight.

Yet she did not know what to do next and could not budge.

She had lost her way once and for all, and at the moment that was restorative. Before her the trees that lined the green, some of their trunks plastered with posters, most of them faded, advertising festivals, concerts, and especially—typical of Vexin towns—flea markets, *braderies*, *vide-greniers*, all of which had taken place months and years ago. One poster, however, announced a concert by Eminem that was supposed to occur the following summer, far from Chaumont, over the French border in Brussels. On one of the benches nearby a suitcase, forgotten or left behind on purpose: any moment now it would explode, sending large and small nails flying in all directions, and that was all right with her. Black flies flitted before her eyes, and when she batted at them they multiplied and multiplied. Out of the corner of her eye she saw a motorcycle thunder across the green, a heavy, imposing one, not a Harley-Davidson but at any rate a Mitsubishi, with "Valter" riding it, or someone with his profile, and if she had still had any strength she would have run after him and jumped onto the back seat for a ride with him across the Balkans and on to the Peloponnesian peninsula. Hopeless, hopeless, hopeless.

That green on the edge of town where she stood motionless, her back perfectly straight, had a round patch, faded to gray, bleached like most of the posters on the trees. A circus tent, a rather small one, had been pitched there at one time, now long ago. And on this very spot—so it had been conceived or daydreamed for the fruit thief's tale—blood was supposed to be spilled. A struggle ensued, perhaps not exactly a life-or-death one, but close to it. That was how the story visualized it and wanted it to happen.

A woman, about the same age as the fruit thief, comes running from between two of the town's last little houses, or from inside one of the houses? and immediately attacks the lost soul standing there. As she lands the first blows, she speaks, but it is hard to make out what she is muttering. One interpretation might be that the other woman stole her husband, or whatever. But what clearly matters in this scene is the corner of the fruit thief's eye again. Even before the first blow she realizes that she knows the woman attacking her. To paraphrase Anna Akhmatova, it is one of many doubles whom, "from the time she was five, she ran into on every street corner," and this is no figment of the fruit thief's imagination. Strange, or not so strange, that all her life these doubles, after an initial phase of wooing, by them, as children, then girls, then women, a veritably stormy, passionate, unconditional wooing—as if the two of them were chosen, meant for all eternity to be friends and the closest of confidantes—every time developed a ferocious hatred for her, the fruit thief. And every time it seemed to her that this hatred—inexplicable as it was, and also never explained, never articulated by the other woman—was something she deserved. She felt vaguely guilty. She had promised her doubles something that she had not fulfilled. She had misrepresented something to them. They were bitterly disappointed in her. In their eyes she was a swindler. A counterfeiter; false through and through; radically false. She deserved the hatred of those she had deceived.

And now, on this otherwise empty green on the edge of town, hatred has become explicit for the first time. Here this particular double's hatred has become action. But why here, of all places, when otherwise the rule prevails, in this story and beyond, that those in conflict with each other in their accustomed surroundings, if they meet by chance in a strange place, impulsively approach each other, at least greet each other, which under everyday conditions they have not done for a wretchedly long time, or even bury the hatchet, and, what is more—this, too, part of the rule—for good? Is this hatred between doubles perhaps the kind that cannot be overcome, and which, on the contrary, when the two meet unexpectedly at a place unfamiliar to one of them, erupts all the more violently, and on the spot, instantly, in a heartbeat, turns into a heartless assault? Is that how it is? That is how it is. That is how it was.

It is also the first time in her life that the fruit thief experiences violence. The boxing she practiced assiduously for a while at her girls' *lycée* was different: it did her good and strengthened her presence of mind to be constantly aware of her opponent's eyes. Here, however: neither eyes nor even a face to be seen. The face of the woman attacking her, beating her, literally fallen away, lacking any similarity to her, the recipient of the beating.

Then she struck back. She landed a blow—and how!—that, too, for the first time in her life. The struggle between her and her double went on and on. In this account, however: brevity. A nosebleed soaking the sawdust in the dead grass of the ring: nosebleed spots not comparable to anything else. The mounting murderous rage of the woman who initiated the violence—homicidal fury, for only a moment, but something the woman returning the blows will not forget for the rest of her life. In retrospect the fruit thief has the impression she never touched the other woman, but instead was transformed into a meteor, spinning out of the sky and ramming vertically into the ground, then, from the force of the impact, continuing to whirl and whirl in the ground, the sharp edges sticking out finally giving her enemy no choice but to flee, howling and gnashing her teeth.

Left alone with the drops of blood, one or two of them still fresh, the others dry, as if long since, not that many, really, or as large as she had thought in the middle of the fight. From which of the two combatants did the blood come? No matter. Did she cry? She did not cry but suddenly was close to tears, that, too, for the first time, no, not in her life, but on this journey. Still. What more did she want for the present? For the first time, too, at the thought of her "doubles on all street corners," no sense of guilt. No, she had not misled them. She was fine just as she was, and she would remain what she was, the fruit thief. "I'm going to remember this green, along with its name!" she thought. But names in her story make no difference, do they? —This one does. The name here does matter. —Name, please? —*Derrière les jardins.* Behind the gardens. And at the same time, that line from Hölderlin: "Make your way defenseless through life and fear naught"? She had defended herself, for the first time, and she was afraid.

Over the bypass, in the middle of the prairie that resumed past the edge of Chaumont, with the Troësne flowing onward in several branches as the prairie river, the barracks complex where the workers lived. There, too, a new town, a *ville nouvelle*, springing up? Possibly. But our tale does not have room for that. We have had our fill of *villes nouvelles*.

A pedestrian crossing, controlled by traffic lights, over the multilane bypass, almost as wide as an expressway. Plenty of time to cross on this Sunday afternoon, with hardly any traffic, to stroll casually over the zebra stripes in emulation of the stride of John Lennon, Paul McCartney, George Harrison, and Ringo Starr as they crossed Abbey Road over half a century ago for the album cover.

But the fruit thief halted on this side of the crossing. Metal bollards had been installed in a row to keep cars from the center of town from turning thoughtlessly onto the main road, or who knows why. Atop the bollards, at hip or chest height, white-lacquered orbs, likewise of metal; the paint on not a few of them partially, and on some of them entirely, scraped, scratched, scrubbed, picked away, by the hands, fingernails, or something else of all the pedestrians who over the years had waited for the green light that would let them cross.

A man in a painter's smock was walking back and forth in front of the bollards. He was alternately taking photos and making drawings of the traces left on the white lacquered orbs by the hands and probably also other things belonging to the passersby at the stop by the light. A Sunday photographer? A Sunday painter? Nothing about him suggested either. The network of images in the white paint on the orbs, which incidentally seemed made for resting one's hand on while one was forced to wait on the edge of wide roads, displayed, the world over, despite all the variations from orb to orb, the same rhythms and patterns. He had been traveling from continent to continent for a long time, in order to document and archive what he had found—the day before yesterday in Beijing, yesterday in Abu Dhabi, today in Chaumont-en-Vexin. He took a particular interest in Chaumont, the town of his birth: these imprints and scars, this unconscious scraping, rubbing, scratching by pedestrians waiting at the light, was, he thought, the only thing that connected Chaumont with the rest of the world, the planet, this town that in his view in other respects lay not only behind the earth's moon but also beyond the moons of Mars and Neptune, farther from Paris than Vladivostok and Ushuaia. In this respect it was appropriate that the orbs had the form of a globe, a child's globe, and the scratch- and rub-marks made by pedestrians on all the globes mimicked the outlines of oceans and continents, different outlines, oceans, and parts of the world on each one. And a special feature was also that the dome of the globe, representing the polar region, was often completely bare, black instead of the prevailing white, as if the pole, the North Pole, had melted, while the rest of the planet was covered in eternal ice and snow. What a series of photos and drawings that would make possible, not today or tomorrow but in ten, twenty years, when he had compiled an anthology of pedestrians' handiwork on street-corner balls, *urbi et orbi*! From time to time a swig from the bottle at his feet further lengthened his perspective. Besides, each of the orbs or globes on earth represented a particular variation—like the one pure white one, not yet touched by human hand, the Little Globe of Chaumont-en-Vexin.

She did not cross the road yet, continuing to watch him until he finally looked up and noticed her. She had needed that. She needed someone who would say or indicate to her how things stood with her and what was in store for her: an oracle. What's going to happen to me now? she wanted to ask the oracle, without actually posing the question, simply by positioning herself silently in front of him. And here she had come to the right place, and in the globe-artist she had found the right person. After the struggle "behind the gardens," the adventure that had brought her to this region had reawakened. It was also not thinkable that her tale should end with the hour of hopelessness. It could not and must not end that way. This was an adventure story, and the adventure had to stay with her to the end of the story. And of course—anything else would be contrary to the nature of such adventure stories—past the end.

At the sight of her, the edge-of-town artist straightened up and first looked long and hard at her, at nothing but her face, and perhaps only her eyes. In taking his own eyes off his work, he had not blinked once, had not had to adjust his focus to register the stranger. Then he spoke: "Wasp stings are very painful at first, more painful than bee stings, but the pain goes away quickly, and besides, except when you're stung on the lips, you don't swell up. It's obvious you're coming from a fight, you've been through a war, a war on two fronts: a physical one, in which you fought well, and another one, which no one can fight, either well or less well, and that one, as it is written, is the great war, the true one: the war with yourself. But that war, too, it seems to me, you've survived for the time being, and both of them together, the physical struggle and the one with yourself, have caused you to blossom. What eyes! What color! Doesn't Ibn Arabi quote the Prophet's phrase about the 'freshness of the eyes after prayer'—or is it 'in prayer'? So why not also the freshness of the eyes after the struggle? You will return—not die in the war, though return to who knows where. How often it's meant maliciously when one person says to another: I know you. I've recognized you. No utterance more malicious. A curse. A malediction. But when I say: I've recognized you, I know you, I mean that in a different sense. 'No one recognizes me': enough of such laments. You're recognized, and not only by drunks like me, you'll continue to be recognized in the future more than ever. Happy the person who will recognize you. He'll be tickled pink. And proud of you the way Louis the Saint was proud of his queen, what was her name again? Though he should also brace himself for various things. To his benefit. The given name Reine—why does it turn up only on old gravestones, or in remote parts of Canada? In Edmonton I knew a woman called Reine. You can dispense with eye shadow. I've counted six freckles on your nose. Or am I seeing double? After you wash your hair, if you rinse with a nutshell solution, it gives brown hair like yours a very special shine. As a child my mother was stung by a hornet once, between her eyes, and for a few days she was blind. She told me three or four hornets could kill a horse, but how could she have known that?"

Later it was not her brother who waited for her in the common room of the workmen's barracks complex but rather she for him. He had set out to meet her, one of his fellow workers told her. But how could he know what direction she would be coming from? And her memory produced a variation on that theme: whenever her brother had had to wait for someone, at a certain point he had always felt compelled to set out to meet the person, whoever it might be.

She was offered a chair to sit on while she waited, after one of the workmen had dusted it off with his bare hand. She sat near the door, where there was a constant coming and going. After her time in the town, deserted on that Sunday afternoon, this hustle and bustle felt good, the more so because none of the workmen was engaged in a job or had a chore to take care of. Although they kept going in and out, they had nothing they needed to do, or at least nothing specific that they had been ordered to do, and though one of them might move faster than another, none of them were in a hurry or under stress. The phrase "chill out" seemed appropriate, in the sense of taking it easy, a buoyant, healthy idleness. Noteworthy, too, that all the workmen, not in work clothes but in street clothes, which seemed particularly suitable for a Sunday, looked handsome to her, projected an elegance different from that paraded by models on the runway. That impression seemed all the stronger because she, her eyes fixed on the door in expectation of someone in particular, her brother, saw each person entering who was not the one she was waiting for with great physical clarity, as someone special in his uniqueness, in his personal light, his nimbus.

The only one who literally tore through the door into the barracks turned out to be her brother. The first impression he made was one of concern, the concern he had felt for her, his sister, and at the same time annoyance at having had to be concerned about her.

A family affliction, worrying about each other? Also setting out to meet each other when happy anticipation suddenly turns into corrosive worry? And likewise calling, from the depths of the soul, for a family member seemingly gone for good—brother, sister, mother, even father—when in reality the person has disappeared for only a moment, having gone around the corner or just into the next room?

That he was upset with his sister turned out to be a mistaken impression. That impression stemmed from the change she saw in her brother's face after a year of not laying eyes on him. He had not only grown a mustache but also seemed to have thicker eyebrows, which now met over the bridge of his nose. Without a word he grabbed her arm and pulled her along to his trailer, where they sat across from each other at the table.

When he finally opened his mouth, his voice sounded surly to her at first, if not unfriendly: just as that morning on the phone, she heard an unfamiliar grating sound—but then it occurred to her that his voice was changing—hardly anything left of the child's voice she had known so well, and not yet that of a man.

Before he spoke he had stared at her a long time, his face expressionless, as if he were waiting for a word from her, a single word, on which everything depended. While she tried to think of one, and tried and tried—she had to find it!—she gazed as if transfixed at the two or three bright red hairs in his dark beard, still patchy, and at the same number repeated in her brother's eyebrows, these scattered red hairs, which she had noticed as a child on her father—in the meantime they had long since turned gray—and that allegedly had also distinguished his father before him, etc., back into the night of time?

"How are you?" she asked finally, though in a tone in which only she, the fruit thief, could pose a question like that. "Comment vas-tu?" Whereupon her brother at first said nothing but just smiled at her, with a smile that initially broke loose in a painful spasm from the dimples in the middle of his cheeks, one on the left and one on the right, but then beamed over his whole face, and she saw before her that Indian mask from the Yukon River in Alaska, with two mice dangling from the mask's cheeks and bobbing around; according to legend they would "devour a person's soul." If such mice had been dangling from her brother's cheeks, now they would have been gone.

Wolfram von Eschenbach's tales, which, just like this one, all take place in France, but verse after verse and rhyme after rhyme are all written in German, not infrequently offer a smattering of French words in the appropriate passages, and for me, writing in German in the French no-man's-bay, *la baie de personne* (at one time a country of immigrants if ever there was one), a word comes to mind / in response to the light, / that now radiates from the face / of the brother, of the heroine / a Wolfram word / a word otherwise never heard from him / and this word is: *fleuri*. / And again: untranslatableness.

The brother, as he now told her in a halting voice, strange to him as well, had thought during their long separation that he had been betrayed by his sister, yes, even by her, his big sister. That "in these times," as he said, parents betrayed their own children, had long ago become a certainty for him—even if that certainty had dissolved into thin air now that he had been living in the country, far from father and mother, as a craftsman among a thousand other craftsmen. "To hell with all certainties!" But before that he had viewed his parents as particularly despicable criminal traitors, a veritable "clique of traitors," "a sneaky traitor-couple," whose treachery consisted in not trusting their child to be good at anything, anything at all, in giving up on him in advance "for today's world," initially with a pitying gaze from a distance, a distance that grew and grew, beyond the dinner table, beyond the office desk, beyond and each time more beyond, a pitying gaze that always just brushed him, until this gaze became a pitiless wound, one without mercy, downright contemptuous of him, his parents' child, condemned to crash and burn, the gaze of traitors, who at the same time were parties to carrying out his sentence, or at least hard-heartedly allowed it to go forward, washing their hands of him. "The betrayal of children by their parents, betrayal in the twenty-first century!" He, her brother told her, would sacrifice himself for his children, as a father should. No matter how they turned out, he would believe in them to the end, as he also believed in such sacrifice. In the twenty-second century: no more betrayal, or a different kind. "But it's a long way till then." And the mother of his children would practice a craft, *un artisanat*, like him. "On my construction site we have quite a few female masons, roofers, electricians, carpenters, all young, more or less, all more or less desirable, *désirables*. But what to call them? *Maçon* or *maçonne*? *Charpentier* or *charpentière*?

But in the meantime his father had written him a letter. He was proud of him, he wrote, and he regretted that he himself had missed out on learning a trade as a young man; true, he'd been a *touche-à-tout*, but his "giving everything a try" had been, as far as physical work was concerned, all for show and nothing but a scam. And here, or "chez nous," as her brother said, their mother had turned up at the barracks the previous day and had slept in his bed, while he moved for the night to a larger building, where a bed was free.

He had just performed the Saturday-Sunday ritual of cleaning his tools in the communal courtyard when a fellow carpenter came and said, "Your mother's here." And there she stood by the window in the barracks, with her back to the wall, and it really was his mother. She seemed tired, dead-tired, as if after a long trip across several continents, and at the same time she giggled "like a young girl." And like "a homeless person," like an SDF, *sans domicile fixe*, the lady banker asked him—first thing—for a bed so she could sleep. It was not only the kerchief that was reminiscent of a woman from the Balkans. Had she perhaps disguised herself as one? On the contrary: the way she presented herself to her son seemed to be her real guise. Later, however, when they had supper together, along with several others from the construction crew, his mother again played the one in control, assigning roles, deciding who would sit where, giving everyone advice without being asked (though not advice on the money market). At the end of the evening mother and son stayed up, sitting on the wooden bench he had built outside his trailer, and she informed him that she had been the one who instigated the game of hunting her down, so as to get her husband, daughter, and son to converge on this region, out here in the country, in the Picardian Vexin, for the family celebration that had not taken place in ages—in her eyes each of them had been living sadly and shamefully alone for far too long—and had to happen now or never; the tent had already been set up, and the party would begin tomorrow (today, that is) at sunset, on Sunday, they knew where. After that mother and son sat a while longer on the bench without saying anything. Heat lightning in the west, then lightning without thunder over the Route du Blues. All around the barracks complex the nocturnal chirping of crickets. Deep down in the prairie grass a couple of fireflies circling each other without ever flying higher. Although the bench was located in the river valley, one had the impression of being on a hilltop. Son and mother, both with their hands on their knees, their palms turned slightly upward, like country folk in old photos sitting on the bench in front of their little farmhouse of an evening.

Her brother had hesitated for a long time before telling her about their mother's visit. At the beginning he had faltered. It almost seemed he was reluctant, the first few sentences coming out in a monotone, as if he were being forced to carry out a duty. But as he continued: "wind in his sails." His breaking voice changed into that of an adult, and apparently for good: from now on, from the moment he found his rhythm, he would leave behind his uneven adolescent pitch and occasional squawks. And as he got into the swing of telling the story, something took place inside him that he had not paid attention to during the event itself. In the midst of his story he made discovery after discovery. And what he discovered this way, painful though it might be, heartrending even, was a source of happiness and enthusiasm. Painful or pleasurable, one way or the other, it acquired value. (A term that might have come from his mother, the *banquière*.)

While her brother told her the story, her eyes were opened—one thing led to the other—to the interior of the trailer, his "living and sleeping system." Of primary importance were his tools, neatly lined up in the corner by the door, ready to be picked up and carried straight to the job site. There they were, the classic carpenter's tools: the level, with the bubble in the middle for establishing true horizontal and vertical. There was the thick pencil with its special red lead, there the carpenter's red chalk with the plumb bob for marking wooden beams and slats. There was the short-handled carpenter's adze. The folding rule. There . . . and there . . . and there . . . And hanging above the tools on a wall hook the carpenter's pants or "work pants," blue, to be pulled on over regular pants. That, too, a motif in old photographs? No. For the colors were what made the difference, red and blue. A black-and-white photo would not have "caught" that. Ah, the international blue of the work pants, intercontinental. Such internationalities: let's have more of them!

These carpenter's tools, though not familiar from old photos, were nonetheless like those of olden times. And how the olden times could come alive from case to case, could be alive, those in particular. And the listener closed her eyes and saw an afterimage of the congregants attending Mass by the Troësne, and among them, wearing a kerchief over her head, her mother. Or was that an afterimage of the Orthodox service by the Yenisei in Siberia? Was she mixing up all the places and times now? So what if she was.

And in the end her brother spoke again: he was looking forward to his workday. And the image epitomizing his pleasure: slipping into his work pants. But what was good about his work? What proved to him that his work was the right work? That it was "a good kind of working"? —"That without intending to, I look up again and again, look around, listen around, for nothing in particular. For something that hasn't the slightest connection to my work. That I pause without taking a break. That I can think about my work and at the same time about something completely different, thanks to this work."

Sunset was still a long way off, and the brother and sister went to see a soccer game, as they had done on at least one Sunday a month in earlier years. The field lay outside Chaumont, not far from the hospital and the cemetery, surrounded by cultivated fields. From a distance lots of shouting, which, as they saw when they arrived, came from the five to seven spectators scattered over the small open-air bleachers, and even more from the twenty-two players on the field. It was a friendly match, which, however, everyone—players and spectators and referees alike—took seriously, and which put everyone in high spirits. The loudest shouts came from a child, sitting as a spectator next to his mother, who was knitting baby clothes; one of the players, almost bald and quite stout even for a striker, was his father, and the little boy kept firing up his father to score. What he shouted provided the only comprehensible words during the game; otherwise the yelling and almost incessant referees' whistle blasts nearly drowned out the boy's shouts, his voice growing progressively weaker. And what he shouted from the bleachers never varied: "Allez, papa! Allez, papa!" (Again, how to translate those four syllables?)

Another spectator was standing at an open window on an upper floor of the municipal hospital. It was a patient, with tubes in his nose, and he was propping himself up on a rolling cart. Time and again he was pulled away from the window, but by whom one could not see, and the window was closed. And every time he reappeared, continuing to watch the game. But finally he fought back, striking out in every direction; all he wanted was to keep standing at the window and watch the soccer game. Now it took more than two arms to pull him away. It was also no longer pulling but yanking, not all at once but little by little, a hand's breadth at a time, as the patient mustered his last strength to resist, but what strength. All the hospital's orderlies were needed to get him under control, to judge by the fingers tugging at him from behind, and from head to foot. And finally he was dragged away, removed for all time from watching, excluded from the game. Never again would he see a penalty kick, a header knocked into the top corner, a cross-field pass, or also just a short throw-in from the halfway line. And his face, visible for a fraction of a tenth, a hundredth of a second, before it disappeared into the dimness of the hospital room, and the window was closed and remained shut. And what did that face express? The eyes opened wide? Pure horror. Mortal terror.

At halftime the brother told his sister about a soccer player the mere sight of whom, if only on television in the canteen, made his heart pound. The player's name was Javier Pastore, and at present he played for Paris Saint-Germain, PSG. Her brother was crazy about Pastore's style, which combined grace with clumsiness whenever he was on the ball. Yet he never set out to make magic. Whether displaying grace or clumsiness, he did neither consciously. When he danced out of the way of four or five opponents at the corner flag, as had happened just before he scored his legendary goal against Chelsea, or when the ball was effortlessly taken away from him—he often seemed to think he was alone with it—without the opposing player's having to attack, just a toe-poke, and the ball would roll away from Pastore's shoe as if he were a complete bungler: whatever the case, he seemed amazed at what had happened without any conscious effort on his part. Another factor was that no one pulled off passes the way he did, sending the ball with the greatest precision to whoever would go on to score: to the left foot of the leftie, the right foot of the rightie, the right or left side of the head of the header specialists among the strikers. Unfortunately his teammates, even those familiar with Pastore, were usually surprised that a pass of such accuracy was possible, and often failed to score, if they even managed to react to the ball's landing at their feet or on their head. More often than not Javier Pastore's teammates failed to understand him. Yet he never played just for himself but rather for the team, though perhaps one that did not exist, or did not exist yet? Or anymore? But on the occasions when he took over as captain for a change, he seemed out of place, playing a different game altogether. And that above all was what attracted the brother to him. The ability to perform wonders while standing outside oneself, and furthermore seldom being understood, even by those closest to one: that was powerful.

Beyond the soccer field, by the wall of Chaumont's cemetery, stood a lone tree that both siblings kept their eye on during the game. It was one of those early apples that have become so rare—yet France had once had the reputation of being the European pioneer in the cultivation of fruit trees—full of ripe apples, billiard-ball white. Another of the fruit thief's recurring dreams, contrasting with the dream of the murderer as the founder of her tribe, had to do with just such an early apple. The family, in her dream far more than just the four of them, were sitting at a table under the tree and enjoying a meal, with the sun and a cloudless space-blue sky overhead, while their feet rested on an otherwise untouched field of snow, glittering like crystal, that stretched all the way to the dream horizon. That was the entire dream, but it continued well past the night. And now, in broad daylight, the actual, real, present early apple tree—there to be touched: without a word, without even exchanging looks, the sister and brother knew what they would do after the match. And this time she, the fruit-thieving sister, would be the one to give him a leg up.

After that they separated until it would be time for the festivities. In parting the brother and sister shook each other's hands, both callused—which hand more callused?—a game that neither of them won.

The place chosen for the party was on the Vexin plateau. So back up to the plateau and then heading west, with the late-afternoon sun straight ahead. During the climb, a long stretch with not a breath of wind. Yet from on high, far above her head, a roar like the sound of a mighty organ that gained strength with every step she took, a wild gallop in the air that left the earth below untouched. No tree, no bush, not so much as a blade of grass on the steep slope stirred, well past the halfway mark. Then, however, as she reached the rim of the plateau: a veritable gale blowing toward her, from one moment to the next. And a moment before that, one step before she reached the rim: an airplane that seemed to shoot up vertically toward the zenith, a spaceship just launched from the high plateau. But what did "space" mean? Where was it located?

Then a child's balloon caught in a bush, with words printed on it: "Frère et soeur toujours," brother and sister forever. A sign? Strange, or perhaps not strange after all, that so many "signs" turned up when one did not need them. By contrast, the utterance of Vladimir Mayakovsky to his dearest beloved before his departure from this world: "Lili, give me a sign!" The sign he sought so desperately did not come.

After the child's balloon, the children who went with it. It was high time, too. During all those days that she had spent on the road, she had not seen a single child—because of the school holidays?—except the one in a dream (another dream . . .), and only now did she recognize how during her travels—the days spent on foot felt after the fact like travels—she had missed seeing a child's face, a child's little body, those dangling arms. Now, however, she at first mistook the children, coming toward her from a distance over the plateau's bumpy surface, with the light behind them, for grown-ups, large ones, gigantic ones. From close up, they turned out to be wee ones, the youngest category of scouts, so to speak, perhaps venturing forth for the first time in their uniforms, complete with little neckerchiefs. In what kind of storm had they been caught that they were spattered with mud up to their heads, beneath this radiant sky? Still hardly more than toddlers and already searching for something, these apprentice scouts, keeping their eyes peeled for hidden objects serving as landmarks. For her, the fruit thief, however, the watchword was: No more searching. No more tomfoolery. Everything was what it was. The branch swaying back and forth was nothing but a branch swaying in the wind on the high plateau. The scrap of clothing blowing across the fields of stubble had nothing to do with her. The shoe in the ditch was a shoe in the ditch. And that over there is that, and this over here is this, and so forth.

As the sun went down, the wind dropped to a mere breath, like the upwind from the sea on the Karst, that other high plateau, above Trieste. From one village on the plateau to the next she kept encountering others who were out and about like her, except that they were not alone but in groups, on the roads, on cart tracks, cutting across fields, also in whole crowds, as if the custom of the Sunday stroll had been reestablished, a corso out in the countryside, and not at night but in late afternoon. The runners, too, at first anomalous figures in this farm country, never appeared singly, but unlike the usual packs of runners they did not have to shout to make themselves heard, and what they had to say to each other sometimes deviated from the usual: "When my father was dying . . ." she heard one of them saying, and another: "What a fabulous taste curdled milk used to have, I'd give anything for some right now . . ." One of them was reading a book while running. Another kept looking up at the sky as she ran. And not a few of them sighed while running instead of panting. And the voices altogether: whether those of people standing still, walking, or jogging, they made themselves heard effortlessly; above all in the villages, which kept out the wind, the voices not only carried far but also seemed to guide and especially to transform what was said and how, in what words and expressions; this effortless audibility seemed to retune the words, replacing them with others, setting in motion a different kind of communication. A powerful peaceableness emanated from the voices and accordingly also made itself heard, word for word. Or were these voices merely creating an illusion? The illusion that no war would ever break out again, and not only here? Praised be such an illusion. Peaceable voices and peace-bringing words: go on creating these illusions!

Something hostile after all: a car raced across the countryside, as if primed to kill, driven by an oldster, coming, however, straight from Mass, supported on all sides? Had he experienced a miracle? Yet one that predestined him to become a headline in the *Oise-Hebdo* as the Sunday killer-driver?

And later another act of war: a drone swooped down out of the clear sky and buzzed past her head, so close that it ruffled her hair. Or was that a tiding of peace?

She did not greet anyone, and no one greeted her. Was she invisible again? Not at all: from the groups whose paths crossed hers she repeatedly heard an "Oh!" often exclaimed in a chorus. Time and again she walked backward, and one person who observed her doing so commented to his people that it would not be long before this type of backward-walking would be accepted as an Olympic discipline, or at least stood a good chance of becoming a popular sport; running backward gave the runner a boost for running forward, for sprinting; the transition from backward to "straight ahead" held the potential for an as yet unresearched source of strength (thus spoke the expert).

Next she was observed leaving a forest plantation with

her arms full of grape clusters, which, although wine grapes had gone extinct in the Vexin after the Middle Ages—all that remained was the *rue des vignes*, Grapevine Street, to be found in almost every village—some vines had spread into the underbrush and survived there. A second time she was seen in a forest, standing for a long time at the junction of roads leading in six directions and finally choosing the seventh. And one last time she was spied in the middle of a field (the grapes had been joined by blueberries from the Buttes de Rosne and wild asparagus growing along the road between Marquemont and Monneville), where she tossed her duffel bag with its contents into a bush, after first stuffing only the absolute necessities under her Alaska trapper's shirt—although, in another version of her story, she had done this long ago, at the very beginning? One way or the other, her pack had come to be unnecessary ballast, useful while she was traveling, walking, riding, and now superfluous.

So no changing of clothes for the festivities? No party dress? —There: she is putting a ribbon through her hair; that will be sufficiently festive in her eyes. —What kind of ribbon? —I'm standing too far away, can only make out that it's yellow. —A yellow ribbon? —Yes, indeed, a *yellow ribbon. She wore a yellow ribbon.*

There was still time, plenty of time, and she delayed her arrival, and kept delaying it. It was as if sunset were also being delayed, as in the Old Testament story, but unlike in that story not for winning a battle. A silence that sounded like sails flapping in the wind. The droning of a bumble bee or of hornets as an opening chord, the opening of a blues piece. A dove chased a falcon, which squawked in terror.

On a village street a dog was lying in the sun, and as she passed, the dog yawned, making her yawn in turn. In the next village the branch of an apple tree, weighed down with fruit, hung over a wall into the cemetery. All the roads had field crops growing on either side, but she had never taken an interest in these fruits, sticking almost exclusively to individual fruits, and only when they were hard to reach, also difficult to see, near the tops of trees.

In the next hamlet a stranger kissed her hand, and in front of the only mansion she passed, a gentleman in a black dress suit and white shirt, his trouser legs flapping in the wind, bowed to her. With a glance at the Buttes de Rosne, where she had lain in the moss and picked the black- or blueberries to bring as her contribution to the feast, she thought: looking at berries from below is different from . . . Drifting clouds against the blue like freshly washed fleeces. A field of honeycomb clouds. A veritable fleet of clouds floating toward us in the country's interior. Then nothing but pure blue overhead, and against the blue a procession that processed and processed—a swarm of birds?—the blue itself was what was processing. The wind in the foliage: stirring it up, putting it in order. Two blackbirds, or some kind of bird, singing in call and response, then one of them interrupting the other: was that possible? Yes. And subsequently a birdcall so urgent, as if it were meant not for a member of the same species but for us, for humans. On an in-between stretch crowded with hunters, a lost baby wild boar weaving back and forth in the fruit thief's lee, with her as protector and escort. The leaves blown onto the roads with the sun at its nadir all feathery, including the oak leaves and even the corn leaves, likewise the ripped plastic bags in the sand along the road. And finally we stopped and peered furtively into the lone, seemingly bare quince trees on the edge of one of the Vexin villages, trying to spy the one fruit, and there it was, there it appeared: a roundish form protruded from the curtain of leaves, the body of a fruit, just one, the only one.

In the party tent at the chosen location her parents were waiting for her. She had not seen her mother in a year, her father, by contrast, barely three days earlier. Nonetheless it felt as though it had been just as long in both cases, very long, longer than just a year. It had been an equally incalculable time since her mother and father had appeared together. Although there was plenty of room in the tent, they had huddled together and hardly budged from each other's side. Her brother had already arrived, accompanied by a few carpenter friends, also a mason and a roofer, all invited by their mother the previous evening at the barracks. For the occasion he had put on his broad-brimmed carpenter's hat, which he wore low on his forehead, with his carpenter's pencil stuck behind his ear. The party was not meant to be for the family only. For instance, a scooter was parked outside the tent by a birch tree, and the old man from Chars had turned up in a canary-yellow dress shirt, and a cat was prowling silently on a leash, the leash longer than a jungle vine.

At the lady banker's direction, all the guests stepped outside to catch the sunset. There was no need to shield one's eyes. As the sun sank over the edge of the plateau, it was half hidden by a distant filigree of trees. We observers could keep our eyes wide open, and as we watched, they opened even wider, if possible, without squinting. With the treetops as a filter, the curvature of the solar orb appeared even more distinctly. The leaves, branches, and limbs of the trees caused the sun's last light to flicker. It flared in dark yellows, then oranges, then reds through the foliage, glittering up and down, back and forth, as if reflected on a distant body of water. As we turned and went back into the tent, we all continued to have a circle of light before our eyes, dancing back and forth for a while, the sun larger in its afterimage than when we had been looking at it directly.

The music began. It came from a battery-operated device—the term has slipped my mind, actually not a nice term, with something like "ghetto" in it—the music sounding more tinny than euphonious. But music was what had been missing all along. It did not really matter what music it was. Everyone who reads this is welcome to imagine any music that seems to fit. The music that played, the tinny quality magnified because the volume was turned up, came from an unconscious sense of lack, also longing, now assuaged by the first few notes, and even more so by the notes that followed; fulfillment through and through, made possible only by the time spent without music, wretched time, the wretchedness perceived only now, after the fact. The music was material in this moment, the essence of materiality, and its materiality assuaged a previously unsuspected hunger, awakening it at the same time, an all-encompassing, elemental hunger. Music that assuaged? Yes, assuaged. The mother sang along, with that vibrato in her voice that had made the brother and sister want to hold their ears when they were young. On this evening it did not bother the siblings, or their father either, who at other times had left the room the moment he heard the first note vibrate.

It was the mother who had arranged for a proper chef to appease the other hunger. This chef, having gone bankrupt, was on the run from the authorities—who in this area, however, seemed more inclined to let things slide than those in the capital—and was hiding out in a shed near the site of the celebration. She had tracked him down there and promised to help him out of his difficulties with an interest-free loan—Crédit du Nord—in return for his preparing the festive meal. Which he had done, and was still doing before our eyes, at the prep table, also organized by the lady banker. The chef, without a toque but in clean clothes, not white but dark, as in Asia? Japan?, also clean-shaven. He did not once look up from the food. What he sliced, he sliced with a knife as long and broad as a sword, tossing the sliced pieces to one side and also over his shoulder, as if in high spirits. And every time his aim was true, no matter how far the toss. He had been through a lot, whether through his own fault or not—but on this evening not one of us had any desire to hear anything said about "guilt," let alone "atonement"—including about the months he had spent in hiding in the shed, where the rain leaked in, his only company a gas-fired hot plate. But starting today, all that was over. He was signed up for the world again, actually belonging now for the first time, as a result of his temporary banishment, returning in good standing as a prodigal son. How his cheekbones gleamed. How his apron billowed around his hips. Without looking up from the table, he kept his eye on the entire tent, as if his hands did the seeing as he worked. Only this much about the dishes and the order in which they were served: nothing was a side dish, everything was a main dish, also our little contributions.

The daylight outside lingered. But we wished it would last and last, though not, unlike in the story in the Old Testament, to win a battle. We did not want the swallows to make way for bats. And at the same time, strange, or perhaps not? No, strange, very strange, we were longing for the night, for moonrise, for the stars that shine so differently on the Vexin plateau from those over Paris, as if there, on clear summer nights like this one, only the stars cast shadows with their light. Besides: August, the month for shooting stars. Not to mention the night wind! More world could not possibly be created than in the nocturnal whooshing, swooshing, and rustling of the trees.

Night fell, and then it was time for one of us to stand up and, however it turned out, make a speech—a party-tent speech. And the one who stood up to deliver the family-celebration speech was, of all people, the father, who all his life had never given much thought to family and such. He, the loner, the lone wolf, the bachelor type, began, without using a word like *family* or *clan*, with *we*, a word he never used, and after that first *we* came an entire litany. From his looks, it was obvious that during the day, and perhaps also in the night just past, the old man, as the explorer he claimed to be, had got himself seriously lost, although he had known this area for many years, and this was not the first time he had lost his bearings. At the same time, the after-effect of his getting lost, including the lost buttons and a missing shoelace, was good: his face presented the expression of someone who had enjoyed going astray. His voice, however, after all the roaming around, quivered. Yet that made it all the more audible. From time to time he had his usual stumbles. But unlike other times, when he would curse malicious objects as "no-goods" and "motherfuckers," this time he apologized to objects, saying, "Pardon me" to the table when he bumped into it, stroking the chair he knocked over. How gray the father looked amid the colors of summer, and that included the eldercurls in his eyebrows.

His speech went more or less this way: "We stateless people, here and today rid of the state, beyond the reach of the state. All the rest turned into sects—states and churches—and . . . and . . . And we? Time refugees, heroes of escape. We without a role, while the state folks stick to their role, steadfastly. We the eternally daunted undaunted. The eternal hesitators and delayers. The impatient in the Lord. The detour-takers. The circle- and spiral-walkers. We over-the-shoulder-into-the-void-lookers. The hereditary guilty ones. The bitterness-lovers. We obsequious ones. We threadbare ones, Counts and Marquises of Threadbare. We incidentals" (someone shouted, "Long live the incidentals!"). "We illegals and desperados. Who have their own law. And having a law means having a fate. We lost-cause defenders." (Another shout: "Long live the lost-cause defenders!")

At this point the father lost the thread—if there had been one in the first place. He went on speaking, but in a muddle, and began to stutter—an old person who stuttered—even stammered, and his voice took on a foreign accent, as indeed the whole family, even the mother *banquière*, French to the core, spoke with an unidentifiable accent:

"Rid of the state? Rid of time, the current one? Never

were we out of danger, nor are we now. We live on the razor's edge, always have. On the razor's edge, and we ourselves are the razor. As babies you children already silently looked around for help. Ah, the traces of dried cold sweat on you, especially your legs. One would like to love it, destiny, but what is it, our destiny, and where? You two wrote in the air even before you'd learned to write. And where are they today, children who write in the air? Thread the silvery trail of a snail into a needle. Long live the pointless—it need only be practiced. Do senseless things and see what comes of it." (A shout: "Develops out of it!") "Yes, my wife and I: we're a couple of cripples, one way or the other, and that's what brought us together in the first place. We're like those flies that live for only one day. But how lovely those flies are. Ah, the tracery of their wings, with the light shining through them, not to mention their antennae, so delicate, tentatively poking at everything." (Another shout: "Long live mayflies!") "But the stranded dugout, with no one at the rudder, rudderless in general! We're the mad ones who fancy themselves passing on the universe in the smallest of spaces. Standing on tiptoe isn't real standing? Sometimes it is. What I thought I'd lost I had in my hand the entire time, and when I opened my hand in the course of searching, I lost it for real. How you children always sat on the edge of your chairs when we were abroad—but never sat up straight! Praised be crooked parts in your hair! Without the Homeric springs, no story. Wolfram, scrape the rust off your storytelling brooch, confront the official version of the story with your crooked one, and pull off your crooked business. Marriage as a sacrament—why is it that I can take that seriously only today, when it's too late?" (A shout? Silence.) "In the city I hear ambulance sirens as owls hooting, and here in the country I sometimes hear the owls' hooting as ambulance sirens. Being in a strange land: sometimes there's nothing better. But for a whole lifetime . . . What a difference between 'I am observed' and 'I feel seen.' My favorite game: Where does the thread begin on the brand-new spool? The policeman said to the thief: 'I've got you now!' but there's also a different 'I've got you now!' The sky seen through a bird's feather. How defenseless you were, children, with your dangling arms—mightily defenseless. We defenseless ones. What fruit is eaten core and all?" (A shout: "Pears!") "What's the chemical composition of the bluish haze on grapes, on plums?" (A shout naming the chemical formula.) "This formula will save the world someday—or perhaps not. The adventure awaits. All the false adventurers, male and female. Serious adventurers! Hermann Lenz's *Nebendraußen*, that's where it's at. Spare us your family stories, I always thought. But now, against my will . . . How much I used to know, after all, and still know. I don't want to know anything now! Interstices and intervals: durable, useful material. Woe and woe again. Against a background of woe, sorrow, and worry: light our vehicle. Our scar is ancient, but it still throbs, and how! Throbs and throbs. Hopelessness, you source of our strength, our weapon, our armor." (A shout: "Our capital!") "The mother is responsible for resources, and the father? For places. And if the places grow dark, turn sinister? Stick with them, stick to them. Who was it who said: How wealthy we are!—let that wealth bear fruit!" (A shout: "That was me!") "Not being coopted—only then can something good result. Hankering for the Balkans. Hankering for Arabic script, from right to left. Russia? Today Russia, Pushkin, Tolstoy, Turgenev, and Chekhov are here with us in the Vexin, in Picardy, the heart of France; even if the time has passed for the kind of stories related in Russia and in the nineteenth century, their tone still matters. And likewise America exists in Picardy today, in the songs of the lost that are uniquely American, hymns, yes, hymns of the lost, thanks to which America will survive. Also triumph? No, survive and remain—America? The world. Why are there no Russian songs of the lost, not even of one lost soul? Why are there no Russian blues? Praised be the killer ancestor in us. Don't try to exorcise him. How loud the peoples have become. Let us be one people today, a different one, powerless, before the clock face of Alternative Time. He who sows the wind shall reap the whirlwind? No, he who sows the wind shall reap the wind. No book leaves one as abandoned sometimes as a sacred one. And let shame return. Falcons, Emperor Friedrich writes in his book on falconry, become restless in the evening and are fearful, and what frightens them most then is a human face. That was already the case in the thirteenth century. Oh, how I'm fulfilled by this place here, by this countryside, as by a book! Sweet shock: love. We illegals. But better illegal than the legal crooks all over the world. The sects everywhere. An empty bird's nest becomes the peacock throne. Overwhelmed by gratitude. Out of sheer gratitude forgetting to say thank you. Out of gratitude grasp even the smallest things with both hands. Or tap you and you on the wrist. To ask the time? Yes, but not the current one. The more you get lost, the more you experience. Do skip-pacemakers still exist?" (A shout: "They exist!") "A toast to the celebration of your birth, children, gentle demons, good ones. Without the demonic nothing can happen. Without demons no true story. Translated from the Greek, though untranslatable, but never mind: children are a person's soul. Pencil shavings in a spiderweb. Amazing what can be a treasure. *Sueño y trabajo*. Dream and work. One of the swinging doors to outside: walking out of the city on a highway as snow begins to fall—but unfortunately winter is still far off." (A shout: "Nonsense!") "And the holy book of the Apocalypse, after execrations and maledictions rain down from black skies all around on page after page: doesn't it come to a close and die away, with the final words 'Mercy for all, *meta pántōn*!'?"

And the mother's reply? She, who had initiated the whole thing, remained silent. For the first time that old word *motherly* fit her, the lady banker. She kept silent in a motherly way.

Music. Dancing. Two who danced around each other looked like three. Someone sang, in the middle of the crowd, but you could not make out who was singing. Everyone's lips were closed. It was clear that the singer was a woman. It was a woman's voice, or a child's?

Later, toward midnight, the fruit thief was still standing alone outside the tent in the chosen place. (Where was, or is, that, by the way? Its name? The name in this case does not matter.) From the distant expressway, or the Route du Blues, a soft whooshing. That, too, was one of the secret sounds of homeyness now. In the night sky above the plateau, close by, the rattling of a helicopter, like a washing machine in the spin cycle, its searchlights sweeping the ground. A search helicopter? Who was being searched for? Who was missing? From very far off the pinging of a Siberian Jew's harp: an auditory illusion?

She wrapped her arms around herself; pressed herself to herself. With eyes closed, she saw the parade of writing again, as fresh as new, bright handwriting against a dark background, repeating the Milky Way, as seen with eyes open. Then the writing changed to black, while the background became white: much empty space, forming bays of light around the indecipherable words. Although at the moment there was nothing more to wish for, she, ever superstitious, slowly untied and retied the bow in her yellow ribbon. A superstitious act after the fact? A wise act, a form of acknowledgment?

She missed fruit-thievery, or rather turning off to unfamiliar orchards, the movement of veering off, fanning out, helping herself. Was it possible for a single person to fan out? It was possible. Even as a mother, a grandmother she would dream of her time as a fruit thief. Found a party? The party of fruit thieves? But didn't that exist already?

Just think of what she had experienced in the three days of her journey into the interior of the country, and how every hour had been dramatic, even if nothing happened, and how at every moment something had been at stake, and after barely three days one bright summery strand in her dark hair: strange. Or not strange after all? No, strange. Still strange. Eternally strange.

CPSIA information can be obtained
at www.ICGtesting.com
Printed in the USA
LVHW100417170423
744523LV00002B/219